THE
AUEN
FOUNDATION

The purchase of this book
was made possible
by a generous grant from
The Auen Foundation.

Barking Up the Wrong Tree

Center Point
Large Print

Also by Jenn McKinlay and available from
Center Point Large Print:

A Likely Story
About A Dog

**This Large Print Book carries the
Seal of Approval of N.A.V.H.**

Barking Up the Wrong Tree

JENN McKINLAY

CENTER POINT LARGE PRINT
THORNDIKE, MAINE

The text of this Large Print edition is unabridged.
In other aspects, this book may vary
from the original edition.
Printed in the United States of America
on permanent paper.
Set in 16-point Times New Roman type.

ISBN: 978-1-68324-703-6

Library of Congress Cataloging-in-Publication Data

Names: McKinlay, Jenn, author.
Title: Barking up the wrong tree / Jenn McKinlay.
Description: Center Point large print edition. | Thorndike, Maine :
    Center Point Large Print, 2018. | Series: A Bluff Point romance
Identifiers: LCCN 2017058241 | ISBN 9781683247036
    (hardcover : alk. paper)
Subjects: LCSH: Large type books. | GSAFD: Love stories.
Classification: LCC PS3612.A948 B37 2018 | DDC 813/.6—dc23
LC record available at https://lccn.loc.gov/2017058241

Acknowledgments

Why do I love my job? Because I get to work with some of the best and brightest in the publishing industry. Thank you so very much to my editor, Kate Seaver, who is always flexible and patient with my process; editor Katherine Pelz, who keeps me on track and sweats the details for me; and copy editor Amelia Kreminski, who fixes the error of my ways. I'd also like to thank the art department and the cover artist, Katie Anderson, for making such spectacular covers for the Bluff Point series. And for the team that has had boots on the ground getting the buzz out about these books, I offer my heartfelt thanks to Jeanne-Marie Hudson, Fareeda Bullert, Erin Galloway, and Ryanne Probst. I am so very fortunate to have such an amazing squad!

As always, I have to thank my family and friends for putting up with me. This has been a particularly busy year, and I appreciate everyone's support and understanding when I canceled dates, missed events, and generally had my head in my laptop pretty much constantly. From those who listened to me whine (Mom) to those who hugged me when I needed it (Hub and Bro) to those who brought me copious amounts of candy when required (Hooligans), I love you all so very much. Plus, you give me endless material for the books, so thanks for that, too!

Chapter 1

"I bet it's a stash of yarn or maybe a collection of troll dolls and bingo daubers," Carly DeCusati said.

"Really? Your elderly neighbor leaves you something in her will and that's what you think it might be?" Jillian Braedon, Carly's best friend for life, asked her.

More accurately, Jillian asked Carly's curvy backside as Carly was half wedged in the narrow closet in her bedroom with her trusty handheld vacuum, attempting to suck up the dust bunnies that had set up a warren in there.

"No, not really. I have no idea what she might have left me," Carly said. "I mean, Mrs. Genaro was my neighbor and I looked in on her and watched some television with her, but I didn't really know her, you know? Honestly, I can't believe she left me anything at all."

"Maybe it's diamonds, a priceless piece of art, or—"

"Her tea cozy collection," Mackenzie Harris interrupted Jillian.

She was standing beside Jilly as they folded the mountain of clothes on Carly's bed in an effort to fit them into the stack of empty moving boxes they had gathered.

9

"She didn't—" Emma Jameson protested but Carly interrupted.

"Collect tea cozies? Not that I'm aware of, but I think that's a safer bet than diamonds or art."

"Bummer," Jillian said.

"Agreed," Carly said. She wiggled backwards, just enough to poke her head out from around the doorjamb, and turned to face her three childhood friends. She gave them a rueful glance and added, "That did not stop me, however, from spending a significant amount of time praying to the big guy that it would be enough cash to pay my rent so I can halt my move back to Bluff Point."

"Is coming home to Maine really that bad?" Jillian asked. "You've been in Brooklyn for a long time, maybe now you'll be happier at home like Mac."

"Mac's happy because she found a hot young veterinarian to warm up those frigid Maine winters," Carly said.

Mackenzie turned a bright shade of red. Her summer romance with Gavin Tolliver had been the stuff of legends, or at least really good chick flicks.

"Please, he's still my baby brother," Emma said with a frown. "Can we not use the word 'hot' when describing him?"

"Sorry," Carly said.

"But he is," Mac said, giving Emma side eye. "Totally hot."

Emma rolled her eyes but she was grinning. As the only happily married one of their group, she had the matchmaker bug going big time.

"See? You have us there, your Maine crew," Jillian said. "Coming home won't be so bad."

Carly looked at Jillian in confusion. "I'm sorry. You've met my family, right?"

"Yes, but—"

"No buts, I love them dearly, but they suck the soul right out of me," Carly said. "You try being the fourth sister in a brat pack of five. It'd make the sanest person cray cray."

"I'm an only child, so I can't really wrap my head around that. But you need to look at the bigger picture," Jilly argued. "Your company downsized and you lost your job. You can't pay your rent and all of your best friends are in Bluff Point, Maine. Clearly the universe is telling you it's time to come home. Besides, don't you want to spend more time with us?"

Jillian tipped her head to the side in a look meant to charm and disarm. Emma and Mac stepped up beside her and mimicked her pose. They were like a trifecta of pretty, exotic, and lovely. Carly sighed. There was no way she could tell her friends the truth—that while she loved each one of them dearly, when she was with them she felt as if she should be carrying a bucket and mop.

The progeny of a black mom and a white dad,

Jillian was tall and lithe with brown skin that glowed, big dark eyes, full lips, and a head of enviable dark curls. If she hadn't been Carly's best friend since childhood, Carly would have avoided Jillian like the plague of good-looking that she was. Truly, no woman should ever have to stand next to a woman as exotically beautiful as Jillian.

Then there was Emma. Petite, blonde, blue-eyed, she looked like someone who was enchanted to life from an old Disney animated film. If that weren't bad enough, she had a huge heart and a contagious laugh and made sure she milked every bit of awesome out of every single day. In other words, she was impossible not to love.

"If I can go home, so can you," Mac said.

Carly frowned. Mackenzie was actually the worst of the three. Medium in height and build with thick, wavy brown hair that hung just past her shoulders and an ability to do mental math that left Carly dazzled, Mac was the sort of hot girl who had no idea she was hot, which was the absolute worst kind because Carly couldn't even be mad at her for being hot since Mac didn't know it herself.

Mac had a smile that lit up rooms and stopped men's hearts. At least, it had pretty much stopped Gavin Tolliver's heart. The man had been in love with her since he was ten years old and Mac had never caught on until just recently—yeah, because she was thick like that.

Being unfashionably short and voluptuous, with a hot temper that frequently beat out her common sense, Carly had always felt like the ugly stepsister when she was with her friends. She had never told any of them, of course, but going home and being with all of them again? Yeah, it wasn't really rocking her self-esteem.

A belch sounded and they all looked at one another. No one asked to be excused so it was pretty clear it wasn't one of them, which left . . .

"Tulip!" Mac cried her dog's name. "Tulip, what have you gotten into?"

The retching noise started shortly after that.

"Oh, no! That's her about-to-hork noise," Mac said. She dashed from the bedroom out to the living room. "Tulip!"

"I'll help!" Emma cried. She glanced at Carly, noting the alarmed expression on her face. "We'll take her for a walk until it passes. We got this."

Carly glanced at Jillian, who was obviously trying not to laugh.

"Can't wait to see them with babies," Carly said.

Jillian lost the battle and cracked up. When she was composed again, she looked at Carly and said, "And there's that. You don't want to miss any of the big life events, do you? It'll be great being together again, I promise."

"Hanging out with you will be a bright spot," Carly said. "But the newly married Emma and the newly-shacked-up Mac are not going to be nearly as entertaining. Why is everyone suddenly hooking up? Don't they know that these are the best years of our lives?"

"We're thirty-two," Jillian said. "I think it's the natural order that we start pairing off and settling down."

Carly fell backwards out of the closet. "Are you trying to tell me something? Oh, no, are you and Sam Kennedy a thing now?"

"What? No!" Jilly protested. "He was just my partner for Emma's wedding. We've become friends—good friends—that's it."

Carly narrowed one eye at her as if trying to determine whether Jillian was telling her the truth.

"I swear." Jillian raised her right hand, forgetting that she was holding a pair of Carly's pink underpants.

"Does holding a thong make it more binding?" Carly asked with a laugh. Jillian dropped the panties and frowned at her. "All right, but if I find out there's been any hanky-panky and you didn't tell me . . ."

The buzzer on Carly's intercom interrupted her. She glanced at the clock.

"Oh, that'll be Mrs. G's lawyer," she said. "He's disgustingly punctual."

Jillian helped her to her feet. Carly stripped off her cleaning gloves and adjusted the red bandana she had used to tie up her long dark curls. With her capri pants and plaid flannel shirt tied at the waist, she felt very much like a nineteen-fifties hausfrau.

"Come on, I'd better let the little badger in before he starts buzzing every door in the building," she said.

"You might try being polite to him, maybe he's going to be your savior," Jillian said.

"No way, he's a lawyer, which in my experience means that this is going to cost me, probably in a pound of flesh," she said. She paused and glanced at her reflection in the full-length mirror, critically studying the generous tits and ass she'd inherited from Nana DeCusati. "Then again, that might not be a bad thing."

"Quit it," Jillian said. She pushed Carly toward the front of the apartment. "You know men drool like fools at the sight of the girls. Those boobies are like your superpower, able to knock grown men to their knees with a single glance of cleavage."

"And that, my dear, is why you are my best friend," Carly said.

She stood by her front door and hit the answer button on her intercom.

"Who is it?" she sang.

"Bartholomew Schuster." The voice sounded high with a little nasal whine to it that reminded Carly of a mosquito.

"Come on up, Barry," she answered. "Door is open."

She buzzed him in and then unlocked the door to her apartment, leaving it ajar before she joined Jillian where she sat on a stool by the kitchen counter. They heard his footsteps on the stairs to her second floor apartment moments before he arrived. He was not a delicate stepper, Carly noted.

"It's Bartholomew, Ms. DeCusati," he corrected her as he stepped inside the apartment. "Or you can call me Mr. Schuster if you prefer. Oh, hello."

Barry froze in his tracks at the sight of Jillian. Carly glanced at her friend, who was smiling at Barry as if she had just happened upon a cute little garden gnome. Barry was only an inch or two taller than Carly, making him pretty short for a guy. It was a good thing Jillian was sitting down or he'd have to work with a ladder just to be eye to eye. As it was, he looked simply besotted with her.

Carly tried not to dwell on the fact that she had met Barry once before and this had not been his reaction to seeing her for the first time. Then again, as she took in the short, paunchy, prematurely gray man in front of her, she did not consider this a loss.

"Barry, this is my friend Jillian Braedon and before you ask, no, she will not go out with you," Carly said.

Jillian shot her a dark look and Barry blustered, looking indignant, which was how Carly knew that was exactly what he'd been thinking.

"I was not . . . I had no . . ." he said but Carly interrupted.

"Yeah, yeah, I have a lot of work to do to get my security deposit back on this place," she said. "So let's make with the paperwork already, unless of course you're telling me that Mrs. Genaro left me a sizeable chunk of money which will allow me to keep my crib."

Barry cocked his head to the side as if he wasn't sure what she was talking about.

"You have a baby?" he asked.

Carly resisted the urge to smack her forehead with her palm. Barely.

"Let's just get on with it, dude," she said.

She figured he would consider "dude" even more appalling than "Barry." She was right. Instead of correcting her, however, he simply sighed as if he were being forced to do community service by helping the rude and sarcastic.

He opened his briefcase and pulled out a stack of papers. "It's fairly straightforward. You sign these documents and the items she has bequeathed you become yours."

"What are the documents for?" Jillian asked.

This earned her a beaming smile from Barry as if she were his favorite student in Estate Settlements 101.

"It's mostly a formality," he said. "The papers will signify that Ms. DeCusati—"

"Ms. DeCusati is my bossy older sister; call

17

me Carly, or even better you can call me Sugar Pants," Carly said. She wiggled her eyebrows at him.

Barry's face flushed a shade of red found only on small, bitter root vegetables. Jillian pressed her lips together to keep from laughing. Carly punched Barry lightly on the arm.

"I'm just funning you, Barry," she said.

He closed his eyes as if he might be able to click the heels of his high gloss Gucci loafers together and escape her. Yeah, that wasn't going to happen.

"The papers are a written record of the transaction," he said. He opened his eyes. "They will signify that you have agreed to accept the object Mrs. Genaro has bequeathed to you and that your association with our office is done."

Carly wasn't sure but she thought he looked a little more chipper at this news.

"Cool, where do I sign?" she said.

Barry put the papers on the counter in front of her. All of the lines requiring her signature had handy little fluorescent stickers with arrows pointing to the corresponding blank space. He pulled a pen out of his Armani jacket and handed it to her.

"Eager to be off the clock, eh?" Carly asked.

He ignored her.

"Don't you want to read through those first?" Jillian asked. "There might be pertinent information in there."

"Nah." Carly waved her hand as she started signing. "I don't have time. Besides, Mrs. Genaro was a sweet little old lady. We watched *Dancing with the Stars* together when she was feeling lonely; she had the hots for Bruno Tonioli. I'm sure whatever it is, it's more a token of affection than a big cash payout."

Carly looked at Barry. His face was a mask of benevolent innocence. That's why she hated lawyers. You could never tell when they were hiding something.

"She wasn't rich, was she?" she asked. "You're not holding out on me, are you, Barry?"

"Uh, no," he said. "Her assets were minimal."

Carly glanced back at Jillian. "See? Told you so."

She signed the last spot and then handed Barry his pen.

"So hit me, what'd she give me?"

"One moment," he said. He walked over to the door and stuck his head out into the hallway. "In here, please."

Jillian and Carly exchanged an intrigued glance.

"Maybe it's a piano," Carly said. "I've always wanted a piano."

"What if it's a leg lamp?"

"From Fragile, Italy?" Carly asked. Then she started laughing. "Yeah, that'd be my luck."

Two burly moving men, wearing brown

coveralls, came into the apartment. One was carrying a large glass bowl filled with water and a very round goldfish, aptly named Goldie by Mrs. Genaro. The other one was carrying a large rectangular case with a fierce-looking reptile named Spike, Mrs. G's pet lizard. Carly felt herself start to sweat. What exactly had she signed?

The men set the pets down on the table and left the apartment. They didn't shut the door, leaving Carly to believe there was more.

"Oh, no," Carly said. She looked at Barry as the panic began to fill her insides like water on the rise. "She didn't."

"She did." Barry looked smug.

"What?" Jillian asked. "What's going on?"

Just then the men returned. One had a pretty golden retriever on a leash; the other carried a large rectangular object, draped with a cloth. The dog, Mrs. Genaro's companion Saul, tipped his head to the side as if considering Carly. She ignored him, hoping with all of her might that there was a huge misunderstanding happening here.

The man set the big object down in the middle of the room and stepped back. Carly grabbed a side of the sheet draped over it and gave it a good yank. Sure enough, there he was in all of his green-feathered glory: Mrs. G's beloved parrot.

"Hello, Ike," Carly said. "Long time no see."

"Oh, for fuck's sake," Ike squawked.

Chapter 2

"Oh, my god." Jillian clapped a hand over her mouth in surprise. "Did he just—?"

Whatever she had been about to say was cut off by the belly laughs of the two moving men as they exited the room. The one with the dog handed Carly his leash on the way out.

"That was awesome," one of them said as they laughed all the way back down the stairs.

Barry was busy stuffing his papers back into his briefcase. Carly frowned at him. She couldn't help but think he looked like a rat scurrying off a sinking ship. Then again, that was unfair to rats; they were cute, Barry was not.

"There's been a mistake. I can't keep these pets," Carly said. "I can barely take care of myself."

"Then you shouldn't have signed the papers," Barry retorted.

"But it never occurred to me that she would . . . wait . . . you mean I could have declined?" she asked.

"Of course," he said. "But now it's too late because you signed the papers."

He gave her a smarmy little smile.

"Can I borrow your pen?" she asked.

"Why? It's too late, you can't cross out your

name and have it undone," he said. He was backing toward the door, clutching his briefcase to his chest.

"I was thinking more about using it to shank you," she said.

At that, he gave her a horrified look, spun on his shiny footwear, and bolted.

"Coward!" Carly yelled after him. Then she slammed her door shut with enough force to make it rattle. She hoped Barry knew that's what she was planning to do to his head if she ever saw him again.

Saul immediately slunk to the floor and put his paws over his head as if he was hiding. Carly sighed. This was bad, so very, very bad. Still, it wasn't the animals' fault.

"It's okay, Saul," she said. She bent over and scratched his ears. "It's not your fault. I'm not mad at you."

Saul immediately rolled over for a belly rub. Carly buried her fingers in his thick blonde coat, trying to keep herself from having a complete and total freak-out.

"Well, it looks like you've got yourself some pets." Jillian stared around Carly's kitchen in bemusement before she approached the birdcage. "Ike, huh? How you doing, pretty boy?"

Ike gave her side eye and sidled away from her on his perch.

"I don't think he likes me," Jillian said.

"He doesn't like anyone," Carly said. "He didn't even like Mrs. G."

As if he understood, Ike fluffed up his feathers and turned his back on her.

"And just what am I supposed to do with all of you?" Carly asked the animals. Saul licked her face, the fish and lizard ignored her, while Ike's response was to begin preening his armpit. She had feeling there was a message there.

"It looks like you have no choice," Jillian said. "You're going to have to bring them home to Bluff Point. Maybe you can find a nice family for them there."

"A nice family?" Carly asked. "For a fish, a lizard, a geriatric dog, and a salty bird? Did you hear what came out of that beak? No family is going to want this foul-mouthed bird teaching their precious munchkins to tell people to eff off."

"Good point," Jillian said. She glanced down but the shake of her shoulders gave her away.

"This isn't funny," Carly wailed. She stood and clapped her hands to her head as she fell back onto her sofa. "I can't even take care of dust bunnies, how am I supposed to take care of this freaking menagerie?"

"A what?" Emma asked as she entered the apartment followed by Mac and Tulip.

Tulip caught one whiff of Saul and began to bark, which caused Saul to bark in return, making Ike screech while pacing on his perch, which only made Tulip bark louder. When the cacophony was too much to bear, Ike puffed out his chest and a ripple ran from the top of his silky green head all the way to the tip of his tail feathers, and in a voice that sounded like a prison warden, he shouted, "Shut your stupid cake hole!"

Everyone froze with their mouths slack. Even Tulip and Saul quit barking. Saul jumped on top of Carly on the couch, while Tulip let out a small whimper and crawled under the dining room table.

"Did it . . . did I . . . where did all this come from?" Emma asked. She put one hand on her hip and pointed at the bird, the fish, and the lizard with her other hand as if she couldn't quite believe their sudden appearance.

"Was this your inheritance?" Mac asked. She was a little quicker at putting it all together.

"Yes," Carly said. Being trapped under Saul, she didn't get up from the sofa but merely lifted her head to look at them. "Emma and Mac, meet Ike, the swearing parrot; Saul, the geezer dog; Goldie, the fish who won't die; and Spike, the prehistoric-looking lizard."

Jillian, who had been making choking noises for the past few minutes, finally lost the battle and a snort came out of her nose that made Tulip tuck her tail in between her legs and hunker lower on her belly. Emma and Mac took one look at their friend and they lost it, too.

Carly stared up at the ceiling. She was pleased that her friends could find amusement in her personal hell, really, she didn't mind. Sure, her life was in the toilet and no one was even offering her so much as a courtesy flush, but yeah, it was fine. She was fine. It would be fine.

She glanced at Ike. He had gone back to preening. Saul was pushing his head into her side. Both the fish and the lizard seemed singularly unfazed by their new domicile. Mac and Emma were now supporting each other as they gasped for air. Jillian had almost gotten herself under control but then looked at the other two and lost it again.

Carly realized that if the situation were reversed, she'd be the one in hysterics and, really, could she blame them? She'd just inherited her own Noah's Ark. It was funny, there was no denying it. For her, however, it was just one more problem on a leaky boat on a choppy sea in shark-infested waters.

It was bad enough she was doing the millennial thing and moving back in with her parents while she regrouped and got back on her feet. Now she was bringing a pack of animals with her, too. There was no way her god-fearing Catholic parents were going to embrace these critters, not to mention Carly's own walk-on-the-wild-side lifestyle.

For the past eleven years, she had managed to keep her family in the dark about her commitment phobia and preference for short-term flings as opposed to full-on relationships. Now, living back in her hometown and under her parents' roof, she was going to have to make a vow of celibacy to keep them happy. The thought had little to no appeal for her.

"I'm sorry, Carly, really I am," Jillian said. She dabbed at her eyes and shook her head in an effort to get it together.

"Me, too," Mac said.

"Me, three," Emma chimed in.

They all piled onto the couch with her, heedless of the half-packed boxes and Saul's hair explosion as they shifted him to accommodate them.

The four of them stared up at the ceiling, looking for comfort, a solution—or possibly just enjoying the thick, creamy paint swirls that covered the ceiling.

"It's going to be all right," Mac said. "We can all help with the pets."

"They are all lovely in their own way," Emma said. "Surely someone wants pets like these."

"I notice none of you are volunteering," Carly said.

"My hours at the bakery make pets impossible," Jillian said.

"I already have a dog," Mac said.

"I'd have to check with Husband," Emma said. "He might be allergic."

"To a fish or a lizard?" Mac asked.

"It could happen," Emma said.

Carly let out a sigh so long and so deep she was sure she was out of oxygen and would expire on the spot. No such luck.

"What's the matter?" Jillian asked.

"I just realized I'm probably never going to have sex ever again," Carly said.

"No."

"Nah."

"Not possible."

"Really?" she asked. "Because I'm going to be living with my parents and my little sister and now I have this furry, scaly, and feathered entourage. What man in his right mind is going to want to come home with me to my parents' house, both of whom would stroke out if I brought a man home by the way, to have sex with me in front of this crew, one of which is a filthy-mouthed bird, who will probably swear at us the whole time we're doing the horizontal mambo."

They were all silent. This really wasn't a glass-half-full-versus-half-empty dilemma. It was more a pour-the-water-out-and-find-a-bottle-of-vodka-and-fill-the-glass-to-the-lip situation.

"I'm doomed, I tell you," Carly wailed. "Doomed."

"Hey, Mac, correct me if I'm wrong, but aren't those your aunts?" Carly asked. "And unless I'm seeing things, it looks like they've had their hair done."

A week had passed and the day of Carly's big move had arrived. Mac had borrowed her boyfriend Gavin's pickup truck to drive Carly, and the possessions she had not put into storage, home to Bluff Point. They had crossed the town line a few minutes ago and were now making their way through the center of Bluff Point on their way to Carly's parents' house.

Mac glanced in the direction Carly pointed and stared at the two elderly women on the town green doing some sort of calisthenic workout with a group of other geriatrics and a guy in basketball shorts and a tank top, who looked ripped enough to bench-press a car.

"Holy hot peppers!" Mac said. "Is that . . . purple in Aunt Charlotte's hair and red in Aunt Sarah's? They told me they had a hair appointment this morning but they did not mention the new colors. My dad is going to kill me."

"He's still not embracing his sisters plowing through their bucket list?" Carly asked. Personally, she thought the two septuagenarians were pretty badass for taking up everything from beekeeping to hip-hop to surfing in their dotage, but that was just her.

"He says it gives him heartburn," Mac said.

"Then don't tell him. Besides, who cares about the hair? Get a load of their buff trainer," Carly said.

"I have to stop just to make sure they're okay.

What if this is some sort of crazy boot camp and they throw out a hip or something?"

"No prob. I'm in no hurry to move back into my childhood bedroom."

Mac pulled into a parking spot on the edge of the green. As soon as she switched off the engine, Saul, who had been dead asleep, popped up in the back seat where he was wedged next to the strapped-in birdcage. He wagged his fluffy tail and gave Carly a soft woof.

She shook her head at him. "We are only stopping for a minute. We just gave you a sniff-and-pee break a half hour ago, you can hold it."

Saul sank back down onto his seat and stared up at Carly. "No, I am not falling for the sad face. Don't waste your time. I'm heartless, remember?"

It was early October and while the days were becoming cooler, today was bright and sunny as the temperature hovered around seventy, making it one of the last gorgeous days Maine would see for a while. They rolled down the windows for the dog, and Carly opened the cover that had been on the birdcage so that Ike could get some fresh air, too.

"Behave," Carly said.

"Bite me," Ike retorted.

Mac snorted.

"Now I know what it's like to have a mouthy teenager on my hands," Carly said.

"So do I," Mac agreed as she gestured to the aunts.

She pocketed her keys as they left the pickup truck and strode over to where the aunts were standing amidst a group of seniors, receiving some sort of workout instruction from the bona fide hottie; at least, he was from the rear view.

"Aunt Sarah, Aunt Charlotte, what are you doing?" Mac asked as she approached the group. Carly could tell she was trying to sound casual like she wasn't worried, but her gritted teeth gave her away.

"Reverse fly," Aunt Sarah said. She tossed her silver bob with the vibrant red streaks in it. The gesture said *duh* clearer than words ever could.

Carly stood beside her friend as she interrogated her aunts, who, to their credit, paid Mac no mind.

Dressed in formfitting black yoga pants with long-sleeved tops that matched the funky colors in their hair—purple for Charlotte and red for Sarah—the two feisty ladies each held small hand weights that they brought forward in front of them before moving their arms back out to the side.

"Just look at the pecs on our teacher," Aunt Charlotte said. Her wavy curls boasted streaks of purple, which Carly thought looked quite lovely amidst the silver. "His name is James Sinclair and he's a physical therapist. He offers free classes to seniors to help keep us limber." She leaned close and whispered so only Carly and Mac could hear her. "Honestly, he can limber me up anytime."

"Aunt Charlotte!" Mac cried.

"What? I'm old, not dead."

"And what did you do to your hair?" Mac cried. "I was gone three days! How am I going to explain this to Dad?"

"Why would you?" Aunt Sarah said. "It's not like you dyed our hair. It's none of his business; besides, I've always wanted to play with the color and I think the red streaks are sexy, don't you, James?"

"Most definitely, Miss Sarah," James called over his shoulder. His voice was low and deep. "I've always been partial to red."

He didn't turn around to look at them as he was helping Mrs. Tillman with the grip on her hand weights.

"See?" Sarah said. "Sexy. I'm going to look so badass on my motorcycle."

"Your what?!" Mac cried.

"Hogs, bikes, crotch rockets, get with the lingo, kid," Charlotte chimed in. "After this class, we're going to buy a couple."

"Over my dead body!" Mac said.

She smacked her forehead with her hand and Carly had to look away so that she didn't laugh out loud. The aunts had been putting Mac through her paces since they decided at seventy-three that they were going to get cracking on their bucket list before it was too late.

Carly glanced over at this James guy to see how he was handling the interruption of his class. He seemed singularly Zen about it. Then he turned slightly and she caught sight of his profile. Wow, just wow. He was not just a stud from the back; his front was looking pretty promising as well. Her dormant sex drive rose to life like a sleeping dragon being poked by a sword-wielding knight. Huzzah!

She glanced down at her baggy sweatshirt and jeans, remembered the do-rag she had tied on her head—oh, and she had no makeup on. Darn it! Who'd have thought she'd meet a man worthy of some effort in the first five minutes she was back in town?

She watched James as he moved to help the Bluff Point postmaster, Mr. Petrovski, who in contrast to him resembled a scrawny plucked chicken, with his reverse-fly posture. Carly had to agree with Aunt Charlotte. James's pecs were drool-worthy, as were his muscle-hardened calves, tight behind, and broad shoulders, not to mention his heroically handsome face, which sported the faintest amount of dark scruff and matched his unruly thick black hair, giving him overall the look of a very naughty pirate.

Carly felt herself break into a light sweat despite the cool breeze. She wondered if she jumped into the class if he'd demonstrate the proper reverse-fly technique to her or, you know, just let her lick his neck and bite his shoulders for a little while.

As if sensing her stare, he turned his head and met her gaze. His blue gray eyes widened at the sight of her. Not a big surprise since she and Mac were easily forty years younger than any of his other students. But there was something in his look, like a flash of recognition followed by a blast of heat, which fueled the fire that was Carly's libido and she gasped.

"That's right," Mr. Petrovski said, mistakenly thinking her gasp was for him. He dropped his free weight on James's foot and curled up his skinny arm in an attempt to bulge a muscle. "Feel these guns. Bet that makes you weak in the knees, Carly, am I right or am I right?"

With a hiss of pain, James hopped back from Mr. Petrovski and tried to walk off the impact of the two-pound weight on his foot. He circled them, shaking out his foot as he walked. Carly wanted to ask if he was all right, but Mr. Petrovski was shoving his arm in her face, demanding her attention.

"You are right, Mr. P.," Carly said. She obliged him by poking his muscle, which was beginning to droop, with her index finger. "Wow, you are built like a brick house."

She glanced over his head to meet James's gaze. He was staring at her with an intensity that made her insides spasm. Huh.

She didn't usually get this sort of reaction from a man when she was makeup-free and the girls were on lockdown. Either James was hard-up or really, really liked the natural look. Never one to pass up an opportunity to flirt, she met his gaze, smiled at him, and then she winked, nice and slow. James's jaw went slack in response.

Carly wasn't surprised. She gave a really good wink and she wasn't afraid to use it. She was about to push Mr. P. aside and make her move, but Mac destroyed the moment.

"Carly, oh, my god, is that Ike?" Mac cried.

Carly whipped her head in her friend's direction and saw her pointing toward the pickup truck.

"Holy crap!" Carly cried. Sure enough, Ike was perched on the half-rolled-down window as he surveyed the town green before him. "He must know how to open his cage!"

"You have a parrot?" Aunt Charlotte asked. "He's cute."

"I like the green feathers," Aunt Sarah said. "Maybe I'll have green put in my hair next time."

"What do we do?" Mac asked. "Can he fly?"

"I don't know," Carly said. "I've never let him out of his cage except to move him from the big one to the smaller one. He didn't fly then."

"I don't mean to alarm you," Mr. Petrovski said, "but there are some eagles in the area who would consider him a tasty lunch."

For a second—the briefest nanosecond,

really—Carly wondered if that was such a bad thing. Then she shook her head; of course it was. Forgetting all about the hot guy, she began to move across the lawn back to the pickup in a sort of trying-not-to-scare-the-bird squat-walk that she hoped looked to Ike like she wasn't really moving when she was actually hauling ass in his direction as fast as she could, given the weird hunched posture she was in.

Ike, not being a stupid bird, caught on pretty quick. He stood on one foot and raised his other in his favorite kung fu pose, and squawked, "Bring it, sister. Bring it!"

Then he flew off the window and up into the sky, where he wobbled awkwardly like an old man who was too blind to drive but refused to give up his license.

Carly froze. Then she yelled, "Ike, you get back down here! Now!"

Ike did a shaky barrel roll, which she figured was the bird equivalent of flipping her off. Saul, still in the car, wedged his nose into the open window and began to woof. Carly wasn't sure if he was egging his bird friend on or trying to call him back.

"So, he can fly," Mac said as she joined her.

"Yeah, sort of like a drunk when the bar closes," Carly said. When she saw Ike heading at top speed for the trees on the end of the town green, her entire body clenched. "Ah, he's going to crash!"

Another bark sounded and Carly saw a blur of motion shoot past her on the left. Ears were flapping, legs were pumping, wheels were turning . . . *Wheels?*

"Hot Wheels, no!" James shouted, and then he started running after the dog in the weird contraption. Carly and Mac exchanged a look and then they began to run as well.

Hot Wheels outmaneuvered them all, however, staying just under Ike, who had not crashed but was now flying low to the ground under the trees, dive-bombing the dog, who continued to bark at him. It looked almost like they were playing, minus the whole snapping teeth and flashing claws thing.

"I think your dog is trying to eat my bird," Carly panted as she caught up to James.

"Really? I think your bird is trying to attack my dog," he said as they raced side by side to catch their critters.

Suddenly, both animals disappeared behind a thick thatch of elderberry bushes. The barking stopped and Carly lost sight of Ike's green plumage. Both she and James froze. Mac joined them, looking equally worried as they all stared at the place in the bushes where the dog and the bird had disappeared.

"Your bird—" James began but Carly shouted over him.

"Your dog—" she began but was interrupted by the sound of a whistle.

"Is that—?" Mac asked, tipping her head to listen.

"Rollin', rollin', rollin'," Aunt Sarah sang as she joined them.

"Keep them doggies movin'," Aunt Charlotte chimed in.

The sound of a soft woof came from the underbrush as Hot Wheels came busting out from under the bushes with Ike perched on his harness whistling the tune to *Rawhide*.

"Oh, my god," Mac said. "Gavin would die, just die, if he could see this."

Hot Wheels trotted to James, clearly proud of his feathered cargo, and for his part Ike looked as if all was right in his world since he was being carried. He continued whistling the theme to *Rawhide* and Carly shook her head.

"This bird is going to be the death of me," she said. "I know it."

Hot Wheels, a basset hound, stopped in front of them and Carly held out her arm in front of Ike, silently praying he stepped onto her hand and didn't fly off again. After a brief hesitation, he deigned to climb on, and when Carly moved her hand to her chest to keep him close, Ike burrowed his head under her chin. She got the feeling that despite his parrot bravado, he had scared himself silly.

She felt her heart melt but then shook it off. Yes, he was an interesting bird and even sometimes he was amusing, but he and Saul needed a forever family and that was not her.

Carly had been lucky to unload the goldfish and the lizard on a couple of teen boys in her building. She had made them take a vow on the life of their Xbox that they would take good care of the pets, and their mother had promised to oversee the situation. So, it was two down and two to go; unfortunately, no one wanted an older dog and a mouthy bird. She couldn't blame them.

James was kneeling down beside his dog, checking his harness and his back legs. The rig the dog was hooked into had two wheels at the back and Carly figured it was to help the dog with his hind legs, one of which looked thinner and less muscled than the other.

The dog was wagging, clearly pleased with himself and his adventure as a rescue dog. Carly approached with Ike still cuddled up against her. James rose to his feet and looked at her. She imagined the relief in his eyes was mirrored in her own.

"I am so sorry—" they said together. They both stopped and laughed. And then spoke together again, "I haven't had him long."

James grinned at her and Carly felt it hook her low and deep. She smiled back at him. She liked this guy, she really did.

"You have a great dog," she said. She glanced

at the pooch. "You are a good boy, Hot Wheels, aren't you?"

He wagged and woofed, his long ears flopping, obviously understanding praise when he heard it.

"And you have a very talented bird," James said. "He's a real looker like his mama—"

"Oh, I'm not his—"

"Carly," Mac interrupted. She took Carly's arm and pulled her aside. "I just got three texts from your mom, asking where we are. She sounds a bit panicked. I think you'd better get home ASAP."

Carly had to force herself to focus on what Mac was saying. She could feel James watching her and all she wanted to do was bask in his hotness for a while. She'd always had a thing for men with dark hair, blue eyes, and rocking bods. Yeah, if she had a type, he was it.

Unfortunately, Saul woofed and Ike ruffled his feathers, reminding her that she had beings to tend to. Mac handed her the keys to the truck and said something about coming by later to get it since she needed to deal with the aunts and their crazy scheme to buy motorcycles right here and now.

Before Carly knew what was what or who was who, she was striding back across the town green toward the truck with Ike. She climbed into the cab and put him back in his cage, making sure it was fastened tight. She patted Saul on the head and then fired up the engine. As she backed out of the parking spot, she glanced up and found James Sinclair watching her with an intensity that made her toes curl. For the first time, she thought coming home might not be so bad after all.

Chapter 3

"Here are the keys to the house," Tony DeCusati said. He handed Carly a set of keys clipped to a World's Best Dad key chain. "Don't worry if you lose them, your mother still keeps a spare under the flowerpot on the back deck."

"I don't understand," Carly said.

She had just pulled into the driveway to find her father, Tony DeCusati, standing in the driveway as if waiting for her. As soon as she parked beside his Buick, he put two fingers in his mouth and whistled at the house. This was his usual signal to Carly's mother that she was needed.

Without so much as a hello, he had yanked the door of the truck open and hauled Carly out as if he was afraid she might change her mind about staying, then he had slapped the house keys into her palm.

"But these are your keys, Dad. Shouldn't I just take the spare? What are you going to do without your keys?"

"Don't you worry your pretty little head about it, sweetie," Tony said. He opened his arms and pulled Carly in for one of his big bear hugs, the sort he gave when he was especially happy.

He glanced behind her and saw the bird and

the dog. Carly knew he was about to start his "no animals" lecture but instead, he just smiled.

"You have a dog and a bird? Nice," he said.

Carly frowned. Who was this man and what had he done with her father?

"She's here! She's here!" Barbara DeCusati cried as she hurried out the front door and raced down the porch steps.

October in Maine was a lovely time of year. The colors of the changing leaves dazzled the eyes, while the smell of wood smoke began to perfume the air as people started to fire up their wood stoves in preparation for winter. Corn stalks and pumpkins decorated porches while the last harvest from the garden was reaped to be pickled, canned, or jellied.

Autumn in Brooklyn was nothing like Maine and Carly had to admit as she watched her mother come toward her that she had missed being home during her favorite season.

"Hi, Mom," Carly said. She stepped forward for a hug, feeling for the first time like everything might be okay, because her mom was here and mothers always made everything better, right?

But Barbara didn't hug her daughter. Instead, she cupped Carly's face and looked into her eyes. "It's good to see you, honey, but now we have to go."

"What? Where?" Carly sputtered.

"Florida!" Barbara said as if it were some magical,

mystical place that was visited by invite only.

She placed a swift kiss on Carly's forehead and grabbed her husband's elbow and dragged him toward the Buick. Carly frowned. What had gotten into her parents?

Barbara DeCusati always greeted her five daughters with kisses all over their faces and hugs that cracked ribs and when she finally let them go, she insisted on feeding them. For Carly, it was always her favorite meatballs and spaghetti because Barbara was sure Carly had lost twenty pounds since she'd last seen her and was convinced that Carly was starving herself, which was one of the many reasons Carly adored her mother.

But not today. Today, her mother gazed at her as if memorizing her face and then she sighed in complete contentment as if she'd just been waiting for Carly to come home.

"We're so glad you're here," Barbara said.

Well, that was more like it, except her parents were still leaving.

"Come on, Tony, I bet we can make it to New Jersey if we put the pedal to the metal," Barbara said.

It was then that Carly noticed that her parents were not dressed in their usual retirement clothes of stretchy jeans and polo shirts and comfortable shoes. Oh, no. They had turned it up a notch with Dad wearing a Hawaiian print under his thick charcoal gray cardigan and Mom rocking her blue wool traveling coat over a pretty pink dress. Barbara DeCusati only wore that coat on special occasions, like winter weddings or holiday vacations. Carly blinked in confusion. What the hell?

"Whooee," Tony said and clapped his hands together. He turned back to Carly. "Great seeing you, baby girl, but we've got to go. Since you're home to look after your baby sister, we are free for the winter!"

"What?!" Carly cried. "You're leaving? No! You can't! Gina and I detest each other! It'll be a bloodbath."

"Stop being so dramatic," Barbara said. "You are sisters and grown-ups, you'll be fine."

"Someone will die, Mom," Carly said. "I am not even kidding."

"Carlotta DeCusati, no one will die or there will be hell to pay," Barbara said. She put her hands on her hips and gave Carly her *do not cross me* look.

"Yes, ma'am," Carly said. Thirty-two years old and she still knuckled under to "the look." "But when will you be back?"

"April or maybe May," Tony said. Then he jumped in the air and kicked his heels together and started to sing, "No snow to shovel, no bitter cold, no wood to chop, no frozen pipes, pour me a piña colada, baby, because I am Florida bound."

On that last long note, he opened the door for

Carly's mom, who climbed into the car, and then he danced—*danced*—around the front and slid into the driver's seat.

As they backed out of the driveway, Barbara stuck her head out of her open window and called, "There's a Crock-Pot full of meatballs for you, dear, love you!"

And her dad cried, "If you need anything, don't call us!"

With a raucous honk, they disappeared down the street and around the corner. Carly stood in the driveway, holding her father's keys and wondering what the hell had just happened?

"And then they just left," Carly said. "Can you believe that?"

"At least your mom left you a Crock-Pot full of meatballs," Zachary Caine said. He was sitting at the counter in Carly's parents' kitchen working on his third serving.

"So you think abandonment is okay if the abandoner gives the abandonee meatballs?" Carly asked. She went to snatch Zach's bowl away but he anticipated her move and looped his arm about it and hissed at her.

"Yes," he said. He glanced at her through the shaggy blonde bangs that hung over his forehead. "I could forgive a lot for a bowl of home cooking."

"He has a point," Sam Kennedy said. He was seated beside his friend and business partner

45

enjoying his second helping while surreptitiously sneaking meatballs to Saul.

"So, it's true what they say about men and their stomachs," Carly said to Jillian, who was fussing over Ike in his cage in the corner of the kitchen.

"Does Ike look all right to you?" Jillian asked. "I think he lost some feathers on his panicked flight through the park."

"It wasn't the park. We were stuck in traffic on I-95 in Connecticut for two hours," Carly said. "I think *I* lost some feathers on that ride."

"Not your tail feathers," Zach said and he goosed her.

Carly smacked his hand away and gave him a reproachful look, although she really didn't mind. Zachary Caine had been her partner in Emma and Brad Jameson's wedding. Because they shared the same phobia of coupledom, they had become fast friends but nothing more, which did not discourage either of them from flirting with the other despite the lack of attraction.

"Come eat, Jillian," Sam said. "Before Zach cleans out the pot all by himself."

Jillian tossed her dark curls out of her face and left Ike with one last worried glance. Like Zach to Carly, Sam had been Jillian's partner in Emma and Brad's wedding and they, too, had become friends. Although, as Carly watched them, she suspected one of them would prefer not to be in the friend zone but sadly the other one was oblivious.

Sam got up from his stool at the counter and offered it to Jillian. She took the bowl that Carly handed her and began to eat. She closed her eyes as she bit down on a meatball, savoring the seasoning that only Mrs. DeCusati could conjure with her Italian mother magic.

"I'm pretty sure your mother is a culinary wizard," she said. Then she gave a little moan while she polished off the rest of it.

Carly was used to Jillian's vocal appreciation of her food and didn't give it much thought, but then she caught the look on Sam's face. He was riveted. When Jillian licked a bit of sauce off her lower lip, Carly could swear Sam's pupils dilated.

Tall and lanky with a thick head of dark brown hair and a boyish face that he tried to make more manly with a beard, Sam was all that was good and kind and reliable. Clearly, he was also desperately in love with Jillian, who Carly knew was completely unaware of his feelings. Oh, brother.

"What. Is. That?"

Carly felt her shoulders snap up to her ears as her little sister's grating voice barked at her from the doorway.

"Hi, Gina. That's Ike, my parrot, and Saul, my dog," she said. She knew the polite thing to do would be to cross the kitchen and hug her sister hello, but she was afraid her hug might venture into a strangle if her baby sister pissed her off, which she usually did in three, two . . .

"Well, they're not staying here," Gina said.

One! Carly curled her fingers into her palms to keep from ripping her sister's curly red hair out at the roots.

"If I live here, they live here," Carly said. She tossed her thick braid over her shoulder and put one foot forward in her fighter stance.

"There is no way Mom and Dad are okay with this," Gina said.

"Actually, Dad met both of them and didn't care one way or another. So there."

Gina crossed her arms over her chest and glared. "Fine. You want them? Move them to your room because I am not dealing with squawking and barking and feathers and dog hair all over my kitchen."

"Your kitchen?" Carly asked. "Since when? And the dog is Saul and the bird is Ike."

"It's mine since Mom and Dad bailed to Florida," Gina said. "I'm the one who lives here permanently so what I say goes."

"Ugh, no," Carly said. "I have five years' seniority over you, so I call the shots and I say the parrot and dog stay wherever they want."

Gina charged forward. She was a taller yet still curvy version of Carly, so in a fight—not that there had been many physical confrontations—they were equally matched. But Gina was a red-head, which Carly believed meant that she was borderline crazy, because every redhead Carly had ever slept with had proven to be a little on the freak side.

Still, crazy quotient aside, Carly figured she could take Gina because she had a few months of life kicking her in the teeth repeatedly to fuel her rage and tussling with her sister might just be the outlet she needed.

"Oh, yeah, that's what I'm talking about," Zach said. He nudged Sam. "Looks like we're getting dinner and a show."

Carly and Gina ignored him and began circling each other, looking for the weak spot. Carly knew she could pull her sister's hair and make her cry, but Gina had her thick auburn hair tied back just like Carly's, making it harder to grab.

"I really don't think your parents would approve of this behavior," Jillian said. Her voice rose with each word. Being an only child, she had no idea how cathartic whooping your sibling's butt could be. She glanced at Zach and Sam. "Do something!"

Zach and Sam exchanged a look as if considering whether they wanted to get involved or go to the fridge and crack a beer and settle in for a good old catfight.

"Now!" Jillian demanded. She stomped her boot on the tile floor, indicating that's what she'd do to their heads if they didn't step up.

"Fine, spoilsport," Zach muttered. He jerked his head in Gina's direction and Sam nodded.

Just as Carly had zeroed in on her target—she was planning to take Gina out in a diving tackle—an arm looped about her waist and pulled her back, thwarting her.

"Hey!" she cried. Zach put her in lockdown with his arms around hers.

"What the hell?" Gina cried. Sam caught her in his arms and lifted her off the ground. She began to thrash and flail. "Put me down, Triple-Shot."

Zach gave Sam a look, and he said, "Barista girl here calls me that because I always order a triple espresso shot in my morning java."

"And if you want it in the future without spit in it, you'll let me go," Gina demanded.

"Nice try but no," Sam said. He pulled her in tighter and pinned her arms to her sides.

"Is this how it's going to be?" Gina cried. "You and your goon friends are just going to bully me whenever you want?"

"Bully you?" Carly snapped. She didn't fight Zach's hold but went limp, hoping he'd release her. He did not. "You want me to get rid of my bird and my dog!"

At this, Ike set to pacing in his cage, bobbing his head and looking like he wanted in on the fight while Saul slunk under the kitchen table trying to make himself as unobtrusive and possible.

"See? You've upset them!" Carly yelled.

"I've upset them? Seriously?" Gina asked. "What are they? The husband and kid you've never had?"

The entire room went still. No one discussed Carly's love life or lack thereof, ever.

A piercing whistle sounded and they all glanced at Ike. He raised one foot with talons splayed and squawked, "She's a cow!"

"Ah!" Gina gasped and wrenched herself out of Sam's grasp. "Did it call me a cow?"

"If the hoof fits," Carly snapped.

"He goes!" Gina roared.

"No, he doesn't!" Carly argued. She shrugged Zach off.

"Fine," Gina said. She pulled out her cell phone, scrolled and tapped, and then held it to her ear.

Carly got the sinking feeling she knew exactly who Gina was calling. The self-satisfied smirk Gina gave her clinched it.

"Don't do it," Carly said. "Do not call her."

"Too late," Gina said. Then she made an over-wrought face and whined into the phone, "Terry, thank goodness you're there. Carly is just being awful to me. She's got a . . . bird . . . and . . . dog . . . and . . ."

Carly dropped her shoulders and stared at the ceiling at Gina's dramatics. Honestly, couldn't Terry, the oldest of the five DeCusati girls, tell when she was being played?

"And it . . . called me . . . a . . . a . . . a . . . cow!" Gina managed to wail the last word, causing both Sam

51

and Zach to clap their hands over their ears as if the frequency was so high it might incur hearing loss.

"Hold me back," Carly said to Zach. "If I get my hands on her, I might just choke her out."

He took her hand in one of his while he scooped another meatball into his mouth with the other.

"Oh, okay, here she is," Gina said. She thrust the phone into Carly's face. "Terry wants to talk to you."

"I'll bet she does," Carly said. She snatched the phone out of her sister's hand. She gave Zach's hand a squeeze and then let go. She strode out of the room, thinking it best to put some distance between herself and Gina. Besides, if she lost her temper, she did not want to be responsible for teaching Ike more bad words.

"Hello, sis."

"Carly, Mom and Dad have been gone for what, an hour?"

"Two, actually."

"And you and Gina are already fighting?" Terry cried. "In two hours?"

"More like ten minutes, since she just got home."

"I told Mom this wouldn't work," Terry said. "Why do you have to pick on Gina? Why can't you be nice to her?"

"Me be nice?" Carly yelled. "She demanded that I get rid of my pets."

"Since when do you have animals?" Terry

asked. "You can't have pets. You can't handle the commitment."

"I inherited them, if you must know, and I'm stuck with them until I can find them a decent home."

"Well, until then, they stay in your room," Terry said. When Carly would have argued, Terry talked right over her. "Do I have to come over there, because I will."

The only thing worse than Gina being a petulant brat was Terry being a bossy butt. Terry loved to lecture, thrived on it, in fact. Her longest known lecture while babysitting her younger sisters clocked in at a little under four hours, the exact amount of time their parents had been out. If she came over now, she might not stop lecturing until April or May.

"No!" Carly said. "I'll move the bird and figure something out with the dog."

"Excellent," Terry said. "And be nice to Gina, she's the baby of the family. She's very fragile."

"She's twenty-seven!" Carly cried. "Maybe if everyone would stop babying her, she'd quit squatting at our parents' house and get on with her life."

"Carly," Terry's voice was full of warning.

"Okay, fine, I'll try to be nice."

"Do more than try," Terry said. With that, she hung up without so much as a *welcome home* or a *how are you* or anything.

Sadly, Carly wasn't even surprised. Terry had always favored Gina. Because Terry had been thirteen when Gina came along as opposed to eight when Carly was born, she had assumed the role of second mother to Gina. She had spoiled her baby sister rotten and their parents had been too grateful for the help to realize the damage that was being done.

Now, as an adult, Gina had zero coping skills. Because of Terry and their parents, she had never wanted for anything, had never known disappointment, frustration, or failure because someone always swooped in and saved the day.

If it had been Gina who lost her job and her apartment, Terry or their parents would have stepped in and paid for her apartment just to keep her from being sad. It was pathetic.

Of course, Gina knew she had it good; so good, in fact, she had never left home to go to college, choosing to commute to a local school instead. Now she worked as a barista in town and appeared to have no motivation to do anything else. And Carly was stuck with her. Ugh!

She turned on her heel and marched back into the kitchen. Gina was helping herself to the last of the meatballs while Jillian, Zach, and Sam were looking anywhere but at her. Carly smiled. At least she had her Maine crew, which was more than she could say for Gina.

"Boys, if you'll give me a hand, I think I'd rather

have Ike up in my room where he can't be con-
taminated by any negative influences," she said.

"Ha!" Gina scoffed. "Terry made you move
him, didn't she? What did she do, threaten to
come over here and lecture you?"

"No," Carly lied. "I'm just being the bigger
person."

"Yeah, by about ten pounds in the ass, I'd say,"
Gina retorted.

That was it! Carly balled up her fist, but Zach
grabbed it and pulled her in for an impromptu
dance around the kitchen. Given that neither
Carly nor Zach could dance, it was a disaster
waiting to happen and Jillian and Sam scrambled
after them, catching the houseplants, trivets, and
kitsch that went flying in their wake.

"Come on, Carly," Zach said. "Let's tuck Ike
and Saul in for the night and head over to Marty's
Pub for a proper welcome home for you. We'll
get you nice and drunk and everything will be
okay."

Carly was certain she'd never heard a better
suggestion in her life.

Upon her second sighting of James Sinclair, Carly
wasn't sure what caught her eye first. It could
have been his lopsided smile, or his big callused
man hands, or maybe it was the thick thatch of
black hair that seemed to stand at attention all
over different parts of his head as if his idea of

combing it was jamming his fingers in it and rubbing, sort of like petting a dog. Charming.

Then again, that wasn't what captured her gaze and held it for several heart-stopping moments at a time. No, his eyes were to blame for that. They were a shade of blue gray hazel, the sort that could switch from bright like a sunny day to foggy like the coldest morning. The fact that they were surrounded by the longest, darkest pair of eyelashes she'd ever seen on a man made them that much harder to ignore, especially when they had been blatantly checking her out all night long.

"So, when are you going to make your move?" Jillian asked. "Or are you two just going to covertly eye fuck each other all night?"

Emma laughed and Mac joined in, as both were shocked and amused by Jillian's blunt turn of phrase. The four women were sitting at a small round table in the front of Marty's while the men had wandered off to play darts in the back of the pub.

"Oh, I'll make my move," Carly said. "I just have to do a little recon first."

"Recon?"

"Yeah, you know, get close enough to determine that there is no ring on his finger or a tan line indicating that there was a ring that's been removed for the evening. Then I have to hear his voice again. I'm pretty sure it was low, but I have to make sure. If it's high-pitched and nasal, that's a total turnoff. Lastly, I need to have him vetted by the boys to make sure he's a good guy."

"Whoa," Mac said. She glanced at the object of Carly's desire. "I had no idea that your criteria for a one-night stand was so strict."

"Of course it is," Carly said. "That's what makes it work; besides, I don't have *that* many."

"You have more than me," Jillian said. Her voice was glum.

"That's because you're the pastor's daughter and you still live in your hometown," Carly said. "If you really want to go girl-gone-wild you have to leave town."

"Someday, I will," Jillian said. "I'll be *fille sauvage*."

"Because you'll be in Paris," Emma said.

She gave her friend a half hug. Everyone knew Jillian's big dream was to travel the world, with Paris being at the top of her list. Unfortunately, her comfort zone was her zip code and no one had managed to talk her into leaving it just yet.

"Back to me, people," Carly said. "I'm pretty sure I want to bag that James guy. Now the aunts seemed to like him, right, Mac?"

"Are you kidding? They adore him, but he is new in town," Mac said. "No one knows his back-story just yet."

"That's okay. I trust the aunts," Carly said. "Oh, excellent, his friend has left him. I'm going to make my move."

"What's your play?" Emma asked. "The standard *don't I know you from somewhere?*"

"Nah, too obvious," Carly said. "Especially since we met this afternoon."

"How about the classic *what's your sign?*" Jillian offered. "It's so old it's making a comeback."

"Please," Carly said. "That's for amateurs."

"How about you look him right in the eye and say, 'Your baby here,' and then point to your belly?" Mac asked.

"Oh, hell no, the man will either stroke out or run as fast as he can and I couldn't blame him." Carly shook her head. "Honestly, do I look like someone who gives off the stank of the desperate?"

"Well, you are—" Emma began but Carly interrupted her.

"Hush your mouth," Carly said. "I've just been having a dry spell, which is why I'm going with my sure thing."

"The one where you ask . . ." Jillian's voice trailed off in embarrassment as she pointed at her crotch.

"That's the one," Carly said.

"Good luck," Mac said.

"Don't need it."

"We'll be here if you crash and burn," Emma said.

"Gee, thanks."

"Find out if his friend is single," Jillian said.

"Roger that."

Carly hopped off her stool and picked up her drink. She polished off her dirty martini in two gulps. Then she shook herself from head to toe to get her game face on.

Carly had known when she went out tonight that she was looking for something, anything, to distract her from the disaster her life had become. The fact that James, the cute physical therapist from the park, was here at Marty's Pub made her think the universe was looking out for her for the first time in quite a while.

Even though it was October, she had pulled together her go-to outfit for pickups, which consisted of a cute floral minidress more suited to June paired with calf-hugging brown leather boots with treacherous heels, and a delicate little sweater that did more to frame the girls than it did to keep her warm.

As she crossed the pub, she hoped her effort had not been for nothing. Judging by the way he watched her walking toward him, it had not. His hazel eyes lit up, making them more blue than gray. He rubbed his hand over his hair as if preparing for her approach—adorable—proving Carly's theory about his style of grooming, casual with a side of sloppy—even more adorable.

She paused in front of his table, pleased to see that his eyes stayed on hers and didn't venture south. He was respectful. That earned him some serious points. She rested her elbows on the table and propped her chin on her hands.

"Excuse me," she said. She made sure she kept her voice low so he had to lean in to hear her. He did. He didn't say a word, but one of his eyebrows rose higher than the other letting her know he was listening.

"My friends and I were having a discussion and I was wondering if you, being a guy, could weigh in on it for us."

"All right," he said. His voice was a beautiful deep bass that made her spine reverberate in response. She had to force herself to stay still and not wiggle with anticipation.

"We were just debating whether men like it better if a woman waxes, shaves, or goes au naturel. Thoughts?"

He didn't move for a second, and then, using his foot, he pushed out the chair his friend had vacated and gestured for her to have a seat. Yep, that line worked every time.

Chapter 4

"Seems to me that is going to require some thought," he said. "What can I get you to drink, Carly? It was Carly, wasn't it?"

She smiled, liking that he'd caught her name this afternoon. Then she gave him a side look as if considering his offer. "A dirty martini would be lovely, James."

He grinned at her, clearly pleased that she'd gotten his name, too.

"Coming up," he said. He stopped the waitress as she passed them, giving her their order.

Carly noted that he was drinking Bluff Point Ale on tap and she knew that Sam, Zach, and Brad would approve of him right away because they co-owned the Bluff Point brewery. She'd have to look to Gavin, who, being a veterinarian, was more of an animal person than a people person and as such had higher standards, to advise her on her catch of the day.

Carly slid onto the seat and faced him.

"Nice to officially meet you, Carly," he said and offered her his hand. There was an intent look on his face that she couldn't read, but she liked it. He was definitely giving her his full attention and what girl didn't like that?

"You, too, James," she said.

His hand swallowed hers up in one gulp and then released it. She'd been right. He had big, manly callused paws that she desperately wanted to feel against her skin. A flash of heat hit her low and deep.

Wow, that was intense. Her life had been swirling in the bowl for so long, she hadn't been attracted to any man in a very long time. Even if it went nowhere tonight, it was nice to feel the fizz and zip of attraction again.

"Carly," he said as if he liked the sound of it on his tongue. "Nice name."

"I was named for my great-aunt Carlotta, who had a wart on her upper lip with two hairs growing out of it," she said. She tapped one ruby red fingertip on her upper lip.

His eyes widened and Carly fought to keep her face straight but when his gaze studied her mouth as if looking for a wart, she cracked and laughed. He gave her an amused look and then he leaned across the table into her personal space.

"Why do I get the feeling you just tricked me into studying your perfectly shaped mouth?" he asked.

"Me?" she asked innocently. "I have no idea what you're talking about. Perfectly shaped, huh?"

"Except . . . wait . . . is that . . ." His voice trailed off as he stared at her mouth with concern.

Carly felt a moment of horror. What if she actually had a wart? Or a pimple? She pressed her fingers to her lips, feeling for any bumps. Sweet chili dogs, she didn't even have an aunt Carlotta. It was just a joke.

Then she noticed the wicked twinkle in his eye. Hot damn! The boy knew how to play.

"Very funny," she said.

He grinned. "For the record, I already noticed your lovely lips." He paused to stare at them, again, making Carly feel hot and shivery, before he added, "As well as your beautiful eyes, gorgeous face, and that figure—well, let's just say you have some dead sexy curves."

Carly started to sweat and her breath was coming in rapid bursts as if she'd just climbed a staircase and was trying to pretend she wasn't winded when she was sucking air big time. She wanted this boy bad.

"Is your dog okay?" she asked. "He really was wonderful with Ike."

"He's fine," he said. "He's got a bum leg, but we're working on it. I think his bird rescue today gave him a nice shot of confidence. How's Ike?"

"He's fine, too," she said. "Maybe a lost feather or two but nothing he won't recover from. So, where did your friend go?"

She hoped he was gone for the night and not just making a pit stop.

"To work," he said. "He's a cameraman on the late news in Portland."

"So, you're all alone now?" she asked.

63

The waitress appeared with their drinks and James waited until she was gone before he answered.

"I am, but I noticed you came in with quite a group, four girls to four guys, unless I miscounted," he said. "This wouldn't be a ploy to make one of those guys jealous, would it?"

"Would it matter if it was?"

"Maybe, not." His full lips curved up a little higher on the right and Carly was charmed stupid by it. "I just don't want to get too attached if this doesn't stand a chance of going my way."

"What way would that be?" she asked. She took a sip from her drink.

"Let's see," he said. "Beautiful girl, gorgeous night outside . . . I see a walk on the boardwalk, a stolen kiss, which wouldn't really be stolen because she wants it, too, and then we see what happens."

They stared at each other for a moment. Carly could feel the blood rushing in her ears. She had never before wanted to leap across a table and rip a man's clothes off, ever, but right now the idea had serious appeal. Man, she'd been out of circulation for too long.

"Those guys are what I call my Maine crew," she said. "Just friends."

"And this night just keeps getting better and better," he said. He looked delighted as he downed some of his beer.

"But, wait, you didn't answer my question," she said.

"Fair enough."

He leaned across the table so that they were just inches apart. Carly felt like she was getting sucked into his gaze as if it were a black hole and she were a passing asteroid.

"I've got to be honest . . ." He paused for so long that Carly felt compelled to say, "Yeah?"

"I don't care what a woman does down there. If I'm lucky enough to be with her, to touch her, to watch her come undone for me, just me, because of what I'm doing to her, then that's good enough for me."

That did it. Carly grabbed him by the shirtfront, yanked him close, and kissed him. It wasn't a nice kiss. It wasn't gentle or timid. It was a full-on assault. She wouldn't have been surprised if James had shoved her off; instead, he grabbed her by the upper arms and pulled her even closer.

Then he took control of the kiss, using his tongue to open her mouth beneath his so he had full access. Carly wasn't sure when it happened—somewhere between his tongue tangling with hers and the way he nibbled on her lower lip—but her brain turned to goo and she was powerless to do anything but hang on while he kissed her senseless.

When they finally broke apart, they were both breathing as if they'd just finished a ten K. Lips were swollen, cheeks were flushed, and deep dark desire clouded any good judgment either of them might have had.

"My car is outside," he said.

"Let's go."

They both got up from the table. James threw down a wad of bills and grabbed her hand as they headed toward the door.

"Oh, my coat and bag," Carly said. She turned and headed toward the table with her friends, pulling James with her.

"Leaving already?" Mac asked.

"James, these are my friends, Mac, Emma, and Jillian. Girls, this is James, okay, bye now," she said. She grabbed her coat and purse and turned back to the door and slammed right into a wall of testosterone.

"Going somewhere?" Zach asked. He crossed his arms over his chest. Sam, Brad, and Gavin fanned out around him.

"Yes, we're leaving," Carly said.

"Not so fast," Sam said. He looked Carly's boy toy over from head to toe as if looking for a police-monitored ankle bracelet or any other indicator that the man was no good. "Name?"

"James, okay?" Carly said.

"James Okay is not exactly what's on my birth certificate, but I kind of dig it. James Sinclair." James extended his free hand to Zach, who gave it a reluctant look before he shook it.

"He drinks Bluff Point Ale, so he's your people, surely that makes him acceptable, yes?" Carly asked.

She was tapping her foot in impatience. Did these men not have eyes? Could they not see that she had bagged a god, or at least a demigod, of hotness? Why, oh why, were they in her way?

"Is that what you think of us?" Brad asked. He looked aggrieved.

"Yeah, like we'd really let you take off with a guy just because he drinks our beer?" Sam asked.

"It's like you don't know us at all," Zach said. He looked at James and asked, "But since we're on the subject, which of our fine brews do you prefer?"

"I'm partial to the amber," James said. "It tastes like it has a hint of nutmeg in it."

The three of them looked at each other and nodded, obviously pleased with James's choice.

"The man clearly has a refined palate," Zach said.

Carly rolled her eyes. She knew they'd be easy to win over. Then Gavin muscled his way forward. He looked forbidding and Carly felt her hopes for a hot night of romance (i.e., sex) get doused like a candle flame being hit with a bucket of water.

"Before you make off with our girl—" he began but Mac interrupted her man and said, "More like make out with our girl—again."

Gavin winked at her. "Exactly, before you make out with our girl again, I'd like to know your intentions."

"What?" Carly cried. She turned to look at James. He was trying not to laugh while she was sure she was going to combust from the hot fire of humiliation that was consuming her.

"You're adorable when you blush," James said, bending low to whisper in her ear.

She blinked at him and felt her face get even hotter. She couldn't remember the last time she had blushed. This sort of thing just didn't happen in Brooklyn.

"Go away!" she snapped at Gavin.

"No can do," he said.

"Dude." She grabbed him by the front of his shirt and pulled him down so they were face-to-face. "I love you like a brother, I do, but you're kind of cock blocking me here."

Gavin burst out laughing, which only made Carly even crankier.

"Wait." James tipped his head to study Gavin. "Don't I know you?"

Gavin stopped laughing and asked, "Maybe, do you have a sick dog or cat that you've taken to the vet recently?"

James shook his head. "I'm new here so I still go to my vet in Portland. I started doing volunteer work for the local animal rescue network though. Last month we broke up an illegal dog breeding syndicate. They had over fifteen basset hounds."

"The place over in Hazelwood?" Gavin asked. "I was one of the vets on call to treat the dogs."

"That's why you look familiar," James said. "You outfitted my boy, Hot Wheels, with his rear support wheelchair. I didn't know you were located in Bluff Point. That's terrific. That'll save me from having to drive him to Portland."

"Hot Wheels?" Gavin asked with a laugh. "Now I remember, you were the one who found the injured dog out in the woods, right?"

James nodded. "That was Hot Wheels. I found him locked in a cage out there. I think the assholes running the puppy mill planned to let him starve to death because of his bum leg."

"You saved his life. We never would have found him if you hadn't gone looking for more dogs." Gavin clapped him on the shoulder. "Nice work."

Carly glanced between the two men. She was all for rescuing animals, truly, but there were pressing matters at hand, or rather, she was quite sure there should be hands pressing her matters by now.

"So, we're good here?" she asked Gavin.

Gavin looked from James to her as if remembering his purpose. He glanced at Mac and shrugged. She nodded in understanding.

Moving to stand in front of James, Mac stood up on tiptoe and whispered in his ear. James's eyebrows rose up to his hairline and he glanced at Gavin.

"Yes, she means it," he said.

"Good to know," James said. He gave Mac a nervous look.

"Carly, can I have a word?" Jillian asked.

If it were anyone else, Carly would have told them where to go, but this was Jillian, her bestie since adolescence. The friend she had woefully misinformed about the actual meaning of the words "blow job" as it had never occurred to her twelve-year-old self that there really wasn't much blowing involved.

"What?" Carly asked.

Jillian pulled her aside while the guys crowded James and asked his opinion on their blonde ale.

"This guy seems different," Jillian said.

"Not as different as he'll seem when we're both naked," Carly said.

"Maybe you shouldn't get naked just yet."

Carly frowned. Mac and Emma joined them and she tried really hard not to feel as if they were ganging up on her.

"What Jillian is trying to say is—" Mac began but Emma interrupted.

"James could be more than a one-night stand."

"No, he can't," Carly scoffed.

"Why not?" Jillian asked. "He's handsome, funny, smart, he rescues animals—what more could you want?"

"I don't want any more, that's the whole point," Carly said. "I don't do commitment of any kind. I can't even commit to a brand of toilet paper. How could I possibly commit to a man?"

"But the right man . . ."

"There is no right man for me," Carly said.

She glanced over her shoulder to make sure James hadn't been chased away by her well-meaning friends with the really lousy timing. Zach was bending his ear, but while James nodded politely, his gaze was on her and she was pretty sure he was picturing her naked, too.

"So, this was fun," Carly said as she fastened her coat. "See you tomorrow."

"Remember tomorrow is your first day of work in the bakery," Jillian said. "If you don't show up, I will hunt you down. I don't care if you and the boy toy are naked or not. I have five special orders, three birthday parties, a bar mitzvah, and a retirement bash to prep and I need you to watch the front counter."

"Gina and I are sharing Dad's old Pontiac," Carly said. "I'll have her drop me off. Don't worry. I'll be there."

She grabbed her handbag, looped her hand through James's arm, and yanked him out the door.

A blast of cold October air hit them as soon as they stepped outside, but Carly was so overheated she didn't care. Neither did James.

He pulled her around the side of the building and pushed her up against the wall.

"I like your friends. They obviously care quite a lot about you," he said. Then he kissed her.

It was just as potent as the kiss in the bar and Carly felt a whisper of caution course through her system. She had a lot of notches on her bedpost and she'd enjoyed pretty much every one, but this, this was different. Jillian was right. *He* was different.

His lips were firm and warm and they fit perfectly against hers. He kissed her with more than just desire. As he breathed her in, it felt as if there was a longing in his kiss, as if he'd been waiting just for her.

Carly broke it off. She was getting lightheaded, clearly, and she was reading way more into this lip-lock than there could possibly be. They'd just met. There couldn't be any longing. And yet, she felt something, something different with him. It was more than desire; it was . . .

"Are you all right?" he asked. "I didn't mean to jump on you, I just couldn't help—"

Carly rose up on her toes, put her hands on his shoulders to steady herself, and kissed him. Was she imagining it? No, there it was, the feeling of connection, like a highly charged wire wrapped around another highly charged wire.

When her lips met his, they fit perfectly together and when she deepened the kiss, he gripped the back of her head and held her in place while he kissed her with a thoroughness that made her woozy.

"—it," he said. He stepped back from her, his hot gaze scorching her from head to toe. "This is crazy, right?"

Chapter 5

"In the best possible way," she said. "So, my place?"

"Only if you're absolutely sure," he said. It looked like the words cost him, and Carly liked him even more for that. "We can call it a night here, and I'll take you home and then we can revisit whatever this might be when we're both feeling more rational."

"You're very sweet," Carly said. "But I'm not a real big fan of being rational." She grabbed his hand and pulled him back onto the sidewalk. "Where's your ride?"

"There," he said. He led her to his car, which was parked at the curb in front of Marty's. He unlocked it and opened the door for her. It was a large SUV but before Carly could hoist herself up, he picked her up and set her on the seat. He closed the door and walked around the front.

Carly glanced behind her and saw that the seats were folded down to accommodate several thick plastic crates full of hand weights, wrist cuffs, stretch bands, yoga mats, exercise balls; truly it was a fitness fanatic's wet dream back there.

As James climbed into the driver's seat, she fished, "So, you're really into the fitness thing?"

He grinned. "Gee, what gave it away?"

"Aside from your perfectly chiseled physique?" she asked. He smiled. "I watched you with Mac's aunts, Sarah and Charlotte, today. You were really good with them. And that's saying something since they can be a bit of a handful."

"I get a kick out of them," he said. "They're very enthusiastic, which is more than I can say for some of my clients."

"Is it hard training people who don't want to work out?"

"Not really. I can be very persuasive," he said. He leaned over the console between them and planted a swift kiss on her mouth, then pressed his lips on the sensitive spot just below her ear before kissing a path down the side of her neck to her shoulder. "Oh, and I believe in rewarding good behavior."

"Oh, my," she breathed.

He winked at her. Then he fired up the engine and left Marty's Pub, following Carly's directions to her house.

The old Pontiac, Gina's car, which was now their shared car, was parked in its usual spot in the driveway and James parked beside it.

"My sister's home," Carly said. "So, we'll need to be quiet."

"You live with your sister?" he asked.

"For now," Carly said. "My life took an abrupt detour off its charted course."

"It happens." He nodded as if he understood. He strode around the front of his vehicle and opened her door. Carly slid out, right into his arms.

James was tall, lean, and muscled. She got the feeling he hefted around the equipment in the back of his truck without even breaking a sweat. Given that she was built strong and curvy, she felt confident that he could handle her. Oh, that thought was a scorcher and so was the kiss they shared.

For the first time in months, Carly felt as if she had some control in her life. Granted it was controlling what happened between her sheets, but it was better than feeling like she was at the mercy of life, which lately seemed to be having a grand old time kicking her legs out from under her every time she turned around.

She led the way to the house. It was dark. Carly knew she had left the porch light on but since it was out, she suspected Gina had shut it off to spite her—man, she could be such a child sometimes.

It took Carly a second of fumbling with her World's Greatest Dad keys to get the door open, but she managed it. She shoved the key ring back into her purse before she had even more explaining to do. It was one thing for James to know she was living with her sister; it was quite another for him to discover that this was her parents' house. A girl could only handle so much embarrassment, after all.

The DeCusati residence was an old farmhouse. The front door opened into a small foyer where an antique coatrack was stationed to hold all of the coats, hats, gloves, and scarves that were required to survive a Maine winter. Since they were just in heavy jackets, Carly didn't bother unloading their stuff on it.

A door on the left led into the front sitting room, which opened up to the large kitchen and dining room beyond. The door on the right was Carly's parents' library with squashy chairs and shelves of books, lining all four walls, which were packed to bursting. Straight ahead was a hallway that led to Carly's parents' bedroom, while just off center was the staircase that led to the five bedrooms above.

The house was over two hundred years old and had been gutted and reconfigured several times over the years, but Tony and Barbara DeCusati had bought it specifically so that each daughter could have her own bedroom. Carly was pretty sure it was the only thing that had kept the girls from killing each other during the teen years.

Since Gina had never left home, she had taken the biggest bedroom at the back of the house as soon as Terry, the eldest, had moved out. Carly was relieved because she had one of the small front bedrooms. If everything went well, Gina would never know that James had been there. Carly never let her partners spend the night, mostly because it would give them the idea that she wanted them to call again—she did not—but also because she really hated sharing a bed.

"This way," she said. She locked the door after him and then took his hand and led him upstairs. She glanced at her sister's door and saw that it was shut with no light shining from under it. Phew.

She pushed open the door to her room. A cold nose shoved up into her palm and she jumped with a little shriek. Saul.

The fluffy golden retriever let out a soft woof and Carly bent over to give him some love.

"Hey, boy," she said.

"You have a dog?" James asked.

"Yeah," she said. "James, this is Saul."

James held out his hand for Saul to get his scent and as if Carly needed his approval of the situation, Saul began to wag. James scratched his ears and Saul wagged even harder.

"Okay, pal, you get to take over the study," Carly said. She opened the door next to hers and Saul trotted into the spare bedroom. Saul glanced at her over his shoulder and Carly nodded, giving him the okay.

Saul jumped up onto the bed, circled around a couple of times before settling down to sleep.

Carly heaved a sigh of relief. She hadn't really thought about the pets when she brought James home but so far so good.

She took James by the hand and led him into her room. Thankfully her mother had turned it into a guest bedroom a few years ago. It was done in pretty shades of blue and white and looked like it could belong in any bed-and-breakfast on Cape Cod.

She switched on the light and ignored the pile of boxes that had been shoved into the corner of her room along with the large cage with the cover over it that was in the opposite corner. Please, bird, do not wake up now.

Instead, Carly turned her attention to James. He was checking out the room as if trying to figure out how it jived with her personality, or at least, what he'd come to know of her personality in the last hour and a half.

Carly could have told him not to bother as they weren't going to know each other that long. To distract him, she gave him a solid shove and caught him off guard. He fell backwards onto the bed with a thump and a bounce.

His look of surprise made her laugh. It had been so long since she'd fooled around with a man, she wasn't sure where she wanted to start. He looked deliciously rumpled. His hazel eyes had deepened to that wicked shade of blue that she found so fascinating.

They lured her in and before she had fully thought it through, she found herself stalking toward him and then pouncing until she was lying on top of him with all of their parts lined up just right.

She moved in slowly to kiss him but he rose up, unwilling to wait, and kissed her first. It was a little rough, a little wild, and more than a little perfect.

James cupped the back of her head with one hand and used his mouth to get to know her. There was no hesitation on his part. He kissed her as if he'd been waiting a long time for this and couldn't wait another second more. It made Carly a little dizzy to feel as if she was the object of his desire not just for the moment but for forever. How did he make her feel that when they had just met?

"You taste amazing," he said. "I think I could spend the entire night just kissing you."

Carly felt her entire body flush with heat. This guy was good, very good, and she wanted more. She unzipped his jacket and pushed it aside. He wore a snug-fitting thermal in the same shade of blue as his eyes. She took a moment to appreciate how it embraced his muscles and then she wanted it gone. She tugged at the hem.

He got the hint and sat up, taking her with him and moving her legs so that they straddled him in the most profound way. Her girl parts were cradling his boy parts and they fit so perfectly, Carly felt herself get hot, wet, and breathless all at the same time.

"Wow," he said. He kissed her while he shoved off her jacket then ditched his own. When the coats hit the floor, his hands found her hips and he rocked her back and forth over his crotch until her vision became blurry and spotted.

"Clothes, must lose the clothes," she panted.

"On it," he said.

Carly didn't have the capacity of speech to clarify that technically she was the one who was on it. Besides, he didn't give her a chance as her cute little sweater went one way and then her dress went another, and she was straddling him in just her boots and underwear.

James dug his fingers into her hair. The long dark curls draped around her shoulders and he used them to pull her close. They were nose to nose and his gaze locked in on hers. He kissed her with his eyes open as if he didn't want to miss a second of her reaction to him. It was crazy hot.

She pressed up against him, feeling slightly naughty at her state of undress while he still had his shirt and pants on. She broke the kiss so she could finally yank his shirt off. He let her and then he pulled her close and rolled so that she was under him and he was pressing her into the soft blue and white comforter.

His lips were moving over every bit of avail-able skin he could find and Carly arched off the bed to meet him. His callused hands moved down her back to cup her backside, pulling her up to meet the hard part of him still zipped into his jeans.

"I'm not going to lie," he said. "It would be powerfully painful to walk out of here right now, but if you have even a smidge of doubt, I'll go. No problem."

Something inside of Carly let loose a soft sigh of appreciation. She was bedding a nice guy. They were few and far between and because they were so rare and precious, she promised herself she'd give him the night of his life.

She reached between them and cupped him with her hand. He bucked and hissed, surprised by the bold maneuver.

"I'm thinking it would actually be a big problem if you were to leave me now," she said. Then she gave him her patent-worthy come-hither look. "So don't you worry. I have no doubts about this, not a one."

James stared at her for a heartbeat. Then he was on her. Carly forgot about the covered cage in the corner of her room, she forgot about her sister down the hall, she forgot what time it was, what day it was, and for a little while what her name was. Yes, he was just that good.

His hands were everywhere at once, drawing

a response from her that she'd never felt before. If it wasn't his hands, it was his mouth. The boy could do things with his tongue that she had previously thought were the stuff of urban legends.

She was sprawled across the bed, completely at his mercy. Somehow, she was only in her boots while he was still half dressed and when she glanced down and saw his thatch of midnight-colored hair between her thighs, she reached down and shoved her fingers into it in an attempt to get a handle on him, on this, on the way he was making her insides clench with spasms of lust and desire.

He was not to be deterred, however. He grabbed her hands and held them at her sides while he nibbled, sucked, and debauched her until Carly was a mindless, throbbing, hot mess.

She arched her back, right on the brink of release, when he pulled his mouth away and said, "Say my name, Carly. I want to know that you know who is making you feel this way."

"James," she whispered.

"Louder," he ordered. Then he put his mouth on her clit and with one stroke of his tongue, that was it.

"James, oh, James!" she cried. She was loud and didn't even care as she was swept under by a riptide of pleasure that seemed to go on and on and on.

When her heart rate finally slowed, she opened her eyes to find him lying beside her with one hand splayed across her belly. Maybe it was because he'd just given her one of the best orgasms of her life, but Carly was pretty sure he was the handsomest, smartest, wittiest one-nighter she'd ever had. And she knew she wanted him to feel the same way about her.

She pushed him onto his back. He let her. She ran her hands over his warm skin, enjoying the sparse hair and firm muscle beneath her fingertips. He let her do that, too. She straddled him, still in her boots, and he cupped her breasts with a reverence that let her know he was a boob guy, thank god—a leg man really wouldn't do her much good.

She let him play for a moment and then she went to work on his jeans. She hiked them halfway down his thighs, making it impossible for him to move.

She pulled away from his hands and began to inch her way backwards, running her mouth over his pecs, which were nicely defined, and lower, the contact giving her the added bonus of making him clench his stomach muscles, which made his hard abs high-def and decidedly swoon-worthy.

She moved lower and lower, working her mouth over him until she noticed that he had gone so still she was afraid he'd passed out on her. She glanced up and caught him watching her with an intensity that almost set her hair on fire. His eyes licked at her like blue flames and when they settled on her lips she could feel the heat.

"Come here," he said.

Chapter 6

Carly, who was usually much more independent-minded, found herself doing as he ordered. Clearly, she wasn't moving fast enough for him as he scooped her close and rolled so that she was on the bottom. He kissed her, long and deep, until her ears started ringing. By the time she came back to her senses, he had kicked his pants off and slid a condom on.

"Last chance to change your mind," he said. His gaze held hers. One look at his face and she knew he would do whatever she asked. Wow.

"No freaking way," she said. Then she reached around him, grabbed his butt, and yanked him forward until he slid right into her all the way, skin to skin, bone to bone. It felt amazing.

"Hot damn, that feels even better than I imagined," he grunted.

He pushed her hair out of her face and kissed her slow just like he was moving down below, in and out, in a steady rhythm that was making Carly sweat and pant.

"Yes, it does," she gasped between kisses. "And it's about to get even better."

She arched her back and clenched her vaginal muscles around his erection as tightly as she could. James grunted and blew out a breath as if it were taking everything he had to maintain control. That really wasn't going to work for Carly. She wanted him to feel just as blissed out and borderline crazy as she had.

"Sunshine, you're not making this easy," he said. "I'm trying to last more than ten minutes here."

"Why?" she asked. She pulled him down so he was pressed flush against her and then she rocked her hips, making him gasp. "There's always round two or three . . ."

"That's it," James said. He reared up and took over. Pushing her legs up high and wide, he put one thumb on her hot spot while he pounded into her. Carly didn't stand a chance.

This time he didn't have to tell her to say his name; she did it on her own, crying out repeatedly, as if begging for more and more and more. The hot swell inside of her was all-consuming. She couldn't think, only feel. For the life of her, she was pretty sure sex had never been like this . . . ever.

"James, oh, James!" she shouted his name while she convulsed around him so hard it almost hurt, forcing him over the edge as well.

"Carly, sweet Carly," he said her name when he collapsed against her, as if these were the last words he would ever utter.

Their hearts were thumping hard; their breathing was staggered. Carly felt as if her limbs had the consistency of wet lasagna noodles and she was betting by the way James was pressing her into the mattress that he felt exactly the same way.

It was a solid ten minutes before either of them moved and then it was James discarding the used condom into the trash can by her bed. He ran his hands through his hair as if trying to kick-start his brain. Then he flopped back against the bed, clearly giving up.

He turned to her and she noticed his eyes were now more gray than blue. They looked content and Carly instinctively opened her arms to snuggle him, which was surprising mostly because she wasn't a snuggler. Then again, when a man delivered the hottest sex a girl could ever remember having, well, a snuggle was surely required.

James paused to pull her boots off, then he drew back the covers and pushed her under the thick comforter. Instead of just letting her collapse on top of his chest, his hands stayed busy stroking every bit of skin he could reach. Carly would have purred but she didn't have the energy, not yet anyway.

"Favorite color?" James said.

"Huh?"

"I want to know some facts about the woman I just defiled," he said. "Favorite color?"

"Well, it used to be green but now it is most definitely a blue gray. Defiled, huh?" she said. She rested her chin on her hands while she studied him. "If anyone was defiled, sir, it was you."

He moved his hand over her backside, down in between her legs and stroked the part of her that he now knew quite intimately. Carly gasped and felt her desire rise up, shocking her with its sharp bite. Usually, after a good tussle she was content for weeks. Not with this man, however; clearly her body had not gotten enough of him just yet.

"You sure about that?" he asked.

She slid one leg over his, until they were intimately lined up. She wiggled her hips and felt him immediately harden. He grabbed her hips, stopping the sweet torture, but not before she noticed that his eyes were shifting toward blue again. She smiled.

"Yeah, I'm sure," she said.

"Don't be," he said. And then, just as before, he took over.

Round two was as hot as before but even sharper because now they knew each other just that much better. The lovemaking lasted only a few minutes longer than the last time but the climax was just as intense as the first, leaving Carly a tousled, sweaty, panting pile of quivering woman.

When James pulled her close to hold her, she didn't even have the energy to boot him out of the bed. As she rested her cheek on his chest, she promised herself that she would roust him out of her bed in a few minutes. Really.

• • •

A bell ringing woke Carly up. It was clanging insistently enough that she couldn't ignore it. She blinked and reached over to shut off her alarm clock, except her alarm clock wasn't there.

She squinted at the nightstand. It was a dark stained maple, not the modern chrome and glass of her own apartment. That's right, she wasn't in Brooklyn anymore. She sighed.

Clang, clang, clang.

The annoying bell kept ringing. She glanced around her room. Sunlight was peeking over the white eyelet half curtains on her windows. She could see the vibrant red shade of the leaves on the maple tree outside her window. It had turned a breathtaking scarlet this year and she had to admit, there hadn't been anything that beautiful outside her window in Brooklyn.

She shifted against her sheets and realized she was naked. In a hot rush, memories of the night before filled her mind. James had been spectacular. She had never had a one-night stand that . . . she felt a warm hand squeeze her hip . . . that was still there in the morning!

Carly sat up and turned to take in the man lying beside her. He was still here! James was still here!

Clang, clang, clang!

"What is that racket?"

The door to Carly's room slammed open hitting the wall. Gina stood there in her pink flamingo pajamas with her hands on her hips and the craziest bedhead Carly had ever seen. James lurched up in bed beside Carly, dropping the sheet off of him and Carly as he blinked at the unfamiliar surroundings.

"Oh, my god!" Gina cried. "You're home one night, one stinking night, and you have a man in your bed! What the hell, Carly? I am so telling Terry on you!"

"Get out!" Carly shouted. She jerked the covers up, covering both James and herself.

As if he sensed his pack was in trouble, Saul chose that moment to sneak around Gina into the room to hop up on the foot of the bed as if to keep watch.

Clang, clang, clang!

"And shut that damn bird up!" Gina shouted. "Some people are actually sleeping in this house."

"Bird?" James asked. He looked at Carly, his eyes bewildered, and then they cleared. "Oh, Ike."

"Yeah, he's over there," Carly said. She turned back to Gina. "Why are you still here? Get out!"

Gina stared at James's muscle-hardened biceps as he reached across the bed to rub Saul's ears then she turned to back Carly looking like she wanted to slap her sister's face.

"I haven't had a date in months and you come home and in less than twenty-four hours, you have a man, a hot man, in your bed. It's not fair!"

"Fair?" Carly asked. "What are you talking

about? This was a one-night stand, no big deal. You have no reason to be mad at me."

"Yes, I do," Gina said. "You always get what you want and I never do."

"Oh, man." Carly dropped her head into her hands. She peeked at James. "I am so sorry about this."

He looked like he was trying to take it all in and trying not to laugh at the same time.

"Do not apologize to him when you should be apologizing to me!" Gina stomped a slippered foot on the floor.

"Gina, you're a spoiled rotten brat. Stop acting like I took something that was yours without asking. I lost my job, my apartment, and my life in Brooklyn, and now I'm stuck here in Bluff Point. What could I possibly have that you don't?" Carly asked.

"Orgasms," Gina said. "By the sound of it, lots of them."

Carly felt her face heat up like it was hit by a blowtorch. She couldn't even look at James for fear that she would implode in a fiery ball of mortification.

"There was none of that here," James said. He slid his hand onto her thigh and she felt him cross his fingers while they squeezed her leg. "I swear we just slept, there were absolutely no shenanigans."

At that point, clearly out of sorts because no

one had lifted the cover off his cage, Ike decided to join the conversation.

In a perfect imitation of Carly's voice in the throes of passion, he squawked, "James, oh, James!"

"Yeah, right," Gina said. The door slammed so hard upon her exit that it rattled on its hinges.

Carly slumped back onto her pillows, pulling the blanket over her head. She was pretty sure she was never going to leave her room ever again in this life.

"Hey, you okay?" James asked.

He tugged at the covers Carly was holding over her head, but she wouldn't let go.

"This is wrong," she moaned. "So very wrong."

"I'm not following. What's wrong?" he asked.

She felt the bed shift as he rose to get up. Thank goodness, he was leaving, and she didn't have to be mean about it. She just didn't spend whole nights with guys. It was a rule. It kept things from getting complicated—like, having her baby sister see her naked with a guy she had just bang-tangoed with complicated.

"You, you're not supposed to be here still," she said.

"Why not?" he asked.

She could hear him moving around the room. How to explain? She figured the direct method was probably best. She didn't want him to get the wrong idea about what had happened last night. While the sex had been off the charts, a one-night stand was exactly that. One night. No strings. No need to exchange last names or cell phone numbers. A young, virile man like James would be thankful to escape any relationship expectations, right?

The rustling in the room stopped. She peeked over the covers to see if he was fully dressed, so much easier to toss him out if he was. Instead, she discovered him standing butt naked in front of Ike's cage. He was looking at Ike, who was giving him side eye.

"Hey there, good lookin'," he said to the bird. "You sure are a handsome fella, Ike."

"James, oh, James!" Ike replied. Then he shook his iridescent green head and raised one foot in what Carly recognized as his kung fu pose.

James burst out laughing. He turned to look at Carly and his grin was wide and warm, causing her to smile back at him even when she knew she shouldn't.

"He sounds just like you," he said. He wiggled his eyebrows. "It's getting me hot."

The look he gave her made Carly's insides spasm in the most delicious way. Uh-oh. She had to nip this in the bud and quick. She glanced at the clock. It was after nine. Saved by the hands of time!

"Oh, dang," she said. "Look at the time. I have to report for my first day of work."

She hopped off the bed, forcing Saul to roll over

as she dragged the sheet with her to preserve her modesty; but really, after last night, who was she kidding? Still, she kept it wrapped around the girls as she bent over to pick up his discarded clothing.

A cold morning draft blasted her backside and she wrapped the sheet tighter. She tossed his underwear at him and he caught it, looking sleepy and surprised at the same time.

She then tossed his pants, shirt, jacket, and socks at him, not giving him a moment to dress, just to snatch his clothing out of the air before it pelted him.

"Okay, good," Carly said. She opened her bedroom door and added, "Bathroom is the first door on the left but don't linger or my sister will likely walk in on you, and in case you didn't notice she is unpleasant in the morning."

"But I . . . shouldn't we—?"

"No time," Carly interrupted.

She pushed him naked out into the hallway and closed the bedroom door. She spun around and put her back to it, trying to catch her breath. Saul was looking at her from under his bushy blonde eyebrows.

"Do not judge me," she said. "I've never spent a whole night with a man before. I have no idea what I'm doing."

Saul gave a sympathetic whine and fell over onto his side.

Jeez, this was awkward. Which confirmed her

reasoning for not letting men sleep over. The morning after was always so much weirder for tossing a man out than the night before.

She glanced at Ike, who was now bobbing up and down on his perch. She got the feeling he was laughing at her.

"It's not funny," she said.

Ike wolf whistled at her and Carly rolled her eyes. This was another man she needed to unload as soon as possible. Surely, he could charm someone into taking him.

"James, oh, James!" Ike cried. Then he cackled. Carly was pretty sure the bird knew exactly what he was saying.

Carly slapped her palm against her forehead. This was a nightmare.

She heard the water in the bathroom running. That got her motivated. She dashed around her room, selecting her clothes for the day.

Jillian's shop was a petite bakeshop called Making Whoopie that specialized in the most famous of Maine desserts, the whoopie pie, and was situated on the town green in Bluff Point. Making Whoopie sold all of Jillian's baked concoctions, from the traditional chocolate cookie with vanilla filling to the more exotic pumpkin spice cookie with blueberry filling. Just thinking about it made Carly drool, and she figured she might need to mainline some whoopie pie filling in order to get her equilibrium back.

She pulled on a pair of skinny jeans, her low-heeled black riding boots, and a tunic-length off-the-shoulder sweater that was as soft as a well-loved bedspread. She finger-combed her tangled hair and braided it into one thick plait that she let hang over her shoulder. She would have killed for a shower but she had no time and she needed to get James gone.

A knock on the door made her freeze. Was it Gina or James? Her brain hoped for Gina but her insides, particularly the lower regions, were rooting for James.

"Carly?" It was James.

"Yeah?"

"Are you all right?" he asked.

"Totally fine," she said. "Just getting ready for work, but you . . . ugh . . . can go on ahead. I don't mind, really." There. She was letting him off the hook from any post-coital weirdness. A guy had to appreciate that, right?

There was silence on the other side of the door. Carly cringed at the awkwardness of the situation. Again, this was why waking up together the morning after was such a bad plan.

"But, hey, thanks for last night, it was fun," she added, hoping that it smoothed things out between them.

More silence.

Carly waited until she figured he had left. Then she sighed with relief. Excellent. Now all she had to do was slap on some deodorant, brush her teeth, feed these animals, and get to work.

She yanked open her door to find James standing there, leaning against the doorjamb with his arms crossed over his chest.

"Sorry, sunshine, but we're not done here," he said.

Chapter 7

"I'm not your sunshine and, yes, we are," she said. She tried to stand firm, really.

"No, we're not." He pushed past her into the room.

"Look, buster, just because we spent a nice evening together does not mean there is anything—" she began to berate him but he interrupted her.

"Nice?" he asked. He paused in front of her and shook his head at her. "Comfortable shoes are nice, hot apple pie is nice, a pretty sunset is nice—what we did last night, that wasn't nice."

His voice got lower with each word until its rough side rubbed against her skin, making it heat up and itch at the same time. How did this man do that with his voice?

He took a step toward her and she took a step back. He did it again and so did she. She was trying to maintain a healthy boundary but he seemed to be having none of that. When her back was at the wall and she had nowhere to go, she steeled herself against him making a move.

She'd let him kiss her, if that was what he wanted. Maybe she'd even let him cop a feel.

That would be a nice parting gift, she thought.

He braced one hand against the wall beside her shoulder, bringing him even closer. She swallowed past the breathless knot of desire in her chest. The urge to launch herself at him was so strong it took every ounce of self-control she had to stay put.

He leaned in even closer until his lips were just a breath away from her skin and said, "What we did was hot."

"Hmm, hot," she murmured.

"Dirty," he said. He moved lower so his mouth was hovering right in front of the girls.

Carly let out a tiny whimper. She didn't mean to; she just couldn't hold it in.

"Delicious," he said. He crouched before her, his hot gaze blasting the crotch of her tight pants.

Carly wanted to bury her fingers into his thick hair and pull him in but she curled her fingers into her palms instead.

James reached behind her and picked up his shoes. He rose to stand and his gaze met hers in a look that pinned her to the wall as surely as if he had pressed her up against it with his own body.

"But it was not 'nice,'" he said. He stepped away from her and sat on the edge of the bed while he pulled on his shoes.

Carly put her hand over her racing heart and tried to get her composure back. Every alarm bell in her system was chiming so loud she had a hard time hearing the thoughts in her head, but it was pretty clear that James Sinclair was too dangerous for her. Period.

Still, she didn't want him to think badly of her. She gulped in a lungful of air and blew out a breath. Maybe if she stroked his ego a little, they could part without this tension between them.

"You're right," she said. "Last night was . . ."

She paused, looking for an adequate adjective.

Ike took the opportunity to fill in the silence with a wolf whistle.

James turned to look at the bird and then he grinned.

"Yeah, that about sums it up," Carly said with a sheepish smile. "It was that."

James bent over and finished tying his second shoe. Then he sat up and looked at her as if trying to make sense of her. Saul butted his hand with his nose and James absently scratched the dog's head while he studied her. She would have told him not to bother but she got the feeling James wasn't the world's best listener.

"But that's as far as you want it to go?" he asked.

"Yes," she said. Relief surged through her and she pushed off the wall, feeling more confident now that he seemed to understand how things were—or more accurately were not—between them. "I don't do relationships."

He pursed his lips and nodded. Saul rolled over to give James access to his belly. Ike clanged the bell in his cage and they both glanced at him.

"Well, you have these two," James said. "So, that's a relationship of sorts."

"Ike and Saul? Yeah, no, I recently inherited them from my neighbor in Brooklyn," she said. "Trust me, as soon as I can find a good home for them, they're gone."

"Hmm," he said. He crossed his arms over his chest and tipped his head to the side. "Just for my own curiosity, have you ever had a boyfriend?"

Carly thought about telling him that it was none of his business—she thought about telling him to get the hell out—but he asked it in such a nonjudgmental way, she felt like she could trust him with the answer even though after eleven years it still caused her great pain and she never, ever, spoke of it.

"I had one once, sort of," she said. "That was more than enough. Believe you me, I will never make that mistake again."

James rose from the bed and moved to stand in front of her. His eyes had spiraled into a soft flannel gray, reflecting the color of his jacket no doubt, but they were full of kindness and compassion and Carly felt a small lump form in her throat.

She glanced away but he was having none of it. He cupped her chin and looked into her eyes and said, "He must have done a helluva number on you. I'm sorry."

Then he pulled her into his arms and just held her. He stroked one of his big man hands up and down her spine in a gesture that comforted and soothed. Carly felt the prick of tears sting her eyes. She blinked. She was not about to cry all over the front of a man she hardly knew— well, except in the most intimate way possible.

She knew she should pull away but instead she soaked up his kindness like a dried-up sponge. It felt so good to be held, to have a man care about her sorrow and try to ease it without looking for something for himself. It was . . . nice.

She almost laughed at the thought but she didn't because she was afraid it might trigger some tears. Instead she leaned against him for just a moment or two. She told herself that it was because this was a much gentler way for them to part company than her throwing his clothes at him, but deep down she knew. She knew she was savoring the feeling of his solid strength and on a day in the future when she wasn't feeling so strong she'd revisit the memory and use it to pick herself up if need be.

After a few minutes, he stepped back and Carly let him. He smiled down at her and said, "So you want this to be good-bye."

"Yeah," she said. "I think that's for the best. I mean, I'm not even planning to be in town that long." She gestured to her laptop computer, sitting on the desk. "I have a goal to send out ten résumés per day, every day, until I get a job back in New York. Really, I'm just passing through."

"Hmm," he hummed noncommittally.

He cupped her face and studied her features as if memorizing them. Carly felt horribly self-conscious about the eyebrows she'd let go, the fact that any makeup she had on was a remnant from last night, and she was pretty sure she was getting a pimple on her chin. He didn't seem to notice or care about any of those things. He smiled at her and it was tender and lovely and warmed Carly from the inside out.

Then he placed his lips on hers in the gentlest of kisses and the impact about took her out at the knees. Without thinking about the consequences, she twined her arms about his neck and pulled him flush up against her. She opened her mouth under his and encouraged him to plunder and pillage with his lips, teeth, and tongue as much as he wanted.

They were both breathless when they finally parted. Carly could feel his response to the kiss pressing up against her belly and she knew from the throb between her own legs that things could go sideways, in the best possible way, if they didn't get away from each other right now.

"One-night stand, huh?" he asked.

"Yeah," she said.

They stared at each other for a moment and the next thing Carly knew, they grabbed for each other at the same instant as if neither of them were quite ready to let the crazy attraction between them go just yet. He hauled her up against him and kissed her while she wrapped her arms about his neck and kissed him back. This time he maneuvered her so that her back was against the wall. His hands stroked her sides, just brushing against her curves but not fully committing to groping. It was maddening.

Carly clutched the back of his neck and hoisted herself up to fasten her legs around his hips while deepening the kiss by thrusting her tongue into his mouth. The contact was electric and this time it was James who let out a moan and curse as he grabbed her hips and drilled up against her even though the barrier of their clothes kept them apart.

"James, oh, James!"

Carly wasn't sure if it was her or Ike squawking. She just knew that it was exactly what she was feeling, as if she could never get enough of this man, ever.

"Carly?" a voice called from the hallway.

Carly ripped her mouth away from James. He fastened his lips on her throat while she clenched her legs around him and yelled, "Go away, Gina!"

"I would but I'm not Gina."

The door to the bedroom was thrust open and there stood Jillian, slack jawed and wide-eyed.

Chapter 8

Carly dropped her legs from around James's waist but he thwarted her escape by cupping her bottom and keeping her pinned between him and the wall.

"Sorry, am I interrupting something?" Jillian asked. She looked like she was fighting a laugh.

"Yes," James growled at the same time Carly said, "No."

Now Jillian did laugh.

"Put me down," Carly hissed.

She could feel her face flaming in embarrassment while James appeared singularly unaffected by their surprise guest. Reluctantly, he released her and a spike of lust stabbed Carly low and deep as she did a slow slide down his body before her feet hit the floor. For a second, she almost slammed the door in her friend's face and jumped James Sinclair's bones for the fourth time.

Thankfully, Jillian's laughter forced Carly's good sense to kick in and she did no such thing.

"What are you doing here?" Carly asked her friend.

"It's nine thirty," Jillian said. "Since Gina didn't drop you off at nine, I thought the two of you might be having issues about carpooling. I told you I'd come get you if you didn't show up at Making Whoopie on time."

Carly glanced at the clock. Yup, she'd blown it. "So you did."

"Making Whoopie?" James asked with a grin.

"It's my whoopie pie bakery on the town green," Jillian said. "I make the best whoopie pies in Maine. You should come by."

"No, he shouldn't," Carly said. "Er, I mean he's all into fitness and whoopie pies are bad for you, really bad, with all that fat and sugar."

She could feel James watching her. She was afraid to look at him for fear she'd get swept into his hotness and do something stupid like give him her number or knock him down and have her way with him. Truly, it could go either direction. This was why one-night stands were not supposed to leak into morning. It was a rule. Damn it!

"Well, I'll take that under advisement," James said. Clearly, he was trying to smooth out the awkward. "I guess I'd better go."

"Yup. Good-bye, James, and, uh, thanks," Carly stammered. She closed her eyes. Good god, she sounded like an idiot. What was she thanking him for? Orgasms? Sheesh!

"James, oh, James!" Ike squawked.

"Oh, my!" Jillian's eyes went wide.

Carly felt her whole head burst into a big ball of mortified heat. Could this morning possibly get any more embarrassing? She didn't think so. She glanced at James to see if he was suffering equally. He was not. In fact, he was grinning.

It made her want to kick him or kiss him—no, definitely kick him.

"Will you excuse us for one second?" he said to Jillian and he gently shut the door in her face.

Carly blinked at him. What did he think he was doing? He couldn't just . . . He began to walk toward her. The look on his face was intensely sexy. It went from her mouth to her eyes and back to her mouth.

"I need to make one thing clear before I go. I know you think this"—he paused to gesture between them—"is done, but it's not. Not even close."

"I—"

That was all she got out before he put his mouth on hers and kissed her with a single-minded focus that made her entire body hum with a desire so strong she was pretty sure she was vibrating.

When he broke the kiss, he leaned back to study her face as if trying to memorize the way she was looking at him right now. His eyes were a fiery shade of bright blue and he ran his thumb over her swollen bottom lip. A slow smile of satisfaction parted his lips.

"I'll see you around, sunshine," he said. Then he kissed her one more time. It was swift and sweet but no less scorching for its brevity.

As he left the room, Carly put her hand over her heart. She was pretty sure she was having a heart attack. Jillian came into the bedroom and her eyes were positively bugging out of her pretty little head.

"Oh, wow, that was totally hot," she said. She looked at Carly in alarm. "You are so screwed."

"Shh," Carly hushed her friend.

They listened to his footsteps go down the stairs and then heard the front door shut after him. Carly collapsed onto the messy bed in a heap of stress and nerves. For the first time ever, she thought she might have taken on a man she couldn't bend to her will.

"I can't believe you let him spend the night," Jillian said. "I never would have come up here, but Gina was in the kitchen and she waved me up. Swear to god, I had no idea he was still here. What was he doing here, by the way? You never let guys sleep over, ever."

"Yeah, I know," Carly said. She draped her forearm over her eyes. What had happened last night? Clearly, she was just in a weird place from moving home, right? Right. "It must have been the emotional upheaval of coming home. I was too exhausted to give him the boot after, well, you know."

Jillian was watching her and Carly didn't like the speculative look in her eye.

"What?"

"Nothing."

"Please, I know that look and it is not nothing," Carly said.

"I just find it interesting that he spent the whole night and you were clearly going to greet the day with your eggs over easy . . ."

Carly burst out laughing. It was part embarrassment and part genuine humor. Jillian had a way of getting right to the heart of it. Last night had been different for her but now that James was gone, taking the fog of lust with him, she could see that her lapse in judgment in letting him sleep over was just an aberration. Nothing more.

If there was a tiny part of her shouting that what she'd experienced with James—the chemistry, the way he made her feel worshipped, adored, and lusted for—was not something she felt with most guys, well, she would just hold a pillow over that tiny part of her until she snuffed it out. Problem solved.

"I think maybe it's just been a really long time since I was with someone, and I got carried away," she said.

"Uh-huh." The disbelief was loud and clear in Jillian's voice, but she said no more. Instead, she leaned forward and grabbed Carly's hand. She pulled her to her feet and studied her face. "Whatever you say but right now we have to go. I have massive orders waiting to be filled, and I need you."

"You could have called me," Carly said. "You didn't have to come over."

"I did but it went right to voice mail."

Carly grabbed her phone out of her purse. She glanced at the display and pressed the button on the front. It didn't respond. Her battery must have died. She tucked her charger into her purse and then shrugged on her jacket.

"No, don't leave me," Ike squawked from his cage.

Carly and Jillian exchanged a glance.

"Did he just . . . ?" Jillian asked.

"No, he can't understand . . ."

"Don't leave me," he squawked. And Saul, as if sensing his pal needed backup, gave a soft woof and then lowered his head, giving Carly a look full of sad eyes. She'd have to be made of stone to resist him.

"Can they?" Carly asked.

Carly patted Saul's head, then she approached Ike's cage suspecting the pretty green bird and his dog buddy were playing her. Ike hopped from foot to foot, bobbed his head, and shook his tail feathers while Saul's gaze remained steadily aggrieved.

"Maybe they're lonely," Jillian said.

"I suppose I could play the radio for them," Carly said.

"Then Ike might start talking like a DJ—or worse, some blowhard on talk radio."

"If Gina would let me put them in the main part of the house at least they'd be able to see

112

the goings-on," Carly said. "Up here, I'm afraid they're going to be sad and bored."

Jillian sighed and then nodded. "Find his travel cage and Saul's leash. They can come to the shop with us. But Saul can't shed all over the food. He'll have to stay in the yard in back. And if Ike poops on anything, he's out and you're cleaning it up."

"I promise," Carly said. "Hey, maybe we'll get lucky and someone will come into the shop and fall in love with them and offer to take them off of my hands for the very low price of nothing."

"A bargain," Jillian said.

Carly put his travel cage on the bed and opened the door. Turning toward Ike, she opened the main door and slid her hand in. She'd been watching the parrot for almost a week now but every time she had to pick him up, she got tense and nervous.

She'd seen him crack a nut with his gray beak like it was made out of paper. She really didn't want him to do that to her knuckles. She took a deep breath and put her finger in front of his belly so he could step on her outstretched hand.

Ike bobbed his head and gave her the side-stare.

"If you want to come with us, you have to climb on," Carly said.

Ike shook himself once more and then stepped onto her hand, the fleshy part between her thumb and pointer finger. She knew it was ridiculous but she was pleased that he trusted her enough to do so.

"I suppose this just makes sense since I have to take him to Gavin for a checkup anyway," Carly said. "Our appointment is at two. I'm hoping he can tell me how to curb his language issues."

"Shut your cake hole," Ike said.

Carly put him in the smaller travel cage and sighed. "That is not going to find you a nice home, Mr. Ike."

"Nice home," he said. "James, oh, James!"

Saul woofed and Carly was pretty sure he was laughing at her.

Jillian snorted, and Carly felt her face get hot as the bird really did do a spot-on impression of her. "Huh, I think I prefer the profanity."

James sat in his car, pondering the extraordinary events of the past twenty-four hours. Carly DeCusati. The name on the mailbox confirmed what he had suspected when he first saw her yesterday at the park, having just hurtled back into his life like a comet scorching the earth. For a second, he considered checking his skin for burn marks but then again even if he was suffering from third-degree blisters, he'd do it all over again. The woman had straight-up blown his mind.

They'd met once before, a lifetime ago, and he had never forgotten her. He could still see her in her red dress with her long dark brown hair loose about her shoulders. She had beamed at him with a smile that stopped his heart even though she hadn't really seen him. No, her entire focus had been on the man she was with at the time. James hadn't even been a blip on her radar.

But for James she had punched right through his chest to imprint on his heart and he had never forgotten her or the time they'd spent together. In fact, it had taken everything in him to do the right thing and walk away from her back then, but he'd done it.

Oh, he'd dated and he'd even managed to fall in love once or twice but no one had ever hit him with the same impact that Carly DeCusati had. He felt as if he'd been waiting forever for her or someone like her to come into his life and then *BOOM* there she was.

Did he believe in love at first sight? Yes, he did, because that was exactly what he'd felt the very first time he'd laid eyes upon her. He had been completely undone by her then and now, after last night, he was even more sure that she was the one.

He caught sight of his reflection in the rearview mirror and realized he was grinning like an idiot. He tried to stop, really, he did, but the smile on his face could not be bent into a scowl no matter how hard he tried. Last night had been a fantasy come true, a night he would never, ever forget.

Then he frowned, remembering what Carly had

said right before they landed in another clinch, a clinch that still had Mr. Happy looking for his new playmate. Carly had been very clear that she wasn't interested in anything more than a onetime-only, no-strings-attached, don't-call-me-in-fact-please-lose-my-number sort of deal. That had been his opening to come clean about their past, the fact that they actually had met before, but he'd been caught off guard and the moment had slipped by him.

He knew he should respect her wishes. It was the gentlemanly, honorable thing to do. He knew that. Yeah, and he had no intention of doing anything even remotely like that. Although, if she did remember meeting him before, things could get complicated, really complicated. He considered the possibility and knew that he'd have to come clean sooner or later, but he simply could not walk away from this woman, not again.

When something this good came along, a once-in-a-lifetime sort of something, it was a moral imperative to follow up on it. Especially since she had walked into his life twice now. Perhaps if they saw each other again, there wouldn't be the same fire-to-gasoline sort of combustion they had shared the previous evening, but he knew that wasn't true. The way Carly affected him every time she crossed his radar proved that one night spent naked and sweaty together was not enough to get each other out of their systems. James suspected that would take a lifetime.

Yes, Carly had made it pretty clear that a repeat was not going to happen as it was not her way. But, she had also let him spend the night and she had been clear that that was not her usual style either. So, he was already off to a good start.

Now he just had to figure out how to see her again. Winter was coming and the tourists were leaving Bluff Point as fast as the leaves were dropping. By the end of October, their town would shrink from its summer seasonal high of twenty-four thousand to a mere eight thousand. In a few weeks, it would actually be difficult not to run into each other. His smile returned with his optimism.

He saw a curtain twitch in the window above and realized that sitting in his car not moving probably looked weird, so he turned the key and fired up the engine. He checked his phone, noting that he had two voice mails and several emails to deal with from work, but first he needed coffee.

Caffeine would help defog his brain and maybe help him come up with a plan to get Carly to see him again. Because, oh yes, he fully intended to see her again if for no other reason than to prove to her that last night had been pure, delightful, most definitely repeatable madness.

The bells on the shop door clanged and Carly shot a glance at it over her shoulder. When she recognized the unkempt, shaggy head of blonde hair and the beaky nose of the man who entered, she felt her heart settle back down in her chest. Zach, of course, it was Zach.

She was not disappointed. She was relieved. Really. She hadn't expected James to swoop into the bakery and sweep her off of her feet. She didn't even want him to. In fact, she was afraid that he would, yeah, that was it. She didn't want to have to endure a prolonged conversation about the status of their non-relationship and have him get all butt hurt and sad.

Because it was just a night of good sex. Okay, that was a lie. It was the best night she'd ever had, with the nicest guy and the hottest sex, but still, Carly didn't do the couple thing. She had learned her lesson and she was never going to let herself be that vulnerable again. Even if James could do the most amazing things with his hands and his mouth, she was not interested. All of a sudden, she felt overly warm and glanced around the shop to see if a fire had broken out in the bakery kitchen.

"Yo, Carly, you in there?"

She glanced up to see Zach standing right in front of her. He was grinning at her, like a dope, and nodding. He turned his head and shouted over his shoulder at Sam, who had followed him into the bakery.

"Oh, yeah, she definitely had the pants-off

dance-off last night, and it looks like it was a good one."

"What?" Carly asked. "How do you know that? Wait, don't answer that. It doesn't matter as it's none of your business."

"You're our friend," Sam said as he joined them. "Of course it's our business." He studied her and then smiled. His Maine accent thickened when he spoke. "Ayuh, looks like someone was up late playing pelvic pinochle."

"Guys! I expect better from you than that," Jillian chastised them from behind the cash register. The shop was mercifully empty of customers, but still Carly was pleased that her friend had her back and was putting the boys in their place.

"What?" Zach cried. "I thought those metaphors were pretty good."

He turned back to Carly and took the napkin dispenser she was strangling in her hands and put it back on the small café table.

"No, not even close, because from what I saw, she was most definitely testing the suspension," Jillian said. Then she wiggled her eyebrows.

Zach hooted, Sam went wide-eyed, and Carly gave her dearest friend a blast of stink-eye that should have fried her hair like a bad perm.

Not one to miss the point, Zach crossed his arms over his chest and looked at Jillian with a smirk. "You saw? Do tell."

"Don't you dare," Carly said.

Jillian ignored her. "Truthfully, it was this morning and they were fully clothed so maybe it was just a good-bye grope."

"Wait!" Sam moved to lean on the glass display counter that housed Jillian's whoopie pies. "Did you say 'this morning'?"

She nodded and he exchanged a look with Zach, who stared at Carly in shock.

"Morning?" he asked. His voice was outraged as he continued, "You let him spend the night?"

"I lost track of the time and fell asleep," Carly said. "NBD."

"No big deal?" Zach cried. "You have just opened the door to a possible relationship. That is a very big deal."

"Oh, my god, you are totally being a drama queen," she said. "We didn't exchange phone numbers, heck, I don't even remember his last name."

"Sinclair," Sam said.

Carly looked at him in confusion.

"What? He told us last night at Marty's Pub, and I happen to have an excellent memory. You didn't think we were going to let you go off with a guy without memorizing his last name, did you?" He jerked a thumb in Zach's direction. "This one even got the license plate off of his car and Brad ran a quick check on an Internet mugshot website to see if he'd been arrested. He hasn't been." He looked at Zach. "I think I'm offended."

"You're offended?" Carly cried.

The bells on the door jangled and Mrs. Finnick and Mrs. Tharp came in. They were two of Jillian's regulars and swore by her version of the Snickerdoodle, a whoopie pie made with cinnamon cake and cream cheese filling.

Jillian gave the three of them a keep-it-down look as she stepped away from the counter and went to greet the ladies. Carly turned her back on the customers and zeroed in on Zach and Sam.

"If anyone should be offended, it's me," she said. "I can't believe you don't trust my judgment."

"You've been having a rough patch," Sam said. "We were concerned that you weren't thinking clearly."

"And if you let him spend the night . . ." Zach began but Carly interrupted.

"So what?" she asked.

"So letting a man sleep over is a game changer, right, Sam?"

Sam was watching Jillian smile at her customers, and it took Zach nudging him with an elbow to bring his attention back to the discussion.

"Right, Sam?"

"Huh?" he asked. He rubbed the spot on his side where Zach's elbow had connected. "Sorry, I lost the thread there."

"Yeah, I noticed," Carly said.

She raised her eyebrows at the lovesick-puppy

look on Sam's face while he watched Jillian. Suspicion that the poor boy was smitten— confirmed. Jillian might think they were just friends but Sam had a whole other agenda going on. He glanced away from Carly's scrutiny and studied the chalkboard menu on the wall behind her. Zach caught on to none of this as he launched right back into his lecture.

"This guy is going to think there's more going on than you do," he said. "That's what happens when you let a man sleep over."

Carly rolled her eyes. "No, he won't. Honestly, it wasn't even that good."

She crossed her fingers, feeling bad about fibbing but doing it anyway so that Zach would stop bugging her. It was then that Ike decided to chime in and expose her for a liar.

"James, oh, James!" he squawked from his cage in the corner. He bobbed his head, his whole body bouncing up and down as if he was acting out what he had heard last night. "James, oh, James!"

Zach and Sam whipped their heads in the direction of the bird. Slack jawed, they swiveled back to Carly, who closed her eyes and prayed for a comet to hit the bakery right then and there. No such luck.

Chapter 9

The big dumb man-boys burst into hearty guffaws and it took all Carly had not to kick them in the privates to quiet them down or take them out, whichever worked most effectively.

"Carly." Jillian's voice was full of warning and Carly knew she was afraid that Ike would freak out her customers with his display of parrot porn.

"I'm on it," Carly said.

"Or, you were," Zach quipped and he and Sam doubled up again.

"Hush," Carly hissed at him.

"Shut your stupid cake hole," Ike echoed her.

"Oh, dear," Mrs. Finnick said. She put her hand to her throat as Ike went back to bobbing up and down and crying out for James.

Jillian looked wild-eyed at Carly. She nodded and stripped off her apron and grabbed her purse and jacket out from behind the counter.

"I'm just going to take him to see Gavin," she said. "You know, an hour early—call me if you need me."

Jillian waved good-bye as Carly hefted up Ike's travel cage and made for the door.

"Has the bird been eating any of the whoopie pies?" Mrs. Tharp asked. "Because I would be very interested in that."

"Me, too," Mrs. Finnick said.

Carly let the door swing shut on Zach and Sam as they hooted with laughter. She could feel her face was hot and a small part of her thought about opening Ike's cage door and letting him fly. She didn't do it but she thought about it.

The cage was large enough that it was unwieldy and she had to carry it all the way across the town green and down a side street to Gavin's veterinary office. Ike wasn't terribly happy about it either as he took his bell in his mouth and clanged it against the side of his cage, like a prisoner running his tin cup across the bars in his jail cell.

Carly passed a couple who was window shopping in front of a bookstore and she had to step out and around them as they decided to smooch right in the middle of the sidewalk.

"Honestly, get a room, people," she muttered. Then she looked at Ike in horror. "Do not repeat that, mister."

He shimmed across his bar away from her as if her crazy might be catching.

"Carly, wait! Carly!"

She turned around to see Zach jogging toward her. Both his coat and his shaggy blonde hair were flapping in the breeze as he ran. Obviously, he hadn't taken the time to get himself together before coming after her.

Carly paused to wait for him. When he stood

beside her, red in the face and panting, she scowled.

"What's wrong?" she asked. "Was there a joke at my expense that you forgot?"

"Aw, don't be like that," Zach said. He straightened up and gave her his most charming lopsided smile. "Who's your buddy?"

She continued to scowl.

"Come on," he cajoled. "Who's your buddy?"

Carly pushed Ike's cage at him, giving him no choice but to carry it for her.

"You are," she said. She gave him her sweetest smile as he staggered with the awkwardness of the cage. Ike squawked and flapped his wings while Zach shifted the cage in his arms.

"Lead on, my queen," Zach said. He bowed his head and Carly forgave him just a little.

They were halfway across the dry brown grass on the town square when Zach broke the silence.

"So judging by Ike's input, last night was way better than 'not even that good.'"

"No."

"No, what? No, it wasn't or no, it was?"

"No, just no, as in, no, I'm not talking about this with you," she said.

She turned and gave him her frantic face. It was the one she formerly used to express her dismay when the purchases of big-girl panties she had made for her middle market department stores went missing or when there was no way she could manage to purchase what the stores required within the budget constraints they had set upon her.

"But we're besties," Zach whined in a falsetto that made Carly's ears bleed. "I'm the man whore and you're the—oh, maybe I'm looking for a different word there."

"You think?" Carly asked. "And you're not a man whore. You're just not interested in a relationship and there's nothing wrong with that so long as no one gets hurt."

"As far as I know, I have never hurt a soul," he said. Ike was giving him a death glare, which Zach gave right back to him. "I swear."

The green parrot seemed unconvinced.

"Well, I haven't either and I'm not going to now," she said. "I mean, James didn't ask for my phone number and I was very clear that it was a one-night thing."

"Was your talk before or after Jillian walked in on your morning round of hide the salami?"

Carly huffed out a breath. She would have slapped him on the shoulder for that but he was carrying Ike.

"It was before, but I don't think that makes a bit of difference," she said.

"Carly, Carly, Carly." Zach shook his head at her. "Don't you know that we men are dumb creatures? We go by actions not words."

"Meaning?" she asked.

"Meaning everything you said to him went in one ear and out the other, while he locked in on the fact that you were warm and willing in his arms *after* your parting speech," he said.

They paused on the edge of the sidewalk. Carly checked both ways and then took Zach by the arm and led him across the street and around the corner to the building that housed Gavin's office.

"Even if that was true, he doesn't have my last name or my number," she said. "He couldn't get in touch with me if he wanted to, which I really don't think he does."

"Yeah, Bluff Point is not Brooklyn," Zach said. "We're a petite hamlet of people who spend a lot of time tripping over each other at Sunday bean socials, which is why I do most of my hooking up in Portland."

Carly heaved a sigh. She knew he was right. The odds of not running into James were not in her favor. Still, if she kept to the shop and home and did her carousing out of town like Zach, surely, she could manage it. Then again, after last night she really couldn't imagine carousing with anyone else.

Carly gasped. Where had that thought come from? She tripped on a patch of sidewalk and went careening forward, narrowly avoiding doing a spectacular face-plant.

"Whoa, you all right?" Zach called out. He

couldn't even offer her a hand as he was still holding Ike.

"Fine, I'm fine." Carly had caught herself on the edge of Gavin's office. She shook her head as if she could shake off the disturbing thoughts rioting through her head.

She was overtired. A night of not sleeping would do that to a girl. Obviously, she would want to hook up with someone again eventually. It was just that she was exhausted and not thinking clearly. Yeah, that was it.

She pushed off the wall and strode forward, stepping on the mat to trigger the automatic doors. She gestured for Zach to lead and she followed, the doors sliding shut behind her.

Jessie Connelly, Gavin's front desk person, was seated at the counter. She glanced up at them over the top of her rectangular-framed black glasses. When she saw who it was she frowned.

Carly and Jessie did not like each other. That was putting it mildly. Seven years ago Jessie had absconded with Mac's fiancé, Seth Connelly, literally driving off with him right in the middle of Mac's wedding ceremony.

As it turned out, Jessie had done Mac a huge favor as Seth was a bully, a letch, and a drunk, but Carly had grudge-holding hardwired into her DNA so while Mac had forgiven Jessie and had even gotten her a job working for Gavin, Carly was not quite so forgiving.

"Oh, it's you," Jessie said. She glanced at her computer monitor with a frown. "You're early, way early."

"Yeah, well, it's an emergency," Carly said.

Jessie hopped to her feet. "Is the bird sick? Should I call Gavin? What are his symptoms?"

"What would you say his symptoms are?" Zach asked Carly as he placed the cage on the counter. "Aural retentiveness? Verbal audaciousness?"

"Silence," Carly said. She turned back to Jessie, who was looking at Ike with concern. "Just call the doc—please."

"Gavin is with another patient right now," Jessie said, her tone matching Carly's overly polite one. "But I can put you in exam room three, if you'd like to wait for him."

She ran a hand through her bangs, which had an unintentional ombre thing going on with her ends being several shades lighter than her roots, and adjusted her glasses.

Jessie had always been one of the pretty girls when they were in high school, but now, wearing scrubs and a cardigan with sensible shoes and a clip that kept most of her hair out of her face, she looked every bit a woman in her thirties just trying to get by. She also looked vulnerable, which made Carly's grudge lessen a bit, but only a bit.

"That'll do," Carly said.

Zach was watching the two women as if the crackling tension between them might be the prelude to a mud wrestling match. Carly would have cuffed him upside the head but she wanted him to stick around and carry the cage back for her, yes, because she could be selfish like that.

"If you'll follow me," Jessie said.

Zach hefted the cage while Carly fell in behind Jessie. She noted the slump in Jessie's shoulders but reminded herself she didn't care. If Jessie wanted people to like her maybe she shouldn't make off with people's fiancés. The best she could manage was to be polite to the woman and that was mostly because Mac had asked her to be.

"Thanks, sweetheart," Zach said as Jessie opened the door for him.

She visibly bristled. "Don't call me 'sweetheart.'"

"I'm sorry?" Zach said it as if it was a question.

"You should be," she said. "Women are not 'sweethearts' or 'honeys' or 'babes.' We're human beings and we deserve to be acknowledged as such."

Carly looked wide-eyed from Zach to Jessie and back. Zach looked stunned while Jessie looked indignant.

"I'm sorry. Do we know each other?" Zach asked. "Because I am quite positive I would remember you if I . . . if we . . . you know."

Jessie pulled her cardigan tightly around herself as if afraid he was going to violate her with his eyeballs.

"No, we do not," she snapped. "Because I am not your type. I've seen your type and I know exactly how you operate, buster."

"Oh, yeah?" he asked. He stuck his jaw out as if he was looking to take a punch and knew he could handle it. "And what's my type?"

"Young and horny," Jessie said. "At least judging by the parade of slores that seem to trip up and down your walkway at all hours of the night."

Zach put the cage down on the counter in the small room and propped his hands on his hips. He looked outraged.

"What do you know about my walkway?"

"Nothing except it runs parallel to mine so I have a front-row seat to the booty parade every night," she said.

"Wait." Zach held up his hands in a stop motion. "You're my neighbor?"

Jessie glared at him. If looks could kill, Zach would be buried six feet under and, judging by the look on Jessie's face, he'd be cradling his privates and crying.

"I'm not surprised you haven't noticed," she said. "What with all the twenty-something hoochie mamas traipsing through your life. Ugh!"

"Hey, don't be mad. You're a little older than I normally go for, but I could probably fit you into the rotation," Zach said.

He looked at her as if he knew he was needling her and was doing it anyway. Carly was surprised

131

Jessie didn't rip his head off with her bare hands. In all fairness, after that last crack, Carly would not have blamed her a bit.

"Oh, please, I wouldn't sleep with you if you were a verified sex god and could make me orgasm just by looking at me!" Jessie declared, emphasizing it with a toss of her head.

"Well, some have hinted that I might be godlike, but the looking thing, that would be new, but I'm willing to try," Zach said with a wicked wink. Clearly, the man had no sense of self-preservation.

Carly eased her way in between the two of them. She was afraid Jessie was a little bit too close to striking range and she really didn't want Zach incapacitated before he carried Ike back to the shop for her.

"You. Are. Repulsive!" Jessie cried. She spun on her heel and slammed the door so hard it rattled.

Chapter 10

Zach gave Carly a wide-eyed look. "Huh. Usually, they aren't that mad at me until after I've slept with them."

"And neglected to call," Carly added for clarity's sake.

"Well, yeah, there's that," he agreed. "What did I ever do to her?"

"I think it's more that you're a man," Carly said. "From what Mac has said, Jessie is not man friendly right now. You know, you could have explained that the parade of girls she sees are your employees, the ones who market your beer to the local bars and restaurants and that they frequently use your house as a stepping-off place."

"I could have, but where would be the fun in that?"

The door to the exam room opened and Gavin came in, shutting the door softly behind him. He gave the two of them a look that was not happy.

"Anyone care to explain why my office manager looks like she's having a meltdown?" he asked.

"She started it," Zach said.

"She did," Carly confirmed. "Apparently, she and Zach are neighbors and she doesn't enjoy watching what she thinks are his extracurricular activities at night."

"Oh." Gavin nodded. "Yeah, that makes sense. Players are not really her jam right now."

He strode over to the sink and began to scrub his hands, pausing to whistle a hello to Ike as he went.

"How does that make sense?" Zach protested. "Even if I am a little bit of a player, I'm not that bad. I mean does she yell at you just because you're a man?"

"No," Gavin said. "She likes me because I'm in a committed relationship with Mac."

Zach frowned. "How is that fair?"

Gavin shrugged as he dried his hands. "So what's happening with my boy, Ike?"

Zach continued to scowl in the direction of the door while Carly opened up Ike's cage so Gavin could examine him. Ike scurried away from Gavin's big hand, but Gavin just rested it in his cage, letting him get used to his presence.

"I'm hoping he'll get curious and come check me out," Gavin explained.

"It's okay, Ike," Carly said. "He's just going to look you over."

Ike squawked and then rudely suggested that Gavin go away, only he didn't say "go away" exactly. Gavin turned his head to keep from laughing and stayed right where he was.

"I see it's more than his feathers that are colorful," he said.

"That's mostly why I'm here," Carly confessed.

"I am not a pet person. I really don't want any and I can't imagine what possessed Mrs. Genaro to leave me her menagerie. I managed to find homes for the fish and the lizard, but the dog is old, and given the bird's vocabulary, it's going to be really hard to find homes for them."

Gavin nodded. "I'd offer to keep them here, but we already have an office cat who is not bird or dog friendly."

"I'd say I'd trade for the cat," Carly said. "But I don't want a cat either."

"Birds aren't really my specialty," Gavin said. "From what I recall there is no way to un-teach them words, but you can make sure not to react to the bad words so he isn't encouraged by your response, good or bad, and you can attempt to teach him more words to try and edge out the bad ones."

While they talked, curiosity finally got the better of Ike and he slid across his perch to examine Gavin's hand. Gavin let him poke and prod his fingers with his beak until Ike seemed satisfied. Then Gavin put his hand in front of Ike's feet, and Ike climbed onto the side of his hand and allowed Gavin to take him out of his cage.

Carly watched as Gavin and Ike got acquainted. She was surprised to find that she was nervous for Ike. She didn't want him to get frightened when Gavin wrapped him in a towel for his examination.

Over the past few days, she had mostly been

grudging about giving Ike and Saul her attention. With packing her apartment and moving back home, her mind had been at capacity. But now, she looked at the parrot as if seeing him for the first time.

Ike was a handsome fellow. He had a dark gray beak and feet, but the rest of him was spectacular. His belly was a vibrant green while his wings were darker. There were aqua colored feathers on his forehead with yellow around his eyes. Tucked into his wings and tail were stray blue and red feathers that popped against the rest of the green.

"He allowed me to towel him easily, so I suspect he's been handled quite a bit," Gavin said. "What's his diet consist of?"

"Pellets and a small amount of cut up fruits and vegetables of the red, yellow, and orange kind," Carly said. "Barry, the lawyer, gave me detailed instructions for all of the animals."

"Have you been keeping him in his cage?" Gavin asked.

"Yes," Carly said.

"You might want to let him out to stretch a bit," Gavin said.

"But what if he flies away again, oh wait, that would solve some problems, wouldn't it?" she asked.

Zach gave her an outraged look.

"Oh, stop," she said and waved her hand at him. "I'm just joking."

Gavin smiled at her as if he knew the thought of Ike flying off horrified her. She didn't know how he could possibly know that when she barely admitted it to herself, but she supposed it was some sort of vet sixth sense. Just because she didn't want to own the bird didn't mean she wanted anything bad to happen to him.

"I'm suggesting you let him out because even a large cage won't allow him to exercise his wings as much as he would like," Gavin said. "You could always clip his primaries and render him flightless . . ."

"No, that's just cruel!" Zach cried. Both Carly and Gavin looked at him and he crossed his arms over his chest in a stubborn stance. "It is."

"If you do decide to do that, you'd need to go to an avian veterinarian for the procedure," Gavin said.

He held Ike firmly but gently and examined him from the top of his head to the tip of his tail. When he got to the feet, he said, "He seems to be in excellent health, but I think his perch may be too wide."

"Really? How can you tell?"

"Well, he has a worn spot on his heel," Gavin said. "That usually means the perch is too wide. You want the perch to be a bit irregular in shape so it doesn't cause wear on their feet."

"You really do know your animal stuff, don't you?" Zach asked. He looked impressed.

Gavin gave him a rueful smile. "I try."

He continued examining Ike and then gently released him from the towel. Ike shook himself from his head to his tail feathers while clutching Gavin's hand for support.

"You okay, Ike?" Carly asked. She wondered if he was going to swear at Gavin again.

"Okay," Ike squawked. "Okay."

He bobbed his head and Carly reached out to rub the back of his neck just where he liked it. He pressed his head into her fingers and she put her hand in front of Gavin's and let Ike climb onto her hand. She held him up so they were nose to beak.

"Lookin' good, handsome," Carly said.

Ike pressed his head against her cheek and gave a wolf whistle. Carly laughed and Ike imitated her, which made her laugh harder. She glanced up to find both Gavin and Zach studying her.

"Looks like someone is getting attached," Zach said.

"I am not," Carly said. "I'm just being kind. I can be kind, you know."

"Uh-huh," Zach said.

"Do you want me to have Jessie get you the number to the avian vet over in Portland?" Gavin asked. "He might know more than I do about Ike's vocabulary issues."

"Yes, please," Carly said. "Come on, big guy, back into your cage."

Ike rode her hand right into his cage. When she latched the door, he said, "Thank you."

"You're welcome," Carly said. She turned and looked at Gavin. "So there are good manners in there, too."

"The more you socialize him and spend time with him, the more he'll imitate you—"

Zach burst out laughing and Carly gave him a sour look.

"What's so funny—or not?" Gavin asked, glancing between them.

"Nothing." Zach shook his head, clearly understanding the dark look in Carly's eyes meant she would hurt him if he told Gavin about Ike's newest vocal trick.

"I'll be sure to work on the socializing," Carly said. "Zach, cage please?"

She gestured for him to pick up the cage at the same time that the intercom in the room sounded.

"Gavin, I have a Mr. Sinclair here to see you," Jessie said. "He doesn't have an appointment but he said he spoke to you last night at Marty's Pub about a rescue dog named Hot Wheels."

Gavin's eyebrows shot up. He looked at Carly, who looked at him in horror.

"What is he doing here?" she asked.

"We made plans for him to stop by before you two left last night," Gavin said. "He wants me to check on Hot Wheels's progress since I initially treated him."

"Why didn't you tell me James was coming here *now?*" she hissed.

"I forgot. Why did you come so early?"

"Or, more accurately, so often?" Zach joked.

Carly glared at him but he just smirked.

It was then that Ike decided to join the convo.

"James, oh, James!"

Gavin's mouth formed a perfect O and his eyebrows rose up to his hairline.

"Yeah, and then there's that," Carly said.

The door to the exam room opened and James popped his head in. "Did you call me?"

His gaze collided with Carly's and he raised one eyebrow as a slow grin spread across his face. Carly had a flash of memory of that same smile looking down on her while he did wicked things to her with his hands. She felt a light sweat bead up on her skin and she had to resist the urge to fan herself with her hand. Was it just her or were the pheromones filling the air thick enough to choke a donkey?

"Well, I'm just gonna . . ." Zach glanced between them, left Ike's cage on the counter, and bolted from the room.

"Me, too," Gavin said. He nudged James into the room, letting the door shut after him as he escaped.

Carly was immediately aware of the fact that the last time she'd seen him, James had her up against a wall. A hot flush of *yeah, baby* suffused her body and she had to clear her throat twice before she could talk.

"Well, this is . . ."

"A delightful surprise and the highlight of your day?" he suggested. He studied her face. "Or maybe you're feeling more painfully embarrassed and agonizingly mortified?"

"Definitely door number two," she said.

He crossed his arms over his chest and his gaze drifted over Carly in a way that hooked her middle and pulled like a magnet. She resisted, stepping behind Ike's cage as if it could keep her from doing something rash, like knocking James to the ground and shredding the clothes right off his body.

When James's eyes lit on the cage, he glanced at Carly in alarm and asked, "Ike's all right, isn't he?"

"He's fine," she said. "Perfectly healthy, you know, other than some language issues. I'm having Gavin check over both pets. Saul gets to come in tomorrow."

"Oh, that's good," he said. He gave her a devilish grin that warmed her all the way to her toes. "For a second, I was afraid we might have caused him a need for emergency parrot therapy."

Carly laughed. She couldn't help it. She noted that James's dark hair was more mussed than usual and his eyes were in the gray zone rather than the blue. She also noticed that his smile was the teensiest bit lopsided, rising a little higher on the right side, and she wondered how she'd missed that last night. It was charming.

"I'm pretty sure Ike has the self-esteem of a rock star," she said. "No worries."

They both glanced at the bird who was clanging the bell on the side of his cage again. He dropped the bell to preen the feathers under one wing as if fully aware that he had their complete attention.

"Glad to hear it." He paused and then said, "I suppose with Bluff Point being such a small town and all, we'll have to get used to seeing each other a lot." When Carly didn't respond, he added, "Or not."

Carly didn't say anything. She was still trying to wrap her head around the fact that he was here and that she was really happy to see him. Happier than she should have been after their close encounter of the naked kind. Usually, after a night with a guy, she was relieved to know she'd never see him again, and if she did run into one of them, she was never happy about it. So, this was new.

"Sunshine, you in there?" he asked.

She blinked. He was looking at her as if waiting for some sort of response.

"No, I mean, yes, I mean, you're right," she said. "It is a small town but I'm sure this is just a freak thing. We won't run into each very often. In fact, probably hardly at all."

"You think?" He sounded doubtful.

"I know," she said.

"Are you all right, sunshine? You seem tense."

"I am not your sunshine and I am not tense," Carly lied. Gah! She felt as surly as Jessie when she'd corrected Zach for calling her sweetheart. It was about boundaries, damn it. She needed to get her boundaries back. "I'm just not used to this, you know, running into a guy after—"

"Sex?" he offered.

Carly felt her face heat up. She was blushing! Again! Carly never blushed. In fact, she was quite certain she hadn't blushed in years. How did the man take a one syllable word and make it sound so delightfully dirty?

"James, oh, James!" Ike squawked.

Carly prayed for a sinkhole to swallow her whole. Sadly, the tile floor beneath her feet looked woefully solid.

The corner of James's mouth lifted when Ike spoke and Carly supposed it was good that he thought the bird was funny as opposed to annoying because she could see how some people might see it that way. But James seemed to genuinely get a kick out of Ike.

"He does that so well," he said.

"Hmm," Carly grunted.

"How many words does he know?"

"I don't know," she said. "I'm just trying to get a handle on the bad ones."

"A little salty, is he?" James asked.

"Like a sailor," Carly said. "It's going to be hard to find him a new home if he doesn't curb his snark."

"If there's anything I can do—" he began but Carly raised her hand as if to ward him off and said, "Stop."

He crossed his arms over his chest, pursed his lips, and lifted one eyebrow higher than the other.

"Stop what?" he asked.

"Worming your way into my life," she said. "We are two ships that passed in the night—"

"I'd say we did more than pass," he said. He was smiling. It was adorable. Carly frowned.

"And we're going our separate ways now," she continued.

James Sinclair was hot, okay, hotter than hot. And, yes, he seemed very nice, and, all right, last night had been amazeballs, but there was no way she was allowing him into her life. Period.

"Separate ways, huh? How about when we run into each other at Marty's Pub?"

"We won't. I'll go somewhere else."

"The library?"

"I have an e-reader," she said.

"Bank?"

"I do all mine online."

"The Grind coffee shop?"

"My sister works there, I wouldn't go there if I were you. She'd probably slip you decaf."

"Really? I thought she liked me, minus the whole yelling-at-me-and-door-slamming thing."

"She did not like you," Carly said. "And even if she did, you can't shag sisters. It's a rule."

"Shag?" He looked appalled. "I would never. I meant she liked me as in she didn't Mace me when she found me in your bed."

Carly refused to acknowledge the ridiculous part of her that was pleased to hear this. It just proved why she never liked to see the guy after they spent the night together. Now she was conversing with him, getting to know him, being charmed by him, caring if he hooked up with her sister or not . . . this was not a part of her plan.

"All right, so this has been the most awkward ten minutes of my life that I'll never get back. I have to go now." She turned her back to him and picked up the cage.

"Bye bye," Ike said. He flapped his wings as if eager to get out of the room full of tension.

"Here, let me help you," James said. He didn't give her much choice as he took the cage out of her arms.

Carly would have told him no, but she didn't want to seem rude; besides, Zach was outside waiting for her so it wasn't like she was stuck having James help her all the way back to the shop. Unless, of course, she was.

Chapter 11

"What do you mean Zach left?" she asked Jessie.

Jessie shrugged. "The door opened, and he walked through it."

"Why?"

"How should I know?" Jessie asked. "Maybe he had somewhere else to be."

"Did you two have another tiff?" Carly asked.

James was standing beside her, shifting the cage in his arms as it was fairly unwieldy.

"I have no idea what you mean," Jessie said.

Carly could tell by the set of her pointy little chin that Jessie was not going to say another word. She handed over her debit card while Jessie processed her bill. When she glanced at James, he and Ike were looking at each other in a *how you doin'* sort of way that she was pretty sure she should discourage. It wouldn't do to have a man get attached to her bird, her *temporary* bird, she reminded herself.

She pocketed her receipt and turned back to James. "Thanks for holding him."

She held out her arms to take the cage and he frowned. "I can carry him to your car for you."

"I don't have a car," she said. "I didn't need one in Brooklyn so I'm hoofing it back to the bakery."

"No, you're not," he said. "I'll give you a ride."

"That's not necessary," she said.

"It's no trouble."

"No, thank you."

"Oh, by all that is holy, let the man give you a ride," Jessie said. "Walking all the way back to Making Whoopie carrying that cage is just dumb."

"Are you calling me dumb?" Carly asked. She was embarrassed and irritated all at the same time and she would have no problem taking it out on Mac's old nemesis.

"Yes," Jessie said. "Because you're being dumb, ridiculous, silly, take your pick."

"Now, let's all just calm—" Gavin began as he stepped out of another exam room.

"I am not! You have no idea what's going on," Carly argued. Deep down she knew Jessie was right, she was being an idiot, but she couldn't seem to stop herself.

"Yes, I do," Jessie said. "I'd have to be in a coma to miss the drama unfolding. Now just accept James's offer of help and stop being such a butt-head!"

"Butthead," Ike repeated. Then he laughed, sounding just like Carly. "Butthead."

"Aw, man, now see what you've done," Carly said. She eyeballed the precocious green bird. "Now there's another bad word in his vocabulary."

She glanced up at Jessie and saw her turn away.

Her shoulders were shaking and for a second Carly thought she was crying. But then a laugh bubbled out of her and she doubled over and slapped her knee.

Carly looked at Gavin in outrage but noted that he had his lips pressed tightly together and looked as if he was having a small seizure. She rolled her eyes.

"Go ahead before you explode," she said.

Gavin burst out laughing, shaking his head as if he was trying to stop but just couldn't.

Enjoying the response, Ike began to repeat, "Butthead, butthead, butthead."

"Oh, my god!" Carly looked in desperation at James. "Let's get him out of here."

James whistled and the basset hound Carly hadn't seen until now came barreling toward them in his harness with his wheels spinning. James picked up the cage and led the way to the door. He paused to call over his shoulder, "Gavin, Hot Wheels and I will be back in a bit."

Gavin nodded while still laughing. Carly gave them one more glower before marching out the door, wishing it wasn't automatic so she could slam it behind her.

James led the way to his car and Carly watched as he opened up the back and put Ike's cage inside. He then secured it with a seatbelt. After the bird was safe, he lowered a ramp from the back of the SUV and helped Hot Wheels up the incline, securing him and his support wheels in the open area in the back.

"I cannot believe she actually called me a b-u-t-t-head!" Carly fumed.

"Butthead," Ike said.

"Uh-oh," James said. "Looks like Ike is a good speller."

"I mean that was out of line, right?" Carly asked. She reached out and let Hot Wheels sniff her hand. When he wagged she gently rubbed his velvety soft ears.

James didn't answer but took Carly's elbow and led her to the front of his car. There he opened the door and, once again, picked her up and put her in the passenger's seat.

"I mean just because she is working for Gavin now doesn't mean she gets to tell people off. I still remember when she made off with Mac's husband. She can call me names but she'll always be a home wrecker to me."

"Mac was married?" James asked. "I thought she was with Gavin."

"She is."

"So, she's divorced," he said. He turned on the engine and merged onto the road.

"No, she never married the guy. Jessie stole him right out of the church," Carly clarified. "Which turned out to be a good thing because Seth Connolly is a horrible, horrible person, a drunk, a letch, a terrible husband, and a lousy father."

"Sort of sounds like she saved Mac a lot of heart-break," James said.

"That's not the point," Carly said. She crossed her arms over her chest and stared out the window.

"Then what is the point?" he asked. "Why did you get so mad when she suggested that refusing to take a ride from me was du— not smart?"

"Nice save," she said. She turned to look at him. "It just irritated me."

"Why?" he asked.

She huffed a breath. She knew she was pouting. She didn't care.

"It just did," she said.

"Again, why?" he asked.

"Because she was right!" Carly snapped. "There, are you satisfied?"

When he turned his head to look at her, his eyes were a scorching shade of blue.

"Not even close," he said.

"Oh." Her voice was little more than a breath-less sigh.

Carly's chest felt tight. She was pretty sure no one had ever looked at her the way James was looking at her now. She ripped her gaze away from his and stared out the front windshield.

She wasn't used to having a man in her busi-ness, knowing about her life, giving her rides, or meeting her friends. It was weird. Her usual compartmentalization was being compromised and she didn't like it.

But the fact was, she wasn't going to be able to hide from this guy—not like she'd be able to in Brooklyn. She studied the town in front of them. In her mind, Bluff Point had always been safe and small. It was the place of her childhood, where she spent summers on the beach and winters on the sledding hill on the outskirts of town.

It was where Friday and Saturday nights inevitably involved mayhem and mischief with her friends at Belmont Park, the small amusement park that sat at one end of the town's five-mile boardwalk, which was where she'd gotten her first kiss, right at the end of the town pier from Johnny Jensen. It had been wet and sloppy, not at all what she had expected, like so much of life.

As she glanced at the mom-and-pop shops that framed the town square, she knew she should take comfort in their constancy. The Millers had owned the dry cleaners for four generations of starched shirts, the Tripletts had opened their collectible shop when she was a little girl. She still remembered going in there with her grandmother and having Nana gasp "Don't touch!" the entire time, making her skittish and nervous to the point where she still got edgy when she went near the shop twenty-five years later.

Bluff Point was the town which boomed with tourists in the summer and contracted in the winter with their departure, leaving only the natives to struggle through the blizzards as best they could, like animals resisting hibernation.

She glanced back at James. His gaze was on the road, and she took a moment to appreciate the stubborn set to his scruffy jaw, the nose that was bent as if it'd been broken, the long eyelashes that were thick and dark and framed his eyes so becomingly, making them soulful when he gazed at her and kissed her with his eyes wide open.

Ack! She did not need to be going there. Carly heard the sound of a record needle scratching across a vinyl album in her head. That was the noise she needed to think of every time her brain decided to revisit last night's sexcapades.

She had to forget all about it. Period. James was right. There was no way they were going to live in a town this small and not run into each other . . . a lot. The only way to deal with the situation was to confront it head on and pretend it had never happened.

He pulled up in front of Making Whoopie and parked at the curb. Before he could hop out to get her door for her, Carly grabbed his arm.

"You were right. We are going to keep running into each other, aren't we?" she asked. "Not on purpose but just while going about our daily lives."

"I'd say that's a safe bet," he said. He didn't sound sad about it.

"Then I think we need to agree to be . . . something else," she said.

"Like pals?" he asked.

"No, pals don't see each other naked," she said. "Well, if they do, it's not interactively naked."

He laughed. "Is that what we were? Interactively naked?"

"What else would you call it?" she asked.

"Lovers," he said. "You know, like a grown-up."

"No, the word lovers implies an ongoing thing," she said. Just hearing the word come out of his mouth made her pant and sweat. "And we are not."

"Maybe," he said, obviously still not conceding his case for more than one night. "But we are going to run into each other, so we will definitely have some sort of association."

"Acquaintances?" she suggested.

"No. Your mailman is an acquaintance. He does not know the thrill of having your thighs wrapped around his head while he—"

"Stop!"

Carly felt a hot flush fill her face and she pressed her hands to her cheeks and gave him a look—with one eyebrow raised higher than the other—that clearly stated *no more of that.*

"Does he?" James asked, looking intrigued.

"I have a mail lady and, no, she doesn't."

"On a very dirty and completely perverted fantasy level, that disappoints," he said. Then he winked at her and Carly couldn't help but laugh.

"Okay, fine, what are we then?" she asked. He shrugged and she said, "Okay, I guess friends it is."

"You're friend zoning me?"

"It sounds so cold when you say it like that."

"Because it was so warm and fuzzy when you said it."

"It's a solid step up from what I usually offer."

"Which is nothing?"

"Exactly. Friends could be good for us."

"I don't see how. I mean, broccoli is good for us, too," he said. He leaned in close so that his lips were just a breath away from her ear. "But last night did not remind me of broccoli, not even a little."

Chapter 12

Carly shivered and turned away to open her door. Last night hadn't reminded her of broccoli either, but she wasn't about to say that. If pressed she would have described the night as one of Jillian's classic whoopie pies, thick rich chocolate cookies filled with decadent vanilla marshmallow cream filling. Her body started to overheat just thinking about it, so she tried to picture Brussels sprouts, cabbage—anything bitter or bland.

James climbed out of his side of the car and circled around to where Ike's cage was strapped in. He opened the door and unfastened the seat-belt that had been holding the cage in place. He lifted the cage out and Carly took a second to lean over the seat and pet Hot Wheels one more time. He gave a soft woof and she smiled.

"I think he likes you," James said.

"He's a good dog," Carly said. "I think he's barking up the wrong tree trying to be besties with Ike, but he did rescue him from the bushes and all."

"So, he's your hero?"

"Something like that," Carly said. She leaned over the seat and kissed the dog on the head. "See ya, Hot Wheels, you good doggy, you handsome boy, you."

When she straightened up, James was looking at her with a weird expression.

"What?"

"Nothing." He shook his head as if trying to clear it. "But if you ever talk to me like that, I will fall to the floor belly-up and let you do whatever you want with me."

Carly rolled her eyes as she led the way into the shop. She tried to squash down the part of her that was ridiculously charmed by his words. James followed with Ike and she tried not to be aware of his nearness. Just friends, just friends, just friends. Yes, this was her mantra now.

The bakery was empty except for Jillian, who was arranging a display of double vanilla whoopie pies in the glass case. She glanced up at the two of them and her jaw dropped.

"Hello," she said, which was code for *what the heck is happening here?* It wouldn't sound like that to anyone else but Carly had known Jillian long enough to pick up the shock and surprise in the not-so-subtle nuance of the way she spoke.

"Hi," Carly said. "You remember James."

"Vaguely." Jillian smiled.

"Hi, Jillian, right?" he asked. She nodded. "And this is your bakery?"

"How did you know?" Her voice was suspicious.

"You mentioned it this morning when you came to pick up Carly," he said.

"Oh." Jillian looked wary. She looked at Carly. "Where's Zach?"

"No idea," Carly said. "He ditched me at Gavin's."

Jillian frowned. "That's not like him."

"I know. I think it had something to do with Jessie," she said. "They don't like each other. I take that back. Jessie doesn't like any men but I think she dislikes Zach more than most, and that's saying something."

"Why? Zach is a sweetheart," Jillian said.

"Unless you date him."

"Oh, yeah, he's not at all datable," Jillian agreed. She looked alarmed. "Oh, did Jessie date him?"

"No, apparently they're neighbors and she sees the comings and goings at his place and does not approve," Carly said.

James stifled a laugh and Carly met his gaze. He shrugged and said, "Phrasing."

"Poor word choice," she conceded. "Apparently, she didn't know that the girls she sees are the brewery's field marketers—you know, the girls who give out samples of beer at bars and restaurants—and that Zach as head of marketing is in charge of them."

"Did anyone inform her otherwise?" Jillian asked.

"It slipped my mind," Carly said, not a total lie since it had never occurred to her to tell Jessie who the girls were, mostly because of the sudden appearance of James.

She glanced at him and noticed that he hadn't moved, but stood holding the cage, looking about the petite bakery as if trying to figure out how to navigate without taking out the furniture.

Making Whoopie was one of the smaller shops on Main Street. It had a row of three booths along the back wall, done in cheery red vinyl, four café tables in the center of the bakery, and counter seating that ran along the windows in front of the shop. On a busy day, they could seat about thirty people comfortably.

The glass display case separated the shop from the kitchen and inside the case were rows and rows of freshly baked whoopie pies. A self-serve soda fountain and shelves of locally made Maine merchandise filled the wall nearest the cash register.

"Here," Jillian said. "You can put his cage right here."

She helped him set the large cage on a table by the window. James stepped back and shook out his hands as if carrying the cage had caused his fingers to cramp.

"You all right, Ike?" he asked the bird.

"Okay, butthead," Ike said. Then he started to sing.

Jillian burst out laughing—then looked contrite, but continued to laugh.

"Turn away," Carly ordered. "Gavin says we

can't encourage any bad words by reacting to them. He said we need to teach him new words and react positively to those and hopefully he'll let go of the bad words if he gets no reaction to them."

"I'm trying," Jillian said, then she laughed again. "Oh, I can't stop."

With a wave, she left the storefront and disappeared through the door that led to the kitchen, still chuckling.

"I think this is going to be harder than I thought," Carly said.

She looked at the green parrot, who was bobbing his head at her in that ridiculously cute way he had. She was torn between wanting to hug him and throttle him at the same time.

"Nah, he's a smart bird," James said. "He'll figure it out."

"I hope so," she said. "I already put an ad in the paper to see if anyone wanted him."

"So, you're really going to sell him just like that?"

Carly frowned and crossed her arms over her chest. She could feel the judgment coming off him and she didn't like it.

"I don't do pets," she said. "The woman who left her animals to me knew that and, yet, she left them to me anyway. I can't imagine what she was thinking. She had to know I was going to give them away."

"Maybe she thought you needed them," he said. "Maybe she thought they needed you."

His voice was so kind and gentle, Carly wanted to punch him in the throat. She didn't need anyone and if the dog and bird needed someone, Mrs. G had picked a bad someone.

"She was wrong."

They stared at each other for a moment. Carly could see that there was more he wanted to say. He opened his mouth; he hesitated; he shut his mouth. Smart man.

Carly took off her jacket and purse and tucked them below the main counter. She began to fuss with the items on display just to look busy. James got the hint.

"I guess I'll see you around," he said.

"Yeah, sure, thanks for your help," Carly said. She forced herself to be gracious and added, "You saved me from a miserable walk back from Gavin's and I do appreciate it."

"What are friends for?" he asked.

Carly walked him to the door. Right now, she needed a snack, a nap, a cup of coffee, and to widen her proximity to this man by an acre or two, and not necessarily in that order.

She opened the door but resisted giving him a hearty shove through it, much as she would have liked to get him gone, for her peace of mind if nothing else.

"Bye, Carly," he said.

"Bye, James," she said.

"Aw, come here, buddy," he said. He opened his arms wide. "Come in for the real thing."

Before she had a chance to track his movement and block him, he swooped in and scooped her up for a hug, pressing her body the length of his and lifting her up off the ground as he did so.

This was not how boy-girl friends hugged each other. Carly knew this because she hugged Zach, Sam, Gavin, and Brad frequently and those hugs never made her want to plaster herself to them, preferably while naked, oh, no, but this one did and it was all James's fault.

When he released her in a slow slide down his body, she wrapped her arms around his neck and hovered for just a moment with her mouth a mere inch from his while she debated planting a kiss on him that would teach the silly boy not to play with matches. Some flicker of self-preservation kicked in, however, and she relaxed her arms and slid to the floor and stepped away from him.

She could see the disappointment she was feeling reflected in his gaze but she knew this was for the best for both of them. She was a commitment phobic train wreck and he was a really nice guy. He deserved a nice girl, someone like Jillian, to complete his life and make everything sunshine and roses. Carly was not that girl. She was more torrential rain and nettles.

James pressed his lips to her forehead. It was

brief and sweet, filled with longing and regret. Then he stepped through the door and left, leaving Carly to watch him walk away. It was cold comfort knowing she had done the right thing.

Chapter 13

"That is disgusting!" Gina said. "How can you let that bird sit on your shoulder?"

Carly was sacked out in the family room with the big-screen TV on, enjoying a bowl of yogurt and raspberries. She, Ike, and Saul had spent a lot of time together over the past few days and had begun to develop their own rhythm.

One of their favorite things to do was watch nature shows together. Ike perched on her shoulder while she fed him fruit from her yogurt bowl while Saul lounged beside her working on his own small bowl of frozen doggy ice cream. The grocery store actually carried this. Who knew?

Together they laughed, sighed, woofed, or sometimes shrieked in terror. Ike seemed particularly afraid of sharks, while Saul was riveted by the big cats.

Carly had begun to appreciate how quick Ike's mind was and how much Saul thrived on attention. She really hoped she could find a family that would give them all of that.

The only downside to her bonding time with her pets was that at some point Gina would arrive, raring to pick a fight. Since Carly was trying to model good behavior to Ike, she'd been biting her tongue, but it was getting more and more difficult not to chomp it in half.

"He's probably going to poop down your back and I'll bet the couch is covered in dog hair. So gross!"

"Shut your cake hole!" Ike squawked.

As much as she wanted to laugh, Carly didn't. Instead, she turned her head toward Ike and in her calmest voice she said, "Be nice, Ike, don't be fresh."

"Like he even knows what he's saying," Gina scoffed. She stood in the doorway with her arms crossed over her chest. "Stupid bird!"

"Gina, watch your mouth," Carly said. "I'm trying to get him family ready, so no insults or bad language please."

"As if that's even going to work," Gina said. She came into the room and frowned at the bird. "Look at his head, he has a brain pan the size of an almond. He's just a chicken with pretty feathers."

"He's smarter than you," Carly muttered. She could feel her temper getting the better of her but she couldn't help it.

"What did you say?" Gina demanded.

"Nothing," Carly said. She spooned some yogurt into her mouth and fed Ike a raspberry, hoping to keep them both from saying something naughty. Saul was busy licking the last drops of ice cream from his bowl and seemed oblivious to the tension in the room.

Gina glared at her, obviously not believing her.

Carly waited but her little sister said nothing more so Carly turned back to the show. It was all about flamingos and she noticed that Ike perked up when he heard them talking. She particularly liked how they trotted around in a big group while selecting their mates. It seemed a festive way to do it.

Saul collapsed against her side while Ike nuzzled into the hair at her shoulder. He'd taken to doing that and she wondered if it was a comfort thing for him. Then she wondered if he'd ever had a mate. Despite the detailed directions Mrs. Genaro had left for her, she hadn't given Carly much of the animals' backstory. She didn't even know how old they were.

"Why don't you put up a flyer at the local college campus? I'm sure some frat house would love to make Ike their mascot," Gina said. "He's certainly loud enough. You know his squawking woke me up this morning—super annoying since I had to work late last night."

Carly turned to look at her baby sister. She refused to acknowledge her suggestion of giving Ike away to a bunch of frat boys. She'd rather set him free than see him neglected but she wasn't going to argue the point.

"Why are you in here? Don't you have lattes to screw up at The Grind?"

Gina gasped. "I'll have you know I make very good lattes."

"Then go make some," Carly said. She was

running out of patience and she knew Gina had to leave before she popped her cork.

Gina slid into the chair beside Carly's, obviously not sensing the peril in which she was putting herself.

"So, I haven't seen that guy James come around. Why not?"

"How is that any of your business?" Carly asked.

"Um, because I walked in on you two after you spent a night doing the—" Gina began but Carly interrupted.

"Yeah, not seeing how that makes it your concern."

"I just want to know if I might have another run-in of the hottie kind," she said.

Carly glanced at her. "You thought he was hot?"

"Totally, I mean he's buff and cute, not my type exactly, but still not hard on the eyes at all, so why aren't you seeing him, like, every night?"

"We decided to just be friends."

"Wow, you're that bad in bed, huh?" Gina snorted and then stole a raspberry out of Carly's yogurt.

"What? No!" Carly cried. "How did you come up with that? What makes you think it was his decision and not mine?"

"Oh, so he's that bad in bed," Gina said. She raised her hand and wiggled her pinky. "Was he an unfortunate disappointment?"

Carly closed her eyes, praying for patience.

"No, he was more than adequate," she said. She noticed her voice dropped an octave when she spoke about James's privates and she cleared her throat.

"Oh, so it was good." Gina wiggled her eyebrows. "Tell me more."

"No."

"Was there some unexpected kink involved that you're uncomfortable with? Did he want to wear your undies?" Gina asked. "We could talk about it if that would help."

"No, there was no unexpected kink." Carly put her bowl on the table so she could press her fingers against her temples to keep her head from exploding or maybe to use her brain waves to make Gina's head explode. It was a tough call.

"Then why aren't you going to see him again?" Gina demanded. She took Carly's bowl off the table and began to finish her yogurt.

"What part of 'none of your business' do you not understand?"

"But I'm your sister. There's like a code that we're supposed to share everything."

"When have you and I ever shared anything never mind everything?"

"Isn't it about time we started?"

Carly glanced away. She wasn't really comfortable with the idea of sharing anything with Gina. She'd probably tell Terry and then, yeah, no. That was not happening.

Ike walked around the back of Carly's head to be on the shoulder nearest to Gina and the raspberries. He started to stretch his neck as far as it would go in an effort to get to the bowl without leaving Carly.

"Give him a raspberry."

"No, what if he bites me?"

"He won't bite you, just hold it steady and he'll take it with his foot."

Gina gave her a dubious look but held out a raspberry to Ike. Sure enough he took it gently from her fingers with his foot and then held it up to his mouth to nibble on. He dripped raspberry juice onto Carly's shoulder but it was an old sweatshirt and she figured both sides would match now.

"He's sort of cute," Gina said. "When he's not yelling at me."

"He wouldn't yell at you so much if you weren't so mean to him," Carly said.

"I'm not mean," Gina protested. "See? You always think the worst of me. Always."

"Maybe it's because I always get the worst of you," Carly said. "You are always taking my things, breaking my things, you have no sense of responsibility—"

"Ha!" Gina cried out through a mouthful of yogurt.

Carly leaned back and looked at her. If her sister was spoiling for a fight, Carly would give her one.

"What was that for?"

"I have no sense of responsibility?" Gina asked. "Who do you think stayed here to monitor Mom and Dad while the rest of you flew the coop?"

"You have got to be kidding me," Carly said. "You didn't stay here to take care of them, you stayed because you didn't want to grow up and leave home."

"Yes, I did," Gina argued. "But who would take care of them if I didn't?"

"I'm pretty sure they could take care of themselves," Carly said. Honestly, was her sister really this deluded? "Which is why they bolted for Florida as soon as I showed up. They are so happy to be free of—"

It occurred to her too late that what she was about to say would probably crush Gina's feelings. She tried to redirect but the damage was done.

"—the winter," she said.

"That's not what you were going to say."

Gina shook her head. Her long red curls flew in all directions and she reminded Carly so much of what she used to look like when she was a kid that Carly had a hard time not talking to her like she was five.

"Yes, it was."

Gina dropped the now-empty bowl onto the table with a thud.

"You were about to say they were happy to

escape me," Gina said. "Is that what you think of me, really?"

Carly sighed. She was in no mood for her sister's dramatics tonight.

"No, I don't," she lied. "I just think that maybe you've lived at home a bit long and might want to consider moving out."

"But you just moved back in," Gina said. "What's the difference whether it's you or me living here?"

"The difference is that I've been on my own for over ten years," Carly said. "This is a temporary setback for me, I've already had two phone interviews for jobs in New York, but for you this has become a way of life."

"But I'm helpful," Gina argued.

"In what way? Do you cook, clean, pay rent, mow the lawn, shovel the snow, or do you let Mom and Dad do all of that for you?"

Gina glanced away and Carly knew the answer.

"Well, Terry says I shouldn't move out until I find a husband," Gina said.

"That's because Terry is a crazy enabler who got married right out of high school, and she thinks everyone should do that. She has no idea about all of the fun she missed out on in her youth."

"She thinks you've had enough fun for all of us," Gina said.

"She said that?"

"Several times over the years."

"Well that's rude," Carly said. She reached up and stroked Ike's head. He nuzzled her hand in a way that was comforting and she wondered if he knew her feelings had been hurt.

"You have to look at it from her perspective," Gina said. "You left home over ten years ago, you rarely come back, when you do you spend all of your time with your friends, and you've never brought a boyfriend around, not once."

"Not every woman wants a boyfriend or a husband," Carly said. "Did it never occur to her that I was happy in my life?"

"No, because Terry doesn't think a woman is complete until she is married and has children. For a while there, she was convinced you were a lesbian."

"So, what if I was . . . am . . . are?" Carly snapped. She was feeling her temper heat.

"I think she would have been happy just to know that you had someone," Gina said.

"Well, that makes me sound pathetic."

Gina nodded. "She doesn't think it's natural for a woman to live alone."

"What century is she living in?"

"Don't be too hard on her," Gina said. "Terry cares for all of us very much in her own peculiar way."

Carly laughed. It was one of the few times she could ever remember laughing at something

171

Gina had said. They had been at odds since . . . well, since Terry had decided Gina was the most perfect being who ever lived, completely forgetting about Carly, who had been the apple of her eye right up until the moment Gina was born.

Carly had never forgotten what it felt like to go from being the sister that Terry doted upon, lavished all of her time and attention on, to the sister that was constantly chastised for being too loud, too annoying, too busy, and too rough with the baby.

Terry had never let Carly hold baby Gina for fear that she might drop her. In fact, Carly had never been allowed to go anywhere near Gina, and when she did, it was a barrage of criticism that just pissed her off and made her five-year-old self even louder, rougher, and more annoying.

For the first time in her life, Carly wondered what her relationship with Gina might be like if Terry hadn't constantly kept them apart and at odds.

"Look, I'm sorry about the other night," Carly said. "It had to have been a bit of a shock to find a man in my room on my first night home. I was working through some stuff."

Gina leaned back in her chair and laughed. "I'll say." Then she sobered and asked, "Is it really so awful coming home?"

"No," Carly fibbed. "I'm just used to being on my own so it's bit of a soul crusher is all."

Gina nodded. She pulled a hank of hair forward over her shoulder and examined the tips. They were perfect; not a split end in sight.

"I'm sorry, too," Gina said. "I haven't been very welcoming to you or the pets."

"Their names are Ike and Saul."

"Noted. Look, I'm sorry. It's just . . . I'm . . . There's this guy . . ." Her voice trailed off. Carly waited but no more information was forthcoming.

"What about this guy?" Carly asked. She noticed that Gina's face turned a bright shade of pink, which clashed spectacularly with her fiery hair.

"Nothing, it doesn't matter," Gina said. She dropped her hair and leaned back. Sharing was new for both of them and it wasn't coming naturally.

Carly studied her sister. It occurred to her that she really didn't know Gina at all. She had spent so many years being irritated by her that she had stopped seeing her as anything more than an annoying piece of gravel wedged in her shoe tread.

The realization did not make her feel very good about herself. This was her baby sister. They should be close, or at least tolerate each other.

"Listen, I was going to go to the Bikini Lounge out on the pier and meet up with my friends," she said. "Do you want to join us?"

Gina looked at her in astonishment. "Are you inviting me to spend time with your elite group of precious friends?"

"See? It's an attitude like that that gets your invitation rescinded," Carly said.

"Sorry, I think I'm just still scarred from all of the years that you threatened to cut off my hair while I slept if I didn't stop following you and your friends around," Gina said. Her tone was rueful and Carly had to admit, she had kept the boundary lines wide and firmly drawn when they were kids.

"Sorry about that," Carly said. "But I was fifteen and you were ten and I had big stuff happening."

"So did I," Gina said. Her voice was soft and when her sad brown gaze met Carly's, Carly felt a punch in the gut as she realized she had failed her little sister spectacularly.

"I'm sorry," Carly said. It was one of the few times in her life that she had apologized to her sister and meant it.

"It's okay," Gina said. She shrugged and stood up, stretching as she did so. "Thanks for the invite but I'm working the late shift tonight. So . . . see ya."

With that, Gina left the room and Carly watched her go. She wanted to call her back and say—what? They had never been close and after twenty-seven years, Carly didn't know how to change that.

She picked up her bowl and let Ike ride on her shoulder as she deposited it in the kitchen sink.

With a soft whistle to Saul, who leapt off the couch to follow her, she made her way upstairs to tuck them both in for the night while she got ready to meet her friends. She wondered briefly if she'd see James, then she reminded herself that she didn't care.

So far, she hadn't run into him in town, which she told herself was a good thing. She'd seen him out and about, sure, she just hadn't been in close proximity to talk, or touch, or . . . she shook her head. Nope, she was not going there.

James sightings, as she called them, happened frequently, as he seemed to be everywhere. Two days ago, he was on the town green, working out with his seniors. Carly had forced herself to look away from him in his basketball shorts and formfitting tank top. She did, however, notice that several women in town took to walking the green with their eyes firmly fastened on James as they did so. Power walking her foot; more like power ogling.

She saw him again walking Hot Wheels along the boardwalk that ran along the beach as he tried to rehab the dog's leg. It seemed that he and Hot Wheels did this every morning, right after James got a large coffee at The Grind, not that she was beginning to track his schedule or anything. It was a small town, she couldn't help it if she noticed the comings and goings of its residents.

While she draped the cover over Ike's cage,

she caught sight of the bed, where Saul was now sprawled, out of the corner of her eye. Had it really been just a few days since James was here with her?

She was surprised by the longing that gnawed at her insides and it wasn't just for the physical gratification that came with spending the night with someone. No, this was specifically for James and for what they had discovered together. She knew, because she had never felt like this before.

If she were completely honest, the man had managed to get under her skin and she had no idea what to do about it. She glanced at her sweatshirt and jeans and the bandana in her hair. Then again, maybe she did.

The Bikini Lounge was where the tourists mostly hung out. If she picked up a guy from away for a little horizontal recreation tonight, maybe she could purge the memory of James from her mind. Yes, that was the ticket.

Carly hurried over to her closet and picked out her sure-thing dress and matching shoes. In her woman's arsenal, this little black dress and black stiletto pumps had never failed to land her a man when she set her mind to it. Never.

"Carly, hurry up," Jillian cried. "It's freezing out here."

"Hang on, the stupid heel on my stupid shoe is stupidly stuck."

Halfway down the town pier toward the end where the Bikini Lounge was located, Carly's heel wedged itself into one of the squeaky old planks.

"That's what happens when you dress like a hooker to go out to a bar perched at the end of a pier," Emma said.

"Listen, married old lady," Carly snapped, "some of us are still looking for love or at least a night of screeching orgasms."

"Really? Because I'm pretty sure you had your quota this week, possibly this month," Mac said.

She was hunkered in her corduroy coat, trying not to look down at the planks since she had a fear of deep, dark water and going to the Bikini Lounge after dark and at high tide always made her squirrely.

"I thought this was supposed to be a girls' night out," Emma said. "No men allowed since our boys are having a poker night."

"Ah," Carly cried as she got her shoe loose. "It is girls' night out, but that doesn't mean I can't find a nice boy to take home later."

The four of them resumed walking and Carly felt Jillian's stare on the side of her face.

"Carly—" Jillian began but Carly cut her off.

"I'm fine," she said.

"Hey, you don't know what I was going to say."

"Yes, I do, Jilly," Carly said. "You were about to tell me you are concerned about me being with one guy a few days ago and being on the prowl now. Honestly, you don't need to worry. I'm fine."

"But James is so hot, and he's clearly interested," Jillian said. "Why would you want to hook up with anyone else?"

"No," Carly said.

"Sorry but I have to agree with Jillian, he is smokin' hot," Emma added. Carly gave her a dark look. "What? I'm married, not dead."

"Stop," Carly said.

"We can't," Mac said. She paused in front of the door to the bar and turned to face Carly. "Listen, we care about you. We don't want to see you make a mistake that you will regret for the rest of your life."

"Oh, my god," Carly said. "Do you people not know me at all? There is no mistake to be made. This is why my life is so perfect. I can do whatever I want, whenever I want, with whomever I want. Now quit worrying. I've got this."

Carly saw her friends exchange an agitated look, but as she showed her ID to the bouncer, and tripped her way into the club, she knew tonight was her night. Tonight she would get the old Carly back and banish any images of James Sinclair from her mind once and for all.

Chapter 14

James finished his beer, planning to settle his tab and go home since his friend Carlos had just left for work at the TV station in Portland. That was the plan. It was a good plan. And then it was shot all to hell.

The door to the Bikini Lounge opened and Carly DeCusati strode in looking like the answer to his every horn dog adolescent fantasy from the age of twelve to, well, now.

In a long-sleeved little black dress that hugged every curve and was cut so low in the front he was surprised he didn't see her nipples peeping back at him, she strode into the room like she owned it.

The dress ended just past her curvaceous derriere and the platform pumps she wore made her legs look like they were five miles of long treacherous road that desperately needed to be wrapped around his waist. Sweat beaded up on his brow and his heart thumped hard in his chest. For a second, he was pretty sure he was having a heart attack.

Then he noticed that he was not the only male in the room watching Carly strut her stuff. In fact, every male in the room seemed to have gone into big-cat mode and was tracking her every move. James felt a sudden caveman-like urge to stomp across the room, throw her over his shoulder, and carry her back to his place where he'd make love to her until she cried out his name in that particularly breathy way she had.

He sat back down, hard, on his bar stool, knowing just how crazy pissed she would be if he tried anything even close to a stunt like that. He signaled to the bartender for another beer and settled in to see what his girl was up to. Yeah, she could deny it all she wanted but she was his even if she was slower on the uptake than he was.

He glanced at Jillian, Mac, and Emma as they trailed behind Carly, who was flirting her way through the bar. Given that the three of them were wearing the more seasonally appropriate attire of jeans and sweaters, and because they kept exchanging worried glances behind Carly's back, he figured they were not completely down with her shenanigans. Good. He knew he liked those girls.

The four of them sat at a small table in the corner. Carly had barely hoisted herself up onto her stool when the first jackass made his move. He was short and had big ears and James figured Carly would shoo him away like a housefly. She did not. In fact, she invited him into their little circle.

James felt something crack in his mouth and realized he was clenching his jaw so hard he might have chipped a tooth. He opened his mouth wide and stretched his jaw while he watched two other guys start to buzz around Carly.

The other girls looked a bit put out, their smiles forced, but Carly flirted with all three of the men, throwing her head back and laughing at their jokes, which judging by the bored expressions of Jillian, Emma, and Mac, were not remotely funny. Suddenly, James wanted nothing more than to turn Carly's curvaceous backside right over his knee. Enough was enough!

He tossed a bill onto the bar, picked up his beer, and made his way over to the ladies' table. Jillian saw him coming and her eyes went wide. She nudged Mac hard in the side and she made the same wide-eyed *oh shit* face. James forced himself to smile at them even though he was pretty sure it was more a baring of teeth and probably the scariest smile he had ever mustered.

To her credit, when Mac elbowed Emma and she saw him coming, Emma sent him a blindingly bright smile. Then she did something that won his heart in friendship for-freaking-ever. She grabbed one of the guys and had Mac and Jillian grab the other two and they dragged them out onto the dance floor, leaving the field wide open for James. This time when he smiled at them, it was for real, and he added a wink, which made all three of them smile in return.

He turned back to the small table where Carly sat alone, looking bewildered, like she had no idea what the heck had just happened. He curbed his grin. He was going to have to play this very, very carefully.

"Hey, don't I know you from somewhere, buddy?" he asked as he slid onto the seat beside her.

Carly glanced from the dance floor to him and her lips broke into the brightest smile he'd seen, well, since the very first time he'd ever seen her. It was like getting blasted by the sun after a long cold winter. Dang, how had he forgotten how potent that smile of hers was? It was the reason he called her sunshine, after all.

He glanced away from her face before he forgot his purpose and did something dumb like drop to his knees and beg her to reconsider her position on one-night stands. Instead he gave her side eye and a low whistle.

"Wow," he said. "You look wicked sexy in that dress, buddy."

"Stop that," she said.

"What?"

"Saying 'buddy' that way."

"And what way is that?" he asked.

"Not in a friendly way," she said. "It reeks of sexual innuendo when you say it."

"Huh, you don't say."

"I do say."

"Whatever you say, buddy."

She huffed with exasperation and leaned close

to him as if she couldn't help herself and then, as if remembering that she had cut him off at one night and should not be in his personal space, she leaned back. She scowled at him and he knew she was recommitting herself to keeping him in the friend zone.

The urge to straighten her out by grabbing her and kissing her until she saw stars, or at the very least saw things his way, was almost more than he could stand. Instead, he chugged his beer hoping it would squelch the fire that was doing a slow burn to his insides every time his gaze veered anywhere near her cleavage. Have mercy!

"What are you doing here anyway?" she asked.

"I was having a beer with my friend Carlos before he left to go into work, and I saw you," he said. "I figured since we're friends, it was only right to come over and say hi."

"Hi," she said. She stared at him. "Now you can go."

"Why?" he asked.

"Because I'm trying to meet someone and having you hanging about is not going to help me," she said.

The waitress arrived at the table and delivered four shots. The liquid was amber and the smell made James's eyes water. These were not girly shots; these were jet fuel. Carly was clearly on a mission tonight. Yeah, he wasn't going anywhere.

"You mean you're planning to pick someone up?" he clarified when the waitress left.

Carly tossed back a shot and then looked at him as if he were too stupid to live. He supposed in many ways he was because after the night they had spent together he couldn't imagine being with any other woman—ever.

If he was honest, a part of him, not just his male ego, was hurt that she would throw herself back out there so quickly after what he considered the greatest night of his life. But when he looked at Carly and noticed the dark circles under her eyes and the frantic set to her face and then remembered the way she had smiled at him when she first saw him, he realized she was here precisely because the other night had been so incredible. It was probably scaring the snot out of her. He knew this mostly because he was terrified, too. He had known from the first moment he kissed her that this girl had the capacity to destroy him and, yet, here he was.

"Oh, well, I don't want to interfere with that," he said. "Let's see if I can help."

"No, I don't need—" she began but he interrupted.

"How about that man bun–wearing stud over in the corner?" he asked. "He looks like he might be interested in getting his banana peeled."

Carly gaped at him. "Did you just—?"

"You know, I have a friend who dated a guy

with hair like that and she let him use her shower. Those hairy beasties will clog up your drains. Just sayin'."

She blinked at him and he had to duck his head and take a long sip of beer to keep from laughing. She looked completely flummoxed.

"No? All right, how about that guy over there? The one in the suit? At least he looks like he knows his way around a comb," he said. He narrowed his eyes and studied the man closer. "Although not a pair of nose hair trimmers, however. Ew."

Carly glanced at the man in the suit then gave James an irritated look because, yes, even in a dimly lit bar at ten feet away, the guy clearly had nostril issues and James knew there was no way she could un-see that.

"I know what you're doing," she said. "And it's completely unnecessary."

"What am I doing?" He blinked innocently. She snorted.

"You're trying to point out what is wrong with every guy in this room so that I won't go home with any of them," she said.

"Me?" he asked. "No, no, I'm just offering some friendly advice."

"Well, don't bother. It's girls' night out. No boys allowed, which includes you."

"Really?" he asked. He squinted one eye at her. "But all your friends are dancing with boys."

Carly looked from him to the dance floor and back. "That's different."

"How so?"

"They're just dancing," she said.

"Oh," he said. "Huh. So, we should dance."

"No, that's not—" she protested but he ignored her.

He stood and shrugged off his coat and dropped it onto the back of the stool, then he took Carly's hand and tugged her out to the dance floor. Her heels, bless them, gave her no traction to fight him so he maneuvered her into the middle of the floor with him.

It was a lively number and Carly began to bust some moves that pushed James back a few feet and made him fear that she might pop right out of the top of her dress. He tried to remember why that was a bad thing even while acknowledging that she was quite possibly the worst dancer he had ever seen. Adorable.

The song ended and Carly flashed him a saucy smile and headed back to the table, but just then the DJ put on "Love Is a Losing Game" by Amy Winehouse and James grabbed Carly's hand and spun her into his arms before she could escape.

"Sorry," he said. "It's a favorite. Dance with me, please?"

It was the please that did her in, he could tell by the way the fire banked in her deep brown gaze as she wrapped her arms loosely about his neck.

He felt like he'd caught a bird in his hands and had to hold her ever so firmly but gently to keep her from flying off.

Other parts of him were more than down with being firm and he had to keep a smidge of distance between them to keep her from discovering what he really wanted to do with her right now. He let his hands stroke up and down her sides, trying to ease the restless heat that was plaguing him. It didn't help.

For her part, Carly seemed to have fastened her gaze on the collar of his shirt and refused to look anywhere else. Interesting. The fact that she couldn't or wouldn't look at him gave James a surge of hope. She could friend zone him all she wanted but he knew the attraction between them was so much more than that.

"Hey, buddy," he said. "Let's kick it up a notch, yeah?"

Carly gave him a bewildered look as he took her hand in his and put his other hand on her waist and guided her around the dance floor in a tight box step that his sister had forced him to learn when they were teens. It was not terribly exciting but better than the middle school sway.

When Carly tried to liven it up with some uncoordinated twirling and dipping, he tightened his grip on her waist and said, "Settle down there, Beyoncé, this is as good as it gets with me."

Carly laughed and fell into step with him. They

matched up perfectly just like he knew they would. Her gaze went from his collar to his eyes to his mouth and then dropped back down to his collar but not before he noticed the pink flush that suffused her cheeks. He forced himself not to smile but it was a challenge.

When the song ended, he reluctantly walked her back to the table where her friends were waiting. They seemed to have managed to shake off the men who'd been hovering and for that James was planning to send each of them flowers the next day.

"Hi, James," they all greeted him with smiles.

"He was just leaving," Carly said. She took a swig from her beer and gave her friends a pointed look that James took to mean they were not supposed to protest.

He made a big show of checking the time on his cellphone, which was ridiculous because he didn't care what time it was. He had no intention of letting Carly out of his sight in that dress, which if he ever got his hands on he planned to hide so she could never wear it in front of anyone but him.

Whoa. He shook his head. His inner caveman was seriously having issues.

"Actually, I don't have to leave just yet," he said. He glanced at Carly out of the corner of his eye. "Besides, how can I go not knowing which lucky dude you're going to drag home tonight?"

He heard Jillian suck in a breath. "Did you tell him that?"

"No. Maybe. Did I?" Carly looked at James.

"You did," he said.

"Oh, huh," she said. She took a long sip from her drink. "That seems bad form."

"Aw, are you talking about my sweet dance moves again?" Zach asked as he bopped up to the table with Brad, Sam, and Gavin right behind him.

Carly narrowed her eyes at Zach. "What are you doing here? This is girls' night out!"

"He's here!" Sam pointed at James.

"He's leaving," Carly said.

Standing behind Carly so she couldn't see, James shook his head at the other men. They grinned.

"We had to come. These two mopes missed their women," Zach said. He pointed at Brad, who had wrapped himself around Emma, and Gavin, who had lifted Mac up, taken her seat, and set her back down on his lap. The four of them were disgustingly lovey dovey and James felt a pang of envy that he tried to ignore.

"This night is a bust, a total bust," Carly said. She looked highly irritated.

"It is that," James said. His eyes were locked on her chest when he said it and she scowled at him. "Chin up, buddy, we'll find someone for you to shampoo the wookie with."

Zach's mouth popped open and then he hooted. "Did he just use a Star Wars reference for sex? Dude, you are our people! Come on, chest bump!"

Without waiting for James, Zach jumped at him and bounced off of his chest. On a scale of manliness, it was a pitiful example, but he liked Zach's goofiness. Carly sighed in defeat and James grinned. He was getting to her—maybe like a hangnail, but he was getting to her.

"So, why are you looking for some gland to gland combat?" Zach asked Carly. James snorted and they shared a knuckle bump. "Correct me if I'm wrong but I thought this guy here already serviced your engine."

"OMG," Carly snapped. "We are not—NOT—discussing my sex life and most especially not in front of the person that I was just—"

"Bone storming," Sam said.

"Lust and thrusting," Jillian offered.

"Organ grinding," Gavin said.

"Roughing up the suspect," Mac said.

"Beard-splitting," Brad offered.

"Slamming the clam," Emma said.

"Yeah." Zach belly laughed with the rest of them. "All of that."

"You know what?" Carly asked. "It's none of your business. It's nobody's business but mine and now I'm going home. Thank you all for nothing."

"Aw, don't go away mad," Zach said. "We love you. We're just teasing you."

"We're sorry," Jillian chimed in. "We just got carried away with the whole euphemism thing. Forgive?"

Jillian clasped her hands under her chin and made with the big sad eyes and the rest of the crew did the same. When Sam elbowed James, he did, too. Carly glowered at them but it had lost its heat.

"Fine, you big jerks are forgiven, but I'm still going home," she said. With a wave, she strode toward the door.

Jillian rose from her seat to go with her, but James waved her back, indicating she should stay.

"I got this," he said.

The group exchanged a look and he realized they were deciding if he was trustworthy or not. Instead of feeling insulted, he was pleased that they were cautious with their friend.

"You seem like a nice guy," Zach said. "So, I'm going to tell you straight-up, don't get your hopes up with Carly. She'll break your heart."

James paused. He suspected that Carly and Zach had a special relationship and now he wondered how special. "Are you speaking from experience?"

"No." Zach shook his shaggy head of blonde hair. "You have to have a heart for it be broken."

His answer was flip—too flip—and James suspected there was some heavy shizzle in Zach's past, but now was not the time. He stepped back from the table and raised his hands in the air as if showing he had no weapons or ulterior motives.

"I promise just to watch over her and make sure she gets home safely."

The group exchanged another glance and then Jillian nodded.

"Phone," she said. James took his out of his pocket and she touched her phone to his, automatically putting her contact info into his phone. "Text me when she's home."

"Will do," he said. Then he turned and bolted after Carly, hoping she hadn't managed to pick up four more guys on her way out.

He saw her meandering her way up the pier. She was gesturing with her hands as if she was having an in-depth discussion with an invisible friend.

"I just don't understand it," she was muttering. "This dress has never failed me. Never. But look at me, I'm going home alone. I think I may have to burn this dress."

James pressed his lips together to keep from protesting. Much as he didn't want her to wear it in public, he also didn't want her to torch it either.

"Hey, buddy," he said. "Do you need a ride?"

"No, thanks. I'm going to call an Uber," she said. She pulled out her phone as if to do just that when James took the phone out of her hands.

"No need," he said. "I'll give you a ride."

She looked at him suspiciously.

"Just a ride," he said. Her eyes narrowed and he added, "In my car to your house, where I will then leave to go to my house."

"No funny business," she said.

"Of course not, buddy," he said.

"Stop that."

James hid his smile as they stepped off the pier and crossed the small parking lot to where his SUV sat waiting. Per usual, he opened her door and gave her a boost into the car.

He tried not to notice how her dress rode up a sweet couple of inches in back before she quickly tugged it down. Tried and failed. As he walked around the car, he pulled on the collar of his shirt, trying to get some of the cold night air to hit his skin and cool him off. It didn't work.

They were both quiet on the drive across town to Carly's house. There were a million things James wanted to say about tonight, but he knew he'd be better off waiting until she didn't look like she wanted to stab him with the business end of her shoe.

"So, how goes the job hunt?" he asked.

"Slow," she said. "I've sent my résumé all over New York, and only gotten two phone interviews. I finally had to send it to a few retail stores in Boston, and I even sent it to Penmans in Portland. I feel like I must reek of desperation."

"Penmans, huh?" he asked. "That's only a half hour away."

"Don't remind me," she said. "It's hard to pretend you're getting away when you look for jobs within fifty miles of the place you're trying to escape. You know, I've been a retail fashion buyer for almost ten years. You'd think that would mean something. Ugh, I can't talk about it. It makes me feel like such a loser."

"Something will turn up," he said. He knew it was a pathetic platitude, but it was all he had to offer at the moment. Besides, it was taking all of his self-control not to do a fist pump of victory that she might stay within datable range.

When they got to her house, he had barely stopped the car before she hopped out and strode up the walkway to the front door. James followed after her, making sure she got in okay.

When he took her elbow to help her navigate the steps to the porch, she turned on him so fast, she wobbled on her heels and he had to catch her before she toppled backwards off the steps.

"See?" she asked. "That's why you're a liar, James Sinclair."

He set her back on her feet and followed her to the front door.

"Okay, I'll bite," he said. His heart hammered in his chest. Did she know how he felt about her staying? "What did I lie about?"

"A 'buddy,'" she said, making air quotes with her fingers, "would let me walk up the stairs by myself and not see me to the door."

"In those shoes with the amount you've had to drink?" he asked. He felt his heart slow down as the panic ebbed. "That'd make me a pretty lousy friend."

She tossed her hair over her shoulder and bent to unlock the door. Once the lock clicked and she pushed the door open, she turned to face him.

"You don't want to be just friends," she said.

"I think I was pretty clear about that," he agreed. "But if that's all you're offering, then I expect I'll learn to make do." He leaned forward and kissed her forehead. "Good night, buddy."

He turned and left, not daring to look at her for fear he'd lose his good intentions and make a move to sweep away their friend status once and for all. He couldn't do that, not until he told her the truth about having met her before. Every step farther from her about killed him, and the only thing that made it even the teensiest bit bearable was the way Carly stomped into the house and slammed the door after him, clearly feeling as frustrated as he was.

James grinned when he fired up his car and drove away.

Chapter 15

The Driscolls—Mom, Dad, Chance, and Lexi—had seen Carly's ad in the paper and had come to the shop to meet Ike. They seemed like a quiet family, so what they wanted with a parrot, Carly could not fathom, but if it got Ike off her hands and in with people who were kind she was A-okay with it.

"Say 'hello,' Ike," she coaxed him.

The Driscolls crowded around Ike's cage in the corner of Jillian's bakery. They watched the exotic green bird in wonder as if he was about to start spouting Shakespeare.

"Hello," Ike said. "Hello."

"Ah!" Lexi, the youngest and most enthusiastic Driscoll, gasped and clapped her hands. "He talks. He really talks."

"Amazing," her mother said with a small smile.

"What else can he say?" Chance asked.

"Oh, a lot of things," Carly said, knowing full well that she was being evasive. "He picks stuff up pretty quickly."

The bells on the shop door jangled and she glanced up to see James walk in with Hot Wheels at his side. Her heart did a stupid lurch in her chest and she could feel her face get warm like she was thirteen and her crush had just walked into the room, instead of being thirty-two and having the last guy she'd seen naked appear on her turf. It was mortifying.

She wiped her hand across her forehead as if she were pink because she was hot and sweaty from working so hard. Given that it was October and the temperature in the shop was cool because outside it was in the fifties, this made a liar out of her, but she hoped James wasn't that observant.

She supposed it was perfectly natural that he had come to see her. They had shared a pretty amazing night together and he'd made it very clear at the bar last night that he was interested in more. She would let him down as easily as she could.

She turned to the Driscolls and said, "I will just let the five of you get acquainted. Let me know if you have any questions."

The family nodded and Carly crossed the room toward James. She was so glad she had taken the time to style her wavy hair into fat curls that bounced across her shoulders, not because she cared what he thought, she assured herself, but because looking her best gave her confidence. Yeah, that was it.

She glanced down in a quick outfit check. She was relieved that she had chosen one of her best outfits today, a low cut ruby red cashmere sweater over a snug pair of jeans and her favorite combat boots. It was the perfect mix of feminine and ass kicker that she strived to maintain.

"Hi, Hot Wheels," she greeted the basset hound first, crouching down to rub his head and scratch his back around the bands of his halter the way she'd noticed that he liked. "How ya doin', boy? Good? Saul is in the yard out back if you want to meet him."

Hot Wheels wagged and gave her a soft woof. She smiled as she stood up to face James.

"Hi, Carly," he said. He kept his eyes on hers but she could tell it was an effort to keep them from roaming over her figure as he'd started to glance down and then forced his gaze back up.

"Hi, James," she said. "I suppose we should talk about this."

He tipped his head and looked at her. "I'm sorry, about what?"

"About you showing up at my work," she said. "I'm flattered but I thought I was clear—"

The door to the kitchen opened and both James and Carly glanced over to see Jillian enter the bakery, carrying a big tray of freshly baked whoopie pies for the display case.

"There she is," James said. He turned back to Carly and squeezed her elbow. "Great to see you, but I need to talk to Jillian." He turned to walk away but then glanced back and said, "You look fantastic by the way. I really love the color red on you."

"Uh . . . thanks," Carly said. She watched as he approached Jillian, with Hot Wheels at his side— yes, even the dog had abandoned her—and almost choked when Jillian put down her tray and greeted him with a hug.

James carried the tray for her and Carly watched as the two of them unloaded the pies into the case while they talked.

What the what? When had the two of them become pals? Jillian threw her head back and laughed at something James said. Carly sucked in a breath through her nose and spun around so that she couldn't see them anymore.

Was something going on between them? How could Jillian not have told her? When could that have happened? James had driven Carly home last night . . . unless, had he gone back to the bar to join the others after taking her home?

Hot, searing jealousy coursed through her veins like lava headed down a steep hill destroying everything in its wake, including her common sense and ability to reason. And yet, even knowing this, she couldn't stop it.

She turned back and marched over to where the two of them were standing. She glowered at them until Jillian finally noticed her and paused in unloading the whoopie pies.

"What's wrong, Carly? Do you need a hand with something?"

"I think the question is, do *you?*" she asked James.

He nodded. "Most definitely, but no worries, Jillian's going to take care of it for me."

What the heck did that mean? Was he hitting up Jillian for sexy time? Carly's head whipped back toward Jillian and she practically shouted, "What?!"

"Well, it's bigger than I'm used to, I admit, but I think I have the skill set to help him out, don't you?" she asked.

"No!" Carly said. Having never perched on the moral high ground before she found the footing treacherous and yet she didn't budge and added, "I don't."

Jillian looked taken aback but Carly kept on going. The green-eyed monster inside of her was out for blood and it wasn't going to stop until it got some.

"How can you even think it?" Carly asked. "Isn't it against some basic set of ethics or principles or common decency?"

"Way to be supportive," Jillian said. She looked quite miffed and a little hurt. "I have been handling stuff like this for years, you know, and what I don't know I'm sure I can look up in a book."

Carly felt as if her eyes were going to pop out of her skull. James just stood there, looking at Jillian as if she was the answer to all of his problems, while Jillian talked about consulting a book on how to handle him. How could a guy find that attractive? The woman was going to consult a manual for goodness' sake.

"This doesn't strike you as awkward at all?"

Carly asked. She gestured from herself to James to Jillian and then back to herself. "See? Weird."

"You're being weird." Jillian nodded. "At least that we can agree upon."

"I am not," Carly said. She wanted to stomp her foot. She wanted to knock over a display shelf of Maine tchotchkes. She didn't. Instead, she just stood there while the two of them went on with their witty banter.

"So, when can I swing by?" James asked.

"The bakery opens at nine," Jillian said. "If you can come by then, I'll have more time to talk to you about what you want."

"Oh, he knows what he wants," Carly snapped.

"I'm not so sure," James disagreed. "Clearly, I don't know what I'm doing."

"Oh, you'll be fine," Jillian said. "I'll talk you through it."

Carly glanced between them. Something here was off. They didn't look like two people who were planning an amorous rendezvous. She was missing something.

"Wait! What exactly are you two talking about?" she asked.

"James is placing a huge order of custom-baked whoopie pies for an upcoming event," Jillian said. "Why? What did you think we were talking about?"

Carly felt her green-eyed monster slink back down inside of her gut with its spiky tail tucked between its legs. Well, wasn't this mortifying? Here she had thought they were hooking up for a little slap and tickle and instead it was a discussion of baked goods. She closed her eyes as she tried to figure out how to backpedal without hurting herself.

James tipped his head to the side as he considered her. His lips curved up higher on the right side and he looked like he was trying not to laugh. She got the feeling he knew exactly what she had been thinking and he was amused by it. That was even more irritating than being wrong.

Jillian, bless her heart, seemed to have no idea. Because it would never even occur to Jillian to make a play for a guy Carly had hooked up with, proving once again that Jillian was a much better person than Carly.

"Are you all right?" Jillian asked. "You look a little pale. Is it the family looking at Ike, are they awful? Do you have to say no?"

Carly glanced at the Driscolls, who seemed quite taken with Ike. She wondered why that didn't make her feel any better. It should. It was her first step toward freedom. She stiffened her spine. Of course she would be thrilled to unload Ike. Thrilled!

"No, it's not them," she said. She scanned her brain for a reason for her boorish behavior, while avoiding James's amused gaze by staring at the wall just over his shoulder. "Gina and I haven't been getting on, it's making me surly."

"Miss!" Lexi called from across the shop. "Can we take him out of his cage?"

"Excuse me," Carly said. "I'd better . . ."

She let her words trail off as she left them. She felt like such a tool. How could she have been jealous of James talking to Jillian? She was never jealous. Never.

Her one very brief relationship had cured her of it. She had spent most of that relationship consumed with jealousy. The sort that festered in her gut like a hot boil, causing her to behave in a variety of horrifying stalkerish ways that ultimately led to her imploding in a big public scene in front of the awful boyfriend and all of his fraternity brothers.

Even the memory left a horrible taste in Carly's mouth. And people wondered why she didn't do relationships. Irrational jealousy was one of the many reasons she avoided them like an outbreak of back acne.

Gah! She hated feeling even a smidgeon of that awful emotion. She shook it off. Obviously, she needed to get back to Brooklyn, where life was normal and she was in control. The first step was to get rid of Ike. Then she needed to find a new job in the city. She had a résumé, a good one. Surely, it wouldn't be that difficult. Feeling better after her little mental pep talk, Carly approached the Driscolls with a big smile.

"You can take him out," she said. "His wings haven't been clipped though, so he can fly. For that reason, you'll want to be very careful not to have any doors or windows open when you grant him a little freedom."

"Of course," Mrs. Driscoll said.

Carly opened the cage. Ike gave her side eye, which she was beginning to believe was his way of telling her he wasn't happy with her. Then he shoved his beak in his armpit, another sign that he wasn't really on board with whatever she had planned.

"Come on, Ike, come out and meet the nice family," she said. She used her softest, most cajoling voice.

"No, no, no, no," he said.

"Ike, come on, don't be fresh," she said.

Carly put her hand right in front of his feet. He didn't budge. She held it there, trying to be patient while she felt the eyes of all of the Driscolls upon her as they studied how to handle the bird. She wanted to admit to them that she had no freaking clue how to manage Ike, but she didn't think that would give them much confidence in her or Ike and they might change their minds.

Instead, she gave them her most winning smile and turned back to Ike. She gave a little whistle that made him pop his head out from under his wing.

"Come on, buddy," she said. "Come meet the nice people."

Ike lifted up one foot as if he was about to step on her hand, but then he didn't. Instead he clawed at the air and started to sing. Carly couldn't place the song. She frowned.

It was James who identified it by singing it with Ike, as he walked toward them. "Everybody was kung fu fighting, those kicks were fast as lightning."

"Oh, wow, he sings, too," Lexi squealed.

The girl's hair was long and messy and her eyes behind her big round glasses with the light blue frames looked huge. Her wool coat hung on her skinny frame and she was pale and bookish looking. Carly figured she would make an excellent companion for Ike.

He must have thought so, too, because he finished whistling and climbed onto Carly's hand, letting her take him from his cage. He glanced around the shop and moved up Carly's arm so he was closer to Lexi and away from the boy named Chance.

"Let's see him fly," the boy said. "Come on, throw him and see if he can cross the room."

Carly glanced at the boy. He was an inch taller than his sister and had the same washed-out, pasty features, but where Lexi had kindness twinkling in her eyes, Chance had a look that Carly thought was mean. He had thin lips that parted over a mouthful of braces in a perpetual sneer. The way his gaze darted around the shop, Carly got the feeling that he was looking for trouble and she suspected that if he couldn't find it, he would make it.

"He's more of a climber than a flyer," Carly said.

"Climber?" Chance scoffed. "That's lame."

"That's enough, Chance," Mr. Driscoll said. He was a portly middle-aged man with a thinning head of gray hair and glasses that kept slipping down his nose. "The bird is for Lexi, to replace her guinea pig who ran away."

"Ran away?" Carly asked. She didn't think guinea pigs were known for bolting for freedom.

"Chance took him outside to let him eat some clover," Lexi said. Her voice was little and sad. "But he ran off when Chance tried to bring him back inside."

Carly stared at Lexi. She was pretty sure her gaze was boring holes into the little girl's head, but she didn't care. She had never seen a guinea pig run but was pretty sure they couldn't outrun a young boy. She wanted to know if Lexi really believed that was what happened. Lexi blinked and looked away. That was all Carly needed to know.

She went to put Ike back in his cage. There was no way she was letting him go to a family where questionable things happened to their pets.

"Come on, bird, fly!" Chance stepped up behind her and yelled at Ike. "Fly!"

He clapped his hands and jostled Carly's arm, trying to dislodge Ike.

"Hey, stop that!" James stepped forward, looking at the kid's parents like he expected them to take action. Hot Wheels began to growl.

"Fly, bird, fly!" Chance shouted.

Carly tried to move away from him, but he grabbed her arm and dug his bony little fingers into her muscles.

"Ouch!" she yelped. "Let go."

"Chance!" his father said. "Behave yourself."

Hot Wheels barked at the boy and then started to charge forward but his wheels got caught on a chair leg.

"Fly, bird, fly!" Chance yelled again.

"Stop it, you're frightening him!" Lexi cried.

"Chance Driscoll, you listen to your father," his mother said.

Carly wanted to run from the lot of them. She glanced at James and he looked as shell-shocked and ill-prepared for this turn of events as she felt.

"Fly, bird, fly!" Chance yelled again. He went to smack Carly's arm, but James got to him first and grabbed him by the back of his collar and hoisted him up onto his toes.

It was too late. Ike had had enough. He arched back and gave an awkward leap into the air followed by a shaky flap of his wings.

He careened sideways, almost smashing into the wall before righting himself at the last second to cross the shop and land on a built-in shelf above the cash register.

"Yeek!" Jillian shrieked in surprise.

"Sorry!" Carly cried out. "There's a situation here."

"Butthead!" Ike squawked from his safe place.

Chapter 16

Silence descended upon the little shop. The ticking of the decorative clock and Ike muttering profanity under his breath were the only sounds to penetrate the hush of awkward that engulfed them all.

"I . . . I'm . . ." Carly tried to apologize. She did. But the fact was Ike was right. The kid was a butthead and she wouldn't let Ike go home with this family even if they were the only people who ever came to take a look at him. She'd rather set him free herself than let this mean little monster do it. There was no way she could fake an apology for what she believed was Ike's own instinct to save himself.

"Obviously, Chance is a little overexcited about getting a new pet. Kids, you know," Mrs. Driscoll said. She fished in her purse for her checkbook. "How much were you asking for the bird?"

"I . . ." Carly stammered. She stared at the family in front of her. How could the woman seriously make an offer for Ike after what just happened?

She glanced up at the shelf where Ike was hopping from one foot to the other, looking like he was striking martial arts poses.

"It seems there's been a mistake. Ike doesn't

appear to like children. I'm sorry but I don't think it would be the best fit for you or the parrot," James said. He let go of the boy with a firm pat on the shoulder. The boy gave him a sour look but James didn't flinch.

Lexi, however, looked crestfallen. Carly felt bad for her, she really did, but it was time she faced the reality that having a pet around her brother did not bode well for the pet and there was no way Carly could be a part of that.

"Miss DeCusati?" Mrs. Driscoll looked at her as if to check that she was okay with James speaking on her behalf.

Not only was she okay with it, Carly was relieved because she hadn't known what to say to these people. Well, she knew what she wanted to say but it would have made Ike's insult seem tame in comparison.

"What he said," Carly said. "No sale."

"But . . ." Mrs. Driscoll started to protest.

As if he'd had enough of the discussion and wanted to weigh in on it himself, Ike took off from his perch and flew back toward Carly and his cage. En route, as he soared over Chance, he let loose with a stream of raspberry-loaded poop, plopping it right onto the boy's head and leaving a spectacular trail of it on the floor, chairs, and tabletops.

"Eeeewww," Chance shrieked. "He . . . he . . . did that on purpose! Stupid bird!"

Chance launched himself at Ike, who took off again, circling the shop, looking for a safe place to land. Hot Wheels, determined to help his buddy, grabbed the boy's pant leg in his teeth and growled.

"Ah!" Chance cried. "Dog attack!"

"Hot Wheels, drop!" James commanded. The dog released the pant leg with a soft woof and James moved between him and the boy and reached down to rub Hot Wheels's ears.

"You need to go," Carly said. Her voice was shrill. Her heart was pounding in her chest from all of the chaos. She began to shoo the family with her hands toward the door.

"No, no, no!" Lexi began to wail. "This is your fault!" she screeched at her brother. "All your fault!"

"Shut up," Chance said. "It is not."

"It is, too," she cried. Her face was blotchy and tears were streaming down her cheeks. "You killed Ollie. He was my best friend and now she won't give me the bird because you've ruined it. You ruin everything!"

She threw herself down on the floor, right into the poop, and sobbed. Her brother, Chance, took one look at her and sneered. His lip curled up and he drew back his foot as if to kick her in the ribs.

James moved swiftly in between the two kids while the parents continued to protest.

"We'll pay you double what you're asking," Mrs. Driscoll said.

"We promise he'll be well cared for," Mr. Driscoll said.

Carly felt as if she was losing her mind. These people had to be kidding. She wouldn't let them have a Chia Pet, never mind anything that lived and breathed.

"Oh, for fuck's sake," Ike cried with a mighty flap of his wings. "Get out! Get out! Get out!"

The Driscolls all went completely still. Lexi pushed herself up off of the floor.

"Did he just . . . ?" Mrs. Driscoll turned to Carly with a wide-eyed gaze.

Carly nodded. "Yes, yes, he did."

"You were trying to sell us a bird that curses?" Mrs. Driscoll drew herself up. Her mouth was puckered into a tight little knot of righteous disapproval.

"He is highly verbal," Carly said.

"These are impressionable young children," Mrs. Driscoll chastised her. She grabbed her children to her bosom as if to protect them from Ike's bad words.

"Yeah, I can see that," Carly said. Her sarcasm was completely lost on the outraged mama.

Carly cast Chance a dubious look and he stuck his tongue out at her as he wiped the bird poop from his head with the sleeve of his coat. Gross!

"We are leaving now," Mrs. Driscoll announced

as if it hadn't been suggested that they leave just a few moments before. "I am very disappointed in you, Miss DeCusati."

"I can live with that," Carly said.

James held the door open for them and they all marched out. Lexi was the last to leave, looking at Ike mournfully as she went.

As soon as the door shut, Ike flew down from his perch and landed on Hot Wheels's harness like he belonged there. Hot Wheels gave his buddy a soft woof and Carly felt her insides melt just a little bit more.

"Aw, look," Jillian cried. "They have a bromance going, how cute is that?"

"Ridiculously," Carly agreed. "I'm sorry Ike got loose."

"It's all right. He did what he had to do," Jillian said. She paused and studied Ike from where he was looking up at them. "Didn't you, pretty boy?"

"Okay. Time for supper. Pretty boy," Ike squawked.

"Oh, no, now he's talking to himself," Jillian said. "I think the rotten boy child freaked him out."

"Maybe it's some sort of self-soothing thing he's doing," James suggested.

"Can you blame him? That family was a horror," Carly said. "Still, he did manage to poop on the awful boy."

"If it was on purpose, he has fantastic aim,"

James said. "Except for the places in the shop that he nailed."

Both Carly and Jillian gave him withering looks.

"I'll help clean it," he said.

"Good." Jillian disappeared into the back room and came back with a tub of antiseptic wipes that she handed to James. To his credit, he said nothing but went right to work cleaning up the mess.

Carly knelt down and held out her hand to Ike. "It's okay, buddy. Everything is going to be all right."

Ike paced back and forth as if unsure. Carly felt terrible because she knew that he was still nervous and she felt like it was her fault. She never should have let that kid get near him but who'd have thought a little boy would be so mean?

She lowered her voice and kept it soft. She kept speaking to him in her gentlest voice, trying to coax Ike from his spot on Hot Wheels's back.

After several almosts, he finally stepped onto her outstretched hand. Carly scratched Hot Wheels's head before she stood and pulled Ike in close to her chest. Ike nestled his head right into her cleavage and let loose a shuddering sigh.

James was cleaning the poop splatters off of a nearby display, and when she moved past him and caught his gaze, she noted his hazel eyes were definitely looking more blue than gray. He looked from Ike, whose head was still nestled against her chest, to her and he grinned.

"Lucky bird," he said.

The mischief in his gaze was contagious and Carly couldn't help but return his smile. They stood staring at each other until Jillian cleared her throat.

"Bird droppings are difficult to clean when they harden," she said. "Just sayin'. I'm taking Hot Wheels out back to chill with Saul. You okay with that?"

"Sure," James said. "He likes other dogs."

Carly turned and walked Ike back to his cage. When he climbed onto his perch, he glanced at her over his shoulder and gave her a wolf whistle. Carly laughed because she knew that meant he was going to be fine.

James had climbed up onto a chair and was wiping off some Ike residue that had splattered the wall. Carly loved that he had pitched in to help without being asked; someone had raised this boy right.

He had shrugged off his heavy jacket and was in just his boots, jeans, and a snug-fitting thermal. He had the perfect shape for a man. Broad shoulders, powerful arms, lean waist, and a seriously cute behind. Carly didn't consider this ogling since she was eye level with the very feature she was pondering. As if sensing her gaze upon him, James glanced down at her.

"Hey," he said. "Is Ike all right?"

"He seems to be," she said. "Thanks for your help but you don't have to do that. I can clean it up."

"It's fine," he said. The wicked twinkle came back into his eyes as his gaze roamed all over her just as his hands had a few nights before. "I like the view from up here."

Again, Carly felt her face heat up. She never blushed. Never. Why did this man affect her like this? She needed to get her equilibrium back. Now.

"The view from down here is pretty swell, too," she said. She tossed her hair and shifted her gaze to his rear, which was perfectly positioned for a grope.

Now it was his turn to blush but he didn't. Instead he hopped down from the chair so he was standing in front of her. Carly's boots had solid heels, but they weren't as high as her shoes had been on the night they met, and James was significantly taller than her. The top of her head reached the base of his throat and she had to crane her neck to meet his gaze.

"Are you flirting with me?" he asked. His voice was a low rumble that resonated somewhere in Carly's tailbone, making her entire body hum like a tuning fork.

"You started it," she said.

"I thought you were set on doing the 'friends' thing, buddy," he said.

"I am," she said. Then she shrugged. "It's just kind of a new thing for me. I usually don't see a man after I've slept with him, but I do enjoy flirting with my guy friends and it's hard to shut off. You're kind of a new category for me."

"I like that," he said.

He was too close. The familiar smell of his soap filled her senses and flipped a switch in her libido that made her want to lunge at him. Instead, she turned away. She had to get a handle on this thing between them before it spiraled out of control—again.

She glanced out the window that overlooked the small fenced-in backyard and saw Hot Wheels cruising around the small grassy area with Saul. They looked to have become fast friends.

"Hot Wheels really lives up to his name," she said. She gestured to the window with her thumb and James glanced out and smiled.

"Yeah, I nickname all of my clients," he said. "I've discovered the name thing builds a rapport."

"What have you nicknamed Mac's aunts?" she asked.

"Spaghetti and Meatballs," he said. "But, uh, not to their faces."

"Ha, my favorite food." Carly hooted. She could just imagine Aunt Sarah and Aunt Charlotte reacting to that. "What do you call them to their faces?"

"Sweet and Sassy," he said.

"You're a smart cookie."

"I try."

"Will you change his name if he gets better?" she asked.

"I don't know. It fits while we rehab his leg," he said. "I guess we'll have to see how it goes. We've got nothing but time."

Carly tried not to acknowledge the *aw* that was swelling up inside of her. So the man cared for a dog, so what? So, it was adorable, that's what.

"That's really nice of you," she said.

He shrugged. "I feel responsible for him."

And the second *aw* about took her out at the knees. Damn it. How was she supposed to maintain healthy boundaries if the guy was determined to be cute, funny, and helpful to injured animals? It wasn't fair.

"So, it looks like we both have animal dependents whether we like it or not. Since the prospective adopters are a bust, what's your plan for Ike?" he asked.

"I guess I have to find someone who doesn't mind a little rough language," she said. "Probably someone without children."

"Mean children at any rate," he agreed.

"Gavin said if I can teach him more words, it might edge out the bad words, but talking all the time is more exhausting than you'd think, plus I swear sometimes, which is not helpful," she said.

James tipped his head to the side and considered her for a moment.

"I might be able to help him," he said.

"In what way?" she asked. Her mind went immediately to naked James even though there was no way that was helpful to Ike—just her, all of her. Oh, boy.

"In rehabilitation, to get some of my less motivated clients on board with their treatments, I use everything I can get my hands on: music, motivational talks, videos, whatever works."

"I can see that," she said. "But how does it apply to Ike?"

"I put together a lot of recordings that I have my clients listen to, so I record MP3s, or CDs, even cassette tapes if that's all they have," he said. "I could help you make recordings of your voice for Ike to learn new words."

Carly considered him. She did not believe for one hot minute that he didn't have an ulterior motive and she was pretty sure it was more in line with her own thoughts of sweaty rumpled sheets than it was about finding a loving home for Ike.

"Why are you helping me?" she asked.

"Wellllll," he said, drawing the word out and gazing at her from beneath his ridiculously long eyelashes. "I like the idea of you owing me a favor."

Carly crossed her arms over her chest and

looked at him with one eyebrow raised higher than the other.

"Would you want a naked sweaty favor in return?" she asked. She narrowed her eyes as if she suspected he did.

"No!" he insisted. "I promise. Unless of course you're into that."

"I'm not," she said.

"Okay, then it's just a favor to be determined."

She stared at him.

"A clothed favor," he clarified.

Chapter 17

Carly stared at him for five seconds and then blinked. "No."

"Why not?"

"Because this"—she gestured between them—"is not normal."

"Normal is overrated," he said. "I have a dog in wheels, you have a bird that swears, I'd say neither of us is really operating under the guise of normal so why should this"—he mimicked her gesturing between them—"be any different? Don't you want to find Ike a new home?"

Carly glanced over her shoulder at Ike. He was preening. He looked to have put the earlier drama behind him. She was glad. She didn't like to see him stressed. It made her worry.

Okay, that was bad. She could not get attached to him or Saul. It would be unhealthy for all of them. She just wasn't the caregiver type, not for animals or people. If James could really help her with this recording then she needed to take him up on it.

Once Saul and Ike had new homes, Carly would be unencumbered once again. She was ready for that. She ignored the tiny pang in her chest. She was sure it was just heartburn from too much coffee. Yeah, she was more than ready to get her life back.

She held out her hand to James. "All right, you've got a deal."

He looked at her hand and pushed it aside. Then he opened his arms and said, "I don't shake hands with my buddies."

Fine. Carly took a deep breath and stepped into his embrace. The familiar scent of him went straight to her head and she had to resist the urge to bury her face in his shirt.

She patted him on the back twice and moved to step away, but he didn't loosen his hold. Instead, he leaned back to study her in his arms.

"Do you want to kiss on it?" he asked. His gaze was focused on her mouth and Carly felt a flash of heat zip through her.

"No!" she said, trying to ignore her reaction to his nearness. She wondered if he felt the same.

"You sure?" he asked. He waggled his eyebrows and even though he was teasing her, she got the feeling that he wouldn't hesitate if she waved him in.

Carly pushed him away. "Are you going to behave this badly whenever we're together?"

"That depends," he said. "Will it get me anywhere?"

"No. In fact, you may find yourself forfeiting a favor to be determined," she said. "No funny business, am I clear?"

"Crystal," he said. "I'll behave, unless I'm clearly instructed otherwise."

"Which you won't be. I'm willing to give this 'friendship' one shot," she said. "So, when do we make this recording for Ike? Do you need me? Can you do it on your own?"

"No, he responds mostly to you so let's make it your voice," he said. "Can you come by my place tonight after eight?"

"Sure," she said. "Where is it?"

"It's in the old lighthouse on Bluff Point," he said.

"Your office is out there?"

"Office, residence, the whole shebang," he said.

"So, you're the one who bought the Bluff Point lighthouse?" she asked. "My mother told me someone from Boston purchased it, but she didn't have a name. Everyone was worried that you were going to tear it down and build some ridonkulous McMansion."

"Nah, no mansion for me. I like the charm of the old building," he said. "I found it a few months ago when I was looking for a space where I could live and have enough room for a rehabilitation center. Someone recommended it and when I saw that the price was right, I snatched it up."

"Small wonder, you know that place is haunted, right?" she asked.

"No, it isn't." He laughed and looked at her like he found her adorable. Carly realized it was a look she could get used to. She shifted away from him.

"Yes, it is," she insisted. She turned to wipe down the tables while they talked. "When Jillian, Mac, Emma, and I were teenagers we used to drive out there late at night and then we would dare each other to go up and touch the side of the building."

James crossed his arms over his chest. "I've been there for a couple of months and there's been no sign of any ghosts, ghouls, or specters. Besides, with the number of workmen I've had coming and going, I'm pretty sure any otherworld inhabitants would vacate the premises to get away from the noise."

"What are you having done to the place?"

"This and that, upgrades mostly," he said. He stepped close and whispered in her ear, "When you come out tonight, I'll give you the grand tour if you're not too afraid."

Carly shivered and it wasn't because of her fear of ghosts.

"All right," she said. "I'll be there. Eight o'clock."

When he stepped away from her, she felt the lack of his warmth immediately. He ducked through the back of the shop to collect Hot Wheels and when the two of them left through the back gate, Carly noticed that James looked pretty pleased with himself.

Carly couldn't figure out if it was because he was going to get her on his turf or because she would owe him a favor. A kaleidoscope of images twirled through her brain as she remembered their night together. How his dark hair fell over his forehead when he was leaning over her; the way his blue eyes seemed to see her, really see her, catching her every expression while he learned who she was, what she liked, and how to make her his. Would her debt include anything like that? He'd said it wouldn't and she had to acknowledge a smidge—okay, more than a smidge—of disappointment at that.

Realizing that he was slyly working his way into her life, Carly felt vulnerable for the first time in forever. In a crushing moment of self-doubt, she wondered if she hadn't just made the worst bargain of her life.

Since Gina had their shared car, Carly borrowed Jillian's Jeep to drive out to the Bluff Point lighthouse. It was on the outskirts of town down a narrow dirt road that wound through a thick copse of trees.

Only, the road wasn't as narrow or as dark as Carly remembered it. The trees had been cut back so that they didn't hang ominously over the road anymore. The road, while still dirt, had been widened and smoothed out so that two cars could actually pass each other without fear of a collision.

A lighted lamppost illuminated a sign that read Sinclair Rehabilitation Center at the end of the dirt road with an arrow pointing to the house that was adjacent to the old lighthouse.

The lot that had once been overgrown weeds and broken bottles from the local teenagers who came out here to party was now a small shell-encrusted parking lot. The two story rectangular white house looked the same, except the broken windows had been replaced and it was sporting a fresh coat of paint. Cheery yellow light spilled out of its windows with a welcoming warmth, and the sound of music was faint over the sound of the waves crashing against the rocks just beyond the lighthouse.

Carly parked the Jeep in between James's car and a sleek black car that looked like the type used by a car service. She checked the time on her cell phone and realized she was right on time. She had a sudden bout of nerves. What if James had forgotten about their plans? She huffed out a breath and glanced at the tall, wide lighthouse beyond the house.

It, too, had a fresh coat of white paint. Even though the light at the top was dark, as the Bluff Point lighthouse hadn't been used since they'd built a newer and bigger one farther up the coastline, it still stood proudly against the star-studded night sky as if ready to be utilized at any given moment. Carly took heart from its strong stance and tightened the silk scarf about her neck as she strode toward the front door.

She rapped her knuckles against the thick wooden door and waited. No one answered. She checked the wall for a doorbell but didn't find one. She knocked again. Still, there was no answer.

She glanced back at the Jeep and wondered if she should just go. Maybe James had gotten busy with work and couldn't fit her in tonight. She glanced back up at the lighthouse. No, a deal was a deal. She was going in.

She grasped the old-fashioned door handle and pressed down on the lever with her thumb. It wasn't locked, so she pushed the door open. Stepping inside, she caught her breath. The place was covered in plastic sheeting, and littered with tools, electrical cords, and sawhorses. Clearly the main part of the house was under construction, but she could see where the open floor design was headed and it made her catch her breath.

It was going to be beautiful. She thought about how she'd thrown rocks at the old windows when she was a wild teen and shook her head. Who'd have thought the old pile of refuse and decay could be turned into such a showstopper of a house?

To her left was a large kitchen; there were no appliances in it, and the cabinetry was only half installed, but the dark wood looked wonderful against the pewter and cream paint. An island separated the kitchen from the large living area. The narrow, old windows had been replaced by huge, floor-to-ceiling windows that overlooked the water. Carly was sure the view by day was spectacular. She crossed the room to peer out the window. She could just make out the lights of a distant ship. She wondered as she always did who was on it and where were they going?

The sound of a door shutting in the distance made her jump and she realized she hadn't announced her presence. She hurried back across the large room, hoping to look like she was just entering before she called out. She got halfway across the room when the sound of laughter stopped her and she whipped her head toward the hallway on her left just in time to see James coming toward her with a woman who was draped across him like a cheap plastic bib at an all-you-can-eat lobster special.

As always, James looked slightly disheveled. He was in a pair of faded, well-worn jeans, but instead of a sleeveless shirt or a thermal long-sleeved shirt, both of which made the most of his ripped physique, he was in a baggy gray sweatshirt with the word "Boston" in big blue letters on the front.

In contrast, the woman didn't look as if she had so much as a hair out of place. Her black hair was styled in a tight topknot on her head. Her workout clothes, a purple sports bra and matching yoga pants, hugged her slender curves and boasted a creative peekaboo cutout over her cleavage. Talk about your mixed signals. Was she here to work out or pick someone up? Carly decided she didn't like this woman.

She crossed her arms over her chest and started to tap her foot. She was profoundly irritated. Here she was on time for their appointment and there was James cavorting with some sexy siren type like he had forgotten all about Carly coming over. She wanted to kick him, really hard.

"James, I can't thank you enough, for everything," the woman purred and pressed herself up against him.

"Any time, Bethany," he said. He was smiling down at her and Carly found she didn't like that at all.

"Ahem," she cleared her throat.

Both James and Bethany jumped and looked at her in surprise.

Really? They had been so caught up in each other that they hadn't noticed she was here? Now Carly was deeply offended.

"Sorry to barge in," she said. "I knocked but no one answered. We had an appointment for eight, right? Unless, of course, you're otherwise occupied."

James looked from Carly to Bethany and back. Then, as if aware of how it looked, he gently extricated himself from Bethany's grasp, moving her hands to the back of one of the bar stools. He went over to the closet by the front door and came back with two crutches and a coat, which he held out to Bethany.

Carly watched as the woman tucked them under her arms and then used them to brace herself. Suddenly, she felt bad for thinking that the woman had been draped on James for reasons other than balance.

"No worries, Carly," James said. "Bethany and I just finished up. I'll see her out and we can get started."

Carly glanced at Bethany, who was looking at her curiously.

"I'm Bethany Wales," she said. She extended a perfectly manicured hand with a ring that had a diamond the size of a walnut on it.

Carly shook her hand and was surprised that Bethany didn't have an icy-fingered, limp-wristed handshake, the sort that Carly found off-putting in other women. Instead, her handshake was warm and firm, letting Carly know that she was a professional who took herself seriously. Now if only she hadn't been draped all over Carly's recent one-night stand, she might even like her a little.

"Carly DeCusati," she said.

"Are you here for rehab, too?" Bethany asked.

"No," Carly said. "I haven't injured anything . . . lately."

Bethany smiled. Then she hugged James close and said, "Well, if ever you do, he's the guy who can fix it. I blew out my knee dancing, but I'm fighting my way back."

"And doing amazing," James said. The affectionate look he cast Bethany made Carly's stomach knot.

"Good to know," she said. She knew her voice sounded frostier than she had intended but she was powerless to change it now, so she tried to soften her words with a smile but she feared it looked more like she was gnashing her teeth.

"You ready, twinkle toes?" James asked. "I'll walk you out."

"Thanks, love," she said.

Love? Carly felt her insides shrink up in disapproval at the endearment.

Bethany used her crutches to push herself up, almost falling onto James when she kissed his cheek. He steadied her so that she didn't tip over and she laughed and said, "There you go, saving me again."

James glanced at Carly and said, "Be right back."

"Pleasure to meet you," Bethany said as James ushered her outside.

"You, too," Carly lied.

For a nanosecond, Carly debated whether spying on them would be in poor taste. Then she realized she didn't care and she hurried over to the kitchen window to peer outside.

When James and Bethany were halfway down

the walk, a man stepped out of the big black car. He was wearing the dress of a professional driver and when he circled the car to hold the back door open for Bethany, that confirmed it.

Carly knew she should step back, but she didn't. She stayed right where she was, waiting to see what sort of good-bye James and Bethany shared. It was not one of her finer moments and even though she didn't even care what his relationship was with the slinky siren, she couldn't make herself back away.

So naturally, when James glanced back at the house, he caught her watching him.

Chapter 18

Instinctively, Carly ducked back out of sight, but she knew it was too late. Even in the dark from a fifty-foot distance, she had felt the intensity in his laser-like blue gaze. She could feel embarrassment warm her face but she refused to let it show.

She had nothing to be embarrassed about. She wasn't the one who was wearing a woman like a necktie. She wondered if he was kissing her good-bye. She leaned forward to peek back out the window. All she saw were the taillights of the car disappearing down the drive. She didn't consider that a bad thing.

When she turned around, James was standing behind her. He had his hands shoved in his back pockets and his head tipped to one side as he considered her.

"Oh, you're back," she said. She tried to sound blasé but the words got caught in her throat and she sounded like she might choke on them.

"Bethany is a client."

"So I gathered."

"She's a ballerina in rehabilitation for her knee."

"So she mentioned."

He tipped his head in the other direction and ran a hand through his hair, making it stick up in back.

"Are you mad at me?"

"Now why would you think that, since I have no reason whatsoever to be mad at you?" she asked.

Carly's voice was tight and hard and she thought the man would have to be as thick as a brick to not register her ire.

"You sound mad," he said. "And I noticed when you met Bethany that your WTF wrinkle got really deep."

"Excuse me?" Carly asked. "What is a WTF wrinkle?"

"You know, that line in between your eyebrows that looks like a V and gets deeper when you're thinking *what the fuck*," he said. He reached out and rubbed her forehead right between her eyes with his thumb. "There, now it's gone."

Carly felt like he had just exposed something in her that she wasn't too happy about letting him see.

"I do not have a WTF line," she said. "If anything it's a AYSM wrinkle because I can't imagine why you have me locked into a favor to be determined since Ms. Wales looked more than willing to do you . . . er . . . to give you any favor that was required."

Gah! Carly wanted to pull out her own tongue. She sounded demented.

"An *are you shitting me* wrinkle? That's a good one. But seriously, she's engaged," he said. "To

Ivan Tudezcu, the director of the Boston Ballet."

"Boston Ballet?" Carly said. She might not know much about dancers but even she knew that the Boston Ballet was a big deal. Still, they were several hours north of Boston. What was Ms. Wales doing all the way up here getting rehab with James?

"Wow, that's a long way to come for rehab," she said.

"Ivan and I go way back," he said. "Bethany's issue is more than her knee. She's having a crisis of confidence as well. Ivan thought I might be able to help with both. Besides, they have a beach house here in town."

Carly glanced around the gutted house. "So that's how you can afford all this. You're the physical therapist to the stars, kind of a big deal."

"Not really," he said. "I'm just good at what I do."

He said it with confidence and yet didn't sound arrogant. She liked that. Carly could feel his gaze on the side of her face. She did not turn to look at him because her mind had slid right to their one-night stand where she felt she could say with more than a little authority that, yes, he was very good at what he did.

"Is it hot in here?" She unbuttoned her coat and slid it off, draping it over her arm.

When she turned back around, he was still staring at her and the heat in his gaze was impossible to miss. James wanted her. The thought made Carly dizzy and now that she was here in his home alone with him, she didn't know if she had the willpower to resist the hot friction that sizzled between them.

"Come on," he said, stepping away from her. "Let me show you the highlights."

Although she refused to admit it, she really hoped he started with the bedroom. She wondered what sort of sleep situation a guy like James required. California king with Egyptian cotton sheets? Maybe just a regular king with flannel. She glanced at him. She could totally see him being a plaid flannel sheet sort of guy.

Wait! What? Why was she even thinking about his bedroom? Seriously, she needed to get a grip. She needed a glass of ice water dumped down her shirt or over her head. She was trying to be friends with this guy. Healthy boundaries needed to be scrupulously maintained. She put a few more feet in between them. If he noticed, he didn't show it.

When he led her down the hallway and pushed open the door into a huge workout room, Carly was hard-pressed to hide her disappointment.

"Unless I am out in the field, helping a client, this is pretty much where I live," he said.

He held his arms wide and Carly took in the large room that was filled with all sorts of exercise equipment, from free weights to parallel bars, and several pieces of medical equipment—stuff she recognized like heart monitors and blood pressure machines, and others she couldn't identify.

He put his hand on her lower back to usher her farther into the room. It felt hot like a brand through her shirt. Oh, jeez, that was not good. The man could accidentally brush up against her and she would catch on fire wherever contact was made.

"This is . . . impressive," she said. She guessed that was what he wanted to hear. Didn't most men?

"You have no idea what most of this does, do you?" he asked with a smile. Busted!

"Not a clue."

"Someday I'll have to get you in here for a proper stress test," he said.

Carly would have said that was a bad idea because any time she was near him she was pretty sure her stress level rose higher than was healthy. But of course she said nothing.

"Come on, let's go to my office," he said. "There's someone who'll be happy to see you."

He led her through the facility to a glassed-in room in the corner. Carly could see a large desk with a computer on one side and a small conference table with chairs on the other.

James pushed the door open and said, "Hey, Hot Wheels, look who's here."

Carly glanced around the room and then heard the scrabble of paws on the hardwood floor. Peering around the desk at her was a big nose and one big brown eye.

"Hey, buddy," she said. She dropped her coat and her purse on a small couch along the wall and crouched beside James.

The dog seemed to recognize her, because he lurched forward and came around the side of the desk. His back end supported by his two-wheel harness, he bounded toward her with the enthusiasm only a puppy could muster.

He stopped in front of them and pushed his head into James's hip, clearly looking for love. James obliged, rubbing his ears and talking so sweetly to him that Carly couldn't help but think that if he talked to her in that voice she would crawl up into his lap and refuse to budge.

She shook her head and focused on the dog. She held out her hand so Hot Wheels could get her scent. After several sniffs and one small lick, Hot Wheels pressed his head into her side as well, then he sniffed her all over and woofed.

"He's the sweetest," she said. "I think he's wondering where Ike and Saul are. Sorry, Wheels, those boys went night-night."

James grinned at her. "I like the way you talk to him and the others as if you expect them to answer."

"Well, Ike usually does," she said. "And if I

understood dog speak, I bet I'd have some great convos with Hot Wheels, too. What's wrong with his leg?"

"Gavin thinks he suffered some nerve damage when he was born," James said. "Because we don't know the circumstances, it's all speculation, but we both think we'll be able to get him walking again. We do exercises a couple of times a day, and the wheels keep him mobile."

While he talked, James unfastened Hot Wheels's harness and helped him out of the rig. The dog shook himself from head to tail as if relieved to be free. Then he limped over to a fluffy dog bed in the corner and flopped onto it, belly in the air.

"Looks like he's done for today."

"He's had a full day," James agreed. He turned to study her. "So, are you ready to make a recording for Ike?"

"Sure," she said.

James pulled an extra chair over to his desk so the two of them could sit in front of his computer. He motioned for Carly to sit next to him, then he positioned a small mic on a stand so it was right in front of her face. An acute bout of shyness hit Carly and she thought about bolting for the door.

"Relax," he said. "This won't hurt a bit."

"So says the man behind the curtain," she said. "I don't think I'm really comfortable like this. I sort of thought I was just going to speak into your smartphone and you could work off a recording from that."

"If you want to give Ike the greatest chance at learning words then the clearest recording possible is your best bet," he said. He opened up a recording program on his computer and then turned to face her.

He was so close Carly was having a hard time concentrating on his words. Did he always smell this good? Yeah, she was pretty sure he did. Damn it.

"Why don't you do the recording?" she asked. She leaned back from him, finding it hard to breathe with him in her personal space. "You'll know better what to say and how to say it."

"No, Ike's clearly bonded to you," he said. "I think he'll pick up your voice more easily."

"He's not bonded to me," she protested. "I'm just the person he sees every day, who feeds him and stuff."

James gently pushed the mic toward her and paused to look at her. His gaze was kind and a little amused but she got the feeling that he saw her, really saw her, more than anyone had in a very long time.

"And stuff," he said.

His voice was low so Carly leaned forward to hear better and he met her halfway. To Carly it felt as if they had no choice in the matter because the pull between them was as much a part of their

240

natural order as the gravitational hold on the planets circling the sun. She bonked her nose on the microphone.

"Oh!" She jumped back.

James shook his head as if trying to get his wits together and then gave her side eye as if he couldn't look at her full-on or he'd risk being sucked back into her orbit. Carly was trying to remember why that was bad, desperately trying.

"You all right?" he asked.

"Fine," she bluffed. "Clumsy but fine."

"Good," he said. "So, what sort of things do you want our man Ike to say?"

"I'm not as clear on what I want him to say as what I don't want him to say," she said. "'Hello, how are you?' would be a solid change up from 'Shut your stupid cake hole.'"

James laughed. "You have to admit the other does have a certain charm."

"Not when you're trying to find him a new home."

"True enough," James said. "How about we start with the basics then? You know, 'Hello, how are you?' or 'Polly, want a cracker?'"

"I am not teaching him that," she said. On this, she was firm.

"Oh, come on," he said. He turned back to the computer and began setting up the recording.

"No," she said.

"But it's a classic. It's what everyone will expect him to say." His voice was a low gruff growl while he concentrated on the task at hand.

She glanced at him and saw the right side of his smile tip up and the wicked glint in his eye, both letting her know that he was teasing her. It struck her that she liked him, really liked him, as a person, which would be absolutely fine if she felt about him like she did Zach or Sam or Brad or Gavin, male friends who were like brothers. But she didn't feel that way, not in the slightest.

"Okay, sunshine, let's do a couple of practice runs, so I can check the sound and quality on my end."

"All right," she said.

She really needed to curb his habit of calling her sunshine. Should she make a big deal out of it or let it go? And why, oh why, was her heart thundering in her chest like this? It was just a word. It didn't mean anything. Right?

Obviously unaware of her inner turmoil, James turned back to her with a smile and said, "Okay, in three, two, one."

Then he pointed at her to go. When Carly thought about it, later, she had no idea what had possessed her, but just looking at him with his roguish grin, baggy sweatshirt, and disheveled hair, well, it made the naughty fly right into her and without overthinking it, she leaned close to the mic and in her throatiest, sexiest purr she cried out, "James, oh, James!"

One moment he was sitting next to her with his hands on the controls in front of him; in the next he was reaching for her with a single-minded purpose on his face that made her breath catch and her heart stop.

He cupped the back of her head and hauled her up against him and then he kissed her, devastatingly and thoroughly. It wasn't a kind or gentle kiss, rather it was a barely restrained plunder of her mouth under his. His lips owned hers, drawing her deeper into the fire that flared up between them every time they touched, leaving her scorched.

Carly didn't remember putting her arms around his neck but when he finally broke the kiss and pulled back to look at her, or perhaps to breathe, she was hanging onto him for dear life since any knowledge of how to sit up on her own had fled the part of her head that retained muscle memory.

Gently, James unhooked her arms from his shoulders and pushed her back into her seat. He cleared his throat and then gave her a sheepish look. He blew out a breath and shoved a hand through his hair, making it stick up on one side.

"Here's the thing," he said. "I can do the platonic thing, I can even hold hands and hug you without losing my mind, mostly, but your voice saying my name like that is my weakness. So if you turn that voice on me and call my name in that insanely sexy way, I am going to kiss you like that every time. Am I clear?"

"Crystal," Carly said, repeating the same word he had spoken to her earlier that day, except her voice came out low and husky. When his eyebrow quirked up at the sound, she cleared her throat and, in a much higher and squeakier voice, said, "Crystal."

"Just so we understand each other, buddy," he said.

He turned back to the computer, but not before she saw him grin as if quite pleased with himself over the response he had drawn out of her. She did not tell him he wasn't the only one, since her survival skills had kicked into high gear and her decided response was to deny, deny, deny.

The next half hour was a blur for Carly. She said words and phrases over and over while James smiled at her and nodded. He seemed very much in control of the recording, while all Carly could think about was his mouth on hers and how much she wanted it there among other places again.

She closed her eyes and repeated the last phrase he asked her to say. Maybe it wouldn't be so bad if she wasn't staring at him the whole time.

"Excellent," he said. He reached over to switch off the mic and was so close his voice sounded in her ear and Carly felt as if he were actually in her head, which would be bad because the dirty thoughts she was having about him were definitely not something he needed to know. "That's a wrap."

"Cool," she said. She was feeling anything but.

"I'll clean it up and record it in a loop and it'll be ready to go," he said.

"Great," Carly said.

"Are you okay?" he asked.

"Yeah, I'm good," she said. Her smile was tight. She could feel it. Thankfully, he didn't press her.

"I'll walk you out," he said.

"No, I don't want to be a bother," she said. She gave Hot Wheels's belly a quick scratch and then grabbed her purse and her jacket and strode to the door. She needed to put some space between them ASAP. "I know the way."

"Yeah, I'm still not letting you walk alone to your car in the dark," he said. "My mama raised me better than that."

Carly didn't want him to walk her anywhere, but he was right on her heels as she left the rehabilitation room and hurried down the hall-way, struggling to yank on her jacket as she went.

"Carly, wait," he said. "Carly!"

She didn't slow down and when she felt her jacket get snagged, she impatiently spun around looking for the object that had caught her. It was

James. He was holding onto one of her sleeves and he didn't look like he was about to let go anytime soon.

"We need to talk," he said.

Chapter 19

"No, we don't," she argued.

"Clearly, we do," he said. He let go of her sleeve and grabbed her coat by the collar, holding it open for her. She slipped into it, then he spun her around and pushed aside her clumsy fingers so that he could fasten it for her. "It was the kiss, wasn't it? It freaked you out."

"I don't get freaked out," she lied.

He gave her a look that clearly said *bullshit,* although he was polite enough not to say it.

"All right, maybe I'm a tiny bit concerned about being 'friends' with a man who kisses me like that when I say his name," she said. There. It felt better to put it back on him. This was his fault, after all. No man had ever gotten her so worked up.

"Oh, you can say my name," he said. "Go ahead, I promise I won't jump you."

Carly stared at him for a moment. Then she cautiously said, "James?"

He didn't flicker so much as an eyelash.

"See?" he asked. "I'm fine. But if you say my name like you're about to debauch and defile me or want me to do the same to you, then you're going to get kissed . . . thoroughly."

There was a buzzing in Carly's ears and she

was pretty sure she had forgotten how to breathe. She blinked.

"Why?" she asked.

"Because you have always affected me that way," he said. His gaze was steady on hers.

"Always?" she asked. She tried to make light of the intensity of the moment. "You make it sound as if I've known you longer than mere days."

"You have," he said. He lowered his eyes and gazed at her from beneath his thick black eyelashes. "You just don't remember me."

"What?" She felt alarm bells clanging in her head. Had she slept with James before and not remembered? She glanced at him. No, that wasn't possible. There was no way she'd forget a man like James.

"It's true," he said. "You and I met when I was visiting my cousin at college, oh, about eleven years ago."

Carly did a quick mental scan. Eleven years ago she'd been getting her undergrad in business at Columbia in New York City. It was also when she'd had her first and only boyfriend, or as she liked to think of it, her life lesson in why she'd never date again.

"Why didn't you mention this when I met you that first day in the park?" she asked.

"I wasn't sure," he said. "You looked familiar, but I didn't put it together until after I was leaving your house the morning after and saw the

248

name DeCusati on the mailbox. Then it all started coming back to me."

"And you didn't say anything?"

"Well, you'd made it pretty clear that we were dusted and done," he said. "I wasn't sure I'd be able to convince you to see me again even as a friend."

Carly was having a hard time breathing; she was sweaty and shaky, sort of like a panic attack but more like a bout of hysteria. She desperately wanted to know who his cousin was but, then again, she was afraid to find out.

She spun on her heel and strode toward the door. She needed some fresh air—right now!

"Carly, wait!" James hurried after her.

Once she was outside, she paused to suck in a deep breath of the cold night air. It helped. There was no avoiding the next question. She had to know.

"Who was your cousin?" she asked. She forced herself to look calm even when the urge to throw up roared up the back of her throat. She closed her eyes for a second, silently begging *Please don't let it be him, anyone but him.*

"Preston Bradley," he said.

Of course, it was him. She turned and hurried to the car, while James fell in beside her.

"Or as he likes to refer to himself, Preston Sinclair Bradley, the third," James said. He seemed oblivious to her distress and Carly planned to keep it that way. "He tried to get us all to call him 'Trey' for a while but my sister kept calling him '*Tres Imbecile*' so he gave up."

"Ha!" Carly forced out a puff of air that she hoped sounded like a laugh.

"I got the impression that you and Preston were together at the time," James said. He glanced at her. "Is it weird that I'm his cousin?"

"Me and Preston? Together? That's a laugh," she said. She wondered if James noticed that she didn't really confirm or deny.

He held the car door open for her, and she slid into the driver's seat as if it were an escape hatch. She could not get away from here fast enough.

"Oh, well, good," he said. "I wouldn't want things to be weird between us."

Carly looked at him.

"Well, any weirder than they already are," he joked.

"No, not weird." She forced a smile while thinking, *Too late*.

"Good. I'll see you around, sunshine," James said.

Carly nodded and started the engine. With a wave, she shot back down the drive. She refused to look in her rearview mirror at him. She didn't want to have an image in her head of him standing alone in the cold, for fear that it would make her turn the car around and tackle him to the groun like her basic instincts were badgering her to do.

She shook her head, trying to get her common sense to wrestle her wayward thinking down to the mat where it could hold it for a three-count and save her from making an ass of herself. They were friends, just friends. And even more than that, he was Preston's cousin, *freaking Preston Bradley,* the bane of her existence! There was no way she could be anything more than friends with James and right now even that was in question.

What if James and Preston talked and Preston told him about . . . no, she couldn't go there. Her shame needed to remain in the past. Given that her time with Preston did not put him in a good light, surely he wouldn't say anything to James. And even if he did, what did it matter?

She had to remember that what she had with James was now no more than an exchange of goods and services. Carly pondered that thought. Was she the goods or the services? Since he was servicing her by making the recording, Carly's undetermined favor must be the goods. Well, that sounded dirty in a decidedly sexy sort of way.

Ugh, everything was sexy when it came to James. She was pretty sure the man could make household chores sexy to her, especially if he did them naked or, even better, in just an apron.

She resisted the urge to do a face palm, barely.

She had to get a grip on this attraction and strangle the life out of it. She did not date, she did not sleep with men more than once; no repeats, that was the code she lived by, and she was not changing it just to shag James Sinclair one more time. Never mind that it would likely be the hottest night of her life. It would only lead to heartache and pain, and she was not going to do it.

Since James was tempting her beyond reason to break her no-repeater rule, there was clearly only one thing to do. She needed to add a layer of protection to keep herself from doing something dumb. She was going to have to break out her baggiest, droopiest cotton underwear, her granny panties, bolstering the foundation layer to keep herself from having a lapse in judgment and encouraging his hands to wander to places that they shouldn't.

As a former lingerie buyer, underwear had been her business, and Carly would rather die than be caught in anything that looked like it was even marginally comfortable. A girl had to have standards after all. But with James around, making her cross-eyed with lust, she needed to add a layer to her no-sex shield. Those droopy drawers of hers were going to be more effective than a chastity belt.

Carly arrived at Making Whoopie bright and early. Jillian glanced up at her as she came through the front door, carrying two large paper cups of coffee from The Grind.

"What?" Carly asked.

"You're an hour early," Jillian said. "What gives?"

Carly shrugged. "Nothing."

"Really?" Jillian tossed her head of dark curls and leveled Carly with an assessing look. "So, you being here this early has nothing to do with James coming in to talk about his special order."

"Is that *this* morning?" Carly blinked. She had forgotten that James was supposed to meet with Jillian. Frankly, she'd been so freaked out about him being Preston Bradley's cousin that she hadn't slept and was barely functional.

"I can't be here," she said. She thrust the coffee at Jillian just as the door swung open and James popped his head in.

"Good morning, ladies," he said. "Am I too early?"

It was nine o'clock on the button. The boy was punctual. Of course he was. Was there nothing wrong with him? Truly, it was maddening.

"Perfect timing," Jillian said. "Come in. I've got a tray of samples for you to plow your way through."

"Excellent," James stepped into the bakery. He inhaled deeply and sighed. "This smells like heaven."

Jillian grinned at him and said, "I think so, too."

Carly glanced between them. They were both tall and lean and would make a spectacular-looking couple. Why couldn't they have hooked up instead of her and James? Everything in her world would be so much easier if she had never decided to have a one-night stand with the hot physical therapist.

"I'll just go tidy up the back," she muttered and stomped into the kitchen.

She knew it probably looked like she was running away. She didn't care. She put her coat and purse in the small office and set to tackling the dishes Jillian had left in the large industrial steel sink. Jillian usually came in at five in the morning and baked straight through until they opened at nine. Since she didn't bake, Carly had taken over the role of chief dish-washer, which was mostly mixing bowls and baking sheets, to give Jillian a break from the kitchen.

While Carly was happy to help her friend in her whoopie pie business—was grateful, in fact, for something to do—the thought of being stuck in this kitchen doing dishes for many more weeks made her want to stick her head in the oven. The only job offer she'd gotten so far was as a buyer for a uniform company. She just couldn't get that jazzed about shopping for polyester slacks and scrubs in every color of the rainbow, plus the job paid nothing and was in a Podunk town in the Midwest. Not to be picky but even scrubbing dishes looked better than that.

She did a quick gut check and realized her self-esteem was about as low as the tide in a hot, dry summer. Seriously, if she didn't get a good job offer soon, she was going to have to go for therapy.

She tied on an apron, pulled on a pair of rubber gloves, and set to work, filling the sink with hot, sudsy water. She hoped scrubbing the batter out of the bowls would calm the paranoid beast still trying to claw its way out of her chest. She had spent the night tossing and turning, wondering how much James knew about her past with Preston. She didn't think she could bear it if he knew the full extent of her humiliation. Even now after all these years, just thinking about it made her queasy.

Full disclosure, at least to herself, she would die, just die, in a complete and total meltdown of mortification, if James knew about the truth behind her relationship with Preston.

"What a mess," she muttered. "Stupid, stupid, stupid."

She took her anxiety out on the bowls, scrubbing hardened bits of batter with the rough side of the sponge. Sweat was beading up on her forehead and it wasn't until she paused to wipe it away that she got the feeling someone was watching her.

She spun around expecting to find James. When she saw Emma and Mac, she felt the tiniest twinge of disappointment, which she was certain was only because she wanted to see James with her new sense of boundaries in place. She wanted to be sure that he knew nothing of her humiliating past, and she wanted to keep it that way.

"Angry at the mixing bowls?" Emma asked.

"They're being difficult," Carly said.

"Well, if you can take a break from scolding them, we want to talk to you about James."

"No." Carly turned her back on them.

"What do you mean 'no'?" Mac asked. She sounded outraged.

Carly wasn't surprised; very few people ever said no to Mac, as she usually had them charmed into her way of thinking before they even realized she'd put the whammy on them.

"I know what you're going to say," Carly said. She glanced at them over her shoulder. "You think I should date him and the answer is no."

"But—" Emma looked at Mac in consternation. She pulled the blue beanie off her blonde hair and shook it out as if she was gearing up for a fight.

"No."

"Just hear us out," Mac said. "He's a great guy. He takes such good care of Hot Wheels and the aunts adore him. He's very successful in his business, he's totally hot, and he owns a freaking lighthouse. What more could you be looking for in a man?"

Carly continued scrubbing the bowl in her hands even though it sparkled and was destined for a spin through the industrial dishwasher beside the sink.

"You can't ignore us," Emma said. "Well, you can, but you know we'll just bug you and bug you and bug you until you listen."

This was true. These girls had staying power, especially when they got their nag on. Carly was pretty sure that coupledom was a disease and once infected the people in them were determined that everyone around them should suffer from the same sad circumstance, sort of like contamination from a zombie bite. No, thank you.

"All right, get it out of your system," Carly said.

She began to load the dishwasher while Emma and Mac moved to stand one on each side of her. They stood with their arms crossed over their chests in identical postures of stubbornness.

"We like James," Mac said.

"A lot," Emma agreed.

"Good guys are really hard to find, and he seems like a really good one," Mac said.

"But that isn't the point," Emma said.

"It isn't?" Mac asked. She glanced at Emma with a bewildered look. "I thought the whole point was that we wanted her to reconsider keeping James at arm's length."

"We do," Emma agreed. "But even more we want her to think about *why* she refuses to be in any relationship ever. I mean it's been years, *years,* since that ass hat ruined her life and it's time for her to rethink it."

"And she's standing right here," Carly said. She loaded a whisk and two spatulas.

They ignored her.

"But we're still for James, right?" Mac asked. "I mean the whole reason we want her to rethink the relationship thing is because we think James is a keeper."

"Yes, of course," Emma said. "But she has to get the root of the problem—"

"Still right here," Carly said. She used her thumb to scrape a cookie crumb off of a baking sheet.

"Sorry," Emma and Mac said together.

Carly put the sheet in the dishwasher and closed it. She stepped back and glanced at her friends. She knew they loved her. She knew that their own happy relationship statuses were influencing their opinion of her life. The truth was she liked being unencumbered and they just didn't get it. She decided to be very clear with them once and for all.

"Listen, even if I were looking for a man, which I am not," Carly said, "I would never ever pick someone like James. He's entirely too nice, too well-mannered—"

"Oh, yeah, that's the worst," Mac said. She looked at the ceiling as if praying for patience. Carly ignored her.

"I'm serious," Carly said. "I like bad boys."

"Oh, right, because the one relationship you had with a bad boy turned out so well that you've never dated again," Emma said.

Okay, that smarted. Carly knew her friends meant well but she felt the need to end this discussion permanently.

"Stop trying to get me to be like you," she said. "I am not you, either of you, and I don't want a relationship. Ever. I like my life exactly as it is. I do what I want, when I want, and with who I want, even if it's a different who I want every Saturday night. I live my life with no compromises, and it's fabulous."

Both Mac and Emma opened their mouths to speak, but Carly cut them off by holding her hand up.

"No. You need to hear me, really hear me, for a change." She couldn't maintain eye contact while she fibbed, so she stripped off her rubber gloves while she spoke. "I don't care how nice James is, I am not now nor will I ever be interested in a relationship with him. He's not my type, frankly, he just doesn't do it for me. Okay?"

She glanced up. Both Mac and Emma were

staring past her at the door. They looked horrified. Carly felt her heart sink into her shoes.

"And he's right behind me, isn't he?" she asked.

Chapter 20

Both Mac and Emma nodded, looking sickly. Carly blew out a breath and turned around with the brightest smile in her arsenal. When she saw him leaning against the doorjamb, studying her, it faltered but only for a second.

"James," she said. "Sorry, I didn't hear you come in."

"Clearly," he said. He glanced at Emma and Mac, looking serious, and spoke in a tone that made his request more of a politely worded order. "Will you excuse us, ladies?"

"Sure."

"You bet."

Both Emma and Mac bolted from the room, practically tripping each other on their way out. Traitors!

Carly sighed and prepared to do triage on the fractured male ego she was certain she had just unwittingly laid to waste. Men could be so fragile—another reason she had no desire to be involved with anyone. She wondered what she could say that would stop the pout and sulk she was certain was coming her way.

She glanced back at James, pulling together a string of adjectives about his performance the other night that would assuage his wounded male ego.

One look at his face, however, and the words stuck to her tongue. Instead of looking irritated or wounded, he was grinning at her. And it wasn't just a grin of amusement, it was a lascivious, naughty, wicked twist of his lips that made her knees buckle just enough so that she had to grip the counter at her back to stay upright.

"I can explain," she said.

He ignored her. He continued to cross the room until he was standing just inches in front of her. Carly felt her pulse pound in her ears and her breathing was shallow, both adding to the dizziness that was already impairing her balance.

"Not your type, huh?" he asked. He leaned forward, resting his hands on the counter behind her, penning her in with a proprietary swagger that she knew she shouldn't find so hot, but it totally was.

Carly tipped up her chin. She knew she needed to put up a barrier here, before this whole thing got out of hand. She didn't want to crush him but then again maybe it was for the best. This would keep him from misconstruing anything between them, inadvertently making more of their one night than he should.

"No, you're not. I'm sorry but that's just the way it is," she said.

She turned away from him and glanced down at the tray of whoopie pies that needed to be taken out front. She didn't hear him move and was startled when he reached around her to take the tray, pressing her up against the table just the slightest bit so that she could feel his front against her backside, causing a flash of heat inside of her that made her think she might spontaneously combust. He leaned closer so that his mouth was just a breath from her ear.

"You are quite possibly the worst liar I have ever met," he said. The feel of his breath in the shell of her ear made her shiver and she was pretty sure she went cross-eyed for a moment. He lifted the tray over her head and stepped back. "And now you're in trouble."

"Trouble?" she asked. Her mouth felt suddenly dry.

"Big trouble," he said. "Because now I feel the need to prove you wrong. I am most definitely your type—well, if the way you cry my name out when you're about to—"

"Point made," Carly said. "No need to revisit the past."

"You sure about that?" he asked. "Because I really wouldn't mind having you—"

"No!" Carly yelped, cutting him off. "I get it and I'll concede that physically we are compatible."

"Really? Compatible? That's your word of choice? I would have said combustible." He drew out each syllable, making Carly sweat, especially since she had just felt scorched by his nearness.

As if he knew what his proximity did to her, a slow smile lifted the corners of his lips, one side slightly higher than the other. The man was too good-looking for his own good, or more accurately, for her own good. He gave her a wicked wink.

"I'd love to finish this conversation but Jillian asked me to get these for her since she's helping another customer," he said.

As he left the room, Carly stood staring after him, thinking he had a lot more bad boy in him than she had thought. Which indicated that there was no way he knew anything about her relationship with Preston; otherwise there was no way he could be interested in her.

Huh. Maybe, just maybe, she could see James again. *What?!* Did she really just think that? What was it about that man that was flipping her script and making her consider the possibility of a relationship when she had never considered one before?

Curiosity compelled her to leave the safety of the kitchen. The bakery was buzzing. She felt bad that she hadn't poked her head out to see if Jillian needed an assist before this. As she watched, James delivered the whoopie pies to Jillian, who thanked him with a warm smile. All of her friends liked James; that had to mean something, right?

She hurried behind the counter and made a

shooing motion at Jillian. "You should have called me for help. Go finish your meeting."

There was no sign of Mac or Emma, but the line at the counter was four deep. Carly set to work helping out the customers while Jillian and James resumed their seats in the booth where they'd been talking.

Carly tried not to pay any attention to them as she helped the people in front of her, boxing up orders and taking payments with a flirty smile. She felt James's gaze on her but she ignored him even while teasing Hank Koslowski, the delivery man who always bought a whoopie pie when he brought a package.

"Look at those muscles," Carly said. She leaned over the counter to squeeze Hank's bicep when he handed her a brown box the size of a loaf of bread. "You are just the manliest man I've ever seen, Hank."

Tall, skinny Hank with the thinning head of blonde hair blinked at her as if uncertain of what to say.

"The usual, handsome?" she asked.

"Yes, please." He swallowed audibly. "Miss Carly, uh, you know I'm married, right?" He handed her two dollars and took the cellophane-wrapped whoopie pie.

"Yes, I do," she said. "And a crying shame it is for women all over Bluff Point."

She gave him a sad smile and he backed away

from the counter toward the door as if he could not believe what he was hearing. He tripped over a table leg and nearly went sprawling but he righted himself at the last minute and bolted from the shop.

"Stop flirting with the customers," Jillian called from the booth. "You're scaring them."

Carly turned toward her friend to make a snappy retort but Jillian's head was down as she was writing on a legal pad on the table beside her. James, however, was looking at Carly, and the look was smoking hot, like he couldn't wait to get her alone and do wicked things to her. Now it was Carly's turn to swallow audibly as whatever she'd been about to say vanished into the air, never to be uttered.

"Carly, I'm going to need you to be the liaison for James's party," Jillian said. She didn't look up as she continued writing. "I already have to be at the Heinrich wedding and can't do delivery for both."

"What about the shop?" Carly asked.

"They are Saturday night events, so we'll be closed," she said. She glanced up at Carly with her delicate brows raised. "It's not a problem, is it?"

Carly narrowed her eyes into a suspicious glower. Jillian was just as bad as Emma and Mac. This was a fix-up if ever she smelled one. She refused to look at James, knowing that he was probably watching her. It was one thing for her to consider having another go-round with James, it was quite another for her friends to try and make it happen. Her contrary nature made her resistant.

"I might have a thing," she said.

"You don't do things," Jillian reminded her.

"I might start."

Jillian rolled her eyes. Carly took a deep breath to argue her case, when James interrupted.

"This could be the return favor," he said. "Packing up one hundred and fifty whoopie pies and driving them to Portland for the party would definitely make us even."

Jillian glanced between them, watching their interaction as if they were her favorite sitcom.

Carly met James's gray gaze and felt a twinge of disappointment. She'd really hoped he was going to pull out something a bit more exciting than delivering whoopie pies as his payback. In all truth, she thought there'd be a lot more whoopie and a lot less pie involved. Which was not to say she wanted more than that—maybe she did—either way she had been so sure that he did. Huh.

"Fine, I'll deliver your whoopie pies," she said. "And then we're square. Agreed?"

His smile was wicked when he said, "Agreed. Of course, given the lateness of the party, I'll have to insist that you stay over in Portland. I'm crashing at the Beaumont Inn, shall I book you a room, too?"

There he was. That was her bad boy with the hidden agenda. She tried to give him a quelling look but it was hard not to laugh at his shenanigans.

Before she could answer, the front door was pulled open and a young woman, who looked to be about the same age as Carly's sister Gina, strode into the bakery, looking out of breath and a bit frantic.

"James!" she cried. "Thank goodness I caught you."

"Lorelei!"

James slid out of the booth with a smile. He looked delighted to see the woman. Carly felt her WTF line deepen in her forehead and she stretched her eyebrows up to stop it. It was an effort.

Jillian looked at her with a questioning glance and Carly shrugged. She had no idea who the woman—now wrapping her arms around James in a big hug that lifted her off her feet—was, but she didn't like her. Of that, she was certain.

Her hair was dyed a deep purple and cut into a shag that bounced around her shoulders. She was taller and thinner than Carly by a few inches in all directions. Carly tried not to hold it against her, but it took some effort, especially since she didn't know who she was or what her relationship to James was. Old girlfriend? Friend? Client? Cousin? Neighbor?

The first option made Carly grind her teeth just the tiniest bit, which she told herself was ridiculous. Of course James had old girlfriends. It was one more thing in his life that was none of her business.

When the woman broke free from James, she stepped back and turned to Jillian and then Carly. Her face was round and bright and brimming with friendliness, and Carly noticed a nose ring in her right nostril and two diamond studs above her left eyebrow.

The girl reeked of free spirit, and Carly couldn't help but respond with a returning smile. When her gaze met the young woman's, Carly noted that her eyes were the exact same blue gray hazel as James's. Sister then? How was it they'd never discussed whether James had siblings or not?

How could she know exactly where to put her mouth on this man to make him grunt and swear and clutch her hair in his fist, but she didn't know if he had siblings? Suddenly, everything felt complicated and weird.

"What are you doing here?" James asked.

"There's been an emergency," Lorelei said. "The hotel in Portland where we planned to host the party caught on fire last night. Everyone got out okay but the place burnt to the ground."

"That's terrible!" he said. "Mom and Dad have been planning this party for months, are they crushed?"

"No, because I have an idea. Instead of having the party in Portland, we should have it at your place," she said. She clapped her hands and jumped up and down in her black Converse sneakers. "Isn't that brilliant?"

"What?" James blinked. "My place? But it's still under construction. I just got my appliances installed yesterday."

"So what? It's a lighthouse," Lorelei argued. She glanced at Carly and Jillian. "Tell him. You can't beat a lighthouse for an eightieth birthday party, you just can't."

"She has a point," Carly said. *Eightieth birthday party?* "It is pretty cool."

James frowned at her.

"Hi, I'm Jillian Braedon," Jillian said as she slid out of the booth. "Chief whoopie maker."

"Sorry." James looked chagrinned but gestured between the women and said, "Jillian, my sister Lorelei."

"Nice to meet you," Lorelei said. She shook Jillian's hand adding, "But everyone calls me Lola, except for Jamie, who insists on using my full name just to bug me."

She turned expectantly and James gestured to Carly. "And this is Carly DeCusati."

"Pleasure," Lola said as she shook her hand. She stepped back and glanced at the two women and gave them a mischievous look that was so like James, Carly almost laughed right up until Lola asked, "So, which one of you is Jamie's girlfriend?"

"Not me," Carly said at the same time Jillian said, "She is."

A faint tinge of pink crept into James's cheeks and Carly knew she looked exactly the same. Ugh, his sister was going to know they'd fooled around. So, this was mortifying.

But Lola just laughed and waved her hand dismissively. "I'm just teasing. James hasn't hooked up in forev—"

"Stop talking, please," he growled at his sister.

Lola gave him a considering glance. "Okay, but only if you agree to have the party at your house."

"Lorelei, no, it's totally impractical. It's still under construction. It'd be dangerous, irresponsible even, to have one hundred and fifty people tromping all over the grounds."

"But Pops is going to be eighty," she argued. "Wouldn't it be great to celebrate it at a lighthouse? You could even light the top in honor of him."

"The top is my bedroom," James argued. "I can't light it up."

She waved her hand at him. "We'll think of something."

"No, we won't," he argued. "You've seen the place, Carly, tell her. It's a wreck."

Lola's gaze turned to Carly. There was speculation in her eyes and Carly knew she was wondering how her brother and a woman working at a whoopie pie shop had ended up at his house.

"He was helping me with an audio recording for my bird," she explained as if that made any sense whatsoever. "His place is a bit of a shambles right now."

"See?" James said.

"But if you moved most of the construction equipment aside, it would make a lovely venue for a party," Carly added just to be difficult.

James gave her an incredulous look as if he couldn't believe she'd rolled over on him. Carly shrugged. Having the party here would make her return favor a heck of a lot easier.

"It still won't work. Bluff Point isn't equipped to deal with this many Sinclairs hitting town all at once," he said.

"Sure it is," Jillian said. "All of the summer tourists are gone and the autumn leaf peepers don't fill up the motels. There will be plenty of room and at a much cheaper rate than the hotels in Portland."

"See?" Lola said. "It's all coming together. So, what flavors are we tasting for the whoopie pies? Pops is a native Mainer so whoopie pies, Moxie soda, and red-skinned hot dogs are all of his favorite things, not to forget the lobster."

She said lobster with an "uh" on the end like a real Maine girl. Carly decided that she liked this firecracker, mostly because she was really spinning her brother's head around. Given that he'd been making Carly crazy for days, she was enjoying his discomfiture, probably more than she should but . . . oh, well.

Jillian led Lola over to the table where the samples were still laid out. While the two of them talked, Carly glanced up to find James studying her with a look of single-minded determination on his face.

"You okay, big guy?" she asked.

His gaze moved over her with a heat that felt almost as hot as the lick of flames. Carly shivered, not in a bad way. She shook it off and met his stare.

"I release you from owing me a favor." He looked mildly panicked. "You don't have to bring the pies to the party. I'll pick up the whoopie pies and set them up myself. What do you say?" James asked. "We'll just call it even?"

"You mean you're not even going to cash in your 'favor to be determined' at a later date?" she asked. This was very suspicious.

"That's what I mean," he said. "I release you from your debt. We're all good."

Carly shook her head. "No, I don't think so. I

always pay my debts in full. I'll be helping with your party, James Sinclair."

His face tightened but before he could argue, his sister leapt up from the booth and crossed the room to join them.

"That's perfect!" she cried. "We need a party planner since none of us know anyone around here to provide the food, booze, music, etc. Oh, Carly, you're a lifesaver!"

"Wait," Carly said. "I just meant dropping off whoopie pies, I didn't mean—"

"Oh, don't say no, there's so much to do and the family will start arriving from all over the country in the next few days," Lola said. She made puppy eyes at Carly. "Please say you'll help. Please."

"I'm a buyer," Carly said. "I don't know how—"

"Same difference," Jillian piped up from the booth. "You can totally do this."

"We'll pay you handsomely for your time, of course," Lola said. "Won't we James?"

He had his head tipped to the side and the panic that had been in his blue gray gaze was gone, replaced by speculation, as if the idea of Carly helping wasn't so terrible. She got the feeling he was revising whatever nefarious plan he'd had. That could not be a good thing.

"Of course we'll pay you," he said. He looked at Lola and asked, "When is the A Factor arriving?"

"A Factor?" Carly asked.

"Yeah, you know, like an X factor, a variable in a given situation which has the most impact on an outcome," Lola explained. "That's our cousin Preston, he's an ass and his impact is usually of the ass clown variety, thus we call him the A Factor, which is short for ass factor."

Cousin Preston had to be Preston Bradley. Carly felt her heart thump hard in her chest. For the first time in years, she was going to be in the same breathing space as him. She swallowed hard, feeling mildly sick.

Lola turned back to James. "He's arriving the day of the party because of course he is entirely too busy and important to help beforehand. Why?"

James nodded and looked at Carly. His look was steady, a challenge even. "If you can handle this party, I'll make you a deal you can't refuse."

"Sorry, I'm not that hard-up for money," she said. Just hearing Preston's name made her rethink her offer. She'd have to do a covert op to drop off the pies without running into him. There was no way in hell she was helping plan this party now. In fact, she might flee the state before Preston arrived just to be sure she didn't run into him.

"I'm not talking about additional money," he said.

"Okay, hit me." She folded her arms over her chest and stared at him. This she had to hear. She expected him to offer her a hot date with endless orgasms. She was wrong. Damn it.

"Coordinate the party and attend it as my date, and if you don't find new homes for Ike and Saul by then, I'll take them," he said.

Chapter 21

James waited. Carly said nothing. He noticed Jillian frowning at her friend and he suspected that Carly was seldom rendered speechless. She blinked at him as if trying to decipher the language he'd just spoken.

"Well?" he asked. He could feel Lorelei and Jillian watching them but the only reaction he was aware of was Carly's.

"You'd give them a forever home?" she asked.

"Yes, I promise," he said. He was dangling the freedom-from-attachment carrot that he knew she desperately craved. Would she take it? He had no idea.

It hit him then that he'd never before known a woman so intimately physically and yet not at all emotionally. Usually, it was completely the opposite, with emotions first and the physical a far, far second. Leave it to Carly to turn everything he'd ever known about women upside down, inside out, and all spun around backwards.

On the one hand, he knew exactly what she was feeling when he pressed her sweet spot with his thumb, and just the thought of her with her lips parted and her eyes half-closed, her back arching to get closer to him, made his crotch tight and he had to shift his stance to make it less obvious.

Lord, she scrambled his brain like no woman ever had. On the other hand, he had no idea what she was thinking or how she felt about his offer and when she was quiet and not sharing, it drove him bonkers.

"All right," she said softly. She held out her hand and he gave her a look. She smiled at him and when he opened his arms wide she stepped in for a hug.

James pressed his cheek to the top of her head, savoring the feel of her body pressed against his and the sultry scent of her hair as it wrapped around him. He had less than a week, four days to be exact, to make her reconsider him, Ike, and Saul. He had never felt so much pressure in his life and he was using every ploy in his arsenal to get her to stay, including calling in every favor he could think of to make it too enticing for her not to stay.

He had to get her to fall in love with him, with her life here, and with the opportunities that were coming her way, because otherwise he suspected she'd leave him and the pets and never look back. He squeezed her tight as if he could literally hold on to her while her past crept inexorably toward them, making her want to flee.

The fact that he had not been completely honest with her when she had picked him up at Marty's Pub—that they had met before, that he was completely knocked sideways by her, and that he knew she'd been involved with his cousin—made him feel a sharp twist of guilt in his gut. But it had been such a surprise to see her and, frankly, she had taken his breath away exactly like she had the first time he saw her. He did not want to lose her again.

Not for nothing, he wondered if he should scrap the plan to romance her into his life and tell her everything. That he had fallen for her the very first time he saw her and that he didn't care what had happened between her and Preston, no matter how awful it was, he still wanted her. No, he couldn't risk it. He suspected that she'd think it was a line, that he was just like his cousin, a user, and he couldn't stand that.

He knew from his work as a physical therapist that pushing through the hurt, the fear, or whatever it was that was holding his client back was usually the only way to get whole again. But Carly, with her refusal to have any relationships beyond friendship, was more broken than most and he had no idea how to help her.

He wasn't stupid. He knew his cousin Preston had done something to hurt her. He saw it in the flash of pain that lit her brown eyes every time his name was mentioned. He'd noticed when he mentioned that he'd thought she and Preston were a couple that she had neither confirmed nor denied their status. He suspected it was because something had happened between them, and knowing Preston, it had been unpleasant.

He would give anything to protect her from her past and spare her the pain, but running into her again after all these years felt like fate. No matter how closed off to relationships she was, he couldn't ignore the hopeful possibility that if he could help her put the past behind her and look to the future, then she might choose to move forward with him.

When he stepped back from her, a long lock of her dark hair brushed across her cheek. He reached up, hooked it with a finger, and tucked it behind her ear. Her hair was so soft, he wanted to bury his fingers in it and pull her close. He didn't.

She glanced up at him and the startled look of want in her gaze made him suck in a breath. The stark need in her deep brown eyes made his heart hammer triple time as if gearing up for a marathon of making her moan his name in that special way she had. James blinked, trying to push aside the memory of her coming undone for him, just him. It about killed him to drop his hands and back away, but he did it.

He forced himself to embrace the bigger picture. If they could get through the next few days and she still looked at him like that then this whole torturous party would be worth it. God, he hoped so at any rate, because now that he'd found her he never wanted to let her go.

He glanced away, afraid that if he didn't, he

might lose control of his good intentions. Instead, he focused on his sister, who was watching them with a dawning look of awareness in her eyes. Uh-oh.

"Correct me if I'm wrong, but you two didn't just meet here at this bakery, did you?" Lola appeared at his elbow with her arms crossed over her chest and her diamond-studded eyebrow raised inquisitively.

Carly glanced at him with a newly resolved expression, sort of like a soldier heading into battle, that morphed into a mischievous grin as she said, "Oh, dear. She's onto us. Shall we tell her how we met?"

James narrowed his gaze. He knew that look of hers. It was wicked and made him want to do deliciously naughty things to her. If Carly wanted to play, fine. He was game if she was.

"By all means," he said.

"We met in the produce section of the grocery store," she said. She waggled her eyebrows at Lola. "We grappled over melons."

James barked out a laugh. It was on the tip of his tongue to ask, "Whose melons?" but sanity prevailed and he said nothing. The image of Carly and her melons splayed out before him on her bed could not be sponged from his brain, however. Man, she was turning him into a pervert.

He felt a bead of sweat run down the back of his neck. A sly glance her way and he saw her bite her lip as if to keep from laughing. Oh, she was wicked. He wondered what it said about him that he liked it, he really liked it. Fortunately, or maybe unfortunately, she was nowhere near done tormenting him.

He glanced at his sister, who was looking at them wide-eyed while Jillian was quietly chuckling because she knew the truth, or thought she did.

"That's not exactly it," he said to Lola.

"That's right!" Carly snapped her fingers. "We actually met on the set of a porno film. Did you know your brother's porn star name is James Wood? I was cast as Handy Hannah, his official fluffer, and, you know, one thing just led to another."

Lola's eyes got huge and then, catching on that Carly was yanking her chain, she tipped her head back and laughed.

"That's hilarious," she cried, letting out a big guffaw.

"It's not that funny," he said. He pretended to look offended. "I could star in a porno if I wanted."

This set all three of the women to laughing, and James turned to Carly and said, "You could back me up a little here."

"Why?" she asked. "Because I have hands-on experience?"

James would have laughed but then he glanced at her and caught her looking at him through her thick dark eyelashes with those big brown eyes that were full of naughty intentions. He let out a hiss of breath as his body reacted over-whelmingly with need. He pulled at the neck of his shirt, trying to get some cool air on his hot skin. It didn't help.

He leaned close and whispered in her ear, "Sweet Jesus, sunshine, you would be the only fluffer in the history of the porn industry who never had to touch a guy to get him in shape—just look at him like that and he'd be rarin' to go."

James forced himself to step back and caught sight of her self-satisfied smirk. That was it. Turnabout was fair play.

"Actually," he said to his sister, who was still laughing. "I came across Carly eating an ice cream cone and when she caught sight of me, she sucked in a chunk of ice cream and started to choke, so I had to give her mouth-to-mouth. It was just like in a movie, with her about to expire and me cupping the back of her head and holding her still while I fit my mouth over hers so that our lips formed a seal so I could breathe the life back into her."

He gave Carly side eye to see how she was reacting. Her cheeks were flushed. Good. A small puff of air burst out of her slightly parted lips and she looked a bit dazed. James smiled, feeling quite pleased with himself.

Carly DeCusati could pretend that whatever was between them was a one-night deal in the past, but he knew it wasn't. If she ever waved him in, and he was going to do everything he could to convince her to do just that, he was going to ruin her, completely ruin her, for any other man. Ever.

Carly cleared her throat and her voice was a bit hoarse when she spoke. "Can a person actually choke on ice cream?"

James grinned at her. He really liked flustered Carly.

Lola glanced between them. Her gaze was shrewd. "You're not going to tell me the real story, are you?"

In perfect sync, they looked at her and shook their heads. "No."

"Fine, keep your secret—for now," Lola said. She sauntered back over to the booth where Jillian sat and the two women began discussing flavors of whoopie pie.

James turned back to Carly and when she met his gaze, he saw the telltale flash of pink bloom across her cheeks. Excellent. She was nowhere near as immune to him as she wanted him to believe. It was a solid start.

"I suppose the most likely story of how we met would be that I came to you as a client and you nursed me back to health," Carly said, keeping her voice low so that only James could hear her. "We could say it was love at first stretch band."

James felt his heart do an abrupt stutter-stop. He could feel the blood drain from his head and for a second he really thought he might pass out. She so blithely tossed out the "L" word in regard to them. She had no idea. None. That he had fallen in love with her at first sight years ago. But how could she when she had no recollection of him?

The reality of the situation, the sudden awareness of the perilousness of his position, hit him hard and it wrecked him. He knew he was making the biggest play of his life here and he desperately hoped it did not blow up in his face.

"James? Are you all right?" she asked.

Her voice was soft. He could hear the concern in her tone and he knew he had to get a grip on the riot of emotion that was rocketing through him. Suddenly, this whole party seemed fraught with disaster. A moment ago, he'd been sure he knew what he was doing but now he wondered if at the end of it, he was going to be the one damaged beyond repair.

"I was just teasing," she said. She looked uncertain. "I mean obviously there is no love here. We barely know each other."

"Right," he said. He forced his lips to curve up in what he hoped looked like a smile but he feared was more a feral show of teeth. "Maybe we should just go with me hiring you for the whoopie pies for the party. You know, keep it simple."

She tipped her head to the side and studied him.

She looked like she suspected something wasn't quite right but wasn't sure if she should ask or not. Her usual sense of boundaries must have kicked in because she just shrugged.

"It's your show," she said. "If you don't want to cop to a smokin' hot one-night stand with me, that's fine."

James took a steadying breath. He had to play this very carefully.

"I like that you admit it was smokin' hot," he said. He glanced at Lorelei, relieved to see that she wasn't paying any attention to them, before shifting his gaze back to Carly. "But I think we should keep our first meeting on the down-low."

There was a flash of hurt on her face, gone before it fully materialized, and James wanted to kick himself. She probably thought he was judging her for how they hooked up. He would never. Not ever.

He just needed more time. He needed her to be more invested in them before he went for full disclosure. She didn't remember meeting him and he was okay with that, but how would she feel if he told her he had fallen in love with her all the way back then, eleven years ago? She'd think he was crazy. She'd be right. He was crazy—about her.

"That's cool," she said.

Carly turned away from him to head back into the kitchen and James knew that he had just lost something, a momentary connection with her beyond the physical. It made him want to curse and turn back the clock one minute so he could not be so ham-fisted and stupid in regard to them, but her past with Preston made that impossible.

She was clearly suspicious of men and relationships and since he didn't know what exactly had happened between her and Preston, wasn't sure he wanted to know for that matter, he had to proceed with caution. Like a tightrope walker in high wind, he would progress this relationship step by step and hope he didn't go splat.

Chapter 22

Carly hadn't really contemplated what all was involved in planning a party at a location that was under construction. The next few days were spent using all of her former buyer skills as she shopped for the party essentials like food and booze. It got more complicated as she looked for a band and photographer, but Emma, having just gotten married, was happy to share the list of vendors she'd interviewed for her wedding.

Of course, helping this much with the party meant that Carly was spending all of her free time at the lighthouse. She arrived when her shift at Making Whoopie was done and didn't leave until well into the night. James seemed more than happy with this arrangement and frequently met her at the door with dinner prepared. The two of them quickly fell into a routine of sharing the news of their days and then working on the party prep.

When the store Penmans in Portland scheduled Carly for an interview, James sat through her practice presentation on sales trends and how her connections from her former position in New York put her in a unique position to buy in-demand items at low cost to the company.

They even did a quick recon trip to Penmans' flagship store in Portland to analyze what was currently on the racks and how Carly could improve it.

James had seemed highly invested in her getting the job, something she tried not to overthink. On the day of the interview, she had left Making Whoopie in her business suit and heels to go to Penmans' corporate offices for her interview, and James had popped into the bakery to wish her luck. When Jillian had observed that it was a total boyfriend maneuver, Carly had ignored her.

Of course, the first person she texted after the interview was James. She tried to tell herself it was because he had put in so much effort on her behalf, but the truth was, she'd been so excited by the company's forward thinking corporate atmosphere, and the possibility of buying for the entire women's department and not just the lingerie department, that she had to tell someone or she feared she'd explode, and that someone was James.

She felt as if he was the only one who truly understood how important it was to her to get this job, to get her sense of herself back. She was a fashion buyer—it was what she loved and what she wanted to do—and she hated that she felt like such a failure at the career she had worked at for so long.

If she was honest, she had begun to look forward to her time with James. She frequently brought Ike and Saul with her, and they quickly formed a pack with Hot Wheels, who was always eager to see his two friends. The third night in a row, the evening after her interview, when she brought her animals with her, James called her out on it.

"You're trying to get them acclimated to their new home, aren't you?" he asked.

"Me?" She put her hand over her chest in a protestation of innocence.

They were sitting at the kitchen counter, sharing lasagna and salad, both of which James had fixed, while the animals cavorted around the newly cleaned and polished great room.

James shook his head at her. Clearly, he wasn't fooled for a hot minute.

"They seem to like it here," she said.

She turned on her stool to watch Ike riding on Hot Wheels's harness while they raced Saul up and down the hallway to the rehabilitation center. James followed her gaze and then turned back to her. His look was considering.

"What about you?" he asked. "Do you like it here?"

She sensed his question had a deeper meaning that she chose to ignore. Instead, she took it at face value and glanced around the room.

James had halted the construction on his home

temporarily so it was free of tools, dust, and thick plastic sheeting. The full potential was just beneath the surface and she could see the gem that it was going to be when it was done. Like it? She loved it. But for some reason, she thought she shouldn't share her enthusiasm with him. She didn't know why, but her sense of self-preservation kicked in and she trusted it.

"It's cute." She shrugged.

"Cute?" He was outraged. "Thanks, that's exactly what I was going for, you know, along with quaint and adorable."

Carly smiled into her glass of wine. It was a luscious pinot noir and she felt it relaxing her, dropping down her first line of defense and making her think it was okay to flirt with James. It wasn't, but she couldn't seem to stop herself.

"Is your bedroom really at the top of the lighthouse?" she asked.

His eyebrows lifted. "Yes, why? Do you want the tour?"

"Well, I was thinking we could light up the top of the lighthouse for your grandfather," she said. "I want to use strings of LEDs to spell out Happy Birthday."

It was a half-truth. She also really wanted to see his bedroom. She wanted to see what it said about James the man. As in: was he messy, neat, somewhere in between? It was none of her business, but she still wanted to appease her curiosity.

"Why do I get the feeling you're scouting the place for your pets?" he asked.

She shrugged. That wasn't it but he didn't need to know that.

"So, you've had no takers so far?" he asked, gesturing at the animals.

"Knees to chest! Knees to chest! Move it!" Ike squawked from his perch on Hot Wheels's halter. She felt her lips curve up at Ike's antics. He was such a funny bird.

"No," she said.

"Shocker."

Carly laughed. It hit her in that moment that she liked James, really liked him. He was funny and patient and kind, and the fact that he was freaking gorgeous did not hurt either.

"Come on," he said. "I'll give you the tour."

He rose from his seat and paused beside Hot Wheels. Ike stepped readily onto James's hand and allowed him to put him in his travel cage. Carly was impressed, as up until now Ike had only let Carly and Gavin pick him up.

She took one more sip of her wine and left her napkin beside her plate. James waited for her by a door on the far side of the kitchen. Once she joined him, he opened the door, which led into a narrow dark hallway.

He flipped a switch and Carly noted that he

had to duck his head to traverse the closed-in tunnel. At the far end was another solid door and James pushed it open. He flicked on another light switch and the spiral staircase in front of them lit up like a runway in a trail of cool blue LED lights that wound their way all the way to the top. Behind the stairs, Carly saw all of the construction equipment that had been moved from the house.

"Convenient," she said.

"Hmm," he hummed as if resigned.

He took her hand and together they climbed the metal staircase to the top. Carly was winded halfway up but pretended that she wasn't by turning her head away and mouth breathing. She noticed that James slowed his pace and suspected she had not fooled him in the slightest.

The stairs wound through the floor to the room above. James flipped another switch and the room was bathed in soft white light from above.

Carly stepped inside and caught her breath. A huge king-sized bed, draped in a navy comforter and pillows, sat in the middle of the room where the old light would have stood, but other than that there was nothing in the room. Nothing.

Carly spun around, taking in the floor-to-ceiling windows and the starkness of the interior. "I'm assuming you do nothing here but sleep."

"There are so many ways to respond to that," he said. "I think I'm going to have to pass."

"I . . . ugh . . . just meant that there aren't any books, or a television, or anything," she said. When had this become so awkward? "Just the bed."

"Which has been known to be used for things other than sleep." He smiled at her and she got the feeling he was enjoying her show of nerves.

Carly felt her face get hot—again. What was it about this guy that made her blush like a middle schooler? She refused to let him get her flustered. She could control this situation. She was a master flirt, all flash and no substance. She just needed to get her head in the game.

"Really?" she asked. She forced herself to sound doubtful. "Your sister said you haven't hooked up in forever. It doesn't sound like you do much up here besides sleep."

Even in the dim lighting she saw his gray eyes deepen into that magnetic shade of blue she liked so well. He took a step toward her.

"Lola doesn't know everything," he said. He gestured between them. "Obviously."

Carly spun away from him to stand in front of the window that overlooked the dark sea. As the wine wore off, her sense of caution kicked in. What had she been thinking, coming up here alone with him? She was way too attracted to him to pretend, at least to herself, that he was just a friend. The reality was the night with him had been one of the best of her life.

If James could make her feel that way when they hardly knew each other, then what would it be like between them now that they had become so much closer? She needed to maintain healthy boundaries around him at all times because her feelings for him might be a slippery slope into lo— She stopped her train of thought right there. She had to maintain control.

Otherwise, she might find herself allowing him to step up behind her and slide his arms around her waist and pull her back against his front. She could then tip her head to the side and let him brush aside her hair so he could place the softest kiss just below her ear. And she might become entranced by their reflection in the window glass and a soft moan might escape her lips as his hands moved forward to caress her curves.

When he turned her to face him, she might not resist him but rather would twine her arms around his neck and pull his mouth down to meet hers while she pressed her body the full length of his. It was the feel of his thick dark hair entwined in her fingers that made Carly realize that this was actually happening. She knew she should pull away and bolt down the stairs, putting space and big bulky furniture between them, but she didn't.

"Carly, are you sure?" he asked, his mouth a whisper away.

"Yes." There it was. No hesitation. No second guessing. She knew she wanted this. Him.

The attraction between them was just too strong to deny so why was she? Because she wanted to be free of attachments and go back to her old life? She did, but when she did, wouldn't it be lovely to have more moments with James to remember him by?

It flitted through her mind that this was just what she needed. They would sleep together. It wouldn't be as good as last time—how could it be?—and then she'd be able to put him back in the friend zone and move on.

He slid his hands to the ass of her jeans and lifted her up, encouraging her to wrap her legs around his waist while he pressed her back against the glass window. Hot, wet, shaking with want from the core of her being, Carly nudged him with her hips, feeling as if she could never get close enough to him.

He responded with a deep groan. He hoisted her up higher until her breasts were level with his mouth, then he pushed aside the fabric of her flannel shirt and hooked her bra aside with one hand while supporting her with the other. As soon as a nipple was exposed he claimed it with his teeth and tongue. Carly arched her back, pushing herself up against him and feeling like the heat inside of her was going to consume her.

"James, oh, James!" she cried.

"Hey, that's what the parrot downstairs said," a voice spoke from below. "What do you suppose James is up to?"

"No idea, Pops," Lola said. "Oh, wait, now I do."

James wrenched his mouth away from Carly. They looked at the railing around the hole in the floor in horror. Lola's purple-haired head was just visible.

"Oh, my god," Carly groaned and pressed her face into James's shoulder.

James reached between them and tugged her clothes into place, then he gently lowered Carly to her feet. He shoveled his hands through his hair and made a quick adjustment to the front of his jeans.

Carly pressed her fingers to her lips—they were as swollen as she feared—and tossed her hair over her shoulder, trying for a poise she did not feel.

Lola climbed into the room with the person she'd called Pops right behind her. Lola was laughing while Pops was clearly trying to act as if nothing was amiss.

James looped his arm around Carly's shoulder and pulled her close as he stepped forward. "Lola, Pops, wow, I had no idea you were stopping by tonight."

"Obviously," Lola said.

"Sorry for interrupting your . . . uh . . . date,"

Pops said. "But I couldn't wait to see the place. We can sneak back out; I don't want to cramp your style."

James groaned and Carly had to bite back a laugh. The devilish grin Pops sent their way could charm the butterflies from the flowers.

"No worries, Pops," James said. "You're fine."

He released Carly and hugged the old man. She watched as James closed his eyes for a second as if committing the moment to memory. She could tell just from the expression on his face that he loved his grandfather very much. It made her like James all the more, which caused her already wobbly sense of boundaries to become even more compromised.

"Let me look at you," Pops said as he stepped back. He patted James's cheek and shook his head. "Still an ugly bugger."

"Ha!" James laughed. "And they say I'm the spitting image of my grandfather."

Pops threw back his head and laughed. It was a wonderfully deep, rich bark of sound that made James grin. Carly smiled as she watched them and as if sensing her gaze, James turned toward her. The wicked twinkle in his eyes made her heart do a barrel roll in her chest and she felt her pulse pound in her throat. How did he affect her so much with just a look?

Lola rolled her eyes. "Ignore them. This ridiculousness will go on all night if we let it."

"No it won't," Pops said. "Not when there is a lovely young lady for me to be introduced to."

"Pops, this is Carly DeCusati," James said. He reached out and brought Carly forward. "Carly, our birthday boy, Pops, also known as the original James Sinclair."

"Nice to meet you," Carly said. She held out her hand but Pops waved her off just like James.

"No, that won't do. If you're dating Jamie, we're past the shaking hands stage," Pops said. He opened his arms wide and Carly stepped close and gave him a gentle hug.

"Welcome to the family," Pops said.

"Oh, I'm—" Carly stepped back and caught James's gaze. He gave her a wide-eyed look and shook his head. She got the feeling he didn't want her to correct the true nature of their relationship. Assuming they would discuss it as soon as they were alone, she said, "I'm honored, thanks."

She felt James relax a bit beside her. Meanwhile her own tension ratcheted up to the breaking point. This was a disaster. His family now thought they were a thing, which was confirmed when Lola spoke.

"I knew it! I knew there was something going on between you two when we met at the bakery," she said. "The spark between you two was incendiary as is evidenced by what we inter—"

"Lorelei," James growled his sister's name, making it clear it was a warning.

She blithely disregarded him. She hooked her arm through Carly's and dragged her toward the stairs. As they started down, Lola called behind them, "Jamie, Mom and Dad are downstairs. I'm stealing your girlfriend so she can meet them."

Carly tripped on the steps, almost taking Lola down with her. Thankfully, Lola was stronger than she looked and grabbed Carly before she bounced down the circular steps like a breakaway beach ball.

His parents were here!

She glanced over her shoulder at James and he gave her a mildly panicked look. They were keeping up the façade then. Okay. She gave him a slight nod to let him know she wouldn't blow their cover, for now.

"You all right?" Lola asked.

"Yeah, sorry, just a long week, I guess," she said.

As they wound their way down the stairs, Carly gave herself a pep talk. She had been in weirder situations, like the time her one and only boyfriend, or more accurately the boy she had thought was her boyfriend, had informed her that he already had a girlfriend and that they were not in fact dating. Good times! Surely, she could finesse the meet and greet with the parents for James's sake.

Meeting new people didn't bother her. She'd been a lingerie buyer for years, so building an instant rapport with all sorts of people had been a part of her everyday life. She knew she could be plunked down into any situation and find common ground with a total stranger. No worries.

As they arrived back in the kitchen through the covered walkway, Lola called out, "Mom! Dad! Look who I brought to meet you, Jamie's girlfriend."

Oh, boy. Carly would have preferred to meet the parentals without the big announcement. It was weird to have the "G" word used in reference to herself, since she really wasn't girlfriend material.

Carly glanced down at her outfit. She was suddenly very self-conscious of her jeans and plaid shirt. She had been dressing down on purpose when she spent time with James, from her big cotton underwear to her scruffy flannel top, trying to shut down any attraction he might feel for her and any temptation she might feel as well. And hadn't that worked spectacularly? She would have upped her fashion game had she known she was going to be meeting his family today.

Suddenly a huge, scratchy ball of anxiety filled up her middle and she found herself looking toward the front door, wondering if she pulled a runner if she'd make it out before his parents caught sight of her.

As if he sensed her distress, Saul came loping

across the floor with Hot Wheels right behind him. He pressed his nose into her hand and Carly let her fingers burrow into his soft fur. It had a curiously calming effect upon her.

"Good boy, Saul," she said. He gave her a soft woof and wagged his fluffy tail.

Not to be denied, Hot Wheels maneuvered himself and his wheels right in front of her. His droopy eyes looked up at her and Carly laughed as she bent over to scratch his back just beneath the harness where she knew he liked it.

"You're a good boy, too, Hot Wheels," she said. When she rose to standing she felt steadier and more centered.

Across the great room, she saw a couple standing close together beside Ike's cage. She could only imagine what Ike had been saying while she was out of the room. She braced herself as Lola gestured her forward, but just before they stepped into the room, James slid in between them.

He put a reassuring hand on Carly's lower back and she turned to smile at him. It was a sweetly protective gesture and she appreciated it. Between him and the pets, she felt as if she had her own support system, which was new for her and she kind of dug it.

"Mom, Dad, there's someone I'd like you to meet," he said.

The couple turned toward them and Carly felt

a hiccup of surprise catch her. James's parents were . . . unexpected. Mr. Sinclair was dressed casually in jeans and a dress shirt and reminded Carly very much of James in that he seemed to have a perpetually rumpled thing going on. When he rubbed his hand in his hair as if to smooth it, he only managed to make it stand on end and she almost laughed out loud because it so reminded her of James. His handshake was firm and warm and his smile genuine.

Mrs. Sinclair, who insisted that Carly call her Emily and her husband Jimmy, was a sight to behold. Blonde bombshell was the description that came to mind, with curves that were showcased in a slinky animal print dress, high heels, makeup that included a sweet smoky eye, and lips done in a deep kissable red. Va-va-va-voom!

Much like Pops, Emily skipped the handshake and wrapped Carly in a hug, although hers was lightly perfumed and she squeezed Carly much tighter. Then she held out Carly's arms and looked her over.

"Oh, Jamie, she's got a fabulous rack and look at those hips, made for making babies," she said.

"Mom!" James smacked his forehead with his palm.

"What? It's a compliment," Emily said with a pout. She squeezed Carly's hands in hers. "You know it's a compliment, don't you, dear?"

Carly pressed her lips together to keep from laughing out loud. Instead of answering, she nodded and smiled, thinking she probably looked deranged, but it was the only way to keep in the belly laughs that were threatening to roar out of her.

"See? She knows it's a compliment," Emily said. She batted her eyelashes at James and he shook his head in resignation. Carly got the feeling that Emily Sinclair had her menfolk wrapped around her little finger.

"I love you, Mom," he said. His voice was full of amused resignation. Then he stepped forward and kissed her cheek.

"I love you, too, baby," Emily said. She beamed at him.

The affection was clearly mutual. Carly liked how James was with his family; there was a closeness there that she thought spoke well of him.

"So, Carly, I hear you're our party planner?" Jimmy turned his attention to her.

"I am, unless someone wants to take over, which would be fine with me," Carly said.

"Oh, no you don't," Lola said. "You've already done so much and now that I know you and Jamie are a couple, I would never replace you. It would break his heart; besides, this is perfect because now you can meet the whole family at the party as his new girlfriend."

"Wonderful," Emily said. She clapped her hands. "Jamie is going to have a date."

"You make it sound like I never do," James said. He looked decidedly exasperated.

"Well, it's not like you've had that many girlfr—" Lola began but her mother hushed her.

James slid his arm around Carly's waist and parked his hand on her hip. Carly noted that his eyes had a mischievous sparkle and she knew he had seen her stiffen when Lola had used the "G" word. Carly refused to let her discomfort show, however. She raised one eyebrow at him to let him know they'd be chatting soon.

"You'll have to give me the four-one-one on James's love life," she said to Lola. She almost laughed when she felt James tighten up beside her.

His parents exchanged a funny look and Carly tipped her head in question. Had she said something wrong?

Emily caught on immediately. "Sorry, dear, it's just that no one in the family calls him James."

"He's been Jamie ever since he was knee-high," Jimmy agreed.

"Jamie," Carly said. She turned to look at her shiny new boyfriend. With his black hair, quick-changing eyes, and lopsided smile, he looked like a Jamie. "It suits you."

"You can call me whatever you like," he said. "Just don't call me late for—"

Carly had no idea what he was about to say but she didn't think it was going to be "supper." In a blind panic to keep him from saying something embarrassing, she rose up on her tiptoes and planted her mouth on his.

Chapter 23

It was supposed to be a quick kiss, not a lingering smooch, but when she would have stepped back, James cupped the back of her head to keep her still while he kissed her with a thoroughness that left her breathless and stammering.

"James, oh, James!" Ike flapped his wings as he squawked at full volume. A room full of chuckles and a snort sounded, bringing Carly back to the ground with a thump.

She broke away from James feeling a hot flush of mortification scald her face. That bird was going to be the death of her. When she finally turned to face his parents, it was to find them grinning at her and James, along with Lola, and Pops, who had joined them.

"Um, well, I . . ." Carly stuttered and Emily laughed.

"I know exactly how you feel, dear," she said. "Thirty-five years married and Jimmy can still make me forget why I walked into a room."

Carly gave an awkward laugh while James hugged her close. She would have buried her face against him but she was afraid if she did, she'd never peel herself off. Instead, she busied herself by moving away from him and tying the cover closed on Ike's cage. She was sure she would expire on the spot if he popped out any profanity on top of his already questionable word choice.

When she glanced at James, she got the feeling he was quite pleased with the situation. She couldn't even yell at him because she was the one who had instigated the kiss. Ugh, what had she been thinking? He probably wouldn't have said anything embarrassing, would he?

"If you all will excuse us," James said. "Carly was just heading out for the evening—"

"Didn't look like out was where she was headed to me," Lola muttered.

"—and I'm going to walk her and her animals out," he continued, ignoring his sister's interruption.

"Of course," his father said. "Take your time."

"We'll just entertain ourselves with the view," Emily agreed.

"Unless, we wander off and get . . . distracted," Jimmy said.

Carly felt her eyes go wide. He didn't mean that they might . . . Emily giggled and looped her arm through her husband's.

"Distracted," Emily said. She winked at her husband. "That sounds like a fine idea."

Jimmy grinned and grabbed his wife by the hand, pulling her toward the wing of the house that included the rehabilitation area as well as a couple of spare rooms. "See you, kids."

They disappeared down the hall, and Carly

turned to James. She opened her mouth to ask a question but he held up his hand to stop her.

"Yes, they're going to do exactly what you think, and, yes, they've always been like that. They are the two most disgustingly in love people I have ever met, truly, it's sickening," he said. He was smiling when he said it so she knew he didn't mean it in a bad way.

"Your Gram and I used to give them a run for their money," Pops said. He looked wistful and Lola wrapped her arm around his thin shoulders.

"You and Gram were the most in love of anyone ever," she said. "Someday, I'm going to find that."

"I hope you do, my girl, I really hope you do," Pops said. He gave James and Carly a steady look. "When you find it you'll know, and if you're smart you'll hold on to it real tight."

James's arm tightened around Carly's waist and she wondered if he was feeling as guilty as she was for deceiving everyone.

"I will," James said. "I promise."

"Excellent." Pops nodded. Then he gave Lola a smacking kiss on the cheek. "And now, I have a Jack and Coke with my name on it."

"To the bar," Lola cried. She took Pops's arm and they crossed the great room to where a bar for the party had been tucked into the corner.

James glanced down at Carly and whispered, "Sorry I got carried away there. I didn't mean to, but I don't think so clearly around you." He sounded sheepish. "And my family can be a bit overwhelming—okay, way more than a bit."

"It's okay. I started it—the kiss, I mean. As for your family, please, I love my sisters, but there's a reason I moved to New York for college and stayed," she said.

"Sisters plural?" he asked. "I didn't realize you had more than one."

"Oh, yes," Carly said. "I am the fourth of five sisters. Teresa, Danielle, Ariana, me, and Gina."

"Whoa. That's a lot of estrogen under one roof. Do they all live in Bluff Point?" he asked.

"Only Terry and Gina," she said. "Danielle is in Seattle working as a weather girl but don't call her that or she'll rip your head off, and Ariana is in Venice Beach doing some nerdy high-tech thing. I pretend to know what she's talking about but the minute she's says the word 'algorithm,' I'm out."

James helped Hot Wheels out of his harness while Saul sat beside Carly, leaning into her as if he, too, was ready to call it a night. Carly bent down to scratch his ears and then rubbed Hot Wheels's back before he limped over to his fluffy dog bed in the corner of the room where he collapsed into a heap of exhaustion.

James helped Carly into her jacket, which had been hanging on a peg by the door. He then retrieved Ike's cage, which he carried to the car for her. Carly helped Saul jump into the back seat of her car as James strapped Ike's cage in to keep it from moving on the drive.

It was dark and chilly and Carly started the engine so that the heater could get cranking as soon as possible. She left the car in park and stood in the open door of the driver's seat so that she could face James. This was the moment of truth where they had to deal with what had happened in there.

James stood in front of her, studying her expression in the glaring light of the lamppost overhead that illuminated the parking area. She could tell he was trying to get a sense of her feelings about the situation.

She wished she could help him out with that, but as it was, her feelings were pretty jumbled. Mostly, she found the whole thing ridiculously funny because of the sheer improbability of her being in a relationship. But then there was this tiny little part of her that seemed to be swept up into the romance of it all.

The idea of a boyfriend, especially if it was James, didn't seem as repugnant to her as it usually did. She figured this was just because her hormones had been hijacked during their recent clinch and she hadn't quite gotten them back under control yet.

"So, this is a hot mess," he said. He put his hand on the back of his neck and blew out a breath.

"No argument here," she said.

"Thanks for going along with it for the moment," he said. "I had no idea they were all planning to stop by tonight, and I never would have put you in that situation if I'd known."

There he was, the good guy Carly knew him to be, taking responsibility for the whole thing as if she hadn't planted a kiss on him right in front of his parents. Darned if his chivalry didn't just charm her stupid.

"I know," she said.

"So, I'm thinking it will be less embarrassing for all concerned if I just go up there and explain to them that we aren't actually a couple, that we just got swept up in a moment, and we're very good friends."

Carly tipped her head to the side while she considered him. "Isn't that going to be awkward?"

"A little—er, a lot," he conceded. "Mostly, because they are all so eager to pair me off. I think they worry about my relationship status a bit too much."

"Why is that?"

"I don't date much."

"Any particular reason?"

"Yes," he said. "I fell for someone once and I've never managed to find anyone else who made me feel quite like that."

Carly felt her heart soften at that. James was telling her the story of her life. She had fallen in love once, and it had wrecked her, utterly wrecked her.

"I'm sorry," she said. "I know exactly how that feels."

He gave her a pained look and said, "Don't feel bad for me. I have high hopes that my luck might change."

The tender way he was looking at her made Carly's toes curl. Was he talking about her? Was he thinking there might be a them in the future that would replace the love he'd lost? Should she discourage him? It occurred to her in a flash that she didn't want to. In fact, for the first time in forever, she wanted something more.

"I like Pops," she said. "I want him to have a happy birthday."

"He will. We'll make sure of it."

"He's awfully fond of you."

"It's mutual. Pops is a great guy."

"He'd be happy if you had a girlfriend."

"Undoubtedly. Gram was the love of his life. I know he hopes that we all find that one true love in our lives."

Carly staggered a bit under that description. It made what she was about to say seem frivolous; still, it would spare them some embarrassment and it might bring Pops some joy and, if she was being honest, it would appease her curiosity about this thing, this insane attraction, between her and James.

"I'll be your girlfriend," she said.

James's eyebrows shot up on his forehead. "What?"

"Let's not tell them that we're just friends," she said. "For the duration of the party, and only for that long, I'll be your *temporary* girlfriend."

He opened his mouth and then closed it. He stared at her as if he wasn't sure if she was just teasing him. Then he lifted his hand and cupped her cheek. His touch was gentle, almost reverent.

"You'd do that?"

"Sure," she said. She tried to make her voice light but it was hard when he dragged his thumb gently over her lower lip, wreaking havoc on her ability to concentrate.

He swallowed hard as if he couldn't quite believe the turn their conversation had taken. He wasn't alone. Carly couldn't wrap her head around it either. She had agreed to go as James's date, knowing there was no way she could avoid seeing Preston. Was she ready for that? Could she handle it? She wasn't sure but she figured she had nothing to lose, except her dignity and sense of self-worth, but hey, those were overrated, right?

At least, leveling up to being James's girlfriend, even if only temporary, made her feel more legit, giving her a stronger buffer between the present and her unfortunate past. Preston could try and shame her—she had certainly given him enough material—but gaining her freedom from the pets would be totally worth it. Eleven years had passed, Preston couldn't hurt her, and even if he tried, the bottom line was that she felt safe with James and didn't that just make her like him even more?

James met and held her gaze, staring into her eyes as if desperately seeking the truth. "Are you absolutely sure about this?"

Carly felt her heart pound hard in her chest. She felt as if James was asking her for a commitment she hadn't really been aware she was making. Could she do this? Did she want to? A tiny voice inside of her, like a match's flickering flame fighting the dark, cried *yes*.

She couldn't give voice to the word so instead she nodded. It was all James needed to see. The grin he gave her was wicked.

"All right, we have a deal," he said. "Does that mean I get to kiss you now?"

Carly gave a startled laugh. Oh, she liked this boy, she really did.

"Sure, why not?"

He needed no further encouragement but pulled her flush up against him and put his mouth on hers, kissing her until she was dizzy and her ears started to ring. When he set her back on her feet, she wobbled and had to brace herself against the top of the car.

"Okay, then, I should go," she said.

He still had his hands on her hips, as if reluctant

to release her. It made Carly feel warm inside. She wasn't used to tenderness like this and even though it made her feel vulnerable, she found she kind of liked it.

"The rest of the family is going to start trickling in," he said. "This was just the first wave. If you're my girlfriend, you'll have to come with me to the family gathering at the brewery tomorrow night."

"What's the matter?" she asked. "Are you afraid I can't be a convincing girlfriend?"

"Nah, I have every confidence in you," he said. "After all, we already know some intimate details about each other, like you know I snore and I know that you mumble in your sleep."

Carly laughed. She did know that about him. How could she have forgotten she had broken the no-sleepover rule with him? Wait, what?

"I do not mumble in my sleep," she said.

"Yeah, you do," he said. "It's rather adorable."

Carly narrowed her eyes. "I think I would know if I mumbled in my sleep."

"How would you? You're asleep; besides, you already told me that you never let anyone sleep over," he said. "Who would tell you if you mumbled?"

They stared at each other for a moment. His hazel eyes were definitely turning a smoky shade of blue and Carly took this as an early warning sign to evacuate the premises immediately or else she might drag him back up to the top of that lighthouse and have her way with him, whether his family was on the premises or not.

She glanced at his full lips, which were curving into a smile, and could almost hear the warning siren in her head. Not one to stand in the path of a tornado, she backed up and slid into the driver's seat.

"I do not mumble," she said. As if repeating it would make it so.

"Uh-huh," he said. "See you tomorrow, girl-friend."

Chapter 24

The night before Pops's birthday party, the entire Sinclair family descended upon the Bluff Point brewery for an impromptu family dinner, barbeque style. Being James's temporary girlfriend, Carly was naturally by his side for the event.

Zach, who was working late at the brewery, caught sight of her and with a nod to James, took her arm and hustled her into a corner for a chat.

"Explain," he said.

Carly shrugged. "Long story short, I'm helping plan his grandfather's birthday party and in exchange if I don't find another owner for them, he's going to take Ike and Saul and provide them with a forever home. Win-win."

Of course, it wasn't that simple, but Zach didn't need to know that. As if he suspected as much, he shook his shaggy blonde head at her.

"You are playing with fire, Carly, and you're going to get burned," he said. He gestured between them. "Remember us? We don't do relationships."

Carly glanced over her friend's shoulder and found James in the crowd. He was standing with a bunch of cousins, holding a beer in his hand and laughing at whatever the guy beside him was saying, but she felt his gaze dart toward her.

He knew where she was, what she was doing, and if she was okay. Before she had always found that sort of attention stifling, but at the moment, she felt protected. James cared about her and she suspected she could come to care for him, too.

"What if I want more?" Carly asked. Her voice was soft.

"Oh, crap," Zach said. "You're falling for him, aren't you?"

"Maybe," she said. It was the first time she'd allowed herself to say it.

"Be careful, girl," Zach said. "If you do this, you are braver than me." He gave her an admiring look. "Know that no matter how this plays out, I've got your back."

"Thanks, Zach," she said. She gave him a big hug and watched as he walked out the door, shaking his head as if he couldn't believe how crazy she was. In truth, she couldn't believe it herself.

"Okay, as your boyfriend—" James said as he walked toward her.

"Temporary boyfriend," Carly interrupted him.

He nodded, acknowledging the status correction.

"Okay, as your temporary boyfriend, how jealous should I be?" he asked.

"Jealous?"

"Of Zach?" he said. He looked uncomfortable but he continued, "You two seem to share a special connection."

"We do," she confirmed. "Zach is as commitment phobic as I am. He gets me."

"And the two of you have never—" James began but then stopped. "Sorry, that's not my business, is it?"

Carly turned to face him. She could see he was trying very hard to be cool and accepting. It was one more reason she really liked James Sinclair.

"Well, technically, if you're my temporary boyfriend it is your business," she said. James looked at her as if he was holding his breath. "The answer is no. Zach and I have never hooked up. We are and always will be just friends."

James looped his arm around her back and pulled her into his side. He rested his cheek on her head, and said. "Thanks for telling me. I like Zach, I didn't want to have to let the air out of his tires."

Carly laughed. "You wouldn't!"

"No, but I'd think about it."

"Couldn't you spend your time thinking about other things?" she asked. She gave him a decidedly flirty look.

He lowered his mouth until it was beside her ear and whispered, "Oh, I am, believe me I am."

Carly felt her insides dissolve into a pool of heat. Zach was right. She was playing a dangerous game with this man and heaven help her she didn't want to stop.

"Come on," James said. "Let me show you off

before I lose all of my noble intentions and try to distract you."

"Okay," Carly said. Her voice was higher than usual and she barely resisted the urge to fan her face with her hand. Oh, this man!

When they rejoined the guests he'd left on the patio, a waiter paused beside them. When Carly opted for the stout beer instead of the wine, James gave her a curious look.

She shrugged and said, "I'm really more of a beer girl."

James looked at her like she'd just handed him a winning lottery ticket. "You really are the perfect woman, aren't you?"

Carly took an enormous swallow, trying to control the ridiculous spike of happiness she felt at his words. He was just being flirtatious and she shouldn't take it seriously, she reminded herself. And yet, she couldn't stop smiling.

Portable gas heat lamps were scattered across the large courtyard and as the sun set and the October air became chilly, the guests moved under the lamps, forming tight-knit groups.

Carly wasn't sure which group to join so she stayed beside James, following his lead. For his part, he seemed happy to have an excuse to keep his arm around her and draw her close to his side.

When she glanced at him in question, he said, "Body heat."

"Uh-huh," she said.

"Jamie, there you are," a pretty woman said. She waved them toward her and her group. "Introduce us to your lovely companion."

James sighed as if he would have preferred to keep Carly all to himself. She shook her head at him.

"This is the reason I'm here," she said.

"I suppose." He took her hand and approached the group.

It was a flurry of introductions and Carly didn't catch any of the names, just that they were his cousins and their spouses and they ranged in age from early twenties to late forties. After the usual chitchat about the weather, one of the women turned to Carly and asked, "So, how did you two meet?"

It took everything Carly had not to look at James. She wasn't sure what made her do it, but meeting at the whoopie pie bakery story be damned, the words just poured from her mouth unchecked.

"Actually, I won him in a bachelor auction for charity," she said. She felt James stiffen beside her as she fought to keep a straight face.

"Really?" The cousins all chuckled.

"Did he command a decent price?" one of the men in the group asked.

"Sadly, I was the lone bidder," Carly said with a shake of her head. "I won him for the bargain basement amount of two dollars and seventy-three cents and a fuzzy Tic Tac, which was all I found in the bottom of my purse."

"Carly." James's voice was a low growl that made her insides hum.

The group laughed and James turned to look at her with one eyebrow raised in question. Carly bit her lip to keep from laughing. She could tell by the twinkle in his gaze that he wasn't mad.

"Two seventy-three? Has he been worth all that?" another man asked.

"And a fuzzy Tic Tac, don't forget. I can't say that he has," Carly said. She leaned forward and whispered in a suspiciously loud voice, "It was a pity bid, really. Probably, I could have gotten him for just the Tic Tac."

The man slapped James on the back and howled.

"Jamie, over here, we want to meet your date," a voice called from another group on the patio.

"Excuse us," James said and steered Carly away from the cousins. When they were a few steps away, he asked, "Having a good time?"

"Most excellent," she said. She nudged him with her elbow and said, "Teasing you is fun."

"Hmm," he hummed but said no more.

They joined the next group and Carly was pleased to see that James's parents were in the mix. They were holding hands and staring into each other's eyes like they were sixteen instead of fifty-something. Adorable.

This time when the question of how Carly and

James had met was posed, James spoke before she could and said, "Jail."

"What?" Emily gasped.

She looked at her husband in horror. Jimmy frowned in concern. Carly whipped her head in James's direction, giving him a wild-eyed look, but he paid no attention to her as he continued his story.

"Yep, I was going into the station to pay a parking ticket when this fine young lady was dragged past me in her orange jumpsuit and handcuffs, and I thought to myself, 'She is it for me.' I badgered the officers until they gave me her name and when she was released, I asked her out."

An awkward beat of silence pulsed amongst the group until Jimmy snorted a laugh.

"You almost had me," he said. He punched his son lightly on the shoulder. "Such a kidder."

Emily looked as if she'd wilt in relief. "James Hardaway Sinclair, it is not nice to tease your parents."

"Or your girlfriend," Carly added. She knew she shouldn't laugh at his malarkey, but the jail bit had been a good one and she couldn't help it.

James whipped his head in her direction. It was the first time Carly had ever said the word girlfriend in the presence of others. She felt the intensity of his gaze upon her and when her eyes met his, her heart kicked up in her chest as if it were trying to take flight. What was even more alarming? She liked it.

"It's nice hearing you say that," he said.

It was a moment of pure honesty, and Carly wasn't sure how to process the raw emotion coming off of him, so she stepped away and said, "Shoot, I have to go call my parole officer. Wouldn't want to get hauled out of the party for failure to check in."

"Oh, my goodness." Emily laughed. She glanced between the two of them and said, "Jamie, dearest, I honestly think you've met your match."

Breaking eye contact with James for fear that she might jump him at the most inappropriate moment (i.e., now) and have her way with him, Carly led the way to the next group.

Through unspoken agreement, when the time came to tell how they met, it was Carly's turn to bust out a whopper. And she did. She claimed that she met James in a strip club, where he'd been stripping to raise money for some new physical therapy equipment.

Again, the story was met with big guffaws and slaps on the back. James laughed harder than anyone, especially when Carly acted out his awkward strip tease and proclaimed that she had stuffed his G-string because she felt sorry for him.

When he hugged her close to his side, Carly felt herself melt into him, and she noticed the family around them smiled and nodded in approval.

They were happy for him. As Carly glanced at the group, she noted that one person was not laughing. In fact, she was staring at James as if she was appalled by his rowdiness. The woman looked pinched as if she had her jaw clamped shut to keep from scolding him.

Carly noted that she was tall and lithe and dressed completely in high-end fashion from her spindly-heeled shoes to her expertly tailored beige suit. She wore her straight, pale blonde hair in a severe bob that stopped at her jaw. She had a gorgeous face, with jutting cheekbones, full lips, and perfectly arched eyebrows over enormous dark blue eyes. She could easily have been a supermodel. Thankfully, when she opened her mouth, Carly saw she had overly large teeth, which gave her a bit of a horsey look.

Still, she had that indefinable air of belonging wherever she chose to be. It was the sort of self-assurance that comes from being beautiful, coupled with a life of privilege spent in big houses, expensive schools, trips abroad, and never knowing what it is to want for anything.

The woman must have sensed Carly watching her, because she stopped staring at James and shifted her gaze to Carly. Her thin nose wrinkled just the littlest bit and her upper lip curled as if she smelled something unpleasant.

Carly felt a moment of self-doubt but then shook it off. Not knowing what to expect tonight, she had chosen a navy blue chemise and matching pumps, paired with a delicate pewter cashmere wrap. It was very Audrey Hepburn with a fit-and-flare style that made it both demure and sexy. Carly had learned early on that when in a fashion dilemma, a girl could never go wrong if she asked herself WWAW: What Would Audrey Wear?

Having reassured herself, Carly tipped her chin up. She had nothing to lose here; if this cow wanted to bring it then so be it.

"James, how amusing you and your . . . friend are," the woman said. "Don't tease us, tell us how you really met. Was she your waitress at a diner or your checkout girl at the market?"

James glanced at the woman, and Carly felt his shoulders tighten just the littlest bit as he registered the woman's *joke?* Carly didn't think she was imagining it when the others in the group swiveled their heads between James and the woman as if watching two fighters square off in a cage match. Okay, now it was all coming into focus; this was an ex-girlfriend. Carly was sure of it.

"Heather," he said. "Nice to see you again."

He couldn't maintain eye contact when he said it, and Carly noted for future reference that he was a terrible liar.

Heather, aka the skinny equine, just stared at him as if trying to bend him to her will. Someone else in the group, a younger cousin in their twenties, jostled James's arm and said, "Come on, tell us the real story."

James glanced away from Heather and back to Carly, who was still tucked under his arm. As he considered her, his gaze went from hard slate gray to a pretty shade of blue, and Carly was quite sure she could spend all day watching the colors shift and swirl in his irises.

"The very first time I saw Carly she was walking across a crowded room in a flirty red dress and matching heels and the sight of her literally made my heart stop."

Carly felt her face get hot. James smiled at her and pressed a kiss against her hair as if to reassure her that he wouldn't embarrass her.

"And I wasn't the only one. Every man in the room watched her, but, as always, she was completely oblivious of how beautiful she was. I remember her hair was in long loose waves and her eyes sparkled with mischief, but it was her smile, which was wide and warm and welcoming, that sucker punched me right in the chest. It was love at first sight."

James turned so he was facing her and Carly swallowed, wondering if it was audible or if she was the only one who heard the lump in her throat going down her esophagus with the force of a plunger. When James lifted his hand to trace the curve of her lips with his fingertip, she stopped breathing and feared she might pass out.

"When I saw Carly smile, when I heard her laugh that beautiful musical sound for the first time, I knew what I wanted to do for the rest of my life."

He paused, forcing Carly to ask, "What?"

James leaned down so his face was just a breath away from hers. "Make you smile and laugh every day just like you did that day."

"Oh." The word was softly spoken on the last bit of breath Carly had in her lungs. The group around them was filled with soft murmurings of appreciation, but Carly couldn't really hear them as she was completely enthralled by the way James was looking at her.

"Well," Heather scoffed, "I think I preferred the story where you were a stripper, Jamie, much more amusing."

She shoved out of the group, pushing through James and Carly, forcing them to step back. Carly felt the loss of James's warmth immediately. She knew he had made the story up, but the way he looked at her. It was like it had actually happened, as if he had really felt all of those things the first time he saw her. Wow.

As the group resumed conversing, James's gaze stayed on Carly. She found herself stepping back into his side, letting him wrap his arm around her. She told herself it was for appearances and warmth, but she knew it was a lie. His words had woven a spell around her and she found she just wanted to be near him for a little while.

As one of the cousins went on to tell how he met his wife in the Peace Corps, Carly stood up on her tiptoes to whisper in James's ear.

"Good story," she said.

She waited to see if he would say more. She wished she remembered meeting him eleven years ago, but she didn't. She had no way of knowing if what he had just said was true. Still, she had to know.

"Was that really what happened the first time we met?"

At that, James moved his hands to her hips and turned her so that they were facing each other. He cupped her chin in his hands and looked at her, really looked at her, then he lowered his head. He moved super slow as if giving her the opportunity to push him away if she chose. She didn't, and after an eternity measured out in seconds, he kissed her.

It wasn't much more than the pressing of his mouth against hers. Lips didn't part and there was no tongue involved and yet, somehow, Carly felt as if it was the most intimate kiss of her life because when he kissed her, James did it with such complete focus, making her feel as if there were no one else on the veranda but the two of them.

He sank his teeth gently into her lower lip in

just the smallest nip and Carly felt as if a flare had been lit in her girl parts. Memories of their night together and what he could do with that mouth of his sent her reeling.

When he leaned back, he caressed the line of her jaw with his thumbs. He studied her face and said, "Yes."

With that, he tucked Carly back under his arm and resumed stroking her side. How could such an innocuous touch make her feel so much, as if his fingers were leaving a trail of sparks along her skin through the fabric of her dress? She shivered and he pulled her even closer. She didn't tell him it wasn't the cold making her tremble. It was him, all him.

Chapter 25

Dinner was catered buffet style, casual with a decided barbeque flair, as the tables were done in red and white gingham with big bowls of peanuts on every table and bales of hay with scarecrows and pumpkins placed just so all over the courtyard as decorations.

James and Carly loaded their plates before finding a spot at one of the more secluded tables set up on the perimeter of the veranda under a heater. Carly wasn't sure but after their run-in with Heather, she got the feeling James was trying to keep her all to himself.

Given how awful the woman had been, she was profoundly grateful.

"I hope you like barbeque," he said. He put their plates down on the table and pulled Carly's chair out for her.

"Are you kidding? They had me at cornbread," she said.

James glanced at the plate he had carried for her, where there were three pieces of cornbread stacked up beside a pile of brisket and green beans. He grinned.

"Now I know one of your weaknesses."

Carly smiled. "Are you planning to use it against me?"

"I might," he said. "You never know what a woman who is desperate for cornbread might pony up in exchange."

Carly grinned at his teasing tone.

"Don't get your hopes up," she said. "I may love a good piece of cornbread but I am not exchanging any sexual favors for it."

"Oh, my god, was I supposed to knock before I joined you two?" Lola asked with a quirk of her diamond-studded eyebrow. She took the seat on the other side of Carly and said, "Just so you know, big brother, that sounded decidedly pervy even for you."

James looked at his sister in chagrin and then threw a green bean at her. It bonked her on the nose and she shouted "Hey!" making both James and Carly laugh.

The table filled in around them with cousins and aunts and uncles that Carly hadn't met yet. She shook hands and tried to catch names, but she figured she'd just have to stick close to James so he could slip her their names on an as-needed basis. She tried not to dwell on the fact that the enforced proximity to James did not feel like a hardship, not at all.

When one more cousin popped up at the table that was already full, James offered the person his seat. Carly glanced up at him in surprise as he stood.

"That's so nice of you," she said.

"Not really."

Without giving her a clue as to his intent, he scooped her up out of her chair and then sat back down, holding her on his lap.

"I . . . uh . . . you . . ."

"Thanks so much, James." The cousin, a darkly handsome man in his late twenties, said as he took his seat and beamed at them. "Clearly, this is the fun table and I would have hated to miss out."

Carly couldn't speak, couldn't chew, couldn't swallow, couldn't move. It was as if every single part of her anatomy was suddenly achingly aware of the man beneath her. She reached for her beer and took a healthy chug. Then she pushed it away, suspecting it might only add fuel to the fire.

"Well, don't you two look cozy," Lola said. She leaned closer to Carly and whispered, "Be careful. Over at two o'clock, you have a mean girl looking like she wants to cut you."

"What?" Carly asked.

She shifted but then was acutely aware of the part of James's anatomy that was intimately pressed up against her backside. She felt a wave of heat scorch her from the inside out and she had to close her eyes for a bit to get her bearings.

"You all right, Carly?" James leaned forward, pressing his front against her back. "You're not eating."

"I'm fine," she said. Then she turned her head so that she could whisper in his ear. "You, however, are in deep, deep trouble, buster."

His arms tightened around her and he pulled her in even closer as he whispered in return, "Hmm, I'm not sure whether I should be excited by this news or dreading it. Give me a hint, what's my punishment going to be?"

Carly pulled back to look at his face. Big mistake. He was grinning and his mouth was just an inch from hers. All she had to do was lean in just a breath—

"See? Look!" Lola jostled Carly to get her attention and Carly glanced back at Lola, trying to remember what they had been talking about. "Two o'clock!"

Carly picked up her beer and pretended to take a sip while glancing over the rim slightly to her right. It was Heather. She was sitting two tables away, facing them while holding her fork in one hand and her knife in the other with her gaze trained on Carly as if she was picturing how to carve her up like a juicy spare rib.

"Yikes!" Carly hissed at Lola. "Is it just me or is it me?"

"Oh, it's you all right," Lola began. "She's married to our cousin. Remember, the one I told you about—the A Factor—and they are a match made in heav— Scratch that, they're a match made in hell."

"Oh, really?" Carly lifted her eyebrows in surprise. So, Preston was married to Heather. Weird. What was weirder was she could have sworn she had gotten ex-girlfriend vibe off Heather in regard to James.

"It's a very sordid story, but Heather married him after—" Lola began but James interrupted.

"What are you two whispering about?"

Lola gave her brother a wide-eyed glance. "Nothing. Not a thing. Not one little pesky nonsensical thing."

Carly glanced between them. Had Lola been about to confirm her suspicion? Had James and Heather been a couple? That would certainly explain Heather's earlier frostiness. Since subtlety was not really Carly's thing, she went there.

"Did you date Heather?" she asked James.

He turned to look at Lola, who was suddenly fascinated by the corncob on her plate as if it were her job to count every kernel. Carly glanced over her shoulder and noticed that most of their table had gone still, blatantly listening to hear how James handled this.

"Yes, we were a couple, but it was a long time ago," he said. "And I've been over it and her for years."

His gaze met hers. It was steady and honest, which was one of the things Carly truly liked about James Sinclair. She realized she trusted him, which was a very new feeling for her in regard to men other than her small circle of friends and her dad.

"Okay," she said.

"That's it?" he asked. "No questions, no opinions, no curiosity? Just okay?"

"Yeah," she said. Then she smiled at him because it was nice to trust someone like she trusted him, really nice.

James returned her grin, then he leaned close so that they were nose to nose. Carly felt her insides flutter as the woodsy citrus scent that was unique to James filled her senses and her mind flashed back to the last time she had been this close to him except without all the pesky clothes in the way.

"I'm afraid I'm going to have to kiss you now," he whispered.

Carly shivered. "I think that's just wise as we want to solidify your status as unavailable, you know, for everyone in attendance. I mean, if we're doing this, we should do it right."

As if she'd flipped a red light to green, James barely waited for the words to escape her lips before he was on her. His mouth molded to hers as he cupped the back of her head and held her still for the onslaught. Using lips, teeth, and tongue, he kissed her with a thoroughness that left Carly clinging to his shoulders for fear that she might melt into a puddle at his feet if she didn't anchor herself somehow.

It took Carly a second to register the sound of shattering glass and even then she didn't care enough to see what had broken as she was too busy trying to catch her breath while admiring the hot blue of James's gaze, which was locked in on her mouth as if just waiting for her to catch her breath before going back for more.

She did that to him. Carly DeCusati made a man's eyes switch colors with desire for her. Hot damn, that felt good! She would have paused to do a fist pump but she didn't want to let go of James.

"Um, you two may want to cool it before Heather smashes something else," Lola said.

"What? Huh?" Carly asked.

"Yeah, James's ex just smashed her wine glass against the table," Lola said. "And I'm pretty sure it was because of the grope you two have going on." She glanced at her brother. "Dial it back, big guy."

James glanced over Carly's shoulder toward Heather and Carly followed his line of sight. Heather was staring at them with a hostility that made Carly's skin prickle.

"Should I be worried that she might boil my pet bunny?" Carly asked.

"No," James said at the same time that Lola said, "I would."

"Okay, then," Carly said.

She turned back to look at James and saw his

mouth turned down in the corners. It was the first time Carly could recall seeing him frown. She didn't like it.

"Hey." She cupped his face and drew his attention back to her. "You all right?"

He clutched her hips as if he was afraid someone was going to take her away from him. His eyes met hers and then he leaned forward and kissed her once on the lips, swiftly and sweetly.

"As long as I have you, I'm fine," he said.

It was the perfect boyfriend thing to say, and Carly heard one of the cousins at the table say, "Aw."

It was exactly what she was feeling on the inside, but Carly didn't dare let it show, because as much fun as being someone's girlfriend for a few days was turning out to be, the experiment might not take and she didn't want to be crushed if it did come to an end.

"Do you need another beer?" James asked.

Carly glanced at her near empty glass. "Yes, please."

"I'll be right back," he said.

He shifted out from under her so that she resumed her seat and then he asked if anyone else needed a beverage. After securing everyone's order, James left their table to go to the bar.

As soon as he was out of earshot, Carly turned to Lola, "So, what's the skinny on Heather?"

Lola opened her mouth and then closed her

mouth. She looked grumpy. "I don't know if I'm allowed to say."

"Oh, come on," Carly said. "I have to know what I'm dealing with. It's only fair."

"She has a point." The good-looking cousin who James had given his seat to joined their conversation.

Carly turned to look at him. He was very handsome, with precisely cut dark hair and bright white teeth. He was also very polished, his clothes impeccably cut, and he had the same lopsided smile that James had. She liked him right away and not just because he was taking her side.

"Mind your business, Tom," Lola said. "Where's John anyway? I thought you never went anywhere without your hubby."

"He's not coming until tomorrow," Tom said. "So I can do family gossip recon before he gets here."

"Excellent," Carly said. "What have you got so far?"

"You mean other than that display?" he asked as he tipped his head in Heather's direction. "Oh, no, I am not giving it up for nothing."

"Fine, I'll go first," Carly said. "See the redhead over there?"

"Aunt Monica?" Tom asked.

"Caught her tossing back a fifth of scotch in the pantry," Carly said. "Your turn."

Tom looked at her with round eyes. Then he

barked out a laugh. "She's never had a drink in her life!"

"If you say so," Carly said. "And see the wrinkled up fella over there?"

Tom and Lola looked to where she indicated.

"Uncle Frank?" Lola asked.

"Saw him goosing the backside of one of the caterers," Carly said. "He almost got a whole tray of sweet potato puffs dumped in his lap."

"Now that one, I believe," Tom said.

They both hooted and Lola gave Carly a half hug. "I like you."

"Then dish!" Carly said. She glanced at where James stood at the bar and knew that time was running out. She gestured to Heather. "And you can start with that one."

Tom and Lola exchanged a glance and Lola nodded.

"Okay, so Heather the Horrible—" Tom began but Carly interrupted.

"Seriously?"

"Quite," Lola chimed in.

"As I was saying," Tom said, giving them both a chastising look. "Horrible was engaged to James—"

"What?" Carly cried.

Tom looked at her. "You didn't know he was engaged?"

"No." She shook her head. She felt stunned. Granted she hadn't really thought about James's previous relationships, but she hadn't envisioned him about to be married, a picture she did not like in the least.

"Remember you did not hear it from me," Tom said. "Anyway, since James decided not to follow in the family footsteps of making more money than a small diamond-encrusted nation, Horrible spent their whole relationship two-timing him with the A Factor, whom she did marry."

"Oh, you call him that, too?" Carly asked.

"We all do," another cousin chimed in from across the table. "He might as well just make it his legal name, he's such an ass."

"Wow, she dumped him for his cousin. James must have been wrecked," Carly said.

"He was," Lola said. "At least, it seemed like he was, but he's over it. Either way I'm so glad he found you."

"Me, too," Carly said. She was surprised at how strongly she meant it. James was a great guy. He deserved so much better than being dumped by a horse-faced gold digger. Even if their situation proved temporary, she'd be a much better girlfriend than Horrible ever was.

Given her own misery at the hands of Preston, the A Factor, she found she was delighted to discover he was married to someone that everyone called Horrible. It served him right. Lola had said he was coming in for just the party. She had shoved aside her dread at seeing him again and now that it was looming, she found she was less nervous than she thought she'd be. She glanced at her empty pint glass; of course, it could be the beer giving her false courage.

"Uh-oh," Lola said. "Don't look now but Horrible is making her move on your man."

"What?" Carly asked.

She glanced up. James was standing at the bar tipping his head down to hear whatever it was Heather had to say to him. While she whispered in his ear, she managed to drape herself across his chest and run her hand up and down his forearm while she spoke. James looked like he was falling back under her spell.

As Carly and the cousins watched, Heather tugged James away from the bar, pulling him around the corner and out of sight. Oh, hell no!

Back during the peak of her own heartbreak, Carly would have given anything to have someone be her wingman and help pull her pride out of the toilet. There were days when she remembered how much she had debased herself for the jerk she'd thought she was in love with and her toes curled with the shame. She was not about to let that happen to James.

Carly was up and out of her seat before she really thought about what she was doing. She stalked across the courtyard, her gaze locked on the spot where James and his clinging vine had disappeared.

She supposed it might be awkward if she walked in on them in a clinch, but she was quite certain that James would thank her later. As she rounded the corner into the narrow service alley, she saw them tucked into an alcove. Heather was leaning forward and James was leaning back, as if trying to get away from her, but the brick wall at his back had him trapped.

Carly was more than happy to help with that. She marched forward. James must have sensed her laser-like stare, because he glanced up from Heather and the look in his eyes went from dead bored to fully engaged in the flicker of an eyelash.

"Carly," he said. He shook himself loose from Heather's hold and opened his mouth to explain but Carly never gave him the chance.

"I missed you," she said with a small pout, using the sultriest voice in her arsenal.

She saw his eyes go wide and he swallowed as if he was nervous, but in the best possible way.

In a move that she knew would insure Heather's enmity forever, not that she cared one little whit, Carly none too gently hip checked the other woman away from James and stood up on tiptoe to press herself against him as she wrapped her arms around his shoulders and pulled him down for a kiss that lost its PG rating in three, two, one. Wow!

Chapter 26

Time and space ceased to have meaning for Carly. She got lost in the scent and taste of James, the feel of his hands on her back as he pulled her in close and held her still while he kissed her. She vaguely heard Heather storm off back in the direction of the party, but she was too wrapped up in James to really register the other woman's departure.

She supposed she should pull away. She'd run her interference. James was safe from Horrible. Still, she dug her fingers into his hair and kissed him until she was breathless and he pulled his mouth away from hers to run his lips down the side of her neck, making her tip her head back and moan.

"Best barbeque ever," he said.

Carly laughed. She pulled away, feeling dizzy and dazed.

"We should go back before we offend everyone with our bad manners," she said.

"Who cares?" he asked. He lowered his head to kiss her again when his attention was diverted by something over Carly's shoulder.

"What is it?"

"Nothing."

His voice sounded tight and Carly turned around

to glance over the decorative hay bales and pile of pumpkins back at the party. The first person she saw was Heather. She was standing in the center of the party, holding her cheek out to be kissed by . . . holy shit!

Carly gasped. No, it couldn't be. He wasn't supposed to be here yet. It had to be someone who just resembled him, but no. She would know that perfectly coiffed head of thick black hair anywhere. Preston Bradley, the bane of her existence and the destroyer of her life, was here kissing Horrible's cheek.

In a flash, the memory of the last time she'd seen him filled her mind. It had been the middle of a frat party; he'd seen her lurking on the fringes of the crowd and then he'd called the cops and had her hauled out of there in handcuffs for violating an order of protection. It had been the single most humiliating moment of her life and it came rushing up on her like the floor in the middle of a faint.

"Oh, my god!" Carly dropped to the ground. "I thought he was only coming in for the party tomorrow."

James followed her down, so that they were both hidden behind the bales of hay.

"So did I. Hey, are you okay?" he asked.

"Nope, not okay, opposite of okay," she said. "I thought I could do this, but I don't think I can."

She was sucking wind as if she'd just sprinted

the forty-yard dash, her hands were sweating, her heart was racing in her chest and she was pretty sure she was going to pass out.

"I'm really sorry, but I have to hand in my notice as your temporary girlfriend. I have to get out of here *right now*," she said.

With that, she hiked up her skirt and started to crawl behind the bales of hay along the edge of the courtyard.

"Carly, wait," James said. He crawled up beside her. "Where are you going?"

"Leaving," she said.

"Really?"

"Yes, I have to," she said. She turned to face him and gave him an apologetic look. "I thought I could handle it, but nope. Can't."

"It's Preston, isn't it? There *was* something between you two, wasn't there?" James looked uncomfortable as he watched her with a decidedly worried gaze.

She stared at him. Did he really have to ask? What sort of history do a man and woman usually have?

"Oh, duh, sorry. Maybe if you face him with me by your side, you'll find it's all in the past." He sounded oddly hopeful about this outcome, but Carly couldn't risk it.

"I can't," she said.

"Are you still in love with him?" James's voice was so low she had to strain to hear it.

She frowned at him. "God, no! Yuck! I'm sorry, I know he's your cousin, but he's an awful person." James looked delighted at this news, until she added, "Honestly, I have to go because I'm not sure if the order of protection is still active." She started crawling again.

"*What?!* What exactly did he do to you? I'll kill him." James grabbed her about the waist, turning her to face him. His look was fierce and it was seriously hot.

"Yeah, no, the order of protection was for me," she said. "Apparently, I have stalking issues. I thought I could bluff my way through this, but it seems I can't. I think I'm having a panic attack."

James's mouth dropped open. He looked stunned.

She broke free from his hold and continued crawling across the edge of the courtyard, hiding behind hay bales and empty chairs until she reached an awning with heavy drapes. It was folded up now, but the thick fabric made for lovely cover. She tucked herself in behind it, hoping to scuttle out the door when no one was looking.

When the drapes were yanked aside, she ignored James as he scooted in beside her. She felt bad that she was backing out of her role as temporary girlfriend, but the reality of Preston showing up here was a total game changer. She could not put distance between them fast enough.

She peered out behind the curtain, wondering if she could make a mad dash for the door without Preston noticing her.

"Carly, wait," James said. He yanked the curtain back over them. "Give me a second to process this."

"No can do. Jail could be imminent. Do you see now? This is why I don't date," she said. "I'm bad at it, really bad."

"I am surprised for a lot of reasons." He blew out a breath. "But mostly by your choice of stalking material. There are so many worthier candidates out there; well, anyone really would be a step up from the A Factor."

"Ha! You think? Here's some TMI for you, he was my first, so I had an unhealthy attachment going, and I might have, you know, called him, emailed him, left notes on his car a few thousand times too many," she said. She moved back to the drapes and looked for Preston. "I have to go before he sees me. This is too embarrassing even for me, and I once peed myself during a coughing fit in a job interview so I know what I'm talking about."

James blinked at her and then he started laughing. Not a quiet chuckle but rather a great big guffaw. Carly put her hand over his mouth trying to keep him quiet but James just shook her off, wrapped his arms around her, and lifted her up off of her feet as he pulled her in for a big smooching kiss.

Carly clung to him for fear that he might drop her, but he didn't. Instead he continued to hold her even after he broke the kiss and pressed his forehead to hers.

"You are an original, Carly DeCusati," he said. His voice was warm with affection and Carly savored it. "For what it's worth, an order of protection usually only lasts a year. Eleven years have gone by, so I think you're good."

"How do you know this?"

"I've had some patients that have come out of some tough relationships," he said. "Kind of like yours, because honestly, of the two of you, it seems to me that you needed an order of protection from the A Factor and not the other way around. And now, I'm sorry but I don't want to let you go."

"I can't believe you still like me after I've admitted all of my crazy," she said. "Clearly, you're defective."

She glanced over his shoulder out at the party. Preston wasn't where she'd seen him last and she scouted the guests, looking for him.

"Damn it," she said. "I've lost visual. I need to know where he is so I can sneak out."

"Don't care," James said. He let her slide down his front and once her feet touched the ground, he kissed her again.

Carly tried to focus on the crisis at hand, really, she did, but James could work some serious mind altering voodoo with his lips and she forgot everything except the need to kiss him back.

He was pressed flush up against her with one hand burrowed in her hair while the other was splayed across her back, anchoring her against him. When she tried to take the lead, he let her kiss him but within seconds, he wrestled control of the kiss away from her and plundered her mouth as if he'd been thinking of nothing else all day.

A tiny sound, a whimper, escaped Carly's lips and she felt James smile against her mouth as he went back in to kiss her again and again almost as if he was determined to coax more sexy sounds out of her. Carly was more than willing to let him.

"Oh, ho, what's this?" a voice cried as the cover of the heavy canvas drapes was snatched away. "Don't tell me Jamie has finally brought a girl to meet the family."

As if it were her own conscience barking at her for the public display of affection, Carly jerked back from James. He was staring at her as if he planned to devour her, and the hot fire of desire raging between them overwhelmed any lick of common sense she might have and she knew that at this moment she would let him do anything he wanted to her. She was gasping for breath and so was he. The rapid rise and fall of his chest made her smile and she put her hand over his heart to see if it was racing as fast as hers.

Suddenly, someone grabbed her arm and jerked

her away from James. She started to protest but then her gaze met a pair of furious pale blue eyes and just like that the past eleven years of her carefully reconstructed life fell away as if it had been clobbered by a wrecking ball.

"Carly? Carly DeCusati?" Preston Bradley was staring at her as if he'd swallowed his tongue.

Carly felt the blood drain from her face as the man—the same man who had shattered her heart and destroyed her trust in men—loomed over her looking like he wanted to drag her out of the party and toss her into the street.

"Hi," she said. She gave him a little finger wave. She was amazed the word managed to muscle its way past the lump in her throat.

The pale blue eyes that had once reduced Carly to a lovesick kitten now made her feel as if she was being impaled by shards of ice.

"What are *you* doing here?" he asked.

The shame that Carly had put years of time and miles of distance behind her rose up like a dark shadow and blocked out the light. She couldn't breathe, her mouth was dry, and her hands were sweating. She felt as if she'd just had her legs kicked out from under her and she was going to fall in a broken heap onto the floor.

Amazingly, James's arms came around her from behind, holding her up and supporting her. She had never been more grateful to anyone in her entire life.

"I . . . I didn't know you were related to James until a few days ago," she stuttered but she didn't know if she was talking to herself or Preston.

"You didn't, really?" Preston asked.

He wasn't looking at Carly but rather at James. There was a tension there and Carly figured it must be because of Preston and Heather shacking up behind James's back. The mere thought of the two of them treating James so badly made Carly's blood boil and she had to take a deep breath to calm her temper.

"She didn't," James said. His voice was cold. "We've never spoken of you before we started planning the party."

He made it clear that he thought Preston wasn't worth the time and Carly almost laughed out loud at the look of disbelief on Preston's face. God, what a narcissist.

"Sure you didn't," Preston scoffed. His gaze was withering. He stepped toward her and he hissed, "I'm Preston *Sinclair* Bradley, a fact that I'm sure you knew when you stalked me after our brief relationship."

"Relationship?" Carly blinked. She felt her temper begin to heat. "That's what you're calling it? Seriously?"

"Listen, I don't know what game you're playing, Carly, but you need to leave immediately."

"Oh, I don't think so," James said. He shifted so that Carly was behind him and he was facing

Preston. "So you and Carly knew each other once. So what? Are you planning to share the details?"

"Do you want me to?" Preston asked. "I could."

"And how would that work out for you?" James asked. "You've already got quite the reputation in the family."

Carly glanced around James to see the two men glaring at each other. Their fists were clenched and their jaws were tight. It was clear that the layers of betrayal ran deep between these two.

"Don't threaten me," Preston hissed.

"Then you'd better watch how you treat my girlfriend."

"Your *girlfriend?*" Preston snapped. "Are you crazy? You can't be serious with that—"

"Tread carefully, Preston," James said. The warning in his voice was unmistakable.

Carly pressed her forehead into his back. She wanted to run, she wanted to hide, she wanted a meteor to hit the brewery and blow them all to bits. Okay, perhaps that was overly dramatic, but she wouldn't have minded if a random fire broke out somewhere on the premises.

"Jamie, you can't date her." Preston gaped. "Don't you get it? She's using you to get to me."

"Wow, there's a level of narcissism you don't see every day. Think pretty highly of yourself there, don't you, A Factor?" Lola asked as she joined them with several cousins flanking her.

"Shut up, Lola," Preston snapped. "And stop

calling me A Factor! What does that even mean?"

There was a ripple of laughter among the cousins, all of whom were watching the confrontation as if they had front-row seats to a show.

Carly felt herself relax just the tiniest bit. They called him A Factor and, boy, they didn't know the half of it. She was here for James not him. She sucked in a shaky breath. She had thought the shame from the past, how small Preston had made her feel, would destroy her if she ever saw him again. But here she was confronting him and she was okay.

Preston Bradley couldn't hurt her anymore. The realization made her feel as if a small car had been lifted off her chest. He had no impact upon her. None. Coming here with James, who was all that was good, had set her free. She was almost giddy with the rush of pure relief that hit her low and deep.

But Preston wasn't about to let it go. He stepped close to James and hissed, "How did she even find you? Did you ask yourself that? Don't you find it odd that she chose to date you of all people?"

"They met at a bachelor auction," Tom called out helpfully. "Carly bagged herself a James."

"No, no, it was in jail," someone else shared with a laugh. "James staked her out when she was released."

Preston glanced around the courtyard, looking

bewildered and frustrated. No one was buying into his drama. The man who had made her final days of college an exercise in heartache and humiliation had no one groveling at his feet, while he kicked her in the teeth for their amusement.

It occurred to her that she had control of this situation, not him. The balance of power had shifted and it made her stiffen her back and stop hiding behind James. She didn't need to hide from Preston Bradley, not anymore.

She stepped forward and said, "I can assure you, Preston, my interest in James has nothing to do with you. In fact, I'm dating him *in spite* of the fact that he is your cousin. I'm here to be with James, not you. Just so we're clear, zero fucks are being given about you."

She leaned into James's side and he wrapped his arm around her, pulling her in close, supporting her and comforting her at the same time.

"I don't believe you," Preston said. "I don't believe you're a couple. It's not possible."

"It's true. Their meeting is a classic," another cousin cackled. "They met when James was working as a stripper. Carly stuffed his G-string."

The twenty-something young woman then busted out what Carly assumed was supposed to be stripper moves but looked more like she was miming riding a rodeo bull, which made everyone hoot with laughter.

"Yeah, and this is why saying we met in the bakery might have been the better choice," James whispered in her ear.

His gruff growl made her shiver and Carly leaned into him, feeling his warmth and strength buffer the humiliation that was nipping at her heels just waiting for her to be vulnerable, so it could sink its teeth into her flesh and render her crippled. She was not about to let it.

"Noted," she said.

On impulse, she rose up on her tiptoes and went to kiss his cheek. James must have anticipated her move because he turned toward her at just the right moment and their mouths met in one of the sweetest kisses Carly had ever received. Again, she was reminded of what a good man James was and she was grateful all over again.

When they broke apart, she gazed up at him, wishing there were words for what she needed to say to him. Instead, she just adored him with her eyes and he did the same.

Carly glanced back at Preston. He was regarding them with suspicion as if he couldn't imagine that they were together. In his designer jeans, loafers, a chunky wool sweater, and without a strand of his thick black hair out of place, he looked so Ken doll perfect that Carly was reminded of how long it took him to get ready for any outing. So very different from James and how he rubbed his hand through his hair and called it done. How

357

had she ever imagined that she was in love with the A Factor?

"Are we done here?" James asked Carly.

"More than," she said, making it clear that Preston's presence didn't bother her one bit.

The dismissal was clearly more than he could take. He looked at James with a sneer full of malice. "Well, if you really don't care that you're fucking my sloppy seconds—"

That was as far as he got before James punched him right in the mouth with an uppercut that snapped Preston's head back and sent him sprawling onto the table behind him. When James looked like he was going to dive after him, Carly grabbed his arm and dug in her heels.

Tom grabbed James's other arm and between them, they weighed enough to stop James's forward momentum.

"That's enough, Jamie," Tom said. "You delivered a good one on the A Factor. Let's not upset the party with an out-and-out brawl."

Preston was lying across a dinner table, flailing as he tried to extract himself from the refuse. Carly thought it telling that no one helped him up, not even Horrible, his wife, who was standing off to the side, looking as if the sight of her husband sickened her.

"Preston?" An older woman with the same ice blue eyes came dashing across the veranda. "Preston, baby, what happened?"

Carly knew without being told that this was Preston's mother.

"Preston bumped into James's fist," Tom said. "Freak accident, truly."

"Uh-oh, you'd better bounce before Aunt Grace figures out that he didn't trip and land on your knuckles," Lola said.

"Agreed. Might be a good time for you and Carly to go do a walk-through of the lighthouse for tomorrow's party," Tom said.

He spun James around and pushed him toward the exit. Tom gave Carly a desperate glance and she tightened her grip on James.

"That's a wonderful idea," she said. "Come on, James, party prep is never done."

He looked like he'd balk but Carly was stronger than she looked; plus, she really needed to get away from here and put a hundred yards or miles between her and her past.

Chapter 27

"This is lovely," she said. "Don't you think?"

James glowered but she knew it had nothing to do with her question so she let him resume pacing.

They had driven to James's lighthouse, but because the main part of the house was full of decorations for the party, they had checked on Hot Wheels, who was fast asleep on his bed, and then retreated up into the top of the lighthouse. While Carly examined the lights she'd strung in the windows, which spelled out Happy Birthday, Pops!, James paced around the room.

"Come on," she said. She pushed him toward the bed in the center of the room and tugged him down beside her.

James glanced back at the stairs as if he was considering going back down to return to the brewery to find Preston and finish what he started.

"Don't even think it," she said. Then she climbed into his lap, straddling his thighs so that he was pinned down and they were facing each other.

The glower left James's face, much as she thought it would, and was replaced by a look of regret. She refused to let him feel badly about what had happened. If Preston had behaved like a nice guy and not, well, an A Factor, then James never would have clocked him. If it was anyone's fault, it was Preston's.

James moved his hands to her hips and leaned his head back as he studied her. It was too dark for her to gauge the color of his eyes, but she suspected they were veering off into her favorite shade of blue.

"Carly, I am so sorry. Preston was so rude. I never should have—" he began but she interrupted him.

"Don't," she said. "It's not your fault. There's no way you could have known what happened between your cousin and me, a fact I'm finding incredibly embarrassing right now."

"I wish things had been different," he said and Carly got the feeling he wanted to talk. She did not.

"Does it matter? We're here right now," she said. She studied his face. It was a good face. Handsome but not pretty, honest but not judgy; yes, she really liked James's mug. In fact, she liked everything about him.

She had never had a guy punch someone on her behalf before and the fact that the guy who got punched was also the one who had all but destroyed her self-esteem when she'd been at her most vulnerable—well, that made James Sinclair something pretty special in her book.

She knew she had drawn the boundary line very clearly between them, and she knew that if it was going to change, she was going to have to be the one to open the border, so to speak.

Carly wasn't one to give out confusing signals, so instead of talking over the situation, she decided the clear way forward was to use action instead of words. She ran her index finger over his bottom lip. When his lips parted in surprise she placed her mouth against his, making it more than clear that the conversational portion of the evening was over.

She felt his hands clutch her hips as if he couldn't decide whether to pull her in or push her off. She knew that as a nice guy, he was probably struggling between doing what he wanted to do—her—and what he thought he should do—not her. She decided to make it harder for him, and by harder she did not mean the decision.

She slid forward on his lap until his guy parts and her girl parts were in perfect lockstep, then she wriggled just the teensiest bit. James dropped his hands from her hips as if she'd burnt him. She smiled against his mouth and then slid her mouth to his ear where she gently bit down on his earlobe.

He hissed out a breath and pulled back to lock his gaze onto hers as if he wasn't sure what was happening between them and was afraid to get his hopes up.

"I didn't think temporary girlfriend meant spending the night together," he said.

"It didn't," she agreed. "But I changed my mind. I don't want my life dictated by my past anymore."

"Oh, Carly, I wish we had met differently."

"Oh, I don't know, I like the way we met." She leaned in close and whispered, "James, oh, James."

"Oh, fuck," he said. "I can't think . . . damn it."

His hands came back to her hips and he locked her in place on his lap while he reclaimed her mouth in a kiss that Carly was pretty sure made sparklers shoot out of her fingertips.

As if he couldn't touch her enough, he let go of her hips and buried one hand in her hair while the other trailed up her side to cup her breast. Carly arched into him. She matched his hunger perfectly, because she felt as if she could never get enough of him, of this, of the way he made her feel.

She tugged up the hem of his shirt up so that she could touch his skin. He hissed a breath and his lips left her mouth to slide down the side of her neck to the base of her throat where her pulse pounded like a bass drum.

Carly closed her eyes, reveling in the feeling of being close to someone not just for a wham-bam-thank-you-ma'am one-night stand, but because she liked him. She genuinely liked James Sinclair. She waited for the panic to set in, the feeling that he was too close, that her potential to be hurt was too great; instead, she felt a sweet sense of connection.

She liked seeing that when she ran her hands over his hot skin, he arched into her touch. And when she skimmed her palm across the front of his pants, he bucked against her and she chuckled. She enjoyed having the knowledge of their previous encounter to make him as crazy for her as she was for him.

"If you touch me like that again, I might lose my mind," he panted. So naturally, she did.

One minute Carly was across his lap and the next she was lying down on the bed with James on top of her. She wound her arms around his neck and pulled him in until they were pressed together from head to toe.

The pale light from the strands of bulbs Carly had strung in the windows washed over them. Carly wanted to see the light dance on James's skin, and she pulled his shirt over his head, tossing it to the ground.

"I was fine, totally fine with my life . . . and then you showed up and changed everything. I told myself that if you waved me in, I was going to ruin you for any other man," he said. He paused to unzip her dress, pulling the top down to pool about her waist. "The first time I saw you, I wasn't looking for this, but I couldn't get you out of my head. It's like I knew deep down that you belonged with me. Now I know it for sure, but really, I've known it for a long time."

It was quite possibly the hottest thing any man had ever said to her, and Carly was pretty sure she melted into a puddle beneath him.

When he unhooked her bra and caught the hardened peak of one breast in his mouth, she moaned his name again and dug her fingers into his hair. Any coherent thoughts she might have had were gone like ashes on the wind under the onslaught of his mouth on her body.

He wasn't gentle, he was ruthless as he employed all of the knowledge he had learned from their previous night against her. He used his teeth to inflict a flash of pain before he ran his tongue over the abused flesh, making Carly writhe beneath him with a longing that was a painful physical ache down deep inside.

The reality that they were in the top of the lighthouse and possibly visible to anyone who cared to look didn't matter. She wanted to belong to James in the most intimate way possible. It was thrilling and terrifying and she couldn't stop what was happening between them if she tried.

He worked his way down her body, savoring each bit. When he reached for the dress still bunched about her waist, she didn't even think to stop him. It wasn't until he paused while he pulled the dress to her knees that Carly could take a deep breath and get enough oxygen into her brain to glance up at him. She found him grinning at her, and the twinkle in his blue gaze made her catch her breath.

"What?" she asked.

"You," he said. "You are a constant marvel to me."

"Oh." She felt her insides flutter at his sweet words.

He pressed his palm right where her heart was trying to beat in a steady rhythm but it kept speeding up and slowing down under the constant whirlwind that was James making love to her.

He trailed his callused fingers across her ribs and around her belly button until they hit the wide stretch of elastic that kept her big cotton granny panties up. Damn it!

"No! Oh, no!" she cried.

Carly bolted upright into a sitting position. She had forgotten. Sweet Jesus on a bicycle how had she forgotten? A hot flush of mortification suffused her face and she pressed her palms to her cheeks as she tried to wriggle out from beneath him and go crawl under the lighthouse to die.

James was not about to let her go, however. He took her hands from her face, then he slowly pushed her back against the bed, holding her hands with one hand over her head while he ran his fingers along the elastic edge of her white cotton shame.

"I didn't think it was possible to actually die of embarrassment, but I'm rethinking that now," she groaned. "You were never supposed to see these. These were my last line of defense in case, well, in case *this* happened. Oh, god . . ."

"Shh," he whispered against her neck.

She could feel his mouth curve up in a smile against her skin but instead of making her feel ridiculed, it made her feel cherished.

"Do you know what makes a woman truly sexy?" he asked as he pulled back to shuck her dress all the way off.

"What?" she gasped. She was struggling to concentrate on his words as James was running his callused hands up her legs from her ankles, pausing to trace small circles at the bend of her knees, and finally resting one on each thigh, gently pushing them wider just below the damned cotton briefs.

"Confidence. A truly sexy woman doesn't need the right hair or makeup or underwear, because she walks into every room like she owns it. She can render a man stupid with the toss of her hair, the curve of her smile, or the swing of her hips," he said.

He lowered himself between her legs while he spoke, shifting to drape her legs over his shoulders, bringing his mouth right in line with her girl parts.

She could feel the press of his thumbs into her skin where he held her still and the heat of his mouth where it blasted through the thin barrier of cotton and torched her clit in a direct hit.

"A truly sexy woman makes a man want to seduce her, possess her, make her cry out his name, just his name, when she comes. And you, Carly DeCusati, are the sexiest woman I have ever known."

He hooked the waistband of her undies with two fingers and slowly, achingly slowly, tugged the droopy drawers down, exposing her wet warmth to his gaze. Carly would have squirmed but the hot blue fire in his eyes didn't allow her to duck or cover or breathe.

When James parted his lips and put his mouth on her, she arched her back and instinctively bucked her hips, trying to get closer to him. He held her still, chuckling against her skin. The low rough rumble made her tremble and then he used his tongue to coax her slowly, inexorably, into a frenzied ball of need.

She cursed, she reached for him, needing to touch him, to bury her fingers in his hair. She writhed beneath him, alternately panting and pleading, and still, he taunted, he teased, he ratcheted up the want in her until she was sure she was at the breaking point.

With his mouth on her, he owned her and he knew it. What's more, he made sure she knew it, too. Only James could do this to her. He hummed against her, and Carly was pretty sure she felt the vibration all the way into her soul. She was close, so close, she was about to start begging or crying, and then he thrust his wicked fingers into her and Carly came undone.

"James, oh, James," she cried as her orgasm washed over her in great clenching spasms of pure bliss.

"Yes," he mumbled against her. "Say it again."

She clenched her fingers in his hair, not sure if she wanted to hold him in place forever and repeat this exact exercise until they both expired or pull him away because the sweet torture was almost excruciating in its intensity.

"James, oh, James," she gasped.

As the orgasm spiraled out of her, James pulled her undies back into place with a wicked smile. He pressed a kiss to her sweet spot through the cotton, causing her to press up against his mouth as if she had the stamina to do this again.

"You must always wear these," he said. He smoothed the cotton drawers with his hand, pausing to cradle the part of her that was still throbbing just one more time. "Promise me."

Carly laughed. She reached for him and pulled him back down on top of her. When she kissed him, she felt her body convulse with an aching need as she realized he tasted of her and it was the hottest thing ever. She reached for the button on his jeans, but he caught her hands in his, stopping her.

"You don't have to—"

"Shh," Carly interrupted him.

With the surge of post-orgasm happy coursing through her, she wanted nothing more than to share the feeling. James, however, had other plans.

"Wait, sunshine. I need you to tell me about Preston," he said. "I need to know what happened between you two."

Like a splash of ice water, Carly felt her lust extinguish with a hiss. Damn it.

Chapter 28

"Are you feeling all right?" Carly asked. She put her hand on his forehead.

"I'm fine. What are you doing?" he asked.

"I'm checking you for a fever," she said. "I think you must be delirious."

"What? Why?"

"Are you really turning down sexy time to talk?" she asked. "Isn't that, like, a girl thing to do? You know, talking about feelings and stuff instead of sharpening the pencil."

James laughed. Then he dug his fingers into her hair and kissed her until she forgot his question, her name, and the fact that she wasn't wearing clothes.

The feel of his skin against hers made her insides tighten and all she wanted to do was wrap herself around him as snug as a sweater. She ran her hands over his shoulders and down his sides, grabbed the waistband of his pants, and pulled him in tight. She could feel his hard length press against her and she wrapped her legs around his waist and locked him up against her.

"You're not going to distract me," he said.

She sensed it was a lie because he was kissing her while he said it. Kissing her and rocking his hips against her as if it were an instinctive response he couldn't control.

She smiled against his mouth. "Yes, I am."

"No, you're not."

James broke the kiss and pulled away. He leaned his forehead against hers and she was pleased to see he was panting for breath. At least it was a struggle for him to stay on task.

"Do we have to talk? I'd rather make you shiver and moan," she whispered in his ear and then she nipped his earlobe, making him groan. It was cold comfort to feel his hands grip her tight as if fighting the urge to spread her wide and plow into her.

"Behave," he said.

With that, he rested his full weight on top of her, trapping her beneath him. He ran his hands over her skin as if trying to memorize the feel of her. Carly could feel the desire that should have been sated surge up again. How did this man wind her up so easily? And why did he want to talk when they could be doing other things that were so much more fun?

"Tell me about Preston," he said. "He'll be at the party tomorrow and it'll be easier to deal with him if I know what happened."

Carly sighed. That's right. She'd have to see Preston again. Ugh. She supposed there was no avoiding the convo.

"All right, fine. But we have to put our clothes

back on because I can't think with you half naked like that," she said.

"I'll put mine on," he said. "But you stay just like that."

She opened her mouth to protest and he took the opportunity to kiss her, stopping whatever argument she might have made. He scooped up his shirt and put it back on, then he resumed his position on top of her. Carly tried not to think about how erotic it was to be nearly naked, down to just her old lady panties, with a fully clothed James on top of her.

"All right?" he asked as he settled down against her.

Carly nodded. He was all warmth and hard angles against her cool softness. She was pleased to feel that his own desire had not diminished at all but rather was a constant insistent nudge against her hip.

"Then start talking," he said.

His gaze fastened on her face but she glanced away, turning toward the window, looking at the reflection of the lights in the glass. Their power was doubled by their reflection, sort of like how she felt when she was with James. There was no question that facing down Preston today had been easier because James had been there. He'd had her back and doubled her strength. She had never felt like that with anyone before.

The realization made talking about the past

seem silly in comparison, as if what had happened so many years ago even mattered now that there was this thing between them. She pushed that thought away, not really ready to evaluate what this thing was. Infatuation? Yes, that would do. There was no need to look too closely at the happy, fizzy, fuzzy way James made her feel, and that wasn't even counting the sex.

She glanced back at James. He was watching her, patiently waiting, not pushing, not rushing her, letting her become comfortable with the idea of sharing. It hit her again how much she liked him—okay, more than liked him.

She cleared her throat. Probably she shouldn't dwell on her feelings for him or she'd jump him and they'd never get this talk out of the way.

"Preston and I went to college together," she said. "We were both getting business degrees and we moved in the same circle of friends. He was so different from anyone I had ever known—so confident and self-assured—okay, kind of a dick actually. He always dressed to impress, had loads of money to burn, and had the best of everything as if it were his birthright. He was the typical arrogant bad boy, and it worked on me like a charm. I had a mad crush on him for two years."

Carly paused. James didn't say a word. His hands moved over her skin as if to reassure her that all would be well, that he was here, that he wouldn't let anything hurt her, not even memories.

"Our senior year, Preston suddenly seemed to take notice of me," she said. "He began to hang around and walked me to and from classes, we studied together, he even took me out a few times. I fell hard and fast. I thought he did, too, but it was a lie."

James's hugged her close as if sensing that what was coming next was the hurtful part. He was right.

"Turns out, at twenty-one, I was the last remaining virgin in our little group," she said. She glanced at James. "Shocker, I know. I wasn't always the sophisticated gal who picked you up at Marty's Pub. Anyhow, apparently, a bet was made on who would be the guy to help me out with that, sort of like capture the flag for assholes."

She glanced at James's face. He looked a little pale and there was a sadness in his gaze that made her feel small. She glanced away. She didn't want his pity. Carly ran her hands over his shoulders and down his sides, trying to soothe him or maybe herself. She wasn't sure. It didn't matter.

"Anyway, Preston always was the most competitive of our cohort. He played to win, and he played me, but hey, I learned later that the prize for my virginity was a whole pizza, so I guess that made it worth it." She tried to keep her voice light and joking, although at the time there had been nothing funny about it.

James went so still that Carly had to check to make sure he hadn't fallen asleep while she was talking. She cupped his chin with her hand and tilted his face toward hers.

"Hey, you still with me?"

His jaw was clenching like a fist and his nostrils were flared. His eyes had gone dark and when Carly looked closely she could see they were slate gray, icy cold, and hard with fury.

"How long did you date him?" he asked. His voice was clipped.

"Not long, not at all, really," she said. "He dumped me via email a few days later."

"That son of a bitch," he snapped.

"Yeah, pretty much," she said. She smoothed his hair with her fingers. She didn't want to ask but she needed to know. "Does it bother you that I lost my virginity to Preston?"

"That depends," he said. His voice was low and rough and Carly got the feeling it was taking everything he had not to lose his cool. "Was it good for you? Was he gentle with you?"

Carly felt her insides sigh and she smiled. James did not. She hugged him close. Leave it to James not to care that she'd lost her innocence to the A Factor—only to be worried about how she'd been treated during the experience.

"Let's just say, it wasn't exactly memorable," she said.

She cringed as she studied his face. Probably there was some sort of rule about telling the guy who had just given you a mind-blowing orgasm that his cousin had been a lousy lover while taking your virginity. Again, more evidence of why she didn't do relationships.

"We probably shouldn't talk about this, should we?" she asked.

James's expression remained neutral, but she got the sense he was working very hard to keep it that way. Oh, jeez, was there any way to save this moment?

"Hey, it was over eleven years ago," she said. "We were young and young people do dumb things. I didn't handle the rejection very well and pretty much stalked him day and night until he hit me with an order of protection, which by the way is definitely the lowest point in my life to date. It also made me realize I wasn't cut out for relationships."

James was silent. He pressed his forehead to hers and his face was full of regret. Carly didn't want him to feel that way about her past, but then she remembered he had his own tough love story. Clearly, Horrible had done a number on him as well. Maybe what she was seeing on his face wasn't pity so much as it was understanding.

"Oh, sunshine, I'm so sorry," he said. "I didn't know. I would never have let you face him tonight—damn it. I wish I'd punched him five more times and curb stomped him, too."

Carly laughed. It felt good to have someone so indignant on her behalf.

"James Sinclair, I had no idea you were so bloodthirsty!" she said. "Thanks for that but I'm all right and, you know, I think it was actually good for me to see him tonight. I realized he has no more power over me. None."

"He is a selfish, narcissistic, ass hat," James ranted. "I always knew it. When he and Heather got together, it was pretty clear that he was the one who had done the pursuing. It hurt and I was angry, but what he did to you, that makes me enraged."

"Don't be," she said.

"But the way he treated you—"

"I'm fine," she said.

"Really?" he asked. "One-night stands and no commitments for the past decade, is that fine?"

They stared at each other. The strings of lights gave them just enough illumination to see each other. James's lips were in a hard, straight line and Carly missed the man who always seemed to have a smile or a laugh lurking just beneath the surface. On impulse she kissed the corner of his mouth, catching him off guard.

"Yes, it's fine. It was my choice to live my life

that way. Honestly, I never wanted anything but a one-night stand," she said. She blew out a short breath and added, "Until now."

James froze. He didn't flicker so much as an eyelash and Carly realized that she'd probably read the situation wrong. He probably wasn't looking for more than temporary arm candy for Pops's party. Oh, god, why did she always throw herself at men who didn't want her for the long haul?

"I'm sorry," she said. She tried to push out from under him, but it was like trying to move a boulder. The man would not be budged. "I don't know where those words came from, honestly, I didn't mean it. Probably, it was just the afterglow talking, you know, I orgasmed so hard I probably lost some brain cells. Forget I said—"

"Oh, hell no!" he said.

Carly's gaze flew up to his but he was already moving in. He cupped the back of her head and kissed her until she saw stars. As if she'd unleashed some sort of sex-crazed demon, James was all over her and it was spec-freaking-tacular. Carly had never, ever, in her whole life, felt as wanted as she did at that very moment.

"Say it," he said as he hopped off the bed and stripped down to his boxers.

"Say what?" she asked.

James yanked off her granny panties and threw them over his shoulder.

"Hey!" she cried out, but her outrage was a lie. She was laughing too hard to make it sound serious. Instead, she reached forward and tugged his boxers off. She threw them in the same general direction as her panties.

"You know what," he said. The look he gave her scorched and Carly almost checked her hair to make sure it wasn't on fire.

He pulled her up and then sat down, positioning her so that she was straddling him. He put his thumb right on her clit and Carly lost her powers of speech as everything went gray and she started to see spots.

"I can't think when you do that," she gasped.

"Tell me," he said. He circled her sensitive spot with his thumb and she arched up against his touch. "Tell me what you want."

"More than a one-night stand," she panted.

"Be specific, sunshine," he growled. His voice was a warning and Carly had a feeling he would do wickedly wonderful things to her if she didn't say what he wanted to hear. It was tempting to deny him, but she had an agenda of her own.

"More than a temporary girlfriend. I want to be your girlfriend, for reals," she said. Her voice was barely more than a whisper but he heard her.

"Yes!" he cried and pumped his fist in the air like he'd just scored a touchdown.

Then he turned back to her and the look in his eyes almost made Carly come on the spot.

No man had ever made her feel like she was everything he had ever wanted and desired. It made all of her hard edges soften and her fiercely protected boundaries fell away, opening just for him.

Before he could regroup and finish what he started, Carly scooted off of his lap and knelt down in between his knees. Now it was his turn to look nervous.

"Strap yourself in, boyfriend." She looked up at him through her lashes as she savored the word she had never used before. "I'm about to have my way with you."

James hissed. That was all he got out before she put her mouth on him. When he fell back with his eyes still locked on her face, Carly knew she had him right where she wanted him.

"Tell me about Heather," she said.

James was sprawled on his back, while Carly had her chin propped on her arms, which were crossed over his chest. They were partially clothed now and snuggled up on the bed, enjoying the sound of the ocean waves breaking on the rocks way down below.

Carly had gotten her way with James, but he had promised retribution once they recovered. Carly was a little alarmed at how much she was looking forward to it; maybe having a boyfriend wasn't so bad after all.

"There's not much to tell," he said.

"Were you very hurt?"

"No," he said. "Which probably should have been my first clue that I didn't love her, not really."

"Then why did you ask her to marry you?"

"How did you know that?"

"Tom and Lola might have mentioned that you two were engaged when we were watching Heather drape herself all over you like a bargain basement suit," she said.

James toyed with a thick lock of Carly's hair. "What else did they mention?"

"That she broke up with you to pursue Preston," she said diplomatically.

"More like she cheated on me with him and when I caught on and confronted her, she dumped me before I could dump her," he said. "Also, she made sure everyone knew about the affair so that Preston had no choice but to marry her to save face."

"No sir," Carly cried out.

"Oh, yes," he said. "It was quite the family scandal."

"How did you meet her?"

"We grew up together," he said. "I've known her my whole life. We dated in high school and then we just sort of stayed together through college, until I found out about her and Preston."

"You never met anyone else that you fancied more than her?"

James was quiet for a moment. When he looked at Carly, his eyes were troubled, and she felt badly for asking what was clearly a painful question.

"Sorry," she said. "That was none of my business."

"Ah, but you're my girlfriend now," he said. "It's all your business."

Carly felt a burst of happiness surge through her. She liked that. She liked that his world, his history, his day to day stuff belonged to her now. She stretched her arms wide and hugged him close, resting her cheek against his chest.

"Still, you don't have to tell me anything you don't want to," she said.

James was quiet. He kissed the top of her head. When he spoke his voice was low and deep as if the memory was being dredged up from down deep inside of him.

"There was one woman once," he said.

He sifted her hair through his fingers, from the base of her scalp all the way to the tips again and again. Carly was sure that if she were a cat, she would have purred. Heck, she might anyway.

"And?"

"I could barely speak to her because I thought she was the most beautiful woman I had ever seen." His tone was rueful.

Carly lifted her head to look at him.

"Are you telling me that you fell in love at first

sight?" she asked. "With someone you'd never met before?"

"Desperately, madly, deeply," he said.

Carly opened her mouth to say something, anything, but she couldn't find the words. It was so romantic and so improbable that she couldn't even wrap her head around it. Finally, she gave up trying and asked, "What happened?"

"Eleven years passed and then on one fine October afternoon, she walked back into my life and stole my heart all over again," he said.

Carly couldn't breathe. "*She* was me?"

"I know you don't remember meeting me when I came to New York to visit Preston," he said.

Carly frowned. She found it inconceivable that she could not remember him.

"Your business cohort was whooping it up, celebrating the end of finals," he said. "You were wearing a killer red dress and you walked across the room like you owned the joint. I thought you were the most spectacular woman I'd ever seen. I felt like Cupid shot me right in the chest."

So, he hadn't been making it up when he told the family how they'd met. Carly shook her head. She had spent so many years burying the memories of that time and place down deep that it was hard to bring it back now.

"Hey, it's okay if you don't remember," he said. "But I am telling you the truth when I say that I fell for you the very first time I saw you and I never ever forgot you."

Carly didn't know what twist of fate had brought her to this space and time, but she knew that she would never forget this moment, she would never forget James or the way he made her feel.

"You're going to make love to me right now, aren't you?" she asked.

"Yep," he said. And then he rolled on top of her, pinning her to the mattress, which was okay with Carly because she couldn't think of any place she'd rather be.

Chapter 29

"But is he eating?" Carly asked. "You know he can be picky."

"You've only been gone a little over twenty-four hours," Jillian said. "Ike is fine. Saul is fine. They even had a playdate with Hot Wheels."

"When?" Carly asked.

She was alone in James's bedroom, talking to her friends on speakerphone and prepping her look for the big dinner to celebrate Pops's eightieth birthday, while James was off enjoying afternoon cigars with the men.

"I brought him over this morning," Mac said. "Ike rode around on Hot Wheels's harness. It was really cute."

Mac and Gavin had taken Hot Wheels for James because he feared the party would be too much for the dog, while Jillian was pet sitting Ike and Saul for the same reason.

"Aw, that's sweet," Carly said. "Thanks for watching the kids for us. I actually called with some news to share."

"Oh, my god, you slept with James again," Jillian said.

"What? How did you get that?" Carly asked.

"Did you hear that?" Mac asked. "She didn't deny it. She slept with him!"

"Hey, I'm on speakerphone here," Carly said.

She switched off the speaker and held the phone up to her ear. "What if someone had been around? Sheesh."

"And still she's not denying it," Emma said. "Oh, wow, is this the first guy you've ever had a repeater with? What does that mean?"

"It's not that big of a deal," Carly said. "It just means he's my buhfurnuh."

"Huh?" all three friends said at the same time.

"Do I have to say it? You know what I mean," Carly snapped.

"Boyfriend? Did that garble you spoke mean 'boyfriend'?" Jillian asked. "As in James is your *boyfriend?*"

"Fine, yes, that's what I meant," Carly said.

"How?" Emma asked.

"When?" Mac chimed in.

"For real?" Jillian asked.

"Isn't it supposed to be who, what, when, where, and why?" Carly asked. "You three would make lousy reporters."

"Details, Carly, and I mean it," Jillian's voice held a note of warning.

"There really isn't much to say," Carly lied. "I thought about what all of you said and I realized you were right."

"Liar!" Mac cried. "You never admit it when anyone else is right."

"Or take advice," Jillian confirmed.

"Busted," Emma sang.

"Okay, fine," Carly said. "Some stuff happened but I can't talk about it now because I need to get ready for the party, so you'll just have to wait until I get home tomorrow for the pornographic version."

"Oh, goody," Emma said. "Will there be visual aids?"

"Shut up," Carly said but she was laughing so it lacked heat. "Listen, that wasn't my news. My big news is—"

"Bigger than James?" Jillian interrupted.

"He can't like that comparison," Mac said.

"Do you want to hear it or not?"

"Yes," all three women said together.

"All right, then, I just got off the phone with Lydia Husser at Penmans. They've offered me a job as a women's clothing buyer, and—"

"Oh, my god, you're staying in Bluff Point!" Jillian shouted.

"Woo-hoo!" Mac cheered.

"Yay!" Emma cried.

"And I accepted," Carly finished. "So, yes, I'm staying."

Her friends started to talk at once, but Carly knew she was out of time if she wanted to look her best for the dinner tonight. She made a hissing sound over the phone, trying to sound like static on a bad connection.

"What?" she said. "I can't hear you. What? We'll chat more tomorrow."

Then she ended the call. She realized she was going to catch hell for that later, but she had a high priority situation here. After spending the day running around like a crazy person, setting up the caterers, the band, the photographer, and every other person involved in this shindig, not to mention fielding a call from her new employer, hallelujah, all she really wanted to do was lie down and nap but there was no time.

Her friends were right; last night was the first time she had spent a second night with a guy and it felt right that it was James even if the man had barely let her sleep a wink, not that she minded.

She used to believe that being able to sleep with her limbs spread out and taking up all the real estate in the bed was way better than having to share space with a man. But having woken up with an arm locked around her middle and her head tucked under James's chin, she had to admit there was a special sort of loveliness that came with feeling cared for that she hadn't realized would be so attractive.

And then there was the sex. They had christened their new status of boyfriend and girlfriend with a couple of screaming orgasms, mostly Carly, and she was pretty sure anyone within a five-mile radius had heard them, which was another reason why she was happily hiding out in James's room.

James's family had arrived earlier, mostly to help with the party prep, but Carly would have to have been blind not to notice the way his parents and sister smiled at her and James, as if they couldn't be happier for them. It added a dollop of pressure to being the perfect girlfriend that Carly wasn't quite sure she could live up to.

In the beginning, she hadn't put much thought into the dress she was wearing tonight. Since her stuff was in storage, she had to borrow from her sister. Gina, being five years younger and having never left home, did not have a lot of formalwear to choose from. Despite being a redhead, or maybe because of it, the one formal dress Gina owned was a deep red number that was off the shoulder and cut low in the front with a snug waistline and a skirt that flared just below her knees.

Carly remembered that James's had said red was his favorite color the very first day she met him when he complimented Mac's aunt Sarah on her red-streaked hair. At the moment, she took it as a sign from the universe that only having access to a red dress meant that dating James was the right thing to do.

Carly hoped cocktail length was okay; since she was on the short side, she really didn't like full-length gowns, especially when they hid her shoes. What was the point of having sexy shoes if no one got to see them? She had borrowed a pair of shoes from Emma, which were sparkly black sandals with an ankle strap that she hoped would invite wicked intentions from James.

She glanced at the clock on her phone. She planned to be ready and out of the room before James returned from coordinating the valet he had hired to manage the parking.

She'd already made plans with Lola to have pre-dinner cocktails in her room before the party. While overseeing the decorating this morning, the two of them had agreed it might take the edge off dealing with the others, and by others, they meant the A Factor and Horrible.

Carly checked her reflection in the mirror. She had done her hair in a half-up half-down do, so it was sophisticated but also playful. Her makeup was a bit heavier than usual, but she had spent hours over the past few months perfecting the cat eye with her eyeliner and she was darned if she wasn't going to use it. Her lipstick matched the red of her dress perfectly and she had lined her lips, making them look just a bit fuller and more kissable.

She stepped into the dress and zipped it up the side, adjusting the girls and smoothing the skirt. Then she put on her shoes and grabbed her black clutch and her phone. She paused one more time in front of the mirror to check her reflection from all angles. It was as good as it was going to get.

She realized that before last night she would have put on the dress and figured James could like it or not, she wouldn't have cared since she was here as part of their bargain, but now everything had changed. Now she was his girl-friend, plus she had the A Factor to contend with so she wanted to make a good impression for James; okay, more than a good impression. She wanted to wow him and everyone else.

She felt a nervous flutter in her belly and realized she desperately wanted James to be proud that she was his date. She put her hand over her stomach. Was this dating then? Caring about someone else's opinion more than your own? Ugh, this sucked ass.

Stepping away from the mirror before she had a total panic-induced meltdown and overthought everything, Carly hurried down the spiral staircase and through the walkway to the main house. She passed the caterers and waitstaff, who were scrambling to finish prepping the last minute details. She smiled at them and noted the looks of approval. Feeling more confident, she strode to the guest room Lola was staying in and knocked on the door.

"Hey, Lola, are we still on for drinks?" she asked.

The door opened and Lola stood there in a beautiful pewter gray chiffon number with a matching beaded top. She looked lithe and lovely and Carly felt a brief pang of envy for Lola's slender figure; then she remembered that James was clearly a boob guy and suddenly she felt pretty good about her curves. It was a nice feeling.

"Oh, my god," Lola said as her gaze took in Carly from her head to her feet. "James is going to have a heart attack, no, an aneurism, no, probably he'll just be sporting serious wood when he gets a look at you."

"Did you just say 'wood' in regard to your own brother?" Carly asked. She tried to sound appalled but it was a lie; Lola's reaction was just what she needed to get through the evening. Well, that and a glass of wine.

"I did," Lola said. She gestured for Carly to enter. "Is that bad form? James says I have no filter but I like to think I'm just being honest. And I am honestly telling you that when he gets a load of you in that showstopper, he's going to be tight in the trous—"

"I got it," Carly said. "And thank you, I think."

"Just speaking the truth," Lola said. She nodded her head in the direction of her room. "Come on, we've got about forty-five minutes until we have to be out there to meet and greet, which is just enough time to have a drink or two, three if we chug."

They sat on the small sofa in the corner of the room. Lola poured them each a glass of wine and then she asked polite but pointed questions, leaving Carly in no doubt that Lola was looking out for her big brother by vetting his new girlfriend even if it was a little late for it.

Carly figured she'd better be square with Lola. If this thing with James did go anywhere, she didn't want to have to clean up a hazardous waste site full of half-truths and evasions. That being said, no one needed to know the specifics of what had happened between her and Preston. James knew about her humiliation and he was one more than enough.

"Did you really pick up James using that line?" Lola asked, after demanding to know the truth about how they'd met.

"I did," Carly said. She glanced at Lola over the rim of her glass. "It works like a charm every time."

"I like you, Carly DeCusati." Lola grinned but then grew abruptly serious. "But I have to warn you that if you hurt my brother, I will cut out your heart with a rusty spoon."

Carly blinked at her. "You know sometimes your honesty is terrifying."

"Which is likely why I'm still single," Lola said. "It'll take a man made of hardy stock to put up with all the truths I have to share."

"He'll be a man worth having then," Carly said. They clinked glasses and polished off their wine.

"I hope you're talking about me," James said as he entered the room.

Carly almost choked on her wine—another good

reason for always wearing red—as she got an eyeball full of the man who from this day forward would be known in her mind as Sex in a Tux.

Lola turned to her with a grin and Carly cringed. "Did I say that out loud?"

"Yeah, you did."

"Do you think he heard me?"

"Let's see. Hey, big brother, did you hear Carly just call you Sex in a Tux?"

"Oh, jeez . . ." Carly felt her face get hot and she gave Lola a dark look. This blushing thing was out of control. She used a hand to fan her face, trying to make it go away.

A wicked smile, just a little higher on the right side, slowly bloomed across James's lips.

"I did not," he said. "Thanks for letting me know."

"My work here is done," Lola said. She set her glass down and rose to her feet. "See you out there, kids."

She headed for the door with an air kiss and a wave. Carly waited until the door closed behind her before she stood and turned to face James.

He looked like he was about to say something and then his jaw went slack. His gaze took her all in and then swept over her, lingering on each part in turn, from the cleavage that showed in the V of her dress, to her nipped-in waist, and lastly her legs, now five inches longer thanks to the high heels she'd strapped on.

Carly supposed it was cheating to make herself taller and thinner than she actually was, but it wasn't like they were permanent alterations—they were more like temporary tattoos. Besides, the cleavage, which was where James's gaze had landed again and again, was real and it was spectacular.

"You are beautiful," he said. "No, wait, that's not the right word. Gorgeous, no, stunning, no, oh, I know . . . incandescent."

"Like a light bulb?" she asked.

"Well, you're turning me on," he said.

Carly giggled. Carly never giggled. She clapped a hand over her mouth as if she could stop the ridiculous noise coming out of her face hole. She couldn't. She giggled again.

James took advantage of her fit to swoop in so that he was mere inches away from her. As if afraid to touch her, he held her by the shoulders as he lowered his mouth to hers in the gentlest kiss Carly had ever received.

When he leaned back, she could feel the buzz from his mouth on hers and she tapped her lower lip with her finger. She looked at him in question.

"I'm afraid I'll mess up your hair or makeup if I do what I really want to do to you," he said. His voice was thick with desire.

Carly shrugged. "It'd be worth it."

James closed his eyes and hissed out a breath. "Nope, no, nuh uh, I'm going to be a good boy and bring you to Pops's birthday bash like I'm supposed to and not haul you upstairs to my room and make love to you until we're both crippled."

"Eightieth birthday party versus losing all feeling in my legs. Hmm." Carly held her hands out as if they were a scale. "Yeah, okay, birthday party it is until the moment it's socially acceptable for us to ghost out of there."

"So sassy, I like it," James said. He swatted her behind as Carly sashayed by him and she yelped.

"Hey, now," she said. "We've never discussed spankings, which for the record I've never tried but would be totally willing to give a go with you."

James froze. He blinked repeatedly and swallowed as if trying to ease a sudden constriction in his throat.

"Okay, I just need a minute," he said. Then he shuddered from his head to his feet and held out one arm to her. "All right, I'm good."

Carly tucked her hand around his elbow, which brought his arm up against her cleavage. He glanced down at where her boob pressed into his arm.

"Eyes up here, big guy," Carly teased him. When his gaze met hers, she leaned close and said, "By the way, Lydia Husser from Penmans called and offered me the job, and I accepted."

James blinked at her once. "You're staying."

It wasn't a question, but Carly nodded anyway.

The next thing Carly knew James had her pinned to the wall and he was kissing her with a single-minded intensity that made her ears ring.

Carly put her hands on his shoulders to hang on during the erotic plundering but when his hands cupped her behind and brought her in close, she responded by twining her arms about his neck and pulling him in even closer.

"You're staying." He said it again as if he had to repeat it to fully grasp the fact that she wasn't leaving.

"I take it that's okay," she said, hissing out a breath as his lips slid up her neck.

"More than okay," he said. He kissed her again and against her lips, he growled, "It's perfect."

As his tongue slid against hers, his busy hands pulled up her skirt until his hands met the bare skin of her thighs. He groaned and it was the most erotic sound Carly had ever heard. When his questing fingers found the edge of her comfy cotton undies, she felt him grin against her lips.

"That's my girl," he said. "You wore those for me, didn't you?"

"Well, you did say last night that I should always wear them," she said. She batted her lashes at him.

"Just knowing that you're wearing those is going to drive me crazy all night."

He began to edge them down to gain access to

her wet heat when there was a knock, causing them both to start.

"James, Carly, are you coming?" Emily, his mother, called through the door.

James met Carly's gaze and gave her a wicked toe-curling grin.

"Two more minutes and we could have been," he growled in Carly's ear and she snorted. He leaned back and yelled at the door. "We'll be right there."

"Your father is waiting, meet us out front," she said.

James pressed his forehead against Carly's and took a deep breath as if he was inhaling her.

"Is it wrong that I wish they'd all go away?"

"Not wrong, exactly," she said.

She reached up to straighten his tie and smooth his hair while he fixed her dress. There was an intimacy found here, in this tender caring for each other that felt more vulnerable than when they bared their bodies to each other. It made Carly's heart melt.

When they were respectable again, James offered her his arm, and they left Lola's room to go join the others. As Carly glanced around the great room, she felt pleased with how it had all turned out. Circular tables were set up all along the perimeter of the room with a temporary square dance floor laid out at the far end.

Large white paper lanterns were strung across

the high ceiling, bathing the room in an ambient glow, while the tables were decked out in royal blue cloths and silver runners.

The band was already warming up on the riser beside the dance floor and the room was filling up with guests. The party stager that she'd hired had placed large bare branches the size of small trees in big pots and decked them in blue and white lights and stationed them all around the room and outside on the large deck beyond.

"Carly, darling, you did an amazing job," Emily said. She hugged her close.

"Truly, it's fantastic," Jimmy agreed, also giving her a quick hug.

"Thank you," she said. She didn't say it out loud, because she didn't want to be braggy, but she totally agreed with them. This felt like it was her finest hour and not just because the party looked awesome and she had a new job and some hot man candy on her arm either.

"It's beautiful," James said. Then he leaned close and whispered, "But not nearly as spectacular as you."

That right there. That's what he did to her, making her heart stutter and her face get hot. She was pretty sure a girl could get addicted to that sort of singular attention.

"You know, it would be a lovely place to hold a wedding," Emily said. James gave his mother a look and she shrugged. "What? It is."

"And your mother is always right about these things," Jimmy said. He leaned in to kiss his wife.

"Uh-oh, here they go again," James said, but he was smiling when he said it.

Carly smiled at the couple. Emily was in a purple velvet wraparound gown that hugged every line of her curvy figure, while Jimmy was in a tuxedo, much like James. Carly could see Emily in James's eyes and chin, but he definitely had Jimmy's broad shoulders and lopsided smile.

"Come on, let's go check out the sunset," James said. He ushered Carly outside.

Carly shivered in her dress and regretted that she hadn't thought to bring a wrap. James put his arm around her waist and pulled her close to his side as they stepped through the open French doors to enjoy the view. His warmth pushed away the evening's chill and Carly realized that this was another perk of a boyfriend. They were always there to keep a gal warm.

The deck overlooked the ocean, and they watched as the fiery orange globe that was the sun slipped behind the horizon line, sending the last of its rays up into the clouds, painting them in luscious shades of pink and orange. It was a breathtaking sunset, the sort that felt like a gift.

"It's stunning, isn't it?" Carly asked.

"Yes," James said.

She turned to find his gaze on her face and she smiled.

"I was talking about the sunset."

"Oh, I was talking about you."

Then he kissed her.

"And they're at it again," Tom said to Lola as they joined them. "I swear they're as bad as your parents."

"That's nothing. You should have heard them last night," Lola said. "They were above me in the lighthouse and still all I heard all night was—"

"Lorelei." James's voice held a note of warning.

"Yes, brother dearest?" she asked, arching her diamond-studded eyebrow.

"You look beautiful," he said.

Lola's eyes widened in surprise. She turned to Tom as if to see if he'd heard James, too, and then Carly.

"I don't think Jamie has ever complimented me before. You are a wonderful influence on him," she said to Carly.

"Love will do that for a guy," Tom said.

Carly felt her heart pound triple time in her chest. The "L" word! Now? She was barely used to having a boyfriend, never mind having the "L" word tossed about as casually as a Frisbee. She was afraid to look at James for fear she'd see the same discomfort on his face that she was feeling.

Instead, he shocked her by saying, "You must be right, Tom. Now excuse us while I go trot my girl around the dance floor. I want to show her off."

"If you weren't so disgustingly perfect together, I swear I'd throw up," Lola said. "Now go away but look for me at dinner. We're sitting together."

"Shouldn't we be mingling, wishing Pops a happy birthday, or at least pretending to socialize?" Carly asked.

"We will," he said. "But first, I just need you in my arms for a minute."

They slipped onto the dance floor amidst a few other couples. James held one of her hands in his and put the other on her hip. While they stepped carefully around the floor, he studied her face. She wondered what he saw when he looked at her. Did he see a woman who was falling in love with him? Is that why he didn't say anything about what Tom said? Was she that obvious?

Because, yeah, she could pretend it was just infatuation, but the truth was she'd never had anyone make her feel like James did, like she was something lovely and precious, a person worthy of being cherished. It was intoxicating and she realized she never wanted to sober up.

Chapter 30

Carly had just found her rhythm with James, who did not like to step out of his comfortable box step, when they were interrupted by Pops.

"Birthday boy privilege," he said. He held up his hand to stop James's protest.

James shrugged at Carly and handed her over to Pops.

"I have my eye on you," James said. He used two fingers to point to his eyes and then at Pops. "Do not try to steal my girl."

Pops laughed. "If I manage to steal her then she wasn't really yours to begin with, now was she?"

With that, he waltzed Carly away from James in a snappy swing step that brought them out to the middle of the floor. Pops kept his hand in the middle of her back, very proper, while Carly kept hers on his shoulder. Although he was a bit stooped now with age, Carly could tell that in his heyday, Pops had had the same broad shoulders as his son and grandson.

When he glanced down at her, he smiled and like most of the Sinclair men, his smile was just a bit higher on one side, giving them all a rakish charm.

"Will you promise me something?"

"Sure," she agreed without hesitation.

"Make him chase you," Pops said.

"Okaaaay."

"You haven't been, have you?" He gave her a friendly scolding look.

Carly smiled. "Probably not as much as I should."

"That's what I figured," he said. He grinned at her. "That's why I cut in. Don't want the boy to get too comfortable."

"Is that what your wife did to you?" she asked. "Make you chase her so you wouldn't get too comfortable?"

Pops nodded. "We were married for fifty-six years, and I spent fifty-five of those chasing that woman. The only time she gave me a break was the last year when she was too sick to run."

There was a sheen in his eyes and Carly felt a lump form in her throat and she squeezed his hand in a show of empathy. Pops squeezed her hand back and they exchanged a look of complete understanding.

"I love all of my grandkids," Pops said. "But James, well, he's something special. He always was. He never let another kid be without a friend, he always had some scraggly critter or another he was trying to save, and when my Ginny was dying, he never went a day without checking on her. He'd spend hours reading her favorite books to her, which was pretty funny because she did love the steamy romances. He even read the racy parts, twice if she asked him to."

A tear leaked out of Pops's eye, and Carly felt her own eyes water up.

"Now don't cry," Pops said. "I don't want him to think I'm saying mean things to you."

Carly snorted as she tried to push back the tears, which made Pops laugh.

"That's better," he said. "Now I'm going to spin you, so he can see how slick my dance moves are. We need to make him worry that he's got some competition so he doesn't get lazy."

Carly glanced over to the edge of the dance floor where James was standing beside his cousin Tom. Tom was talking and James was nodding, but his eyes were trained on Carly and Pops.

"He's not looking lazy now," she said.

"And he won't be for the remainder of the evening," Pops said. He waggled his bushy gray eyebrows at her and Carly narrowed her eyes at him.

"What are you up to?" she asked.

"Me?" Pops blinked at her. He was the very picture of innocence. "Not a thing."

He spun her right into Jimmy's arms, who shared a grin and a look of understanding with his father before he whisked Carly away.

And so it continued for the next several songs, as Carly was passed from father to uncle to cousin to cousin to uncle to friend of the family and lastly to cousin Tom, until dinner was announced.

During the course of the dances, Carly learned that James had been a champion skier until he fractured his leg, he was a straight-A student and graduated top of his class—except for art, apparently he couldn't draw to save his life— his favorite dessert was brownies, he once backpacked from Maine to Florida all by himself, he loved motorcycles, and when he was a little boy, he had a plush golden retriever stuffie that he took everywhere with him and it was named Woof.

When Tom spun Carly into James's waiting arms, she was numb from the knee down but felt as if she now knew the man standing before her better than she knew even her closest male friends.

"Hi," she said.

"Hi back," he said. "I missed you, sunshine."

She grinned. "I think that was Pops's plan."

James cast his grandfather a mock dark look but Pops was busy checking out his four-tier whoopie pie cake, which Carly had spent most of the afternoon putting together, and wasn't paying them any attention. Carly laughed when Pops tried to stick his finger into the thick white filling of one of the pies but Emily snatched his hand away before he could connect.

"I like your family," Carly said. She smiled up at James and he hugged her close.

"I'm glad," he said. He put his arm around her

waist and led her to the table where Lola was waiting with Tom and the other cousins who Carly suspected were favorites.

Dinner was all of Pops's favorite dishes, which meant lobster and steak with hardly a vegetable in sight. One of the cousins who was vegan looked grumpily at her salad as she eyed the lobster tail on the plate next to her.

"I swear Pops is trying to crack my resolve," she said.

"Mine, too," James whispered in Carly's ear.

She glanced at him and smiled.

"He loves you very much," she said. "He told me so."

"I love him, too," James said. "Both he and Gram were always in my corner, you know? When I couldn't talk to my parents about what was happening in my life, I could always talk to them."

"Pops told me how good you were to your Gram when she was ill," Carly said. She put her hand on his arm. "He said you were very kind, especially about reading her favorite books to her."

James leaned over and kissed her. It was swift and chaste but Carly got the feeling that if they hadn't been at the dinner table with eight others, it would have crossed over into the hot and raunchy zone in a nanosecond.

"There was nothing kind about it. Do you know

how much I learned about women by reading those books to Gram? Hoo dang, it was like an accelerated class in sex ed, but, you know, it was the stuff you really need to know, not the other junk."

Carly burst out laughing. Then she leaned close and whispered in his ear, "So, is that where you learned to do that thing with your mouth and your fingers?"

James turned to look at her, bringing his face just an inch from hers. He studied her mouth as if thinking about what he wanted to do there, and then a slow smile spread across his lips and he said, "Yep."

"Oh, my," Carly sighed and his grin deepened.

As the plates were being cleared, James excused himself for a moment. Carly watched him leave the room, admiring the way his tuxedo molded itself to his tall, lithe form. She'd been right before. The man was definitely sex in a tux.

"Carly, how about a dance?"

She glanced over her shoulder to see Preston standing there. His nose was swollen. She tried not to feel too much satisfaction in that and failed miserably. He was staring at her with a confused look on his face, as if he was missing something but he wasn't sure what.

"Um, I don't think that's a great idea," she said.

She noticed that half of their table had already left to go back to the dance floor and the other half was deep in conversation. Without Lola, Tom, or James, she really had no buffer against Preston.

He seemed to realize the same thing at the same moment and his smile turned cold and a bit cruel. How had she ever found this man attractive?

"Come on," he said. He held out his hand and when she didn't take it immediately, he leaned over her and hissed, "It would be a shame for everyone to find out about the order of protection I took out on you, wouldn't it? Bet Pops wouldn't be so enamored of you then, would he?"

Carly blew out a breath. She took her napkin off her lap and tossed it onto her plate. Even though James knew about the restraining order, she would be absolutely mortified if anyone else found out. How could she possibly explain it in a way that made her sound not crazy? She couldn't.

She put her hand in Preston's cold, soft one and immediately missed James's callused warmth. She knew as she followed him out onto the dance floor that this was going to be the longest dance of her life.

He held her too close. She pushed him back. His hand felt clammy through the fabric of her dress and she tried not to think about whether she'd be able to get sweat stains out of Gina's favorite dress, which she didn't exactly know that Carly had borrowed since Carly hadn't asked her beforehand.

"So, you and James, huh?" Preston asked.

Carly said nothing. She'd found that while men often complained about overly emotional women, much like Preston had about her when he'd dumped her a few days after sleeping with her, they were completely stymied when it came to women who didn't offer any emotion at all.

"How long have you two been together?" he asked.

Carly maintained her stony silence and continued to stare over his shoulder at the other people on the dance floor. Despite the obvious amount of booze he had consumed, Preston managed to maneuver around the floor like a man who had taken his fair share of dance classes. She wondered if that had been Heather's doing.

"Really?" he asked. Now he sounded irritated. "You're not going to speak to me?"

Carly didn't say anything but she did turn to look him in the eye. She hoped all of the contempt and loathing she felt for him was flashing like a neon sign. Of course, since he was such a narcissist, it was unlikely he would read it that way.

"Listen, I get that you're pissed at me," he said. He ran his hand up and down her back in what she assumed was supposed to be a soothing gesture. It only annoyed. "What I did was a dick move."

Carly lifted her eyebrows. Was he about to apologize? She might go into shock.

"But you made it way more than it was supposed to be," he said. "I never really asked you out. I was pretty clear that I was just after one thing."

Carly tripped and he caught her around the waist, using the opportunity to pull her up against him. Carly felt her gag reflex kick in. She pushed back against him, trying to put some space between them, but he was bigger and stronger and had locked his hands together behind her back.

"Let me get this straight," she said. "Are you saying that I deserved what you did because I didn't pick up on the fact that you were just out to win a bet to relieve me of my virginity?"

Preston shrugged. "Yeah."

Carly glanced over her shoulder. The urge to knee him in the junk was almost more than she could endure. She forced it back down, refusing to make a scene at Pops's birthday bash.

"I followed you last night," he said. "I saw you and James in the lighthouse."

"Oh, my god," she said. "You watched us?"

"Yeah, it was totally hot," he said. He pressed his crotch up against her and Carly felt his erection through his pants. "I bet it would be way hotter between you and me, just like it was that last time, right?"

"Are you insane?" Carly asked. He danced her into a corner and she shoved him off her, sending him into the wall. "I wouldn't sleep with you again on a bet. Oh, wait, that's right. That's *your* game, not mine, you manipulative prick."

She turned and began to walk away from him, but Preston pushed off the wall and grabbed her arm.

"Don't you walk away from me," he said.

"Remove your hand or you'll pull back a bloody stump," she said.

"Always so dramatic," Preston mocked. He used his other hand to cup her breast and he squeezed it. "You know you still want me, and I can totally have you if I want."

"No. You. Can't," Carly snarled. "Because no means no, asshole."

When she tried to shake him off, he refused to let go, leaving her no other choice. She stepped in close and at the last second she jerked her knee right up into his privates.

Preston dropped her arm and doubled over. His pale face turned a mottled shade of burgundy with a nice tinge of green. He was cradling his nuts with both hands and gasping like a fish out of water. Carly did not feel badly for him, not even a little.

"Carly, are you all right? What the hell just

happened?" James shouted, looking like he wanted to rip his cousin apart.

"Preston walked into my knee," Carly said. "Isn't that right, Preston?"

"Argh," Preston choked. He shoved his hand in a nearby water pitcher and grabbed some ice cubes, which he then held over his crotch. "You're pissed at me for manipulating you? Well, wake up sweetheart, I'm not the only one."

"What?" Carly asked. Maybe his brains really were in his pants because right now he wasn't even making sense.

"Ask him," Preston wheezed as he jerked his head at James. "Ask him abou—"

"Don't!" James snapped at Preston. "Don't say it."

He hooked Carly by the elbow and started to pull her away.

"Don't say what?" Carly glanced between them. "What are you talking about, Preston?"

"Ask him about that job offer you got today," Preston said. "Ask him about Pops's being on the board of Penmans."

Carly's eyes went wide.

"That's right," Preston said. His tone was mocking. "We all know about your new job because James made it happen. He had Pops call in a few Sinclair favors. Congratulations."

Carly glanced at James and saw his nostrils flare; he looked like he wanted to punch Preston again. She felt her heart sink as the truth of the situation flattened her spirits. Of course James had gotten the job for her. She should have known that the job, much like this relationship, was too good to be true.

Chapter 31

"Tell her, Jamie, tell her the truth." With a laugh that resembled a villain's cackle, Preston scuttled off in the direction of his table.

A large whooshing noise filled Carly's ears and she looked at James, really looked at him, so she could see the truth in his eyes.

"Say it isn't so," she begged him. "Please."

"I wanted to talk to you about it first," James said. "But—"

"But what?" she cried. "You couldn't find the time? No, we've had plenty of that. You couldn't find the words? No, your powers of speech are just fine. So, why? Why didn't you tell me?"

"Listen, I really didn't do that much," he said. "The résumé was all yours and you wowed them at the interview—"

"Did I, really?" she asked. "Just how much did you have Pops grease the wheels to get them to hire me? I probably could have shown up in a Viking hat and a wet suit and gotten the job, is that it?"

"I didn't," he argued. "I told Pops you were interviewing, and he merely suggested to Lydia that she might want to look at your résumé. He just got it in front of the right pair of eyes."

"Seriously? That's the best you've got?"

"Hey, you two, come on," Lola shouted as she dashed past them. "Pops is about to start dividing up the cake. You'd better hurry because I am not saving anyone a whoopie pie!"

"Can we talk about this later?" James held out his hand to her but Carly shook him off.

"I need a minute," she said. She turned and headed toward the bathroom, grabbing her purse off the table as she went. Her throat was tight and she was sure she was about to dissolve into a puddle of tears. When James went to follow her, she turned back and snapped, "No."

He sagged against the wall, looking upset. Too bad.

She didn't go to the bathroom. Instead, she walked past it, out the front door of the house, and into the front yard where the hipsters in the family were vaping. Tom was among them and he waved her over when he saw her.

"Having a good time?" he asked.

He puffed out a plume of vapor that hit the night air like a fine mist. A fine mist that smelled like bubblegum. Carly wrinkled her nose.

"It's disgusting, I know," he said. "But much better than the smokes I used to puff."

"I suppose," she said. She rubbed her arms with her hands. It was freezing out here and she had no idea what she was doing or why she was out here.

"Oh, hey, here," Tom said. He shrugged off his

jacket and draped it around her shoulders.

"Oh, you don't have to do that," she said. "I'm fine."

"No, you're not. You're clearly freezing. Besides, what sort of gentleman would I be if I didn't have you wear my coat?" he asked. "A lousy one, that's what. I insist."

He gave her no choice but to accept. Carly snuggled into the coat, appreciating the warmth.

"Hey, you guys, you're going to miss singing and cake!" a cousin whose name Carly didn't remember cried from the door.

"Oh, right then, let's go," Tom said.

They all put away their paraphernalia and headed toward the door. Tom glanced at Carly and she gave him a weak smile.

"I'm right behind you," she said.

He nodded and the rest of them went inside. Carly felt the unmistakable burn of tears and she tried to push them back before they ruined her perfectly applied cat eye. Sensing failure, she checked Tom's pocket for a hanky or a tissue. There was nothing. Nothing but a claim stub for the parking valet. Interesting.

Without overthinking it, Carly handed over a small blue slip of paper and the valet nodded at her and said, "Right away, miss."

He opened a box and matched the ticket to a set of keys and then dashed off into the parking area.

"Your car, miss." In minutes, the valet appeared

in front of her, driving a brand-new bright green Hellcat. Carly tipped her head to the side as she considered it. Yes, it would do.

She opened her purse and pulled out a fifty-dollar bill. She handed it to the valet, whose eyes went wide as she shrugged off Tom's jacket and handed that to him, too.

"Please see that Tom Sinclair gets his jacket back," she said.

She climbed into the driver's seat of the car, adjusted the seat, and strapped herself in. Thank goodness her father had insisted that all of his daughters learn to drive a stick shift in case they found themselves in an emergency where that was the only viable means of transportation.

Carly pushed in the clutch, put the car in gear, and stomped on the gas. She sprayed some gravel, making the valet jump back. The sports car had a lot more life in it than the Camaro her father had taught her to drive. She waved an apology, shifted into a higher gear, and shot down the long drive.

At first she was terrified by the raw power under the hood, but by the end of James's private road, she felt as if she was getting the hang of it, plus it suited her reckless mood. She was getting the hell out of here, away from James and whatever his dubious plans involving her had been, the sooner the better.

She stopped before turning onto the street that

would bring her back to town. She heard her phone ring in her purse. She opened it and snatched it out. It was James, shocker. She switched her phone off and tossed it back into her bag.

Then she drove, just drove. In the silence, the memory of that night so long ago began to fill in the void. It was eleven years ago, when she'd been dating Preston or, more accurately, when she thought she'd been dating Preston. Their business major cohort had gone out for beers at a pub in New York. They'd been celebrating getting through finals by drinking themselves stupid.

She'd been feeling very full of herself not only because she had aced her finals but also because Preston Bradley had finally noticed her. He'd been hanging around her for weeks, they'd studied together, had a few meals together, he'd even kissed her twice. She was pretty sure they were dating, and she was certain she was in love with him.

Carly had worn a red dress and left her hair loose the way she knew he liked it. When the hour grew late and the group began to pack it in one by one, Preston had a surprise visitor. He was about their age and cute in a laid back sort of way; Carly didn't really pay attention because all of her focus was on Preston. It did register that the guy was a relative and he seemed very intent on talking to Preston, who in his usual arrogant way did not seem to care.

While Preston played one more round of darts with his friends, Carly had made small talk with the cousin. The cousin, who was studying to be a physical therapist. It was James! The memory hit her like a slap across the face and she struggled, trying to remember as much as she could.

It was hard bringing the fuzzy details into sharper focus. She hadn't paid much attention at the time, because it was difficult to converse with anyone while fixating on Preston. Eventually, the dart game wound down and the group left the pub and headed home. When they reached Preston's apartment, he insisted that everyone come in for more drinks and the party had continued on.

She had seen Preston in an intense conversation with his cousin and shortly thereafter, James had left the party, but not before pausing beside her. He had looked her right in the eye and said, "You deserve better," and then he had left.

She realized that James's conversation with Preston that night had likely been about Heather. Irrational or not, she really wished he had mentioned the other woman to her that night. Clearly, his desire to meddle in her life hadn't reached full bloom until now.

How could he have had Pops intervene on her behalf? He knew she had busted her butt to put on the presentation of her life. Did he think she couldn't get the job on her own? Why would James have called Pops to manipulate the whole thing for her if he thought she was any good at what she did?

Clearly, he didn't believe in her. And that's what hurt the most. She had really thought that he saw her as a professional woman, who knew what she was doing, but no, she was just another "rescue" of his.

He'd ruined everything. She didn't know if she got the job on her own merit or if the mighty Sinclair name had done the trick for her. The mere idea of getting the job because of connections made her want to throw up. And the real pisser was that she'd been so excited about this job. She was going to be buying for the entire women's department, not just the lingerie.

The people she'd met at Penmans had been so welcoming and with such a positive corporate outlook that she'd been willing to overlook the fact that she'd be staying in Maine. But now, that was all tainted by James and his need to "fix" things. Grr.

Carly gripped the steering wheel. Now she was sorry she'd only kneed one Sinclair man in the crotch tonight. She flipped on the radio, using the button on the steering wheel to change the stations until she found a tune that was blare worthy. As Taylor Swift wailed about her ex, Carly sang along, promising that she and James were never, ever, ever getting back together.

In fact, now that she had been burned by two Sinclair men, she was quite certain she was never ever going to let any man into her life ever again, except for the ones who really were her friends.

"Oh, my god!" Zach cried into the phone so loudly that Carly had to hold it away from her ear. "You stole a car!"

"Borrowed," Carly corrected him. "I borrowed it, there is a difference."

She stared at the red traffic light, willing it to turn. She could not put enough distance between her and James.

"Tell me it was a minivan or some other useless POS," he said. He sounded as if he was begging.

"Hellcat, green, SRT, six-speed, V-8," she said.

"Holy crap!" Zach said. He gave a low whistle. "This I gotta see. Where are you?"

"I'm driving to the bakery," she said. "I'm parking it there for the night. Can you pick me up?"

"On my way," Zach said.

He ended the call and Carly put her phone away. It was the first time it had been active since she'd left the party. She'd lost track of the time as she drove around town, trying to get her head together. A quick glance told her there were three voice mails and five text messages, all from James.

The light turned green and she shut her phone

off again and tossed it back into her bag. She continued on to the bakery, hoping Tom forgave her for borrowing his car, but given the circumstances she didn't really care.

A few minutes later she pulled into the small lot behind Making Whoopie. She switched off the car and waited for Zach to arrive. It wasn't long before a pair of headlights flashed over her; she stepped out of the car, locking it and taking the keys with her. She'd have Zach deliver the keys to Tom later.

Zach parked his pickup truck beside Carly. She opened the passenger door and climbed in, not giving Zach a chance to open the door for her. She handed him the keys to the Hellcat.

"I'll need you to deliver those to James's cousin Tom for me," she said. "He's a nice guy and I'm pretty sure he won't punch the messenger in the face."

"Especially if I give him a ride back to his car." Zach looked past her at the Hellcat in all its beautiful sublime green glory. "You know there's probably a warrant out for your arrest right now."

"Wouldn't be the first time," she joked.

"Is it wrong that I have more respect for you than ever before?" he asked.

"Probably," she said.

"Where to, my dear?" he asked.

"Home," Carly said. "I need to go eat my feelings."

When they arrived at her house, Jillian's Jeep

was in the driveway. She glanced at Zach and he shrugged.

"I might have called the girls."

Carly reached over the console and hugged him. "Thanks."

The front door flew open before Carly was even out of the car. Jillian, followed by Mac, was racing toward her.

"What happened?"

"Did you really steal a car?"

"Where is he? I am going to crush him."

"Let's go inside," Carly said. "I cannot stand to be in this dress for another second."

"Good thing, since it's my dress," Gina said. She was standing on the front steps with her arms crossed over her chest, looking highly irritated.

"I'm sorry," Carly said. "I should have asked before I borrowed it." Her voice cracked and a tear slipped down her cheek.

Gina dropped her arms and tipped her head to the side. In one step, she pulled Carly close and hugged her hard.

"It's okay," she said. Her voice was gruff. "I don't care about the stupid dress. I'm just glad you're okay."

"Tears," Zach said with a nod. "That's my cue to leave. Call me if someone, and by someone I mean James, needs a beating, okay?"

Carly pulled out of Gina's arms and hugged Zach hard. "Thanks."

Zach hugged her back and kissed the top of her head. "Anytime, kid."

They watched him leave and then the friends stormed the kitchen, pulling all four tubs of ice cream out of the freezer as they sat down at the counter with spoons at the ready.

"Start talking," Mac said. She spooned up a mouthful of Maine blueberry before pushing the carton at Carly. "We have all night."

Chapter 32

Carly shoved a scoop of mint chocolate chip into her mouth. The sweet mint cream and chocolate chips made her taste buds happy and for a few seconds she was pretty sure she could shake off her upset. Then she swallowed and the happiness went with it. She knew it would take every bite in the half gallon to make her feel better, but once the ice cream was gone so would be the happiness.

She jammed her spoon into the ice cream and turned to Jillian. "Where are Ike and Saul?"

Jillian and Mac exchanged a worried look, and Carly felt her heart plummet down into her shoes.

"Did something happen to them?"

"No, not exactly," Jillian said.

"They just got attached," Mac said.

"Meaning what?"

"Show her," Jillian said.

"Follow me," Gina said. "For the record, I tried to discourage this."

Bewildered, Carly followed Gina and Mac down the hallway and into her parents' bedroom. Mac stepped up to the door and eased it open and peeked in before turning back to them and putting her index finger over her lips to indicate they should be quiet.

One by one they tiptoed into the room. There, on a doggy bed, released from his wheelie harness, was Hot Wheels. He was lying on his side, snoring, and pressed back to back with him was Saul. And there, wedged between their noses with his beak tucked under his feathers, was Ike.

"Ridiculously adorable, right?" Mac whispered. Neither the dogs nor the bird moved.

Carly felt her heart expand in her chest. She fell for the man and her bird and dog fell for his dog. In any other scenario, this would be the perfect happy ending. Instead, it just indicated more pain. She didn't know if she could take that.

In unspoken agreement, they left the room in single file, closing the door behind them.

Gina led the way back to the kitchen and handed Carly her spoon as if she knew her sister was going to need it. Carly dug out a scoop of raspberry cheesecake and shoved it in her mouth, hoping it would freeze the part of her heart that hurt right now.

"Sorry," Jillian said. "We didn't plan for a sleepover, but Hot Wheels seemed to miss James, and Ike and Saul clearly missed you, so Mac brought Hot Wheels around the shop and the next thing we knew the three of them were homeboys and we figured they'd be happiest here."

"A bird and two dogs, isn't that against the laws of nature?" Gina asked.

"I think that's more a bird and a cat," Jillian said. "Those three are ridiculously cute."

"I suppose," Carly said. "Too bad it's doomed."

"All right," Gina said. "We've been patient, really we have, but you have to tell us what happened between you and James before I go crazy."

"It's a long story," Carly said. She shoved more ice cream in her mouth to avoid answering in greater detail.

"Put down the spoon," Mac said. "You can start by telling us why Zach brought you home."

"Where's Emma?" Carly stalled. "I don't want to have to tell this story twice."

"She's on her way," Jillian said. "Don't worry. We'll catch her up to speed when she gets here."

Carly went to dig out a scoop of butter pecan, but Gina wrestled the spoon out of her hand. For such a petite thing, she was surprisingly strong. Carly glanced around the table to find her friends and her sister regarding her with expectant expressions. She wasn't going to be able to put this off any longer.

Then the doorbell sounded and Carly jumped off her stool, hoping to avoid the awkward conversation looming in front of her like a bout of indigestion.

"That'll be Emma," Carly cried. "I'll get it."

She hurried out of the kitchen before any of the others could beat her to it.

"This conversation isn't over!" Jillian called after her.

Relief propelled Carly swiftly down the hall. It wasn't that she minded sharing her latest relationship fiasco with her friends—that's what friends were for—it was more that it was just so fresh and she was feeling so raw that she didn't particularly want to relive each detail right now. She knew she'd be doing plenty of that in the weeks to come.

She stopped in the foyer and took a deep breath, putting her everything-is-fine smile firmly in place. She didn't want to upset Emma, since she was by far the most fragile of all Carly's friends.

She yanked open the door, and said, "Hi, Em—"

"You were expecting someone else?"

James stood in the doorway, arms crossed over his chest, his bow tie undone and hanging loosely about his open collar. His hair was standing on end and his mouth was compressed into a firm line. In short, he looked pissed.

"Emma, actually," Carly said. She began to close the door but James stuck his foot in the way.

"Oh, no," he said. "You don't get to close the door on me until you tell me why you left. Nice exit by the way. I think Tom had a small heart attack when you spewed gravel and punched it out of the driveway."

"Tell Tom I'm sorry," she said.

She stared over his shoulder while she spoke. She refused to make eye contact in case the sight of him weakened her resolve and she did something crazy like throw herself in his arms because he looked just that good.

"Carly, we need to talk about this," he said.

"Really? *Now* you want to talk?" She was furious.

She went to close the door again and James stepped forward, blocking it with his shoulder.

"I'm sorry," he said. "I should have told you about Pops's connection to Penmans. I didn't know Preston would find out about your job offer and say something before I could."

"So, you were just going to let this big lie sit between us?" she cried. "For how long, James? Until I passed probation on my new job?"

"I never lied to you," he said.

"Oh, my god, yes, you did!" she cried. "A lie of omission is still a lie."

"What was I supposed to say, Carly?" he asked.

"How about 'Hey, is it okay if I have Pops put in a good word for you at Penmans, because he happens to be on the board?' You know, asking my permission first. But you didn't, did you?"

James put his hand behind his neck. "I was just trying to help."

"Bullshit," she spat. "You were meddling in my life without my consent, and I know why. You're trying to keep me here instead of letting me go back to New York, where I clearly belong. You had no right."

There was a gasp and Carly looked over James's shoulder to see Emma standing on the porch. A glance back and she saw her squad all crammed in the doorway to the foyer, watching her with wide eyes.

James took advantage of her distraction to come into the house. Emma slipped in behind him and shut the door.

"Carly, I can explain," he said.

She held up her hands in a *back off* gesture. "Really, not necessary."

"Yes, it is," he insisted. "There's so much I need to tell you."

"Zach has Tom's keys," she said. "I parked his car at the bakery. It's all locked up. Hot Wheels is here, so you'd better collect him. Apparently, our pets have formed a pack but I expect they'll get over it. We all will."

"Carly, please, all I'm asking for is five minutes."

She didn't want to give him five seconds, never mind five minutes. Just being this close to him made her long to forget everything she had learned and jump into his arms and the heck with it all, but she would hate herself for it just like she hated her heart for cartwheeling about her chest at the sight of him.

"Five minutes and if at the end of it, you don't believe me, then I'll never bother you again," he said.

She glanced back at her friends. They were all staring at James as if they weren't sure whether to hit him or hug him. Carly understood exactly how they felt. She glanced at Mac, the accountant, the one who could always be relied upon to weigh the pros and cons before making a decision. Mac blew out a breath and then jerked her head in the direction of the living room. It was obvious she thought Carly should at least hear James out. Fine.

"Five minutes and not one second more," Carly said.

She felt her friends crowd into the foyer as if they thought they were coming, too. She shook her head no. Emma stomped her foot but they all stayed back. Carly gestured for James to go first and then she closed the door behind them.

They were both silent. Carly refused to speak first. She was not going to make this easy on him. If he wanted to confess that he had manipulated her for whatever reason, then he was going to have to choke out the words all on his own.

When James just stared at her, saying nothing, Carly got impatient. She glanced at the clock. "You only have four and a half minutes left."

"I'm sorry I didn't tell you that Pops is on the board at Penmans and that I asked him to recommend you," he said.

She snorted. "It was a little bit more than just a 'recommendation,' wasn't it?"

"No," he said. "It really wasn't. Look, my family has connections, no doubt, everyone loves Pops, but they wouldn't have offered you the job if you weren't the best candidate."

"Even if that's true, here's the problem, I don't believe you," she said. "By not telling me, you've made what I thought was a victory into a sham, and instead of boosting my confidence, you've gutted it."

"I should have told you," he said. He took a deep breath. "I get that now, but in my defense, you seemed so broken. You were struggling so hard to believe in yourself and your abilities, that I thought maybe I could fix you."

"Fix me?" Carly echoed. Her temper flared and her voice came out as a screech. "I'm sorry, did you just say 'fix me' like I have a flat tire or something?"

"No . . . maybe? I mean, look at your life. So much of it is because of my family."

"How do you figure?" she asked.

"You thought you were in love with my cousin when you lost your virginity to him on a bet for a pizza. How could that not mess with your head? Your relationship track record is all one-night stands, no commitments, never letting anyone get close enough to make you feel vulnerable," he said. "And when your company downsized and you lost your job, it was another blow to your self-esteem."

Carly couldn't argue that point.

"If Preston hadn't messed with your head," he said. He paused and clenched his fists as if he really wanted the chance to punch his cousin one more time. "Hell, if I had warned you away from him more strongly the night I met you eleven years ago, I could have spared you so much hurt."

"You're assuming I would have listened to you," she said.

"I should have said something more. I wish I'd made a bigger scene. I was there to chew him out about him and Heather and if I'd knocked him out like I wanted to—" He shook his head. "I just thought if I could get you a job here and you stayed in Maine then it would give you a do-over in both your personal and your professional life."

"Oh, my god, so I'm your charity case?"

"No! Carly, it's not like that, I swear. I think you're amazing, and I have from the moment I set eyes on you eleven years ago, really, but I'm a physical therapist. I fix people, it's what I do."

"So, this whole thing, starting up a relationship with me, dragging me to Pops's birthday party, making me face down Preston, *Preston Bradley* of all people, getting me a new job as a buyer at Penmans, all of it, was your idea of 'fixing me'? Tell me, was it because you care about me or was it because I just presented such an irresistible challenge, seeing as how I am so 'broken' and all?"

He glared at her, clearly frustrated, and then took a deep, calming breath.

"I know how it looks," he said. He rubbed his hand through his hair and she felt her chest compress at the familiar gesture. "But I swear, I was just trying to help y—"

"I'm sure you were," she interrupted. "But you never asked me if I wanted help."

"Because you would have said no," he protested.

"Exactly," she said. "And you should have respected that."

Anger unlike Carly had ever felt before pulsed through her. She had trusted him, she had fallen in love with him, and he had lied to her from the start. He opened his mouth to speak but she held up a hand, stopping him.

"I trusted you," she hissed. Then, without conscious thought, she shoved him, hard, throwing him off balance so that he landed on the couch in a heap. Carly loomed over him and spat, "And just so you know, I was never broken. Not until now!"

With that, she stormed out of the room, pushed past her friends, and raced up the stairs to her bedroom, where she slammed the door so hard it rattled.

Chapter 33

James took Hot Wheels with him when he left. Ike was put in his cage in the kitchen with no argument from Gina but with much protesting and a little profanity from Ike. Carly could hear all of this happening from her bedroom, but she stayed on her bed, letting her pillow soak up the tears that spilled from her eyes in what felt like an endless waterfall.

She hadn't cried over a man since Preston, and looking back, she realized she hadn't been crying over him at all, more like the idea of him. But these tears, these were real. This time Carly knew exactly what she had lost, and it hurt so freaking bad she kind of wished James's sister had cut out her heart with a rusty spoon. She was certain it would hurt less.

There was a soft knock at the door and Carly squeezed her eyes shut, wanting whoever it was to go away. She knew if she was one of the crew she'd be on the other side of the door, doing the gentle knocking, so she tried to rally, really she did.

"Yeah?" she called. Her voice sounded as if it had been scraped raw and she cringed.

The door was pushed open and a shock of red hair appeared. Gina. "Are you okay?"

"Not really up for seeing anyone right now, okay?"

"I figured," Gina said. "That's why I kicked them all out, but I live here so you're kind of stuck with me."

Carly stared at her baby sister. She was still wearing Gina's dress, which she was sure she had crumpled beyond repair at this point.

"I'm sorry. I think I've ruined your dress," Carly said.

Gina stepped into the room and softly closed the door behind her. She crossed over to the bed and nudged Carly until there was enough room for her to climb up beside her.

"I don't care about the dress," Gina said. She reached out and smoothed Carly's hair down her back. It was the softest of touches, like a mother soothing a child. It made Carly's throat grow tight again. "I care about you. Are you okay?"

"Not really," Carly said. She closed her eyes tight. "I was such an idiot."

"No, you weren't," Gina said. "You fell in love—"

"No, I didn't," Carly protested.

"Puhleeze." Gina rolled her eyes. "I know what love looks like in all of its many torturous forms. For what it's worth, I think James loves you, too."

"No, he doesn't," Carly said. "I was such a moron. His Pops even told me that James is a fixer, a gatherer of wounded animals and people,

439

the friend to the friendless, he fixes them up and then releases them back into the world."

"Well, I'd say you're the wild one he didn't tame," Gina said. "Judging by that shove you gave him at any rate."

Carly grunted. She could still feel her hands connecting with his chest. "I feel a little bad about that. He didn't deserve it."

"Hmm, the girls and I were listening at the door, and I didn't catch all of it, but let me sum up, if I may," Gina said. "The two of you actually met eleven years ago, about the same time you lost your virginity while dating his cousin Preston, on a bet over a pizza, setting in motion your no-relationship lifestyle. How am I doing so far?"

"Pretty good. For complete disclosure, I have to be honest and say that while I thought Preston and I were a couple, he never did, not really," Carly said. She didn't look at her sister while she spoke, not wanting to see the pity on her face. "Thus when he ditched me, I did some light stalking and he hit me with an order of protection. Good times."

Gina blinked at her. The shock in her eyes almost made Carly laugh—almost. It came out as a strangled sob instead. Gina squeezed her hand and shook her head as if she couldn't believe what she was hearing.

"Okay, if I ever see that rat bastard, I may have to punch him in the junk," Gina said.

"Already took care of it," Carly said. A ghost of a smile passed across her lips and Gina high-fived her.

"That's my girl," her sister continued. "Now we fast forward eleven years, you move home, run into James, have a torrid one-night stand—"

"It was not all that—"

Gina shook her head, sending her red curls in all directions. "I was down the hall, I heard the whole thing. Torrid is a mild term for the sexual shenanigans I heard that night."

"Fine." Carly felt her face heat up so she grabbed a pillow and plopped it onto her face.

"So, after your one-night stand when you give him your standard heave-ho," Gina continued, reaching over and taking away the pillow, "James pursued you in the guise of friendship, which turned into something more, because why wouldn't it? I mean look at him, he's a god and he's a sweetheart. Then at his grandfather's birthday bash this weekend, you faced down Preston and also discovered that this new job you've been offered at Penmans came about in large part because James's grandfather is on the board and he used his connections to encourage them to hire you."

"Yeah, that's the part that sucks the most," Carly interrupted. "I thought I got that job on my own, and I needed that, Gina, I really needed that boost to my confidence."

"How do you know you didn't?"

"Because Preston all but said that James manipulated the whole thing," Carly said.

"Preston?" Gina asked. "The jerk who got a pizza by deflowering you?"

"Did you really just say 'deflower'? What does that even mean?" Carly asked.

"I was trying to be delicate," Gina said.

Carly rolled her eyes.

"You know what you need to do," Gina said.

"Quit the job I just accepted a few hours ago," Carly said. "Yeah, that won't make me look like a psycho."

"No," Gina said. "You need to go in and talk to your new boss and explain that you want the job but that it has to be on your own merits. Give them a chance to tell you exactly why they hired you, and if it turns out that the Sinclair family was the leverage that got you the job, then you can quit. But you owe it to yourself to find out exactly why they offered you the job, don't you?"

"Maybe," Carly said. "But then what? Do I take the job and stay?"

"Do you want to?" Gina asked.

"I don't know," Carly hedged.

Gina gave her a look like she wasn't smart enough to use grown-up scissors. "Come on, you know that what you have with James isn't something to just walk away from."

"Do I?" Carly countered. "I mean, maybe I'm just a fix-it project to him."

"I doubt that," Gina said. "Maybe I'm wrong, but I still think he's in love with you."

Carly thought back over her time with James. He never said "I love you" directly to her but he had told her that he'd fallen in love with her on first sight. Had he? Had James been telling the truth?

"No, it's not possible," Carly said. "No one falls in love at first sight."

"Mom and Dad did," Gina argued.

Carly glared.

Gina ignored her and said, "You know it's true. We have to hear the story every April twenty-fourth on the anniversary of the day Dad first saw Mom. She was waitressing at the ice cream parlor, and he saw her through the window and thought he was having a heart attack because his heart stopped at the sight of her." She paused and the sisters shared a smile and finished the story together. "So he went inside and sat in her station and ate four hot fudge sundaes in a row, until he was stomach sick but had finally worked up the courage to ask her out."

"Dad is a freak," Carly said.

"Well, yeah, but—"

"No, I can't talk about it anymore."

She couldn't bear to hear Gina argue with her conclusion, as she was sure her chest might actually explode from the pain she was feeling. Because while James would say that what he had done came from his feelings for her, and while Gina and the others might believe it, Carly couldn't.

Because the one thing she had learned from Preston, the most valuable lesson she had learned from his cruelty, was that true love didn't manipulate. True love was honest, it didn't maneuver or coerce an outcome. Simply put, James had played her to make himself feel better. She had thought that what they had was the real deal. She'd been wrong, so very wrong.

"When I told her to make you chase her, I didn't mean across town," Pops said.

"And I didn't think she'd steal my Hellcat," Tom said. "Tell her that's my new nickname for her, would you?"

"Yeah, if she ever speaks to me again, which isn't likely," James said.

He studied the contents of his coffee mug. He wasn't usually one to get depressed, but the look on Carly's face when she had shoved him away had been so devastated it had broken his heart wide open. He had hurt her. The one thing he had never wanted to do. He was the guy who fixed things; how could this have happened?

"She'll speak to you again," Pops said. James studied the face so like his own. He couldn't quite tell if Pops was bullshitting him or not. He was pretty sure he was.

"Did you really not tell her that you had Pops put in a good word for her?" Tom asked. "As a businessperson myself, I've got to say that would piss me off."

"Very high-handed of you," Pops said.

"I know, I'm an idiot," James said. He hadn't told them the worst of the situation about Preston and Carly and their past. It may have been too little too late, but he figured he could spare her that indignity.

"Can't argue that," Pops said. "Although, I might have called you thick instead."

James sent him a dark look and Pops shrugged.

"So, what's the plan?" Tom asked.

"I have no plan," James said. "I asked for five minutes. She gave me five minutes and tossed me out. She clearly hates me, so, yeah, I'm pretty sure I am without a plan."

"Well, that disappoints," Pops said.

He poured the last of the coffee from the pot into his mug and topped it off with three teaspoons of sugar and a less than healthy dollop of half-and-half.

"So sorry," James said. "Got any bright ideas?"

He was pretty sure his sarcasm could have curdled the cream. Pops raised one gray eyebrow at him but said nothing.

"Really?" James asked. "You've got nothing?

You had to chase Gram for fifty-plus years." He could hear the desperation in his own voice and he didn't even care. "Surely, you have something to offer me: advice, counsel, commiseration, something?"

"Nope," Pops said.

James exchanged an incredulous look with Tom.

"Fear not," Tom said. "I hear a but in there—of course, it could be just a butt."

"Don't be fresh," Pops said but his voice lacked heat as he tried to hide his smile. "First of all, you blew it. Bad."

"I got that," James said.

"Do you?" Pops asked. He sipped his coffee and then gave James a steady look. "What do you think you did wrong?"

"I should have told her the truth about you being on the board at Penmans," James said. "None of this would have happened if I'd been straight with her."

"Maybe," Pops said.

"What do you mean maybe?" James asked.

"Yeah, I'm lost," Tom added. "I thought lying was the issue."

"The problem isn't totally that you didn't tell her the truth about the job," Pops said.

Now James was confused. Of course it was. He wondered if turning eighty had caused Pops to start getting dotty.

"The problem is that you see her as someone

who needs to be fixed and you, quite arrogantly, figure you're the man for the job," Pops said. "No woman wants to be with a man who thinks she is less than."

"But I don't," James protested. "I think she's amazing. She's everything I ever wanted in a woman and more."

"Yes, but she's not going to think you feel that way when you manipulate her life for her. She's not your client," Pops said. "You know, you're really not helping my theory that brains skip a generation; even your dad has never made this much of a boneheaded maneuver."

James dropped his head into his hands. Pops was right. It wasn't just that he'd hurt Carly by not telling her the truth, he had made her feel like he found her lacking. His stomach twisted into a knot. He felt queasy.

"Buck up, buttercup," Tom said. "You'll figure it out. You always do."

"Not if he doesn't get his head out of his rear," Pops said.

James glanced up at the man who'd had his back his entire life. Pops was quitting on him. That stung.

"Thanks for the support," he said.

Pops held up an age-spotted hand. "Wait for it."

Tom gave James a concerned look. "He's talking like a hipster. Do you think he's had a stroke?"

"Nah, his face isn't sagging and he still has control of his fine motor skills," James said.

"Ha ha, very funny, I'll show you my fine motor skills when I flip you off," Pops snapped. "Now do you want my advice or don't you?"

"Hit me," James said.

"Don't tempt me," Pops returned.

Tom snorted and they both gave him a dark look.

"Carly is angry because she believes that you were trying to fix her, correct?" Pops asked.

James nodded.

"Okay, so the first order of business is to make sure you don't do anything that makes you look like you're trying to change her in any way," Pops said. "If you love her, you have to love all of her, even the quirks."

"I do," James said. "It's just the commitment phobia, no-relationship thing that's working against me here."

"Well, get over that because if you want her, you're going to have to prove to her that she doesn't have to change for you," Pops said.

James's eyebrows shot up to his hairline and he was pretty sure *he* was about to have a stroke.

"You do know what commitment phobia is right, Pops?"

"Sure." His grandfather shrugged. "She's afraid to settle down with just one guy, she doesn't want to be vulnerable, she doesn't want to have to compromise her life for some loser, makes perfect sense to me."

Tom clapped one hand to his cheek and stared at their grandfather as if he'd never met him before.

"So, what?" James asked. "I'm just supposed to be okay with her shacking up with different guys all of the time? News flash! That. Is. Not. Okay. With. Me."

"Of course it isn't. So you'll just have to run interference with any guys she hooks up with and be the better option," Pops said. He winked at James and said, "It's called romancing her, dummy, and you need to go big here. Believe me, it worked for your Gram and me. Ha! You should have seen me when I had to win her over during her cowboy phase. I had to wear a Stetson and I had a pair of assless chaps—"

"Stop!" James and Tom shouted together.

"I'm just saying, keeping a lady happy can be more fun than you'd think," he said.

James stared at Pops as if he had sprouted horns. He glanced at his cousin and noted that Tom was doing the same thing. Oblivious, Pops finished his coffee and rose from his seat to rinse his mug out.

Tom elbowed James hard in the side. "That was information I did not need to know about our grandparents. Tell the Hellcat she owes me a few therapy sessions now, too."

"Let's roll out," Pops called from the doorway. "I want to get back home in time for lunch. I hear lobster bisque is on the menu at the café."

Tom rose from his seat and followed their grandfather out the door. Dazed and a bit bewildered, James trudged after them, turning over and over in his mind what Pops had said.

By the time they reached the bright green car, he understood what Pops was telling him; not only that, he had a plan. Before Pops could climb into the car, James hugged him close.

"I take it you're getting up to speed now?" Pops asked. He leveled James with a pointed look. "Be the man she needs you to be, go all in on loving her and she'll be yours."

"I think I'm catching on," James said. He rubbed his hands together and added, "Good thing you have all those smarts, so you don't have to get by on your looks."

Pops barked out a laugh. He pointed to James and then himself, and said, "Acorn, meet oak."

"Pot meet kettle, yada yada," Tom said. "Jamie, don't screw this up. I don't want to have to drive back here with him. It's Frank Sinatra the whole way, and he sings."

James laughed. "No worries. I got this."

Chapter 34

"Give me one good reason why I shouldn't punch you in the mouth," Zach said.

They were standing in the restaurant portion of the Bluff Point brewery. The place was empty, save for Carly's friends and her sister Gina, all of whom had agreed to meet James after hours without Carly. So far it hadn't gone as well as James had hoped.

Gina had barely acknowledged him, Jillian looked disappointed in him, and Zach was glowering at him, looking like he was going to punch him in the mouth no matter what he said. James figured it was time, as Pops said, to go all in.

"Because I'm in love with Carly, and I want her back," he said. He was relieved that he didn't sound as pathetic as he felt.

"Aw," Mac and Emma said together. Jillian looked concerned while Gina said nothing as she continued studying her manicure as if unaware of James's existence. The girl had an advanced degree in giving the cold shoulder.

"Assuming we believe you, and that's a big assumption," Sam said. "Why should we help you?"

"Because Carly is in love with me, too," James said. "She just won't admit it."

The Maine crew was quiet, glancing at James and then at one another as if trying to decide whether going behind Carly's back to help him win her back was a betrayal of their friendship or not. James said nothing. He had pleaded his case; now it was up to them to decide whether they were in or out.

He figured it would be easier if they helped, but he was really just doing this as a courtesy. He had a plan and he was going to put it in motion and win Carly back with or without them.

"I believe him," Gavin said. "I think Carly is in love with him, and I think we should help him."

James turned a surprised glance at the veterinarian. He hadn't expected Gavin to be the first one to speak up.

"I've seen how you are with Hot Wheels." Gavin shrugged. "Carly could do a lot worse."

"Thanks, I think," James said.

"I agree," Mac said. "I think we should help. Sometimes a relationship needs a kick in the pants from the outside."

She slid into Gavin's side and he pulled her close and kissed her. James had a feeling there was a story there but now was not the time to ask.

"Shall we vote on it?" Brad asked. Emma's husband was the most pragmatic of the group; well, he was the most skilled at adulting at any rate. James had noticed the few times their paths had crossed that he was the one who mediated the group's shenanigans.

"All right," Emma said. She glanced around the room. "All in favor of helping James, raise your hands."

Mac and Gavin did so without hesitation, Brad and Emma followed, Sam raised his hand but it was at half-mast as if he still wasn't sure, Jillian nodded slowly and raised her hand. That left just Zach and Gina.

Gina glanced up from her manicure and stared at James with brown eyes so like Carly's it made his heart hurt.

"Why?" she asked.

James raised his eyebrows. "Why what?"

"Why do you love her?" she asked.

"I don't know," James said. "I just do."

"Oh, well, I'm sold," Zach said. He clenched a fist and James was pretty sure his beat down had arrived. "Carly's my best friend—we're kindred spirits, she and I. I get her. Do you?"

James turned and faced Zach so that they were squared off. He was vaguely aware of the rest of their group slowly lowering their hands and leaning forward as if getting ready to jump in and separate the two men if warranted.

Was Zach in love with Carly? James hadn't thought so. They'd always seemed to have a brother-sister thing going. But really, could he blame Zach for being in love with her? Carly was amazing. Who wouldn't fall in love with her?

"Yeah, I get her," he said. "I get that she's scared and vulnerable and lost. I get that someone she once trusted used her and crushed her spirit, and that I unwittingly have done the same stupid thing.

"If I could take it all back and start from the beginning and spare her all of the garbage she went through, I would. But I can't, so now I have to fix this—I have to fix us—because honestly, I let her slip away once, and it was hard, but if I lose her again, well, I just don't think there's going to be any coming back from that for me."

The two men stared at each other and Zach unclenched his fist and slowly raised his hand in the air. James studied the guy in front of him. With his shaggy surfer dude hair and YOLO attitude, he seemed like a perpetual child, but James got the distinct feeling that there was a hell of lot more to Zach's backstory than that.

Now there was only one person left to convince. He turned to Gina and met her dubious gaze. Fine, if she wanted him to break it down for her, he would.

"Why do I love your sister? Here's the high-lights reel. I love that she walks into every room like she owns it, I love that she can't dance for shit, and I love that she gets a little WTF line in between her eyes when I say something stupid. I love that she secretly adores a parrot that swears like a pimp and lets Saul sneak up onto her bed, pretending she doesn't see him, and I love that it was her kindness to a neighbor that got her stuck with those two."

Gina opened her mouth to speak, but James held up his hand, stopping her.

"Wait, I'm on a roll. I love that her smile is like sunshine and can light up the darkest day. I love that the sound of her laugh makes my spine vibrate when she chuckles low and deep. I love that spaghetti and meatballs is her favorite food, and I love that she enjoys her food. I love that she is fiercely protective of her family and friends, loving them with all that she has and all that she is. But mostly, what I love about Carly is the way she makes me feel when I am with her. She makes me feel like my life means something, that it's worth something, because she makes me the best version of myself—you know, when I'm not being an idiot. She makes me want to be a better man for her for the rest of our lives together."

James was winded when he stopped. He could feel everyone staring at him and he knew he couldn't have exposed himself more if he'd pulled his pants down. To his dismay, Gina still didn't raise her hand. She took two steps toward him and he wondered if she was going to take a swing at him. Instead, she threw her arms about his middle and hugged him tight.

"Excellent! You have my vote," she said. Then

she laughed and added, "Okay, peeps, let's help this loser win my sister back."

Carly dashed into The Grind. She was not having a great day. She had overslept and was late for her shift at Making Whoopie. Given that this was her last week, she'd wanted to help Jillian as much as possible to alleviate her guilt about leaving her friend to go to work at Penmans.

Instead of calling to discuss the job offer, Carly had driven to Portland the day before and had a one-on-one meeting with the head of the purchasing department, Lydia Husser. She had gently but firmly insisted that she wanted the job, but only on her own merit. To her surprise, Lydia had been incredibly impressed and had assured her that after her interview Carly had been her first pick for the position and now she was even more certain. Pops's recommendation had just reinforced Lydia's own instincts about Carly.

Feeling a renewed sense of herself and her career, Carly had returned home to Bluff Point victorious. Her Maine crew had taken her out to celebrate but halfway through the evening, Carly couldn't help but feel that something, or rather someone, was missing. James.

She had cut the evening short and gone home to snuggle Saul and Ike, eat a half of a pumpkin pie with whipped cream, and try to put the man out of her mind. She should have known that in a town this size, it wouldn't be that easy.

She had no makeup on and her hair was in a mangy snarl on the top of her head. Her laundry had piled up, leaving her no choice but to wear one of her frumpiest outfits: overlarge jean overalls on top of a bulky sweater, which made her feel as sexy as a pair of dirty sweat socks. And she wasn't sleeping because she missed sex—not James, just sex, on that she was very clear.

"Gina," she called to her sister. "I need a pu—"

"Here you go, one extra-large pumpkin spice." Gina put a to-go cup of coffee in front of her and Carly smiled at her.

"Well, hey, that was fast. Thanks, sis." She opened her wallet but Gina shook her head at her.

"It's already paid for."

"What? Oh, that's so sweet, but you don't have to do that," Carly said.

"I didn't," Gina said.

Carly frowned. "Then who?"

Gina tipped her head in the direction of a table at the back. Carly swiveled around and there he was. James. Her heart felt like a fist knocking on her ribcage. He glanced up and met her gaze and her heart started banging triple time.

The weather had gotten colder over the past few days and he had a scarf the same shade of gray as his eyes draped casually around his neck.

His hair was mussed and he looked tired, but still he smiled at her as if the sight of her was what he'd been waiting for all morning. His lips curled up just a little bit more on the right, making her sigh. He was so freaking adorable, it hurt.

Carly whipped her head back toward Gina. "I can't take coffee from him. We're apart, as in not together, as in he should not be doing stuff like buying me coffee."

Gina shrugged. "Maybe it's just a peace offering."

Carly glanced at the cup in her hands. Okay, that made sense. Did she have to thank him? Probably. Maybe she could just yell it across the coffee shop on her way out. Yeah, that would work.

"Okay, then," she said. She glanced at her sister. "See you at home?"

Gina nodded and Carly spun back toward the door. She strode across the room, dodging other customers. When she got to the door, she lifted her cup in James's direction and yelled, "Thanks!"

He winked in return and she tripped over her feet as she rushed out the door. A wink. What did that mean? That wasn't like a return wave or a shout of "You're welcome." No, there was something decidedly calculating about his wink. What was James Sinclair up to?

By mid-afternoon, Carly had her suspicions. The flowers began arriving as soon as she got to work, each bouquet being delivered by one of her friends. It started with Mac and the flowers kept coming, arriving every hour on the hour, brought in by Gavin, Brad, Sam, Emma, Gina, Zach, Aunt Charlotte, Aunt Sarah. Even Mr. Petrovski, the postmaster, dropped of a bunch, and Jillian produced the final bouquet from her office when they were getting ready to close.

Lush bouquets of wildflowers, fragrant garden roses, and even her favorite, hydrangea, all filled the petite shop. The cards tucked into each bunch of flowers were addressed to her and read Happy Anniversary, but they didn't say who they were from. There were eleven bouquets in total. Eleven bouquets for the eleven years since the first night they'd met.

Carly would have had to be made of stone not to feel touched by the gesture. She knew James was trying to tell her that had things been different, had they met under better circumstances, then they likely would be celebrating an eleventh anniversary. It was a lovely thought; she'd give him that.

"James isn't going to be brushed off as easily as you thought," Jillian said as they locked up. "He wants you back, and we're all hoping you give him another chance."

Carly surveyed the bouquets. She had put one on each table in the shop and a few on the counters. They really were stunning.

"I appreciate that you guys want a happy ending, but I'm pretty sure that's not in the cards for me and James," Carly said. "In fact, I'm going to make sure of it."

They stepped outside as soon as Jillian hit the activate button on the alarm. Carly stood in the dark, stamping her feet while Jillian locked the door.

Jillian frowned at her. "What are you thinking?"

"Nothing," Carly said. "At least nothing that I wouldn't be thinking if this was any other evening."

"Oh, no. You're going on a man hunt, aren't you?"

"Maybe." Carly shrugged. She had run home at lunch to change her clothes and put on some makeup. As each bouquet had arrived, she'd realized she needed to put some serious distance between her and James and the best way to do that was to get back in the game. "Come on, the crew is waiting at Marty's Pub, which, come to think of it, is a great place to pick up guys. Let's go."

As Jillian dragged her feet, Carly looped her arm through her friend's, pulling her toward the pub.

Parker Barton was as easy a pickup as Carly had ever had. She had smiled at him from across the room, he made a beeline for her, and Carly had been unable to make a move without the scrawny, beanie-wearing millennial by her side ever since.

She finally sent him to the bar just to get a

break from his eagerness. She watched as he tripped over his overly long pointy-toed shoes while crossing the room. After James's muscular build, sleeping with this guy was going to be like snuggling a pencil. She sighed.

While she waited for Parker to return, she sat with her friends. Gina, Jillian, Emma, and Mac were holding the fort while the boys were playing darts.

"How goes the conquest?" Jillian asked.

"He'll do," she said. "Although, I don't know. He seems . . ."

"Underdeveloped?" Mac offered.

"A poseur?" Emma suggested.

"He sort of has an underfed Ashton Kutcher thing going," Gina said. "Maybe it's just the beanie."

"I don't know, he kind of reminds me of Alexander Skarsgård," Jillian said. "You know, without the muscles, if I tip my head to the side and squint."

"Oh, I see that," Mac agreed. "It's the cheek-bones—no, the full lips."

"Really?" Carly asked. "I was thinking he more resembled Jesse Eisenberg, you know, total nerd boy."

They all looked at Parker again.

"Yeah, he's pretty geeky," Jillian said. "But in a very pretty way."

Carly dropped her head to her chest. A few

months ago, heck, a few weeks ago, Parker would have been just fine to take home. Now he was more like yesterday's Kung Pao chicken, a congealed mess in the bottom of a plastic container she was afraid to reheat. She just wasn't interested.

"So?" Emma asked. "Are you going to tap that?"

Carly waffled. "No. Maybe. Should I?"

"Why not?" Gina asked. "You're single."

"Yes, but—"

"But what?" Mac asked. "He's totally into you. I bet you could take him home now if you wanted, you know, for a little rec sex."

Carly blinked. She could. She knew she could. Why then was every single cell in her body rejecting this idea? *Weird!*

"You know, you don't want to take too much time finding a new boy toy," Gina said. "You'll end up in a dry spell and it could go on for months; trust me, I know this to be true. So, why not do a little palate cleansing?"

"You did not just say that," Carly said. "A man is not a sorbet."

Gina shrugged.

"She's right. You're in a small town now. It could be a while before another boffable man comes along," Jillian chimed in. "You don't want to let your pilot light go out."

"Agreed. If it does you'll just end up fuckstrated: sort of like being hangry but it's over sex instead of food," Mac said.

They all laughed; well, everyone but Carly. She was finding nothing funny about this conversation.

"Seriously? Since you all did a round at floral delivery today, I thought you were all Team James."

"We are," Mac said.

"This is reverse psychology," Emma added.

"Is it working?" Gina asked.

"No, and it would serve you all right if I did take Parker home and to hell with James!" Carly snapped. At the wide-eyed looks on their faces, she got a sick feeling in her stomach. "He's right behind me, isn't he?"

"To where with who?"

Carly whipped around and sure enough there was James, looking as yummy as ever. Damn it. How long had he been there? What had he heard?

"Nowhere with no one," she said.

"Really?" he asked. "Because it sounded like you were trying to decide whether or not to make a move on the swizzle stick over there."

Carly heard one of the girls (*Gina!*) snort behind her but she refused to acknowledge her.

"So, are you thinking you're going to date him?" he asked. He sounded very calm about her hooking up with another guy given that he had sent her eleven bouquets today. Eleven!

"I don't date, as you know. I'm more of a smash and dash kind of girl," she said.

"Is that so?" He studied her for a moment and

then reached up and smoothed the frown line between her eyebrows with his thumb. Carly shivered.

"What do you want, James?" she asked.

"I thought the flowers would be a clue," he said. "You. I just want you. I'm sorry I wasn't straight with you from the start. I'm sorry I hurt your feelings. I just felt like we got this amazing second chance and I didn't want you to go back to New York before we really gave it a go. I want us to be together however you want us to be. Even if it's just one-night stands that you want, you can have them, so long as they're all with me."

Carly stared at him, feeling like her brain had flatlined. She could not wrap her head around what he was saying. Heck, she could barely process the fact that he was here, with her, within reach.

"How could we possibly work after everything that's happened?" she asked.

"We should play to our strength," he said.

"We have a strength?"

"Yep, and it's not our ability to talk," he said.

Then he leaned down and kissed her. It was a swift possessive press of his lips against hers and it hit Carly like a lightning bolt. Before he could back up, she grabbed him by the front of his jacket, pulling him flush against her as she opened her mouth beneath his and deepened the kiss. He responded by locking his arms about her and plundering her mouth with his. Still, it wasn't enough, it was never enough.

Self-preservation and a lack of oxygen made her jerk back and put some distance between them. Over his shoulder, she saw Parker leaving the bar, looking decidedly grumpy. So there went her night's entertainment. She felt curiously relieved.

"You were right, what you said before," James said. "You weren't broken; you were protecting yourself. I get it. I had no right to say that, just like I had no right to think you needed me to fix you. You don't need fixing. You're perfect just the way you are."

It hurt. It was a physical ache in her chest to hear him say the words she wanted to believe so very badly. And that was the problem. She wanted it, him, too much. She'd been the same way with Preston, only seeing what she wanted to see and not really seeing the truth. And the truth was that James would always view her as someone who needed fixing no matter how much he denied it.

"James, I appreciate what you're trying to do, I really do, but I think it's best if we just let it go. Maybe in time we can be friends, real friends."

He stared at her, looking frustrated. "Do you kiss all of your friends like that?"

Okay, she had to concede that point—or did she?

"Oh, yeah," she said. "Jillian and I make out like that every time we see each other."

"Carly," he said her name in that deliciously reproving way he had and she felt her face get hot with a blush. Damn it.

"What?" she asked. "You know friendship is more than I offer most men I've slept with."

"Ah, but there's the problem," he said. He reached up and tucked a stray hank of hair behind her ear. "I'm not most men and I have no interest in being just friends, which is why I've made up my mind."

"About?"

"I'm going to woo you."

Chapter 35

"Woo me?" Carly made a scoffing noise, even as she felt as if her insides had just burst into flame.

"That's right," he said. "You know, you were my girlfriend for reals for just twenty-four hours, which is hardly enough time to romance you like I planned, so I'll pick you up at seven tomorrow evening for our first official date."

She blinked at him. "I'm sorry, but I don't think so."

She stepped away from him and he let her. Then he gave her the lopsided smile that she had grown to love and said, "We'll see about that, sunshine."

It could have been the singing balloon telegram he sent to the bakery the next day that chipped away at her boundaries, or perhaps the ten-pound box of chocolates, or maybe it was the limousine that arrived at her house that night to pick her up for a night on the town in Portland. Then again, it could have been the ruby earrings and necklace he gifted her with during their romantic candlelit dinner at a five-star restaurant that overlooked the water. Maybe it was one of those moments that opened the way for Carly to yield, or perhaps it was the combination of all of them, she didn't know. She just knew that James was getting to her and she had no idea what to do about it.

The truth of it was that Carly had no real experience with dating, and she wasn't sure she liked not having control. Sure, it was lovely to have someone put so much thought into making her happy, but it didn't feel right. It was uncomfortable, like a shirt that was too tight.

When she frantically group texted her friends from the ladies' room at the restaurant, they assured her that yes, this was what dating was all about. When she offered up the possibility that James was just doing this to get into her pants, ever helpful Gina pointed out that he already had, so really any maneuvers from him to that end were superfluous at best. Carly had no idea what to do with that.

Over the course of the next week, which included a candlelit dinner at home of spaghetti and meatballs, her mother's recipe no less, where her friends ran the kitchen and served while Ike, Saul, and Hot Wheels joined James and Carly for dinner and were outfitted in matching bow ties, she determined that it wasn't the big gestures, nice as they were, that were breaking her down.

It was the little things, like the way James always opened the door for her or pulled out her chair. He listened to her when she spoke, asking questions about her childhood, and he laughed at her ridiculous tales of the five DeCusati sisters.

He asked about her new job, showing that he cared about her world and wanted to hear more. He asked what she thought she wanted to do in the future, without ever telling her what he thought she should do.

He was goofy and funny and self-deprecating in a way that charmed her silly. It was clear that he knew he had blown it but was doing everything he could to get her to give him one more chance. He never did more than kiss her swiftly on the lips at the end of their dates. He was so respectful, in fact, that Carly was beginning to wonder if he still wanted her in *that* way.

After a day trip to Bar Harbor, where he had behaved like the absolute most perfect boyfriend ever, he walked her to her door and kissed her once again, gently on the lips, keeping his behavior above reproach. Carly had been so frustrated, she had taken the opportunity to press herself up against him, pleased to discover that his attraction to her was self-evident. Still, he declined her invitation to come inside or to come at all. In a lust-fueled haze of want, she did not think she was overreacting to think that their new relationship was reaching a tipping point.

On the morning she awoke to the sound of something that resembled a cheese grater being dragged over a rock, she glanced out the window to discover a thick frost had formed the night before, coating everything in a thin blanket of ice. And there in her driveway was James in his gray scarf and thick wool coat, scraping her car clear of the frost that had formed.

He wore a hat but his thick black hair shot out from under it, refusing to be tamed. His cheeks were ruddy, giving him a decidedly New England manly sort of look. He hummed softly while he prepped her car and when he was finished, he checked it over and then got into his own vehicle and drove away. He was looking out for her and that meant the world to Carly because no man ever had before.

Something cracked inside of her at that moment. Perhaps it was her own coating of ice, the one she'd kept her heart in for so long, she didn't know. Either way, Carly felt something inside of her soften and settle. It was clear James had been showing her what sort of boyfriend he intended to be. He had asked her to give him a chance to prove himself and she had. It was decision time.

Ike and Saul watched her as she fluffed her hair. She turned away from her reflection and asked them, "What do you think? Can I win him over like this?"

Saul thumped his tail on the bedspread and Carly ruffled his ears. He licked her wrist in return. Ike gave her a wolf whistle and bobbed on his perch as if in agreement. Carly reached up and rubbed the back of his head just the way he liked it. He turned and pressed the top of his head into her palm. It was a gesture of total trust and Carly knew that it wasn't just her relationship with James that needed to be decided.

It hit her then that she couldn't imagine her life without these two guys in it. They had managed to wag and flap their way into her heart and she knew there was no going back. She was theirs, and they were hers. Her guys, her fellas, her special boys.

"All right, so I suppose I should declare it out loud so we're all on the same page," Carly said. "I love you, Ike and Saul, and, well, I think you're stuck with me because I can't bear to let you go."

Ike stretched his back and flapped his wings as if celebrating the best news ever while Saul rolled onto his back and thrust his belly into the air.

"I take it you're okay with staying with me?"

Saul gave a soft woof and Ike squawked, "You butthead."

Carly laughed, not a delicate little chortle, oh, no, this was a full-on guffaw. Yeah, they were hers, all right. Maybe Mrs. Genaro really had known that Carly needed them as much as they needed her.

She glanced at the ceiling and said, "Thanks, Mrs. G."

Now she just needed to figure out what to do about James. She had a plan. She was wearing her unstoppable little black dress and her super-high heels. Her hair was done in tousled curls that fell around her shoulders and her makeup was light but she'd gotten some pointers on how to do the smoky eye from Lola and Emily; yes, she'd called James's family to let them know what she planned. Thankfully, they were all in.

It was dance party night at The Grind, and the Maine crew was meeting up to kick off their night there. Carly planned her arrival so she'd be the last to show. She wanted to sneak in and get the lay of the land before she made her move.

She parked her car in the lot in back and ducked into the coffeehouse, using the rear door. The staff knew she was Gina's sister and they called out a greeting as she slipped through the kitchen to the front using the Employees Only door.

Carly perched herself on a stool by the wall where she could watch the room. The crew was in a booth by the window while James was out on the floor dancing with Mac's aunts, Sarah and Charlotte. The three of them were doing some crazy hip-hop moves to "Can't Feel My Face" by The Weeknd. When James clapped his hands to his face and swiveled his hips in a seriously seductive way, Carly choked on the espresso Gina had just handed her.

"Nice," Gina said. She grabbed a rag and cleaned up Carly's mess. "Very ladylike."

The Grind was Bluff Point's only coffee shop

and it thrived by hosting loads of entertainment, including a nightly DJ or band, as well as poetry slams, art shows, and board game and trivia nights, essentially whatever seemed interesting and fun. Carly looked at her sister and noticed for the first time how in control she was of this place of business.

She jerked her thumb at the dance floor and asked, "Was this your idea?"

Gina shrugged. "I've been known to have a few."

"I'm impressed," Carly said.

Gina blushed and looked away and Carly realized she liked her baby sister, really liked her.

"I probably should have noticed how cool you've become a lot sooner," she said.

Gina's eyes shot up to hers and Carly smiled. Gina beamed back at her and said, "Thanks."

They both glanced back at the dance floor and Gina leaned close and asked, "So, how long are you going to torture the poor boy?"

Carly looked at her as if she had no idea what Gina was talking about. Gina raised one eyebrow and shook her head at Carly.

"Don't even," she said. "It's so obvious that he is crazy in love with you. If you don't feel the same way, it's time to cut him loose."

"But—"

"No buts," Gina said. "You're better than that."

A customer signaled for Gina's attention and

she left, leaving Carly to watch James dance with the aunts. When he glanced up at her and caught her watching him, his lopsided grin made her heart somersault in her chest. When she considered cutting him loose, she felt the exact same wrenching pain she'd felt when she thought about letting go of Ike and Saul. This was it then. Decision time.

James delivered the aunts back to their table and joined Carly by the counter. The crew at the booth had busted out a Scrabble board. Things looked to be getting heated as they bickered over whether the word "muggle" from Harry Potter was considered legit.

"Sick dance moves, James," she said.

"Thanks."

Carly turned to face him as they were tucked in the shadows of the shop, with the counter beside them and the wall behind her.

"I meant sick as in stomach issues and have to use the bathroom not sick as in cool," she clarified.

"Ouch! Harsh," he said. He laughed and added, "It was the gyrating hips, right? Too much?"

"Yes, you are too much," she said.

He tipped his head to the side as if he could tell there was a double meaning there, but he didn't want to interrupt her by asking what she meant— just one more of the many things she loved about him. He was really good at being still and listening.

Carly leaned back so she could meet his gaze and then she sighed. Her hands were shaking, and she thought she might throw up. She was scared shitless right now, but she knew Gina was right, and it was now or never because she didn't know if she'd ever get the nerve up to talk to him like this again.

"I was fine, totally fine with my life . . . and then you showed up and changed everything," she said.

James went completely still. Did he remember saying those exact words to her? He looked at her as if he did, which made her feel safe enough to keep talking.

"And you messed up everything," she said.

He nodded as if he was familiar with the feeling and she had to check the urge to give up talking and hug him tight.

"Why are you wooing me?" she asked. "Why didn't you walk away? Leave? Find someone else?"

He reached out and cupped her chin with his hand. Carly was relieved to see he was shaking as badly as she was.

"Because I can't let you go," he said.

His voice was so soft she had to strain to hear him and just like that Carly felt the last of her resolve melt.

She huffed a breath and met his gaze and asked, "You know, don't you?"

"Know what?" he asked. He looked confused and a little wary.

"That I'm in love with you," she said.

He stared at her for a full three seconds as if it took that long for her words to fully register and the next thing Carly knew her back was to the wall and James's mouth was on hers as he clutched her close with one hand on her hip and one buried in her hair.

The kiss was like liquid fire, scorching Carly from the inside out as his mouth took possession of hers, making her cling to him as she met his hunger in equal measure.

Then James wrenched his lips from hers and said, "Did you really just say that? Say it again."

"I love you," she said. His eyes were bright blue and glittered with relief and happiness as they moved over her face as if he was reassuring himself that she had really just said it.

Carly decided to help him out and said, "I love you. I'm in love with you. I, Carly DeCusati, am completely, wildly, madly, exasperatingly, head over heels in love with . . ." She lowered her voice, making it seductive, and said, "James, oh, James."

That was as far as she got before he kissed her again. It was long and thorough, cementing the new status of their relationship, and Carly found she was okay with that, more than okay. She was giddy. She had a boyfriend again.

When they came up for air, he cupped her face with his hands and said, "I'm in love with you, too. Crazy in love with you, so much so that I have to ask you this right now before another second passes." He took a deep breath as if he were bracing himself for a dive into deep, dark water, and asked, "Carly, will you marry me?"

Just when she thought the man could not surprise her any more, he took her out at the knees.

"You don't have to answer ri—"

"Yes," she said. Then she giggled. She clapped a hand over her mouth. Carly never giggled. Then she giggled again, and said, "Yes, I'll marry you."

James kissed her, a swift and possessive meeting of their lips, then he whipped around toward the booth with their friends, and shouted, "Did you hear that? She said she's going to marry me!"

There was a moment of stunned silence and then a whoop, from Zach, sounded and the crew poured out of the booth to come over and congratulate the happy couple.

Gina brought a bottle of champagne out from the back, bubbly was poured, toasts to the happy couple were made, and all the while, James never took his hands off Carly. It was as if he needed to be touching her at all times to reassure himself that this was real, they were real, and that she wasn't going anywhere.

Carly wasn't, not ever. She was going to marry this man. She felt her heart clutch in her chest. She had never known this sort of happiness was possible. She glanced at her friends, Emma and Brad, and Mac and Gavin, and she got it now. This was true love, the I-can't-live-without-you love that the songwriters gooped on about, and it was hers. Still, she had made a promise to Pops.

Slyly, she slipped out of James's hold. She gestured that she needed to use the bathroom and he reluctantly let her go, kissing her before he released her. But instead of going to the bathroom, she ghosted through the front door, standing just outside the shop where she could see him through the window, then she texted him.

Catch me if you can.

She watched him get the text. He looked up from his phone and glanced around the coffee shop and then saw her through the window. The lopsided grin he sent her was blinding and then with a singleness of purpose that left her breathless, he was striding toward her.

Carly laughed as she turned and began to jog down the street. She planned to let him catch her at the corner, but just this time, because they had a whole lifetime to spend chasing each other and she couldn't wait for it to start.

| Books are produced in the United States using U.S.-based materials | Books are printed using a revolutionary new process called THINKtech™ that lowers energy usage by 70% and increases overall quality | Books are durable and flexible because of smythe-sewing | Paper is sourced using environmentally responsible foresting methods and the paper is acid-free |

Center Point Large Print

600 Brooks Road / PO Box 1
Thorndike, ME 04986-0001 USA

(207) 568-3717

US & Canada:
1 800 929-9108
www.centerpointlargeprint.com